Pine Creek
COURTSHIP

Pine Creek
COURTSHIP

AMITY HOPE

Entangled Publishing, LLC
10940 S Parker Road
Suite 327
Parker, CO 80134
Visit our website at www.entangledpublishing.com.

Amara is an imprint of Entangled Publishing, LLC.

Edited by Stacy Abrams
Cover design by Elizabeth Turner Stokes
Photograph by Tom Hallman
Interior design by Toni Kerr

Print ISBN 978-1-68281-568-7
ebook ISBN 978-1-68281-590-8

Manufactured in the United States of America

First Edition April 2021

AMARA

GLOSSARY OF AMISH TERMS

Ach: oh
Appendlitch: delicious
Ban: a shunning or excommunication
Banns: marriage announcement
Boppli: baby
Bruder: brother
Canna: cannot
Danki: thank you
Daed: dad
Daedihaus: small house on the property typically used by aging parents
Dummkopf: a disparaging term for someone without sense
Englischer: non-Amish person
Frau: wife
Goot: good
Goot mariye: good morning
Goot nammidaag: good evening
Grossmammi: grandmother
Hallo: hello
Jah: yes
Kapp: prayer covering for the head
Kaffi: coffee
Kinner: children
Maidel: an unmarried woman
Mamm: mom
Meidung: shunning or expulsion
Mudder: mother

Nammidaag: afternoon
Nee: no
Ordnung: a set of rules
Rumspringa: a rite of passage during adolescence
Schweschter: sister
Sohn: son
Vadder: father
Wunderbaar: wonderful
Yummasetti: a casserole made with ground beef and other ingredients

*For Zack and Nick, who bring so much love,
laughter, and adventure into my life.
I'm so blessed to be your mom.*

CHAPTER ONE

As the buggy's wheels rattled over the gravel road, Levi's mind skimmed over the past hour. It had been a torturous one, one he knew he would never forget. He had angled himself so that he could see Emma Ziegler from across her father's gravesite. As the funeral had progressed, he'd wanted nothing more than to hurry to her side, to support her.

He couldn't do that.

Instead, he'd watched his childhood friend as she stood stoic, never taking her eyes off the casket as it was lowered into the ground. He'd always admired her courage before, and her strength had not wavered then. At least not in front of all those watching over her—and on the day of her father's funeral, there were a great many people surrounding Emma and her siblings.

The spring breeze had managed to tug a few wisps of her chestnut hair from her *kapp*. She hadn't bothered to tuck it away. Or maybe she couldn't. She had been wedged between her sister, Sadie, and her brother, Ezekiel, both clinging to her like darkness grasping a winter morning.

"Looks like the entire district is here," his father proclaimed now.

Levi gave a nod to *Daed*, who sat beside him. "It sure does."

Buggies were hitched along the pasture's fence posts. Neighbors were milling about the yard. Others were on a slow progression into the house. He didn't see Emma anywhere.

"It's not a surprise so many people turned out for the funeral," his mother, Diana, said from behind him. "Paul was a kind man, had a lot of friends. Emma takes after him. Everyone wants to show their support. She's going to have her hands full trying to raise two teenagers and keep up the farm."

Moses, his father, shook his head. "It's a lot for anyone to take on."

"Paul knew his time was coming," *Mamm* reminded them. "It's unfortunate he didn't find a husband to look over Emma, though he tried."

Levi clenched his jaw to keep from speaking as he drew the buggy to a halt. Not quite a year ago, Paul Ziegler had contracted pneumonia. The man was more stubborn than Abram Graber's entire team of mules. By the time Emma finally convinced him to see a doctor, he was in need of hospitalization. It was only by the grace of God that he pulled through.

Unfortunately, he never fully recovered.

When it had become apparent that his health would continue to deteriorate, Paul had asked Ivan, Levi's brother, to marry his daughter. The Bontrager and Ziegler farms shared a border, so the families knew each other well. Ivan had agreed. And Levi had been crushed. No one knew, not even Ivan, how deeply his feelings for Emma ran.

"We must not fault Ivan for the broken engagement," his mother continued. "He's so happy with Miriam."

"They make a *goot* pair," Levi said. "Emma and Ivan never made sense to me. If he hadn't been so ill, Paul never would've tried to match them up."

"*Nee*, I don't suppose he would've," his mother admitted. "He simply wanted to see his daughter cared for. He was a *goot* man."

Paul Ziegler had been good at a whole lot of things, but resting had not been one of them. There were fields that needed tending, a family that needed raising, and a good Lord who needed praising. He'd pushed himself when he should've been allowing time for recovery.

Complications of the pneumonia had caught up with him.

Now his children were on their own.

Nee, Levi silently amended as he hopped down from the buggy, *that isn't true*. Like all Amish communities, the residents of Pine Creek were a close-knit group. The Amish took care of those in need, just as they knew the Lord had intended. Emma, Sadie, and Ezekiel would be tended to. The women would be sure they were fed. The men would be sure help was given in the fields, if need be.

"*Hallo, bruder*."

Levi, satisfied that his gelding was secure, pivoted on his heel. Ivan and Miriam had taken their own buggy and had also just arrived.

"*Hallo*, Ivan." He nodded in deference to his brother's new wife. "Miriam."

He was only vaguely aware of her return greeting, as his attention had skittered elsewhere as he searched for Emma. While *Daed* helped *Mamm* down from her perch, Levi took off toward the house.

Friends and neighbors were scattered about the lawn. The men had already set out tables and benches, the women set to work carrying out food. He knew his mother and Miriam would be rushing to help. It was his fault they were at the back of the procession of buggies. He'd wanted to buy some time as he tried to decide what to say to Emma.

No words of condolence seemed to be enough.

He caught sight of her through the crowd, still wedged between her siblings as she greeted people on the front porch. Dark crescents rested beneath her eyes. His heart ached for her, as he could only imagine how difficult this had to be. With Paul's health failing steadily over the last several months, he was sure Emma had not been afforded much rest as of late.

"The poor girl," his mother said as she rushed up beside him, "she does not look well. If she's not careful, she may wear herself out, make herself ill, just like her *daed* did."

Emma, usually so strong, did look frail.

"That," Levi said, "will not happen. I will not allow it." With those words, he set off, weaving his way through the crowded yard.

• • •

Emma could barely stand the weight of the heavy, worry-filled stares. She knew everyone present had respected her father. They were here to lend their support.

But she had heard the whispers. Well-meaning people wondering how she could manage the farm, harvest the syrup that was her family's primary source of income, as well as raise her siblings. Truth be told, she wondered the same thing, but she couldn't bring herself to admit it. Not out loud, anyway. But the bothersome question swirled in her mind, crisp and annoying, like the sound of dead leaves rustling in the wind.

"Ezekiel, Sadie, I will help you dish up some food. I know you have not eaten much today." Their older cousin, Amelia, held out her hands to the teens. She caught Emma's eye and gave her an apologetic smile. "My *mamm* would like to speak with you."

"Now?" Emma asked.

"I am afraid so. She would like you to meet her on the back porch."

Thirteen-year-old Ezekiel's fingers squeezed Emma's with a strength she wouldn't have thought his small, bony body capable of. Sixteen-year-old Sadie leaned in on her from the other side. The pressure of supporting her siblings should have crushed her. Instead, it gave her strength.

She needed to be strong for them. They were counting on her. She was all they had left.

She would not fail them.

She untangled herself, giving each a gentle nudge toward Amelia. "Let Amelia help you with the food. I won't be gone long." She twisted away from them before they could protest. Then, with downcast eyes, she hurried to the backside of the only home she had ever known.

Aunt Naomi was her father's sister who lived in a district in the southern part of the state. She had arrived earlier in the week, jumping in, taking charge. For the most part, Emma hadn't minded. She was grateful for the help. Aunt Naomi seemed to flourish when she felt she had a job to do.

Emma climbed the steps that led up to the back porch. "You wanted to speak with me?"

"I do." Aunt Naomi turned to face her. Wispy strands of silver hair were tucked tightly beneath her black *kapp*. Her face was lined with age, her hands callused with hard work. "You know I am unable to stay with you and the children indefinitely."

"I never expected you to stay," Emma demurred. "I've been running the farm on my own for some time now. *Daed* was so ill much of this past year, he could barely get out of bed."

"*Jah*," Naomi said, "I know. It's a shame you had to do it all on your own. A woman your age should have a husband by now."

Emma hung her head, trying to ignore the heat that filled her cheeks. She was four years past twenty, practically a spinster. While her friends had been courting, she had been busy raising her siblings.

Aunt Naomi was not wrong. She *should* have a husband by now. That was what her father had wanted for her. He'd even asked Ivan Bontrager to be her groom. And Ivan had agreed.

But that plan had fallen apart. This past winter, Ivan had told her he didn't think he was the right man for her. He had told her that it was best for everyone. She had demanded to know who he meant by "everyone," because surely, he could not include her in that proclamation.

She wasn't sure if she had loved him. She had,

however, felt a companionship with him. She enjoyed his company. Most of the time. Although if she were to be honest with herself, he could be a bit of a bore. Even so, he was known for his fairness and honesty. He was a hard worker, and she knew he would've been a good provider and a faithful husband.

He was proving this to be true already. He'd recently wed Miriam, and the couple seemed undeniably happy together.

Now here she stood, alone, with no husband and two siblings to care for.

And a farm to run.

And maple trees to tap.

Fortunately, the syrup was harvested for the year, the sap having been boiled down and bottled at the end of the cold months. The community had come together to help because her father had been too ill.

Next year, Emma knew it would be an enormous undertaking, but one she was willing to tackle on her own.

"Ivan and I were not a *goot* match," Emma murmured.

"Your father thought you were. It's unfortunate Ivan changed his mind. I wonder what caused him to do such a thing."

Emma's eyes flickered to her aunt's before dropping to the porch railing again. "I don't know."

She was ashamed of the fact that she'd nearly begged Ivan to reconsider, arguing it was what her father had wanted. But Ivan's mind had been made up. There had been no changing it back. He'd begun courting Miriam, and Emma had no choice but to accept his decision.

He hadn't so much broken her heart as he had wounded her pride. And, since being prideful was a sin, it was possible she held a bit of a grudge. She was miffed that he'd brought that undesirable quality out in her.

"The circumstance matters not," Naomi said, heaving a weary sigh. "The end result is the same. This farm is too much for you to run on your own."

"I'm not on my own. Sadie and Ezekiel will help me."

"Sadie?" Aunt Naomi scoffed. "That girl has her head in the clouds. She's a dreamer, that one— spends too much time playing with animals or with her face stuck in a book. And Ezekiel, that child has been spoiled all his life. He's frail, just like your *mamm* was."

Emma sent up a quick prayer, asking God for patience. Aunt Naomi said "frail" as though it were an insult. Emma knew she really meant "weak."

"My *mudder* was a *goot mudder*." Emma's voice was low and steady, but there was fire in her eyes.

"She was frail, unable to withstand childbirth," Naomi *tsk*ed. "That brother of yours has been coddled since the day he was born. He's scrawny. He should be working the field at his age. If he doesn't learn to earn his keep soon, when will he? That boy is destined to remain as fruitless as Barbara was if he continues to be overprotected."

Her *mamm*, Barbara Ziegler, had withstood great heartache. She had difficulty carrying a *boppli* to term. Their family was smaller than most in the community. She had been heartbroken over her losses, and though she tried giving the pain to God, she never seemed to recover. During her pregnancy with Ezekiel, she had been nervous, making herself sick with worry. Ezekiel's birth had been too much for her. She had died shortly after holding her only son for a few short minutes.

Emma thought it was no wonder God had taken her. Perhaps He thought her mother belonged in Heaven, caring for her lost little ones. And now *Daed* had joined his beloved Barbara.

"Ron is a hard worker, a *goot* man," Aunt Naomi said of her husband. "But his age is slowing him down some. We could use the help around our place. It would do Ezekiel well to put in a full day's work."

"The children will stay here." Emma's tone held no room for argument, though her heart lurched, then began to race at the very thought of losing them as well. "They'll help me work *this* farm."

Aunt Naomi was determined to argue regardless. "This farm? You need to use your head, girl. I wasn't going to mention this yet, as we are all in mourning, but perhaps this is the time. Marvin Stoltzfus is looking to set his son up with his own place. We've been talking. I believe the Stoltzfus boy would be a *goot* match for you. Marvin wants to buy the farm; you'd be allowed to stay on, of course, as Amos Stoltzfus's wife. Ezekiel and Sadie will have to come with me. You can expect only so much of a man."

Amos? He was a bit older than her, but quite a few unpleasant stories had drifted her way. She fought back a shudder.

Her voice trembled when she spoke. "My *daed* has only been gone not even a week and you've made arrangements to sell our farm…*and* marry me off?"

"I'm only looking out for you," Aunt Naomi coaxed. "This is the best solution for everyone. You'll be allowed to stay in the home you grew up in. You'll have a husband to take care of you."

"And if I stay on, where does the money from the sale of the farm go?" Emma clenched her hands at her sides, sure she knew the answer.

"Your uncle and I will need the money. We'll use it to help raise the children." Naomi wore a determined look. "I grew up in this house as well."

Emma shook her head. "*Nee*. It will never work. I *canna* marry Amos—I barely know him. I…I…" She trailed off, knowing there was no argument that would win her aunt over at the moment. She could tell by the stubborn set of her jaw that she would not let this go.

Marry Amos Stoltzfus? The idea was absurd. Even more absurd was the idea that she would *ever* give up her siblings. After everything they'd been through, the three of them belonged together.

"I understand you're going to need a bit of time to get used to the idea," Aunt Naomi said, as if Emma's agreement was as good as given.

Emma struggled to find a reason her aunt would accept. Amos Stoltzfus was not a kind man—though she tried to whisk the thought away. Judgment was not hers to dole out. Yet the thought would not recede. She was not judging, simply remembering things she had noted about Amos in the past.

"*Nee*," she said quietly, not wanting to argue with Naomi but needing to express her feelings on the matter. He was the only man—young or old—in their community who had gotten into a physical altercation with a tourist. On many occasions he had been known to imbibe alcohol while stumbling down the streets of Pine Creek. "Amos is not the sort of man I can marry. He has a querulous way about him."

"Emma!" Aunt Naomi exclaimed in indignation.

"He has been known to be cruel," Emma whispered. "When young Eli Graber's new pup got loose and ended up in Amos's yard, he beat the poor creature with a rake."

"Well, Eli should've taken better care to contain the animal," Aunt Naomi argued. "Plus, people should not be gossiping. *You*, Emma, should not be gossiping. I knew Marvin when I was younger; we grew up together. He's a fine man, and I'm sure his son is a decent boy."

Naomi had been away from Pine Creek for a long while. Though Amos's father was an upstanding member of their congregation, Amos was not. Emma could continue on with her valid accusations, but her aunt was clearly in no mood to listen to them. Or to believe her.

Not wanting to be scolded again, Emma's mind whizzed into action. Perhaps she needed to try a different approach. She had to do *something*. She was not going to simply agree to this…this nonsense! If she were to lose the farm right now, her heart would shatter all over again.

But marrying Amos, of all people, was simply not an option. She couldn't do it.

She *wouldn't*.

She furrowed her brow and lowered her voice, trying to reason with her aunt. "How will it look if I begin courting him now? I should be in mourning."

"Under the circumstances, it would be understandable. No one would expect you to run this farm alone. You need a husband."

"It is *goot* to hear you say that."

Emma startled at the sound of the familiar voice.

Levi Bontrager edged his way through the screen door. "I'm sure you'll excuse my interruption. I came to see how Emma was faring after such a trying morning. I didn't mean to overhear your conversation…but perhaps it is fortunate that I did."

"Why is that?" Aunt Naomi asked with a delicate sniff.

"Stoltzfus *canna* court Emma." Levi's voice was firm.

Emma nodded in agreement. She and Levi had been friends since childhood. And though he had done her wrong in the past, she had forgiven him and moved on. However, their friendship had never been the same.

Perhaps he was trying to right his wrongs by offering her support?

"I do not believe this is up to you," Naomi said.

Levi raised his hand to Emma's elbow and gave it a squeeze. She shot him a peculiar look, surprised by the unprecedented act of familiarity, then quickly realized the gesture was one of warning.

"It is," Levi started, and then proceeded more firmly, "it is because she is courting *me*."

The blood in Emma's veins felt as if it turned to ice. How could he say such a thing? *Why* would he say such a thing? What right did he have to do so? She opened her mouth to protest but quickly snapped it shut again when Levi gave her elbow another gentle squeeze.

"I didn't realize," Naomi said coolly.

"How could you have?" Levi asked, his tone casual.

Emma blinked at the both of them, too flustered to say a word. The Amish did not flaunt their courtships. She realized that it would be all too easy for Naomi to believe this fallacy.

But lying was a sin. She couldn't allow it.

Or could she? Aunt Naomi had said she needed a husband. Surely she wasn't too picky about *which* man filled that duty. If Naomi thought she was with Levi, that should satisfy her. Shouldn't it?

She blamed her momentary lapse of judgment on her grief. She had just lost her *daed* and wasn't thinking clearly. Her lack of sleep was making it hard to organize her thoughts into words that would make sense. Perhaps...perhaps she could just remain quiet.

"I love Emma deeply," Levi said quietly.

Emma's cheeks instantly flamed red. She gasped in outrage. How dare he lie not only once, but twice? And on her behalf? It was scandalous.

Aunt Naomi must have assumed the gasp was that of surprise. Amish men did not, as a general rule, blurt out professions of love. Not even when they were courting.

"So you see," he continued, "I'm afraid that you are going to have to let Mr. Stoltzfus know that a mistake has been made. Emma is not free to court his son."

A protest was brewing in Emma's head, but Levi's next words put a halt to her thoughts.

"She *canna* have the children taken from her. They belong here, at the farm. They've all three already endured a tremendous loss; it wouldn't be right to take them from one another." Levi held his gaze steady as he met Naomi's.

The children. Losing the children would be an even worse fate than having Amos as a husband. For them, she would keep quiet. For now. Just until she had time to get her thoughts in order.

"And what of the maples?" Levi demanded. "Amos knows nothing of producing the syrup."

Naomi held her head high. "He has no interest in the trees, only the farm. It is my understanding that he would sell off the surrounding land."

Sell the land? Emma's heart slammed against her rib cage. A thick forest of sugar maples skirted the property on two sides; it was the reason her father's family had purchased this property decades ago. Her family had harvested syrup since before she was born. It was an arduous process, and because of that, a case of syrup brought in a pretty penny. The Pine Cone Lodge purchased the syrup in mass quantities to serve to the guests in the café, and the gift store was another outlet. Tourists loved genuine Amish goods.

The syrup was not only their livelihood, it was her father's legacy. She could *not* let it fall into someone else's hands.

By not speaking, she knew she was lying by omission. She sent up another silent prayer. *Please, God, forgive me for this sin of silence. Forgive me for feeling so attached to this worldly possession. For now, I canna bear the thought of parting with my father's beloved trees.*

Another frightening thought weighed her down. If Amos was cruel to animals, how kindly would he treat her? What kind of father would he be? He did not strike Emma as the sort of man who tolerated children well. The very thought of having children with Amos sent her stomach roiling. She dared not voice her fear, worrying that Naomi would accuse her of passing judgment.

Naomi eyed them warily. "You are truly courting?"

Levi did not hesitate in giving a response. "We truly are."

"And your intentions are to marry my niece? To help her run the farm, to harvest the syrup, to raise the children?"

Emma expected Levi to falter under her aunt's scrutiny. "It would be an honor, someday, if she will have me." He turned to Emma. "But I do not believe now is the proper time for this discussion. She has guests to tend to."

"I suppose she does," Naomi grudgingly admitted.

Emma could only dip her head slightly.

"We will speak again soon," Levi said.

Emma gave him a sharp, quick nod before slipping back into the security of the house. "*Jah*, indeed we will."

CHAPTER TWO

Levi dropped by the very next morning and every morning after for the next several days. Aunt Naomi met him at the door each time, telling him that he should come back another time. She insisted that Emma must be left alone to properly mourn.

Emma had overheard the exchanges as she worked at the gas stove, cooking breakfast for her family. She briefly wondered if keeping Levi away was supposed to be a punishment of sorts. Naomi had been clearly ruffled when she realized the sale of the farm was not to take place. Perhaps she wanted to make Emma regret going against her wishes.

Emma was sure that Naomi meant well, even though her methods were rather abrasive. She knew her aunt didn't see it that way. Naomi always did what she thought was best.

When her cousin Amelia asked her mother what length of time she considered respectable, Naomi refused to give an answer.

Naomi could have continued to stonewall Levi for quite a bit longer, but an opportunity arose that Emma had not expected.

"Emma!"

"What is it, Sadie?" Emma continued to scrub the kitchen floor as her sister skidded to a stop in the doorway.

"Levi is coming down the lane," Sadie said.

"Is he?" Emma dropped the scrub brush into the bucket of water and scrambled to her feet. She dried her hands on her apron before straightening her *kapp*.

"*Jah*, he is," Sadie said. "I was hanging the laundry on the line when I saw him."

"I suppose it's time that I speak with him," Emma admitted.

"Aunt Naomi won't like for you to speak with Levi alone," Sadie warned.

"It's a *goot* thing you're here, then," Emma reminded her.

The last few days, Emma had been given a reprieve. While she knew she needed to speak with Levi at some point to discuss the fib he'd told, she had been in no hurry. She'd had days and she was still unsure of how to address the situation.

He was about to knock on the door when she flung it open and stepped onto the porch.

"Emma," he said in surprise. Most likely he had assumed Naomi would cut him off, as she always did.

"We don't have long," Emma warned. "Naomi went visiting this morning but she could return at any moment."

"All right, then. How have you been?"

Emma hesitated for a few heartbeats. "I've been managing."

Levi studied her face.

Emma knew he would see the shadows under her eyes belying the sleepless nights she'd endured. While she knew her father's death was God's will, she missed him with an ache that had yet to fade. She tried not to worry about the future but the responsibilities placed upon her seemed too much to bear at times.

Though she knew she must bear them, for that, too, was God's will.

"Emma," Levi began, "I hope you are not angry with me. I know I may have spoken out of turn, but I meant well."

"You did more than speak out of turn," Emma corrected with a scowl. "I know that you were trying to help. I was not thinking clearly the day of my father's funeral. If I had been, I wouldn't have allowed you to tell my aunt such a tale. God doesn't approve of liars."

"I know," Levi agreed. "Lying was not my intention; I truly don't know where the words came from. I heard Naomi say she wanted you to marry Amos, and I know what sort of man he is. It was already a difficult day for you. Her words made it only harder. I was trying to help, Emma. I did not mean to engage in a falsehood."

She could hear the honesty in his voice, see it in his eyes.

That didn't make the situation right.

A lie was still a lie.

"I appreciate your concern," Emma said firmly, "but I will not lie to my family. Nor will I lie to this community. They have done so much for me." In the time since her father's death the women had stopped by frequently, often bearing baked goods, canned fruit, or some other small token of their thoughts. Several times friends of her father had stopped by to see if any repairs were needed. "I won't repay them with dishonesty. What would my *daed* think? What would God think? I *canna* live this lie you've told."

"Emma," Levi said gently, "take a breath. Calm yourself down."

"*Ach.* Calm down?" she huffed. "How can I? You made a liar of me." She was trembling with frustration. "Aunt Naomi will be home soon. We need to decide how to fix this."

"What do you suggest?" Levi wondered. "Are you going to tell her you're free to marry Amos?"

Emma winced. She had spent days thinking about it and she could see no way past this complication.

"I will tell her that I do not need a husband at all." Emma's voice was firm. "I can run the farm and harvest the syrup on my own."

"Do you think she'll let the idea go?" Levi asked. He spoke before Emma could answer. "I don't think she will. Naomi isn't the sort of woman to give up easily. If she knows you're free to marry Amos, she will be relentless."

"I will have to make her see that I am capable," Emma said stubbornly. "Now that some time has passed, perhaps she's had a chance to see that I can run this household."

She wanted the words to be true, but she wasn't so sure. Levi was right about Naomi—the woman could be unyielding. She adhered to the belief that a young woman needed a husband, a man to take care of her. While Emma disagreed, she didn't believe she would truly be able to sway her aunt to her way of thinking.

"I can tell by your hesitation that you know I'm

right," Levi gently prodded.

Emma sighed. "Perhaps you are. Yet that does not justify a lie."

Levi shifted from one foot to the other. He wore a pinched expression that Emma couldn't decipher. He wouldn't meet her gaze when he spoke again.

"If you let me court you, it won't be a lie." His tone was low, and she had to lean in to hear him.

"Let you court me?" Emma laughed. When Levi didn't even smile, her laughter quickly faded. "You *canna* be serious."

"Why not? Do you have a better idea? Can you think of a way to save the farm? Can you think of how to save the maple trees? Do you think she'll happily leave Sadie and Zeke here knowing you have no intention to marry?" He hesitated, giving his words a moment to take hold. "You know as well as I do that if Naomi thinks you are unattached, she'll march you right to Amos Stoltzfus's front door." He rushed on, not allowing Emma to protest. "I saw the look on your face when she said she would take the children with her."

"I think she wants them only because she needs the help," Emma said quietly. "She is not very kind to either of them. I fear how she will treat them if I'm not around."

"You see," Levi pressed, "this could solve your problems. Let me court you. Then it will not be a lie. Surely, Naomi will need to return to her husband soon."

Emma nodded thoughtfully. "Just last night she was saying she had already been gone too long." Emma wouldn't admit, not even to Levi, that she was ready for her aunt to be on her way. Naomi had been of great help while planning the funeral, but as of late, the woman had done nothing but complain. She missed her husband and yet she refused to leave. She freely criticized the way her brother had raised his children. She felt Emma should be married, Sadie should act like more of a lady, and Ezekiel, she could not seem to find a single kind thing to say about the boy.

Still, she hesitated.

"Emma, I know I made a terrible mistake in the past. It made your life more difficult. Are you still angry with me? Is that why you're refusing?"

She shook her head. "*Nee*. I forgave you." For sure she had. Forgiveness was the Amish way. But more than that, though Levi had hurt her, she hadn't wanted to hold a grudge. Not when she knew Levi was truly repentant over what he'd done.

"*Danki*. Please let me do this for you. We were friends once, *jah*?"

"We were." They had been friends as children. They had explored the woods together, gone fishing, picked berries and eaten them off the bushes by the handful. But that was when they were much younger, before it became improper for them to spend time alone together.

It seemed to Emma like forever ago.

"Then let me do this for you."

• • •

Levi's heart pounded as he waited for Emma's reply. She could have no idea how important her answer was to him. The thought of her marrying Amos, it felt as if a mule had kicked him in the stomach. He couldn't let it come to that. She said she had forgiven him, so surely, she had. Not only was it the Amish way, but it wasn't in her sweet nature to hold a grudge.

Emma tilted her head to the side as she squinted at him. "Why are you so insistent?"

He couldn't tell her the truth. Could he? Could he tell her that he'd been in love with her for as long as he could remember?

The words were right there, dangling on the tip of his tongue. In some ways, it would be easier if he just admitted it. He was weary of hiding it, of holding such an exhausting secret. Yet he and Emma had drifted apart. He wasn't sure how she would take the news. Plus, it wasn't that long ago that she had been engaged to his brother. He didn't think she'd loved Ivan, but what if she had?

Or what if he confessed his love and she felt pressured to love him back? He didn't want her to agree to be with him out of a sense of obligation. But he also couldn't bear the thought of her rejecting him.

No. He couldn't tell her. Not now. Not while she was still in mourning. She bore a heavy enough burden already.

If she agreed to his plan, he would win her over. That's what he would do. *Then* he would tell her his true feelings.

For now, he would part with as much of the truth as he dared.

"I care about you, Emma, and don't want to see you hurt. I don't want to see you tied to a man like

Amos." His eyes searched hers. He saw her expression softening, and it gave him hope.

"I care about you, too," she admitted.

"We were friends once—close friends. I miss that. I made a mistake in the past." He could admit that. "I didn't mean to spread lies about you. I was worried. I thought my words were the truth at the time, but I never expected a rumor to spread."

"You had people believing I was in love with an *Englisch* boy." Her tone still held the hurt she felt. Her father had been angry; the other teenagers in their community had teased her, ignored her, nearly ostracized her for her perceived indiscretion.

It had been all his fault.

Levi hung his head. "It was a misunderstanding. I saw you with him. You were in his arms."

"For a moment. Only a brief moment!" Emma exclaimed. "I was upset and I wasn't thinking clearly. Several *Englisch* girls had been mocking me, poking fun at my plain clothes, my *kapp*, the way I talk. It wasn't the first time. Usually I was able to ignore them, but that day they were particularly relentless, following me around town as I did my shopping. Tourists laughed with them, and I let my pride get the better of me. I was in tears as I walked out of the general store." She shook her head. "But that day, I couldn't ignore them, no matter how I tried. Darren saw how upset I was. He was trying to comfort me."

Jealousy swirled in the pit of his stomach. He wanted to be the one to hold Emma, the one who comforted her. He could still envision the way the boy had pulled her close, held her in a way that Levi had only dreamed of. He held his tongue, afraid that if he spoke, he wouldn't be able to hide his feelings.

He knew the *Englisch* boy Darren. They all did. His father drove a cab that many of the Amish in the area used. On many occasions, Darren filled in for his father.

When Levi said nothing, Emma continued as if uncomfortable with the silence. "I shouldn't have allowed him to embrace me. It happened so quickly, I didn't have time to think. If you had stuck around at all, you would've seen that I immediately stepped away."

"I know that now. At the time, I was afraid he'd take you away from us." Levi hesitated, gathering courage to say words he'd held back for so long. "I was afraid he'd take you away from me."

When this happened, Emma had been of the age to go on her *rumspringa*. It was a time when the rules of the Amish were loosened so as to allow their young people to make their own choice as to whether or not they wanted to commit to the Amish way for life. He had worried that she was spending secret time with the *Englisch* boy and had feared Darren would influence her decision on being baptized. Looking back, he knew Emma's heart had always been steadfast. He'd had nothing to fear.

He never should have doubted her. In trying to protect Emma, he had managed only to push her away.

Emma lifted her eyes to his. "I wish you would've spoken to me directly."

"*Jah*. I made a mistake. I was worried for you. I went to some friends asking for advice. Judith Graber overheard," he said with a scowl. "She's the one who got people talking. Yet I take responsibility for speaking of it at all."

Emma sighed. "That's in the past. It's time to move on."

"I would like that." He bolstered his emotional fortitude and admitted another sliver of truth to his friend. "I've missed you, Emma. Missed talking to you, spending time with you." While she had been courting his brother, he had barely been able to sit in the same room as them. His jealousy toward the *Englisch* boy paled in comparison to the soul-crushing jealousy he'd felt toward his brother.

Never mind that jealousy was a sin. He couldn't control it, no matter how he had tried.

But her relationship with Ivan was in the past as well. A wave of gratitude flooded through him. He couldn't imagine going through life with Emma as his sister-in-law, watching from a distance as she shared a life, had children, built a family with Ivan.

Now he didn't have to.

A horse nickered in the distance, pulling their attention to the gravel road.

Naomi and Amelia were returning.

"So, what will your answer be?" Levi wondered. His heart rattled so fiercely, he feared she would hear it. "Are you willing to give courting me a try?"

Emma's gaze was on Naomi as she and Amelia neared. "I am still not sure that I understand how this will work. It seems to me we will be courting but it will be for appearance only."

"If that's the way you would like to look at it."

"How long do you see this carrying on for?" She bit her bottom lip and he knew she was seriously mulling it over. It made his heart trip in his chest.

He shrugged. He wanted to say, *As long as it takes for you to fall in love with me.* Instead he said, "I suppose it will depend upon what Naomi expects of us."

"She's expecting marriage," Emma reminded, her voice low as she watched Naomi clamber out of the buggy. Amelia remained behind to take care of the horse.

"Let's not worry about that quite yet," Levi soothed. "She doesn't expect us to wed next week, so we can take things slowly."

Her words came out in a rush, as if she were afraid she would change her mind. "All right then, I will agree to court you."

Naomi marched across the lawn. Her features were fixed in a scowl, her eyes set upon her niece.

"What is this?" she demanded as the gravel crunched under her feet. "Levi, I have told you Emma is not ready for your company yet. I go away for just a few hours and return to find the two of you alone?"

"They're not alone," Sadie declared. She pushed her way through the screen door while holding a large glass of iced tea in each hand. "I've been here. I went inside to prepare them something cool to drink." She turned her back to Naomi as she handed Emma a glass. "I saw them coming down the lane," she whispered.

"Thank you," Emma whispered back as she took the drink her sister offered.

Levi took the other.

Naomi climbed up the steps. Her irritated gaze

swung between Emma and Levi. "Well then, as long as you are both here, I believe it's time to iron out this situation. Have a seat."

Levi dropped onto the porch swing, Emma hesitantly settling in beside him.

Naomi eyed up Sadie. "Where's that *bruder* of yours?"

"Last I saw him, he was in the barn mucking out Ginger's stall."

"You should join him. Take over for Amelia, please."

Sadie hurried down the steps, looking anxious to get away.

Naomi took a seat on the wooden bench that rested against the porch railing. Her spine was ramrod straight as she eyed Levi.

"Tell me about this man," Naomi said to Emma. "Does he own a farm of his own?"

Emma shook her head. "He does not. He does carpentry work on the side, as do many of the men in our community."

Naomi's mouth puckered in displeasure as she narrowed her eyes at Levi. "He works for the *Englisch*?"

"There is no shame in that," Emma said. "We sell our syrup to the *Englisch*. If not for them, we would not have enough income to get by."

"Pine Creek's new bishop seems terribly…lenient."

Bishop Yoder wasn't exactly new. He'd been the bishop for nearly a decade, but Naomi had left Pine Creek long before that. Levi admired their bishop, and it bothered him to hear Naomi insinuate that he wasn't doing a good job. Working for the

Englisch—in any capacity—was forbidden in some districts. The Old Order Amish adhered strictly to keeping separate from the rest of the world.

But here in Pine Creek—where the New Order Amish resided—their bishop allowed leniency out of necessity. There were families who needed the extra income to get by. He considered explaining this to Naomi but decided she wouldn't care to hear it.

"Does he know how to work the land?" Naomi continued.

Irritated at being ignored, Levi chimed in. "I do. I grew up on the next farm over. My *daed* still works our land, my *bruders* and I helping out as needed. I work on a carpentry crew because I don't like to be idle and my *daed* is still capable of running the farm on his own, for the most part. I'll be taking over the farm someday, but my *daed* isn't ready to give it up yet."

Amish tradition dictated that as the youngest son, the farm would become his. Just as Paul's farm was expected to go to Ezekiel. When the time came, his parents would move into the *daedihaus*. For now, Levi was living in the smaller structure off the main house, to garner a bit of privacy. He worked part-time for an *Englisch* man because he enjoyed having a paycheck of his own. While he was anxious to own his own farm, his father was nowhere near close to retiring.

Naomi said nothing for several drawn-out minutes. When she spoke again, she continued to direct her attention to her niece. "Tell me honestly—do you think your father would approve of this man?"

"He would," Emma said assuredly. "I know he would. My *daed* knew Levi well. For as long as I can remember, he's helped with the fires to boil down the syrup. *Daed* always appreciated his help."

Levi's hand clenched the iced tea, condensation making the glass slippery. He waited in silence for Naomi's inquisition to continue. He was as surprised as Emma when the older woman rose to her feet.

"Very well, then. I expect to see you here for supper tonight," she told Levi.

"I would enjoy that very much," Levi said as his tension eased.

Naomi turned to Emma. "You know the rules of courting. It is not appropriate for the two of you to be without a chaperone." Her angry gaze bore into them.

"We were not alone," Emma murmured. "Sadie and Ezekiel were here."

"We will take greater care," Levi quickly assured when he saw Naomi's ire flare.

"See to it that you do." Without another word, she rose and entered the house.

"My goodness, Levi, I didn't think she was ever going to leave!" Emma whispered. She clapped her hand over her chest. "My heart hasn't pounded this hard since the Weavers' bantam rooster got loose and chased me across the schoolyard!"

He chuckled. "Seems to me I saved you that time, too."

She giggled at that. He'd chased after the rooster while the rooster was chasing after Emma. He managed to peel off his jacket while he ran, and when he got close enough, he'd thrown it over the bird. But somehow in the melee he'd tripped, landed on the creature, and had ended up with a bloody peck to his cheek.

In fact, he still bore the scar, and though it was small enough most people wouldn't even notice, it made him grin every time his finger accidentally traced it.

It had been worth it. Emma had been just fine.

The curtains behind them were tugged open, causing them to bounce apart from each other and chasing away their laughter.

Emma cleared her throat. "I wonder how long she'll stay."

"She may stay until we are wed," Levi said with a grin. He wiggled his eyebrows at her, earning him a smack on the shoulder.

"You are hopeless," Emma groaned.

He shrugged, even as anticipation flowed through him. "We could be wed this fall. Would that be so bad?" He said the words, testing them out, getting a feel for Emma's thoughts on the matter.

"This isn't a time for teasing," she scolded, though her lips twitched.

"Perhaps I'm not teasing," he said with an honesty Emma was oblivious to. "You could become my wife. I could take over the farm until Ezekiel is old enough to rightly claim it. By then, perhaps my own *daed* will be ready to hand off the family farm to me."

"I don't find this nearly as amusing as you do."

He wasn't trying to be amusing. But he found no reason to push the matter. Her mind was set, believing his affection was for show. He knew her well enough to know that no words would convince her of his true intentions.

Only time and his actions would prove to her that he was worthy of her trust and her love.

"I don't see how this charade could possibly end well," Emma lamented.

"Don't think of it as a charade," Levi ordered. "I asked if I could court you. You said that I may, so I intend to do so. You should expect to be seeing a lot more of me."

Emma smiled at his enthusiasm. She clearly thought he was joking, simply being silly. He intended to prove her wrong…and quickly. He was going to do everything within his power to show her that he was worthy of being her husband.

"Speaking of seeing a lot more of you," Emma said as she got to her feet, "supper is served promptly at six o'clock. Do not be late or Naomi will likely give you a tongue lashing you will not soon forget."

Levi grinned. "I don't doubt it."

"I should go inside—I have bread rising. It needs to be put in the oven." Emma turned away from him but hesitated with her hand on the front door. "I honestly don't know if this is a brilliant idea or if it's completely terrible. Either way, I need you to know that I appreciate what you are doing for me."

"It's my pleasure, Emma," Levi said as he stood to leave. "I'll be seeing you soon."

She nodded and went into the house.

He stood on the front porch for a moment, trying to wrap his mind around all that had happened. When he showed up here today, he expected to be sent away again. He knew full well Emma had agreed to his plan only out of desperation.

As he descended the steps—grinning like a child with a piece of toffee—he thanked God for the opportunity that had been given to him. This might be his only chance to win Emma's heart...

And he was not going to waste it.

CHAPTER THREE

Emma readjusted her freshly starched prayer *kapp*. Her stomach felt as squirmy as a bucket of worms as she waited for Levi's arrival. Despite their earlier conversation, she couldn't help but feel uneasy. How long could she put her aunt off?

In their community, weddings took place only two times a year. The spring weddings had already occurred, and the fall weddings would not take place until late October, after harvest. But Emma knew time had a sneaky way of flying by quickly. Naomi would surely expect them to wed this fall. If they did not, what would become of the farm? Of her siblings? Of her?

Would Naomi revert back to her plan and insist on selling the farm to Amos? If Naomi moved forward with that plan, Emma knew *she* would not be part of the deal. She could never wed a man she couldn't love. Even if it meant being left homeless.

And giving up the maples.

She abhorred the idea of living without her siblings. But if they had no home, where would they go?

As kind as Levi was for offering to court her, she knew it was a temporary solution to a problem that would not recede. In all honesty, she believed he still felt guilty about the rumor he had spread. Most likely, this was his way of making it up to her.

A gentle knock on her door pulled her from her worries.

"Who is it?" she called.

The door creaked open and Amelia stepped inside.

"You look lovely," her cousin said with a kind smile. "Are you nervous about supper?"

Emma shook her head. "*Nee*. I've known Levi a very long time."

"I wasn't wondering if you were nervous about Levi. I was wondering if you were nervous about my *mamm*," Amelia said conspiratorially.

Emma clapped her hand over her mouth, but not before her giggle slipped out. "Amelia," she scolded good-naturedly.

Amelia looked unrepentant. "She can be a difficult woman."

Emma didn't know what to say. Naomi had grown up in Pine Creek. She had met her husband, Ron, years before Emma was born. Ron had been visiting from his home community on the state's southern border, and they were wed soon after. Naomi had returned to Pine Creek only a handful of times over the years.

Emma had met her cousin Amelia once, prior to this visit, back when they were very young, but they'd kept in contact via letters over the years. Emma felt close to her cousin in a way she could never feel close to her aunt. The two got along well though they'd had little chance to speak without Naomi looming in the background.

"I love my *mamm*," Amelia said on a weary sigh, "but she's insistent that it's improper for a woman to remain unmarried."

"*Jah*, she's made that clear to me."

"It's not only you. It's any woman of age."

"She believes you should remarry."

Amelia nodded before moving back to the door. She carefully closed it so as not to be overheard. "She feels my Gideon has been gone long enough, and it's become her mission to find me a new husband. I have come to dread visiting Sundays. For the past year, not one has gone by that hasn't included entertaining a man in hopes that I'll agree to court him."

Emma winced. The Amish attended church services—held in homes—every other Sunday. The Sunday not spent at a service was often referred to as a "visiting Sunday." It was a day to spend with friends and family, or in Amelia's case, potential beaus who may come calling.

"Her attempts are in vain and it's exhausting," Amelia admitted.

"You don't want a new husband," Emma surmised. Her heart ached for Amelia; the pain in her eyes was clearly evident. Gideon had been killed in an accident more than three years ago. Ample time had passed. It would be expected by many that Amelia would marry again.

"*Nee*," Amelia agreed. "I do not. I loved my Gideon with all my heart, and when I lost him, it was as if my heart had been ripped away. I do not want to feel that sort of pain again."

"Amelia." Emma sighed. "You deserve to be happy."

Amelia forced a smile. "I can be happy. I am happy to serve the Lord. I am happy to help out around your farm. Zeke is turning into a fine young man and Sadie is so kindhearted and nurturing."

"She is," Emma agreed.

"I am looking forward to the chance to get to know all of you better. I would like to stay in Pine Creek when *Mamm* returns home," Amelia admitted, her voice full of hope. "Harmony holds too many memories. If you'll have me here, I would appreciate a chance at a new start."

Emma reached for her cousin's hand. "*Jah*, we'll have you! We'd all be delighted." Relief and happiness swept through her. It would be lovely to have her cousin here for support and friendship. "You can stay as long as you like."

"*Danki*." The relief was evident in Amelia's demeanor. "I've spent the afternoon trying to convince *Mamm* to return home. *Daed* misses her. Her garden is surely a fright, though my *schweschters* did promise to keep an eye on it."

"You would stay, and Naomi would return?" Emma asked.

"That is my hope."

Emma had to bite back a smile.

"*Mamm* doesn't think it would be proper for you to court your neighbor while living here alone. Much of the community would agree," Amelia reminded her. "But if I were to stay, there should be no complaints on the matter."

"If that is what you wish," Emma said, "then of course."

Amelia grabbed her hands and squeezed them in her own. "You *canna* know what this means to me."

Emma thought perhaps she could. Her own father had been a kind and loving man. He'd run his household with gentle authority, always guiding his children, yet never oppressing them. Emma wanted to raise her siblings—and someday her own children—in just such a manner. However, Naomi, it seemed, ruled her household with unwavering authority.

Even her grown daughter was expected to abide by her wishes.

"You've already spoken to your *mamm* about this?" Emma asked. "She approves?"

Amelia nodded. "*Jah.* I believe she has already begun arrangements for her departure."

Naomi would need to line up a driver to bring her to the bus station. The bus would deliver her to a town near her home where another driver would be waiting.

"*Daed* will be glad to have her back."

"I'm sure he will," Emma agreed. "She's been gone quite some time."

It was hard to believe her own *daed* had been gone so long already. Before his passing, he had told her he had no fear, that he'd led a good life, and heaven would be his reward. She would see him again someday. Until then, she needed to concentrate on not letting his death hurt so much. Because right now, her heart continually ached in his absence.

"I believe I hear a buggy approaching," Amelia stated. She moved toward the open window. "It's Levi." She twisted around with a merry twinkle in her eye. "He is a handsome man."

Emma raised her hand to fidget with the strings of her *kapp*. Was he handsome? She had never really noted whether he was or not. She moved closer to the window, standing by Amelia to watch his approach.

He had a sturdy build, wide shoulders, and a tapered waist. She suspected nicely shaped arms, too, from his hours spent lugging shingles to rooftops and tossing hay bales. Dark hair was hidden under his straw hat. She could picture his pale blue eyes, always full of merriment and mischief. Perhaps Amelia was right in her assessment. Now that she'd given it a moment's thought, she realized he *was* a handsome man. Emma wasn't sure when that had happened. So often she still thought of him in his boyhood, but he was no longer a child, and neither was she.

"Emma, Levi has arrived!" Sadie called as she swung the door open. "I'll let him in, but you should come downstairs right away." She scampered off without waiting for a reply.

"She's right," Amelia said. "No need to leave Levi alone with my *mamm*. There's no telling how uncomfortable she'll make him."

"I'll be down in a minute," Emma assured. She watched as Levi leaped from the buggy. He hitched his gelding, Blaze, to the fence post, stopping to give him a gentle pat, and the horse nuzzled him affectionately. Emma thought you could tell a great deal about a person from the way they treated animals. Especially when they thought no one was looking.

She had never doubted Levi's kindness. Nor had she doubted that he was a hard worker, a man of God, or that someday he would be a caring husband and father. It was surprising that one of the women in their community hadn't won his heart yet. Still, today, she was grateful that they hadn't. Because without Levi stepping in, she'd be facing a very different future right now.

• • •

Levi scrubbed his sweaty palms on his dark pants as he made his way to the front door. He'd courted in the past, but no girl had grabbed his heart the way Emma had. One had been too bossy, another too needy. Another interested only in making his friend jealous. But Emma? She was the perfect combination of independent yet nurturing. It was embarrassing, the way his nerves were setting to work. He'd made his way to the Zieglers' front door countless times before and he'd never felt as rattled as he was just now.

"*Hallo*, Levi."

Levi glanced over his shoulder as Ezekiel raced toward him. "Zeke, I have not seen you in a while."

The boy fell into step beside Levi as he gave the farmhouse a wary glance. "I've been staying out of Aunt Naomi's way," the boy admitted. "I don't think our barn has ever been so clean."

Levi chuckled at Ezekiel's candor.

"Are you and Emma truly courting?" Ezekiel demanded.

"*Jah*. We are." His heart thumped out an anxious beat, as it did every time he thought of this new development between them. He had a chance with Emma, something he felt he'd been waiting for his whole life.

"*Goot*." Ezekiel grinned at Levi as they clomped

up the steps. "Maybe you will marry her soon so Aunt Naomi will go home." He ducked his head. "I shouldn't have said that. I didn't mean to show disrespect."

"I won't say a word," Levi assured him with a clap on the back.

The front door swung open and Sadie ushered them inside, where they were greeted by the aroma of pork chops and freshly baked bread.

"Emma will be down in just a moment," Sadie said. "I have the table set."

"We should not let the food get cold," Emma proclaimed as she hurried down the stairs. "Levi," she said with a shy smile, "I'm sorry to keep you waiting."

"It wasn't for long." His gaze swept over her, taking in her sage green dress covered by a white apron. As always, her chestnut hair was tucked neatly under her *kapp*. She was so pretty, he wished he had the nerve to tell her so. He would someday soon. Just not in a room full of her family.

Levi gave a warm greeting to Naomi, who nodded at him in return. As they sat at the table, he was relieved to find himself between Emma and Ezekiel. Emma slid him a sideways glance, her lips curved up ever so slightly, but the forced smile didn't hide the sadness in her eyes. He knew she was still hurting over the loss of her father. It was a stark reminder that their dinner together wasn't exactly a cause for celebration—at least, not for Emma. And if not for Emma, not for him, either.

The heavy farmhouse table was laden with food. Pork chops, herbed fingerling potatoes, fresh bread with Emma's whipped maple butter. After a silent prayer, the food was passed around.

Naomi did a fine job of commanding the conversation. She spoke of her visit with Mary Kurtz, complained of how the town of Pine Creek had grown, and once again proclaimed the new bishop too loose in his rulings.

Levi was relieved that none of her grumblings seemed to require a response of any sort. He glanced at Emma every now and again. She appeared resigned to listening to her aunt, and he realized this was what meals had been like since her father's death.

It was vastly different from when Paul had been alive. Conversation had been lively and compliments had been tossed about freely. Laughter had been the norm and not something to be avoided.

"This meal is *appendlitch*," Levi said. He'd been waiting for a lull in Naomi's monologue and jumped in before the moment passed. He kept his eyes averted so as to avoid the scowl he was sure she was shooting his way.

"*Danki*," Emma said.

"We have rhubarb pie for dessert," Sadie interjected. "I picked the rhubarb today. Emma makes the most *wunderbaar* pie crusts. So light and flaky."

"It's unfortunate she hasn't taught you how to make a decent pie crust," Naomi chided.

Sadie frowned. "She's tried."

"So, the fault is your own?"

Sadie sighed. "I'm not so *goot* in the kitchen."

"That's not true," Emma argued. "Your goat cheese is always delightful."

Sadie brightened at her sister's compliment.

Levi knew Sadie had been making cheese for years, that it was her specialty. She had a love for animals that Paul had decided to nurture. He had purchased chickens and goats for her, knowing she would enjoy caring for them, but also knowing she could make a profit as well. Sadie had been selling her goat cheese to other Amish families since she was eleven years old. And the *Englischers* loved the unusual eggs her Marans laid.

"The girl needs to learn to make more than cheese," Naomi said. "Perhaps she should spend less time playing with those silly animals of hers and more time working in the kitchen. She'll be of courting age soon. A hardworking husband deserves a wife who can put up a *goot* meal every night."

"I've had Sadie's blueberry cobbler before," Levi interjected. "It was some of the best I've ever had."

Sadie beamed at him as Emma shot him a grateful look.

"Sadie is learning her way," Emma said to Naomi.

Her aunt frowned. "I still think she should spend less time out in the barn. And him!" She pointed her fork toward Ezekiel. "That boy—"

"*Mudder*," Amelia gently scolded, cutting off what was sure to be a scathing remark, "the children are doing fine."

Naomi harrumphed.

Out of respect, Levi fought to hold his tongue. Sadie and Zeke had just recently lost their father after worrying about his health for nearly a year. The children, who were barely children anymore, were well behaved. They were polite and they were kind, which was more than Levi felt he could say for

Naomi. Yet he knew it was not his place to say so. Not yet.

He gave Emma a sympathetic look. It had to be hard on her, hearing her aunt's unending criticisms. He knew how much she loved her siblings, and Naomi's words had to hurt her.

"What time is your driver arriving?" Amelia asked.

Naomi's brow furrowed. "He will be here at seven tomorrow morning."

Emma and Levi shared a questioning look.

"Tomorrow?" Emma echoed.

Amelia gave her a small smile. "I mentioned that *Mamm* would be heading back to Harmony."

Levi watched as Emma struggled to keep her expression even. "I didn't realize that she would be leaving so soon."

Leaving? Levi wanted to whoop with joy.

"I see no need to stay any longer," Naomi said. "As you know, Amelia has kindly agreed to stay on."

Levi, curious as to how Amelia felt about this assignment, turned to her with a questioning look on his face. He received his answer when he noted her pleased smile. Her eyes seemed to twinkle with excitement.

"You're happy to be staying in Pine Creek?" he asked.

"*Jah*. I am. I am looking forward to meeting new people."

"Perhaps you can find yourself a husband." Naomi stabbed at another pork chop and hoisted it onto her plate. "When I spoke with Mary today, she said there are quite a few eligible men in town. I asked her to be sure to speak to a few of them on your behalf."

Amelia ignored her mother. "I'm looking forward to getting to know my cousins better."

"We are happy to have her," Emma said.

Levi didn't doubt her. He knew she would never say the words, but he was sure Emma was relieved to be bidding her aunt farewell.

"I will be leaving everyone in Amelia's care," Naomi continued. "Perhaps she can teach Sadie how to make a decent pie crust. Surely, she can ensure that Ezekiel learns how to do something other than loaf around."

Levi noted the way the boy's face fell. He could not remain quiet.

"Zeke is a fine helper. I hear he's been cleaning the barn. And when it comes time to tap the trees, he hammers in the spiles along with the rest of us, then trudges through the snow to collect the sap." Naomi had grown up on this farm. Levi knew she had to be aware of how difficult the collecting of sap could be, especially in the years with heavy snowfall. "The boy never shies away from the fires that burn continuously until the syrup is boiled down."

"What of the fields?" Naomi asked.

"He's learning," Levi assured.

"At his age, he should be doing a lot more than he is. My Ron would never stand for a child to be so useless. Our boys were never afraid of a hard day's labor."

Ezekiel's chin dropped to his chest as his hand clenched his fork. Levi wanted to say more in his defense, but he feared it would only backfire, causing

Naomi to plow ahead with more criticism.

"Who is ready for dessert?" Amelia interjected.

Levi appreciated her interruption—he didn't want to get into an argument with Naomi. Not on her last night in the Ziegler home. She would be gone soon enough, and they would no longer have to listen to her grievances.

"I would love some of Emma's rhubarb pie," Levi said.

"I'll get it." Sadie bolted to her feet.

Ezekiel leaped up to help.

"Sit down," Naomi snapped. "A man's place is not in the kitchen. What has this family been teaching you?"

Ezekiel dropped back in his chair. His cheeks burned with shame, and he couldn't meet his aunt's glare.

Levi wanted to tell her that he had eaten many a meal here in the past. He had seen with his own eyes that Paul had no trouble retrieving something he wanted from the kitchen. Whether it be a butter knife or an extra piece of cake, he didn't wait for one of the girls to wait on him. Levi tapped his hand against his thigh. Judging by Naomi's expression, she felt the bishop was not the only one who was too lenient.

They had endured weeks of this woman. Now they had to get through only one more night.

The group ate their dessert in relative silence.

When the plates were ready to be cleared, Amelia stood.

"Sadie and I can clear the table and wash the dishes." She looked to her mother. "I believe it would be all right if Emma and Levi sat on the front porch for a while?"

Naomi frowned over the idea but apparently could think of no reason to object. "I suppose they could. I have some packing I must finish."

Levi nearly sighed in relief. He led the way to the front door, wishing he could whisk Emma away from the house, but for now, the front porch would have to do. As they settled onto the porch swing, he was painfully aware that Emma had scooted to the farthest edge of the space.

"Are you happy that Amelia is staying?" he asked.

"I am," she admitted. "She didn't want to return to Harmony."

"I'm surprised by that. Harmony, from what I've heard, is a fine community."

"It is," Emma agreed. "Unfortunately, it holds painful memories for her."

She explained to Levi that Amelia had been married, but her husband had been killed while walking home from a neighbor's farm one night after he'd helped deliver a calf that had been born out of season. It had been snowing heavily, the roads were slick with ice, and he'd been hit by a car. The driver was a young *Englisch* girl who had just gotten her license. The sun had set and she did not see him dressed in his dark jacket and pants.

Levi winced. "How long ago?"

"It happened three years ago this past winter," Emma said quietly. "It's been long enough that her *mamm* thinks she ought to remarry."

"Amelia disagrees?"

"She does. She doesn't feel she could ever love someone else as much as she loved her Gideon." Emma hesitated before adding, "Nor can she stand the thought of losing someone again. Naomi doesn't understand her hesitation."

"Amelia needs some time away from such pressure." After the meal tonight with Naomi, he thought that having her as a mother would be a trying affair. It was no wonder that Amelia wanted to stay in Pine Creek.

"Does your family know?"

"Know what?" Levi grinned at her. He knew what she was asking, but he wanted to hear her say it.

"Do they know that we are…courting?"

"*Jah*. Everyone, especially *Mamm*, is pleased."

Emma nodded, not looking the least bit pleased herself.

He wondered yet again if she was disappointed about not marrying Ivan, though it was a question he couldn't imagine asking her. His brother didn't seem to think Emma ever had strong feelings for him. It was part of the reason Ivan broke their engagement.

But there was more to it than that. Levi knew he needed to talk to Emma, needed to admit what he'd done. He was not looking forward to that conversation, though he was sure it had all worked out for the best in the end.

While he desperately wanted Emma for himself, he wanted her happy above all else, and he wasn't sure that Ivan could've made her truly happy. If they had wed, Levi knew Ivan would've remained faithful in deed, but his heart would've strayed. He'd been in love with Miriam for quite some time but was never sure if she felt the same way.

It wasn't until after Ivan ended things with Emma that he had the nerve to approach Miriam. Now the newlyweds exuded happiness. They had the sort of marriage that Levi longed for someday.

In that regard, everything had worked out for the best.

He lowered his voice, even though the window was closed. "Is Naomi always so unkind? Or was she unhappy that I came to supper?"

"This is her usual way," Emma admitted. "Amelia has told me many times not to take it personally. I don't mind so much when she criticizes me, but I wish she wouldn't be so harsh with Zeke and Sadie."

"She's very different from Paul."

Emma gave him a wobbly smile. "I have thought that many times. *Daed* was so gentle, so caring. Sadie takes after him in so many ways."

"As do you," Levi said.

She dropped her gaze and sighed. "I miss him terribly. The farm should belong to Zeke someday, but I'm afraid I won't be able to manage it on my own until then. What if I lose everything?"

Levi could only guess at how difficult it was for Emma to admit such a thing. He was touched that she was comfortable enough to share such vulnerability with him.

"That won't happen." His tone was firm. "This farm has been in your family for generations. It's not going anywhere."

"I want to believe that."

"Then believe it," he said simply. "You have the entire community supporting you. Nobody wants to see you fail."

Least of all, Levi.

He would do whatever he could to ensure Emma's happiness.

CHAPTER FOUR

Emma hummed a hymn as she peeled the potatoes. Naomi wouldn't have approved, but Naomi was no longer here. Already Emma felt a new lightness about the place. She tried to banish the thought, but her aunt's presence had been wearing.

"Is this thin enough?" Sadie held the rolling pin in the air.

Emma leaned over to inspect the pie crust. "It looks perfect. You can line it in the pie plate and start on the carrots."

"Are we having Levi over again tonight?" Sadie wondered.

"Not tonight." Emma wasn't sure when she would see him again. She felt an unexpected twinge of anticipation when she thought of Levi. She had missed her old friend.

She glanced at Sadie as the girl carefully lifted the crust into the pie plate. Her brow was furrowed in concentration, worried the crust would tear. When it was pressed into place, she relaxed.

"I love potpie," she said. "Perhaps I can perfect this one meal and find a husband who will be happy to eat it every night."

Emma laughed at her sister's reasoning. "You are a fine cook, Sadie. The few things you make often, you make well. Everything takes time and practice."

They worked together to finish the meal preparation. When the potpie was in the oven, Sadie gave

Emma a sly look. "I like Levi," she said.

Emma continued to scrub down the kitchen counter. "We all do. He's been very kind to us."

"I didn't know you two were stepping out before *Daed* died."

Emma continued to scrub. She would not lie to Sadie but wasn't ready to part with the truth, either.

Sadie continued on, unbothered by Emma's lack of response. "I'm happy you two are courting. I always thought Levi was a better match for you than Ivan. He's been smitten with you for such a long time, it must have been hard for him when you were with his *bruder*."

Emma laughed. "He's not smitten with me."

Sadie arched an eyebrow. "That's a silly thing to say."

Emma immediately realized her error. "What I meant to say was that he was not smitten with me when I was courting Ivan."

Sadie shook her head. "I'm not so sure about that. Levi's always had googly eyes when he looks at you."

Amused by her sister, Emma swatted her with the dish towel. Sadie laughed and leaped out of the way. "You are such a tease," Emma said with a smile. "Why don't you go outside and weed the garden?"

"I checked the garden this morning," Sadie said. "It doesn't need weeding yet."

"It's a beautiful day," Emma continued. "I'm sure you can find something to do outdoors."

Still giggling, Sadie rushed past Emma and headed outside. Emma knew Sadie probably thought she would change her mind and put her to work indoors if she hesitated too long.

Sadie, as Naomi often pointed out over the past month, lived with her head in the clouds. Emma didn't have time for such nonsense. She busied herself preparing a salad with produce from the garden. Supper was almost done, so she didn't dare stray too far from the kitchen.

The sound of the buggy alerted Emma to Amelia and Ezekiel's arrival. They had gone to town earlier in the day, as Amelia hoped to find employment. Emma had tried to tell her it wasn't necessary, but Amelia insisted that she wanted to contribute to groceries and whatnot.

Emma was setting the salad on the table when Amelia hurried into the kitchen. Emma smiled, reading her excitement. "I take it you have happy news?"

Amelia nodded. "I'm allowed to work at the Pine Cone Café. *Mamm* was right—your bishop is much more lenient than ours."

"I've heard he's more lenient than most," Emma confided. "He is a fair man and tries hard to do what's best for the people in this district."

Amelia nodded. "I was hired to do the baking. They need me several mornings a week. It's perfect—not too many hours so I can still help around the farm."

Emma was not surprised. Serving tables, or even seating people, the bishop would not have approved of. The Amish believed in staying apart from the rest of the world. Yet, often people in their district needed to find work to help supplement their incomes. Baking, where Amelia would be out of sight in the kitchen, seemed to be the perfect compromise.

"I'm happy for you." Emma had suggested the Pine Cone Café to Amelia because she knew of other Amish women who worked there. "It sounds like work you will enjoy."

"*Mamm* will not be pleased," Amelia admitted.

Emma cocked a curious eyebrow. "How will she know?"

"I've no doubt Mary will pass along the information." Amelia winced. "You do know that *Mamm* asked Mary to keep an eye on you and Levi?"

Emma shook her head, frowning. Perhaps she should not be surprised. Mary Kurtz was a spinster who lived in their district. Emma didn't know the woman well, but if Naomi had asked her to keep an eye on her and Levi, she suspected she'd be seeing quite a bit of the woman. Not that she would mind getting to know Mary better, but she did not like the circumstance thrust upon her.

Amelia made an apologetic face. "She did. *Mamm* might have left, but she still wants to keep her nose in everything. If it makes you feel better, Mary is to keep her informed about me as well. She wants Mary to pass along information on any acceptable suitors for me. I told her not to bother, but she won't listen."

"She certainly is determined." Emma took a moment to digest this news. While courting was often done in private, it seemed word always had a way of getting out. If she and Levi didn't step out together every now and again, Mary might start to wonder why. She would undoubtedly pass that information along to Naomi.

It looked as if she and Levi would have to do

their part and make a show of courting.

"Supper smells *wunderbaar*," Amelia said.

"It will be ready shortly. Where is Ezekiel? Is he rubbing Ginger down?"

"No, I did that," Amelia said. "What do you mean where is he? I just returned from town. I haven't seen him."

"He didn't go to town with you?"

"*Nee.*"

Emma pulled the oven door open. As she placed the hot pie plate on the stovetop, she said, "You've been gone for hours. I haven't seen him. We assumed he went into town with you."

"I haven't seen him since this morning," Amelia admitted. "I wouldn't have taken him for the day without making sure you knew."

Emma went out on the porch. Worry nipped at her, but she was trying not to panic. Amelia followed close behind.

Sadie was sitting on an overturned bucket, her favorite Marans hen nestled on her lap. A few other chickens were wandering around, pecking at the ground, keeping their lawn free of bugs. The Marans laid unusual, deep brown eggs that were popular with some of the townspeople. Whatever eggs they were unable to use for themselves, Sadie was easily able to sell. Naomi had not approved of Sadie's affection for her chickens, but Emma was happy her sister had something that brought her so much joy.

"Sadie," Emma called as she rushed up to her.

The chickens scattered, squawking and making an interminable racket that set Sadie's goats to bleating.

Sadie carefully placed Gretel on the ground before she stood. "What is it?"

"Ezekiel wasn't in town with Amelia. Do you have any idea where he could be?"

"I'll check the barn. Maybe he's in the hayloft." She hurried away.

"Where has that boy gone?" Emma asked as Amelia came to her side.

"He's a young boy. Isn't it possible he started wandering through the woods and lost track of time?"

"It's possible," Emma admitted. "But he's been gone nearly all day. He didn't come in for lunch." Besides, her brother had never been much for solitude. Anxiety sizzled up her spine.

"He's not in the barn," Sadie called as she ran up to the other women.

Emma cupped her hands over her mouth and shouted, "Ezekiel!" She waited a few moments, her heart beating frantically in her chest, before trying again.

When there was no response, the women looked at one another, fear creeping into their eyes, into their bones.

"Perhaps he's just too far away to hear. There's a bit of a breeze. Maybe your voice isn't carrying over the sound of the rustling leaves," Amelia suggested.

Heart pounding, Emma darted off toward the woods.

"Sadie and I can look through the northern part of the property," Amelia offered as she hurried behind her. "You take the south."

Emma didn't argue. She knew the woods well,

and so did Sadie. Amelia wouldn't get lost if she was with her.

None of the women had a timepiece, but Emma was sure nearly half an hour passed before they met up again. Her heart was clanging in her chest, and it wasn't from exertion.

"Maybe he's at the Bontrager farm," Amelia suggested. "At supper last night he seemed rather taken by Levi."

"He's never run off before," Emma said. "Not for more than a short time. Certainly not without telling us where he was going." She looked down the gravel drive. "I suppose it's possible he went to see Levi." She found herself clinging to that hope because if he wasn't there, she had no idea where else to look.

"I can hitch Ginger up," Amelia offered.

"It's not that far to the farm. I can be there before the buggy is ready." She took off at a run. It wasn't entirely ladylike, but she didn't particularly care. She was sweating and gasping for air by the time she reached the Bontragers' front porch.

"Emma?"

She spun around and spotted Levi coming out of the barn. He began jogging toward her.

"What is it?" he demanded.

"It's Ezekiel. He's missing." She pulled in a breath. "I thought he went to town with Amelia after breakfast, but she returned earlier and he wasn't with her. We've searched the property. I was hoping he was here with you."

"I saw Ezekiel this morning," Diana said.

Emma spun around again. She hadn't heard Levi's mother come onto the front porch.

"When? Where?" Emma pressed her hand against her chest, willing her heart to slow.

"He was riding that old bike of yours down the road. He had a fishing pole."

"A fishing pole?" Emma echoed. "Why would he go fishing and not tell me?"

"Come on," Levi said, "I just got home. I haven't unhitched the horse yet."

"I should tell Sadie and Amelia. They're worried as well."

"You go find your *bruder*," Diana said. "I'll walk over to your farm and tell them what I saw."

Emma thanked her for the offer before she and Levi rushed to the buggy and climbed up.

"He had to have gone to the river," Emma said.

"It sounds like it."

"I *canna* believe he took the bicycle," Emma said. "I didn't realize it was missing."

Her *daed* had purchased the used, three-wheeled bicycle in case of an emergency, should one ever arise while the buggy was in use. Several districts didn't allow them, but even though theirs did, they used it sparingly.

"He's been gone since this morning. What if something happened to him?" Emma worried.

"Remember all the times we fished when we were *kinner*?" he reminded.

She nodded, recalling how much she used to enjoy the activity in her youth. When they were young and carefree, back before her *mamm* had passed, she and Levi could fish an entire day away.

"Then you must remember how easy it was to lose track of time." His tone was soothing, as was the way he gave her shoulder a gentle squeeze. She wanted to lean into him, to rely on his strength, but fear continued to niggle at her.

She hoped he'd simply lost track of time. Ezekiel wasn't a strong swimmer. It was hard not to worry that he'd fallen in and been swept away.

Levi's horse trotted along at a steady pace. Emma wanted to beg him to go faster.

Finally, the buggy turned off the main road. The gravel drive led to a picnic area along the river, where children sometimes swam or fished. There were a handful of picnic tables higher up on the riverbank. It was tucked away, so it wasn't often in use. The moment they rounded a bend in the road, Emma let out a sigh of relief.

She spotted Ezekiel standing at the edge of the riverbank. He glanced over his shoulder when he heard the buggy approach.

A smile broke out from one ear to the other when Zeke spotted Emma. He went to the water's edge and tugged at something, and she realized a creel of fish was dangling from his hand. Under other circumstances, she'd be impressed. Right now, she was just plain miffed.

"Look how many I caught, Emma." Ezekiel was buzzing with excitement. "I caught enough for our supper."

She leaped from the buggy before it had come to a complete halt.

Levi called after her but she ignored him. Hurrying to her brother, she said, "What are you doing here?"

"I'm fishing." He frowned at Emma's confusion.

"Fishing?" Emma cried. "You've been fishing all day? It did not occur to you to tell me where you'd gone?"

Her voice was shrill, and she knew perhaps she was being unreasonable. The arched-eyebrow look from Levi told her so. But her heart was still pounding; she'd been so afraid he'd fallen in the river. Or... something.

She dug her fists into her hips. "Well?"

"I'm sorry I didn't tell you. I just…"

"Just what?" Levi prodded, far more gently than Emma was capable of in that moment.

"I was afraid I wouldn't catch any."

Emma motioned for him to go on because that did not seem like a good enough explanation.

"I didn't want anyone to know that Aunt Naomi was right. That I'm not *goot* for anything."

Emma's heart immediately plummeted to her stomach.

Zeke raised his chin defiantly. She knew it wasn't a defiant gesture toward her, but likely defiance toward the tears that were threatening to fall. He was a thirteen-year-old boy, standing before his older sister and a man. Crying would be mortifying.

Levi stepped forward and put a hand on his shoulder. "There is no shame in trying." Emma saw his fingers give her brother's shoulder a gentle squeeze, to push the point home. "There is failure only in not trying. Do you understand?"

Ezekiel nodded.

"You scared your *schweschter* senseless."

Ezekiel nodded again. He raised his eyes to Emma and said regretfully, "I'm really sorry. I didn't mean to be gone so long. I guess I lost track of time."

Emma closed her eyes and pulled in a breath. When she opened them again, she felt more composed. "I'm sorry if I sound unreasonable. But after losing *Daed*…when we couldn't find you…when no one knew where you'd gone…I was afraid…" Her own voice trembled, leaving her unable to speak in complete sentences.

Ezekiel lowered his gaze once more.

"I was afraid of losing you."

He moved forward and wrapped his arms around Emma's waist. She hugged him tightly. Relief spilled through her, drowning out any frustration she'd felt.

"I'm sorry. I didn't know."

She gave him one final squeeze. "Now you do. So don't do it again." Her tone was firm but there was a gentleness to it this time. "As for Aunt Naomi, we know she means well, but she can be"—Emma struggled for a fitting descriptor—"harsh."

"You," Levi said firmly, "are not worthless. You are one of God's children. He loves you wholly and completely. You are not worthless to your family, either—they love you. They worry about you."

Ezekiel studied his sister's face.

She nodded. While pride was a sin, Emma was certain that God did not want his children to feel badly about themselves, either. Naomi's words had caused Ezekiel to do just that.

"You are a *wunderbaar* young man," Levi continued on. "With a lot to offer. Don't forget that. And next time you go fishing, do *not* forget to tell your *schweschter* where you are going."

"I won't," Ezekiel said firmly. "I'm sorry, Emma. I

didn't mean to scare you."

"Apology accepted." She motioned to her brother's catch. "It sure does look like you have a knack for fishing. Look at all those."

Ezekiel grinned shyly at the compliment.

Levi let out a low whistle. "Now that we have that all straightened out, do you know how to clean them?"

Zeke's smile slipped and he shook his head.

"I'd be happy to show you, if Emma doesn't mind."

"I would be grateful," Emma honestly replied. She was also grateful for how Levi had handled the situation with her brother. He had been firm with him while not being unkind, and Zeke had responded to his attention so well. It caused a new concern to flutter through her. Her brother was still so young, and to be without a father would be particularly hard on him. Emma was so relieved that Levi was here to be a role model, at least temporarily. She ignored the pang of melancholy that arose at the thought of Levi flitting out of her life again.

"You've got enough for tonight and I'd guess at least one more meal."

"Can you stay for supper?" Zeke asked, his tone hopeful.

Levi looked at Emma, his mouth twitching and his eyes twinkling. "I don't know. *May* I stay for supper?"

Emma felt a smile tug at her lips. "I think that would be only fair."

She didn't mention that supper was already prepared at home. They would simply save the potpie for tomorrow. Ezekiel was so happy to be contributing, she didn't want to ruin the moment for him.

• • •

Levi was relieved that Emma's ire had faded as they bounced along the road to the Ziegler farm. He'd carefully placed the bicycle in the back. Zeke had been fishing all day, without food, in the hot sun. He knew the boy must be famished.

"What did you use to catch those fish?" Levi asked.

Zeke glanced at Emma, then quickly looked away. "I dug some night crawlers out of the garden."

Emma shot him a look. "You were digging in my garden?"

Levi grinned. Her anger had subsided and now her tone had taken on a teasing nature. This was the side of Emma that he was so fond of.

"I was careful," Zeke said quickly. "I didn't disturb any seedlings."

"I should hope not," she huffed with a twinkle in her eye.

Levi chuckled and Emma raised an eyebrow at him.

"I've forgotten how feisty you can be." He hadn't spent much time around Emma and Ivan, but when he had, he'd noticed Emma's personality was much more subdued. As if she was always minding her manners and holding herself in check.

He never wanted her to do that with him.

She opened her mouth, most likely to give a feisty retort, but then snapped it back shut when he continued to chuckle. The smirk she wore let him know she was having trouble holding back.

"Levi?"

Levi tossed a glance over his shoulder to look at Ezekiel.

"Do you think you could go fishing with me sometime?"

Emma turned to him with a curious expression.

He would be happy to go fishing with Ezekiel. He knew he could never replace Paul, didn't want to, but thought the boy could use some time away from a house filled with women.

"I would enjoy that," he said.

He was rewarded with a soft smile from Emma. It pleased him that she appreciated his offer.

The rest of the ride home was filled with Ezekiel's chatter. He told the tale of each fish he caught, and of those he released. By the time they reached the Ziegler farm, Levi thought he had never heard the boy talk so much in his life.

It was not a bad thing.

The more the boy chatted, the happier Emma looked.

"Thank you," she said when Ezekiel ran toward the house to tell Sadie and Amelia of his fishing adventures. "He misses *Daed* terribly. He's so quiet, sometimes I think I overlook him. It means a lot to me that you're helping him with the fish tonight."

"Didn't your *daed* teach him how to clean fish?" Levi's tone was curious, not accusatory.

"*Nee*." Emma shook her head. "He didn't have much time for fishing. He always said he didn't like the taste of them, even when he did catch a few."

"*Jah*," Levi said. "Now I remember. When I used to take you fishing, Paul always insisted I bring the entire catch home with me."

"I never minded. I liked fishing with you; it was always fun. But I never told you I was afraid of cleaning them." She shuddered comically. "I was more than happy to let you take them all."

"Ah, now I see." He laughed. "I thought you were being kind. But you were actually being a scaredy-cat."

"I'm not a scaredy-cat! I'm just…" She wrinkled her nose. "Not fond of fish guts."

"But if I do the work, you'd be happy to eat them?"

"For sure." Emma grinned. "Feel free to take Ezekiel fishing anytime, now that he'll be learning to clean them so I won't have to."

He chuckled. "Fishing is not a hardship. I don't know why I don't do it more often. I'll be glad to take him."

"*Danki*. I'm sure he tires of spending his time with us women." She hesitated, looking contemplative. "This past year, when *Daed* was sick, I am just realizing that Zeke was on his own much of the time. Naomi accused us of coddling him, but I actually don't think we coddled. I think we neglected him."

She wrapped her arms around her waist, hugging herself. It was clear the revelation bothered her. He didn't want her to feel guilty for it. Paul's illness had affected all his children and had taken its toll on the family. They had handled it the best they could at the time.

"That's in the past," Levi gently reminded. "The

boy is still young, but perhaps it's time to start giving him more responsibility."

The screen door slammed and Ezekiel pounded down the steps.

"Time to get these fish cleaned," Levi said.

"I'll get some potatoes peeled and set to boiling. Bring the fish in when they're ready," she said, grateful for his help.

Less than an hour later, Levi found himself, once again, seated at the Ziegler table. After they each said their silent blessing, the meal was passed around. He helped himself to a heaping serving of mashed potatoes, buttered peas, a dinner roll, and the freshly caught fish.

The scent of homemade brownies hung in the air, promising a satisfying dessert.

"Amelia is going to start baking for the Pine Cone Café," Sadie said.

"Is that right?" Levi glanced at Amelia.

"It is."

Sadie passed him a container of fresh herbed goat cheese. He took it and gladly spread some on his dinner roll.

"That must mean you're planning on staying in Pine Creek awhile," Levi assumed.

Amelia nodded. "I would like to stay for as long as the family will have me."

"We love having you here," Emma assured her.

Her presence brought some comfort to Levi. He knew it would be good for Emma to have the company. Yes, she could use the help, but he also felt better knowing there was another adult in the house.

He was grateful that he lived right down the road

and could come to Emma's aid at a moment's notice. He knew she was capable of taking care of matters on her own, yet she shouldn't always have to. He would be much happier if they were wed and he was a permanent part of her life.

As he watched her smile at something her brother said, he asked God for guidance, for His blessing, for a way to make that happen.

CHAPTER FIVE

Emma stared at the letter in her hand. Amelia had taken Sadie and Ezekiel to town with her to run errands, and Emma couldn't remember the last time she'd had an afternoon to herself. Amelia had suggested she read a book or take a leisurely walk. She'd walked as far as the mailbox and now wished she hadn't.

"This can't be." Tears stung her eyes, blurring her vision. She hastily blinked them away so she could read the letter again. But it was as she feared. She hadn't misunderstood. "Oh, *Daed*," she moaned. "How did this happen?"

Clutching the letter and a seed catalog in her hand, she trudged back to the house. She resisted the urge to go up to her room, toss herself on the bed, and have a good cry. Instead, she went to the kitchen and sat at the table. She placed her head in her hands as she tried to come up with a plan.

Much too soon, she heard the sound of buggy wheels and stifled a groan as she wiped away an errant tear. She had hoped for a little more time to pull herself together. She darted around the room, trying to figure out where best to hide the letter.

"Emma?"

She whirled at the sound of her name.

"Levi!"

He took in her disheveled state as he strode into the kitchen. With a look of concern, he said, "I knocked and when no one answered, I let myself in because the front door was open."

She hadn't heard him knock. She had probably been busy blowing her nose. Or stifling a sob.

"What's wrong?" His clear blue eyes studied her face.

She was too distraught to even try to pretend she was okay.

"Emma, you can tell me anything."

His gentle tone was her undoing. A sob broke loose. Despite pressing her fingers against her lips, she couldn't stop another one from breaking free.

"*Ach*, Emma." Levi crossed the room in two quick strides, pulling her against his chest. She didn't have the energy or desire to protest. For once, it was a relief to not have to be the strong one.

She sobbed quietly for a few moments, simply taking comfort in Levi's arms around her, accepting the support he was so freely giving. It was utterly inappropriate to be in Levi's arms, and in her kitchen of all places. But she couldn't force herself to peel away.

"I know you must miss your *daed*," he murmured.

"I do, Levi. More than you can imagine," she admitted. "But it's not just that."

Reality came crashing down on her again. Her gaze slid to the drawer where she'd hastily stuffed the envelope from the county. With a shuddering breath, she moved away from Levi, averting her gaze.

He reached for her, encircling her wrist. "Talk to me. If it's more than missing your *daed*, maybe I can help."

She didn't want to turn to face him, but she knew she owed him an explanation. She shook her head. "You can't help."

Using the pad of his thumb, he brushed the remnants of tears from her cheeks. His hand lingered, his palm gently cupping her face, and her heart picked up speed. His concerned eyes studied her, and she saw so much compassion there. In that moment, she longed for a real relationship, a husband. But she would have to settle for a friend.

Levi said, "I might be able to help, but first, you have to tell me what the problem is."

She stepped away from him, tugged open the neatly organized junk drawer, and pulled out the envelope. She held it out to him, silently encouraging him to read it because she didn't want to have to explain it. "Please don't tell my family about this."

Clearly confused, he took the letter. It took him only a minute or two to read it and to understand the enormity of what it said. "Emma…"

"I know."

"That's a lot of money," he said. "Did you know your *daed* was so far behind on property taxes?"

Emma bit her lip and shook her head. She'd had no idea. Now she owed not only the back taxes, but fines and interest, and the total came to thousands of dollars. While the amount wasn't insurmountable, it was certainly more than she could imagine coming up with in the timeframe given.

"You could go to the bishop," Levi suggested.

"*Nee.*" Emma's refusal was immediate.

He hesitated, as if choosing his words carefully. "This isn't a time to be prideful. This notice says you have only ninety days to get caught up. If you don't—"

"I'll lose the farm," Emma finished for him. "I know. But it's not about pride. Our community has already done more than enough. Emergency funds were given to us to help cover the hospital bill." She blew out a breath. That bill had been enormous. The Amish did not believe in insurance, so she'd been beyond grateful for the community's help in covering her father's care. "I believe we nearly drained the fund dry. I *canna* ask for anything more." She paused, gathering her resolve. "I need to take care of this myself."

"How?"

Levi's question was blunt.

She didn't have an answer.

"I don't know," she admitted. "But I have some time. They won't come after the farm for a while. I'll simply need to come up with the money on my own." She took the envelope from him, shoved the letter back in the drawer, then said, "I don't want to think about this anymore today." Thinking about it meant she'd have to address the fact that Naomi might have been right. That she wasn't capable and the only logical thing to do was sell the farm.

But she did not want to sell the farm.

She wouldn't.

"I have some money set aside—"

"No." She cut him off with a sharp shake of her head.

He seemed to debate arguing but decided against it. "You should come with me," he said. "*Mamm* sent me over to ask if you'd like to come for a visit."

Emma had been so flustered by the letter that she hadn't even questioned why Levi had stopped by. She nodded. "I would like that. Can we go right now?"

When Levi offered her his hand, she took it.

• • •

Levi hated seeing Emma so upset. He wished he knew how to take this burden from her. But she didn't seem to want his help. The buggy ride back to the farm was a quick one.

"Emma!" his *daed* called as he strode out of the barn. "What a nice surprise!" He closed the distance between them in no time. "How is everything going?" Before Emma had a chance to answer, he said, "If you need help with anything, you just let us know."

She nodded and forced a smile for his father. "I will. *Danki.*"

"I'll take care of the horse." His *daed* pointed toward the house. "Diana has a special treat for you, I hear. You should probably go on in and not keep her waiting."

"We'll do that," Levi said.

They found his mother in the kitchen. She was sitting at the table, right where Levi had left her. Her arm pumped round and round, cranking the ice cream maker.

"Emma!" she said, her eyes lighting with delight. "Am I ever happy to see you!"

A genuine laugh escaped Emma's lips. "I'm sure that you are." She crossed the room, making a shooing motion with her hands as she neared the table.

"Gladly," Diana said. She slid out of the chair, giving her arm a good, comical shake.

Emma slid into the chair Diana had just vacated. She immediately took over the tedious task of turning the crank. "I didn't know you were making ice cream today."

His mother laughed. "Neither did I. But Jessa," she said, mentioning one of her daughters-in-law, "dropped off a bucketful of strawberries. I didn't want to break tradition, so I sent Levi down to the basement for the ice cream maker. He already took his turn churning." For as long as Levi could remember, they had made ice cream with the first strawberries of the season. She gave Emma a gentle smile. "I still remember the day I found this old ice cream maker," his mother said.

He knew the story well but also knew Emma liked hearing it.

"My mother thought you were a bit silly for buying it," she said.

Diana nodded. "We were at a flea market. It was filthy and broken. The container was missing a few wooden slats, the crank missing a few screws. But it was so *hot* that summer. I didn't have much money with me, but the person selling it took pity on me."

"Or maybe he knew you'd be the only one silly enough to buy it," Emma said, repeating her mother's words from long ago.

"That's probably just it," Diana said. "I brought it home and scrubbed it down. Then my Moses fixed it right up. Now we've used it every summer since."

Emma's smile slipped as she continued to churn the ice cream. She looked as if she were lost in time, or perhaps only lost in her thoughts about the letter.

His *mamm* shot a worried look over Emma's head. Levi mouthed, *Later*. Emma had asked him not to tell her family about the letter but hadn't said he couldn't talk to his. He was close to his parents, he valued their opinions, and they'd never led him astray.

"Well then," Diana said as she wiped her hands on her apron, "I think I've had enough churning for the day. There's about twenty minutes left, if I'm not mistaken. I'll leave you to it. I need to speak with Moses. Jessa invited us for supper tomorrow, so I should let him know." She patted Levi's shoulder as she walked by. He knew what she was up to, offering him some time alone with Emma, and he was grateful for it.

Levi leaned against the kitchen counter. "How's the churning?"

"I can't believe that when we were *kinners* we used to fight over who got to turn the crank." She frowned comically. "My arm is already burning."

He pushed off from the counter. "Want me to—"

"*Nee*," she said, shaking her head firmly. "You already had your turn."

He settled against the counter again, fighting down a smile. Emma could be so stubborn.

Her arm continued, round and round, spinning the inner metal container through the ice and rock salt that surrounded it, freezing the mixture within to a divine consistency. Homemade ice cream was a lot of work. And though it was delicious, for his family and Emma's it was more about tradition. Making ice cream always created a feeling of nostalgia.

"Sadie and Ezekiel will be disappointed they missed out," Emma said as she switched, churning awkwardly with her left hand now instead of her right.

His biceps still burned thinking of his own turn earlier that day. Even though he was used to lifting hay bales and pallets of shingles, the ice cream crank never failed to do him in.

"I'm sure *Mamm* will send the leftovers home for your family," he said.

He watched, trying to hide an amused smile as Emma's strength began to wane. Neither of them ever wanted to admit that they were about to be outdone by the antique gadget.

"Remember how we always used to talk about all the flavors we'd make someday?" Emma asked. "Peanut butter banana was at the top of my list."

"Peanut butter jelly."

"Pumpkin spice."

Levi wrinkled his nose. "I was never interested in that one. I still think we should make mint chocolate chip."

"I think peach would be *appendlitch*," said Emma. "The *Englischers* have them shipped up to sell at Saturday Market in the fall."

It was a running joke between them. They would never make anything other than strawberry. It was a once-a-summer treat. Levi knew that they made electric ice cream makers, but that was out of the question. He also thought if he looked hard enough, he could probably find a new manual one that was not so cantankerous, so hard to churn.

But that was part of the charm of this one. It held

so many memories.

"We're almost there," he said. "I'll take out some glasses."

The consistency of the dessert fresh out of the container was like that of a milkshake. They could put it in the gas freezer to firm it up, but no one ever wanted to wait that long. He pulled four large matching glasses out of the cupboard, then grabbed some spoons.

When he turned around, Emma had switched back to her right arm and was wincing.

Levi reached for the crank, but Emma playfully pushed his hand away. "I'm almost done."

"You have three minutes left," Levi said. "Let me help you out."

Emma maneuvered her body, blocking the machine from him.

He tossed his hands up in the air and laughed. "Suit yourself."

A few minutes later, Emma let out an exaggerated groan. "I think we're done."

She rubbed her aching muscles with her other hand.

Minutes later, they had the four glasses filled.

"We have to eat these outside," Emma said. That, too, was tradition.

They each took two glasses and headed down to the barn. They gave Levi's parents each one, then, without needing to discuss it, they moved to the swing set.

Emma giggled and said, "Do you remember the time—"

"*Jah*," Levi said, cutting her off with a smirk.

"You don't know what I was going to say," Emma argued with a laugh.

"Of course I do," Levi said, grinning at her. "You were going to ask if I remembered the time the swing broke and I landed on my backside in the dirt." He gave her a questioning look, daring her to deny it. She did *not* deny it. "It's a little hard to forget something like that."

He wished he could forget it. That day, they were sixteen, almost old enough to start courting. He had brought Emma out to the swings, where he had planned to tell her how he felt about her. He had hoped to ask if they could court as soon as their parents allowed it.

Instead, he found himself laid out on the ground, with Emma standing over him, the broken swing swaying in the breeze. The wooden board had snapped and sent him toppling. As soon as she realized he hadn't damaged any bones, and that the only thing that hurt was his ego, she'd laughed so hard she'd had tears in her eyes. He knew he must've been a sight. Flat on his back, staring up at the sky with a bewildered look on his face.

He had always wondered where they would be right now if he'd managed to get the words out that night. Then again, they had been young. Maybe too young. He believed that God had a plan for his life, and he had to believe that he'd landed in the dirt because the time for telling Emma how he felt hadn't been right.

But now here they were.

He had replaced both wooden swings with new, sturdy pieces of wood long ago. He also tested the ropes every summer. He knew they were sturdy and would not break this time.

He eased himself onto one of the swings, Emma carefully seating herself on the one next to him. She wrapped her arms around the ropes so that she could still eat her ice cream. With one foot, she gently set her swing into motion.

"I had such a crush on you," Levi blurted. He pushed himself off, causing his own swing to gently sway.

"Oh, you did not," Emma scoffed.

"I did," Levi said. He wanted to add, *Still do*, but the words wouldn't come.

Emma gave him a teasing smile. "Growing up so close to me, you didn't think of me as a *schweschter*?"

His face scrunched. "A *schweschter*? *Nee*." He laughed. "I did not." Not even close. His laughter quickly cut off as a troubling thought struck. "Did you think of me as a *bruder*?" What if she had and still thought of him that way? That possibility was like a kick to the head.

She laughed. "*Nee*, Levi. I have never thought of you as a *bruder*."

"Well," said Levi, "*goot*."

"It seems to me you had quite the crush on Betsy," Emma pressed ahead.

"Betsy? *Nee*." He shook his head and swirled his spoon around in his glass. Betsy was the first girl he'd ever courted. He hadn't known what he was getting into.

"*Nee*? You courted her for quite some time."

Should he admit to Emma that he stepped out with Betsy only because she'd been quite forward and had asked him? He had been too flustered to come up with a kind way to turn her down. One buggy ride had turned into another and another. After that, she always glued herself to his side at singings, and if he so much as glanced at another girl—only Emma, really—she gave him a look that could have sent him into the ground.

"She made it very hard to say no," Levi admitted.

"How so?" she wondered.

"You know what she's like," he said. They had all gone to school together. "She's very…"

"Intimidating?" Emma offered.

"Scary," Levi said. "And bossy. From the start, she had our entire lives planned out. She wanted me to buy a farm because she was not about to wait for me to inherit this one. I was to plant her four apple trees and two cherry trees. She wanted five *kinners*—no more, no less. She even had names picked out. She wanted seven chickens and knew exactly how she expected me to build her henhouse." He raised his eyebrows at her. "She wanted it to be two stories, with a ramp, if you can believe that. It took a lot of resolve to tell her I didn't want to see her anymore." He had thought maybe she'd chase him off her father's property with a pitchfork. Instead, she'd chased him away with a glare and some harsh words.

He'd gotten off easy.

"How very brave of you." Emma smirked.

"She still gives me the evil eye every time I run into her," Levi confided.

"What about Trisha?"

Levi fought down a shudder. "Ah, Trisha," he said.

"She's very pretty."

It was her looks that had drawn him in. He'd soon realized *that* was a big mistake. Trisha was very attractive, but she was also very needy. "Almost every time we were together, she would ask if I saw a future with her. She would get all teary if I took too long to answer."

Emma smiled sympathetically. "Poor Trisha. She's always been an emotional one."

That was for sure. She would frequently ask him where he saw them in a year. He always struggled to answer because he could hardly envision himself past the next week. Ending things with her had been rough, because the tears had been immediate. Luckily, he'd thought to bring a hankie.

"And Faith?"

He laughed. "Faith spent time with me only because she wanted to make Timothy jealous. It worked, and now they're wed."

"That wasn't very nice," Emma said.

He shrugged. He had asked to court Faith only because Emma was courting someone and he was trying to take his mind off it. So really, it had worked out just fine. "What about you? You didn't court Aaron for very long."

Her smile slipped. "Aaron thought I spent too much time taking care of Sadie and Zeke. He told me I needed to make more time for him. When I couldn't do that…" She shrugged, letting him infer the result for himself.

"He ended your relationship because you're too kind and caring." He shook his head.

"I don't think he saw it that way," Emma

admitted. She took a bite of her ice cream and he did the same.

"Was there anyone else?" Levi asked. Courting was often carried out in secret, though word usually got out. Still, if Emma had been stepping out with anyone else, he wasn't aware of it.

"Just Aaron, and then Ivan," Emma admitted. "I thought maybe he was right. Maybe it wasn't fair of me to start a relationship with someone when so much of my time was devoted to my family."

"What isn't fair," Levi said, "is for a man to expect you to choose between the two. You should be able to see someone and still let your family be a priority."

Emma studied him a moment. "You really think so?"

"I do. That's one of the things I admire the most about you: you put your family first. You know what's important in life," Levi said.

"And you've courted no one since Faith?" Emma wondered.

"Most everyone has married off," Levi said. "There's really no one left to ask." No one but Emma, the only one he had ever really wanted.

Emma's smile seemed to falter.

Had he said something wrong?

She quickly turned her attention to her ice cream, frowning as she took a bite.

His gaze wandered to his parents. They were both leaning against the fence, eating their ice cream. He could hear his mother's laughter. At one point, *Daed* leaned in, presumably to swipe a smudge off *Mamm*'s face. He had always known how lucky he was to have such a wonderful family. He'd been especially aware of it because Emma had such a large piece missing from hers. Maybe someday they could create their own.

Whoa.

He needed to rein in those thoughts. He was happy they were spending time together, but they were a long way from spending *forever* together.

He glanced over at her. She was watching his parents with a look of longing on her face. It made him think maybe that's what she wanted for her future, too.

"Does your *daed* still enjoy farming?" she asked.

"He does," Levi said. "I don't think he's ready to give it up anytime soon." He didn't have to explain to Emma what that meant; she already knew. As the youngest son, he would inherit the farm someday. Just like Ezekiel would inherit Paul's. That day was a little too far off in the future for his liking.

"I'm thinking of buying my own farm," he admitted.

"Really?"

He turned to Emma and found that she was studying him with a look of curiosity.

"I'm grateful to have a job on the carpentry crew. I've learned a lot. But..." He shrugged.

"But it's not what you want to be doing," Emma said. "You would rather be farming."

"I would," he admitted. "I've been putting money aside. Just for something real small for now. Then when *Daed* is ready to retire, I could sell my place and take over this one."

"It sounds like a logical plan," Emma said.

"It will be a while still," Levi replied. "I have some savings, but not quite enough yet." He dug his toe into the dirt, stilling the swing. "It's just as well. Right now, I'm exactly where I want to be. With your farm right down the road, I like being nearby to help if you need it."

He thought maybe she would argue, tell him she was completely capable and didn't need his help.

Instead, she pushed herself off with her toes again and said, "Thanks, Levi. Thank you for the offer. And thank you for today."

He nodded. "Anytime, Emma. Anytime at all."

CHAPTER SIX

The Pine Cone Lodge rested at the edge of town. Over the winter months, it stayed busy with snowmobilers and downhill skiers. In the summer months, it was just as busy, filled with people wanting to enjoy the abundance of lakes in the area.

It seemed to Emma that regardless of the time of year, the tourists were taken with the Amish. She had a hard time understanding this, as it just didn't make sense to her that being a good servant was spectacle worthy. She knew that Amish settlements everywhere gathered attention, that the *Englischers* would pay good money for tours through Amish communities. She thought it odd, but it was something she had gotten used to.

As Levi's buggy rolled into the small town of Pine Creek, she felt the stares of the tourists. She kept her eyes averted, not wanting to give them a chance to snap pictures with their phones. Though the Amish believed the Bible warned against taking photos — creating graven images — many *Englischers* did not seem to care, completely disregarding Amish belief.

She kept her head lowered as they were brought to a private, corner table in the Pine Cone Café.

"Can I get a cheeseburger?" Ezekiel asked.

"You *always* get a cheeseburger," Sadie admonished.

"So?" He frowned.

"So, you may get a cheeseburger," Emma agreed.

"That sounds *goot*," Levi said. "I think I'll have the same."

"Perhaps I will, too," Emma said. "I *canna* remember the last time I had one. They always taste better when someone else makes them."

Her friend Rachael Esh worked in the kitchen, as did two other Amish women she knew.

"What are you going to have, Sadie?" Levi asked.

"I suppose I should have a cheeseburger as well," she answered primly.

Ezekiel snickered. "It's a fine choice."

An *Englisch* waitress took their order, complete with chocolate malts for everyone. Sadie and Ezekiel asked if they could be excused to look through the gift shop that was connected by the lodge's lobby. Emma gave them permission and they hurried away.

"Does Amelia enjoy working here?" Levi asked.

"So far," Emma said. "She's left the house at five o'clock every morning this week and has had nothing but kind things to say. The Hansons are fair employers."

"I've heard that from several people," Levi said. "Does Naomi know about her new job?"

A smile tugged at Emma's lips. "If she does, it's not from Amelia. Nor has Amelia told her *mamm* that she's overtaken our bicycle. She rides it into town every morning. I wouldn't doubt Naomi will hear about it from Mary."

"Ah, Naomi's childhood friend." Levi nodded. "Is she keeping Naomi updated about all the goings-on in town?"

"I would imagine," Emma admitted. "Naomi warned Amelia that she would."

"I have news that might please her," Levi said. "And hopefully you as well." He glanced around the café to ensure no one was within earshot. "I think it may help with the *problem* with the county."

She waited expectantly for him to continue.

"Harvey Larson asked me about buying your hay," Levi said.

"Harvey?" He was a local *Englisch* dairy farmer. For several years now he'd purchased hay from Paul to keep his cows fed throughout the winter. "Why you?" Emma wondered, feeling a bit put out. "Why didn't he just come to me?"

In the past, Harvey would've spoken to her father. It irked her that he went through Levi instead of coming to her.

"I ran into him at the feedstore. He knows we're neighbors." Levi frowned. "I'm sorry—I should have directed him to you."

She waved a dismissive hand. "It's all right." It wasn't Levi's fault. It wasn't as if he'd searched Harvey out without her permission; the man had come to him. "What did he say?"

"He asked if I thought you would be willing to let him bring in the hay for you. The first crop will need to be cut by the end of the month."

Emma was aware of this and had been trying not to fret about it. It was a big job and one she'd never taken part in. In the past, Paul had borrowed a friend's draft horses and equipment to first cut, then bale the hay. Before she left, Naomi had suggested that Ezekiel be given the chore, but Emma was not sure he could handle it. It was a grown man's job, and even then, it was strenuous work.

"He'd like to buy all the hay, probably at a discount for doing the work," Levi said.

"All the hay?" Emma wrinkled her nose in confusion. There were several local *Englisch* farmers who had purchased hay from Paul. "He never buys all of it."

"He expanded his herd this year. He's anxious to secure a food supply for the winter," Levi explained. "It's several days' work."

"It might be worth it," Emma said. It would simplify the process if he cut, dried, baled, and transported the hay himself. "I'll have to get approval from the bishop, I would imagine." She wasn't sure if he would approve of an *Englischer* haying her field with his own equipment.

"Harvey said he was really sorry to hear about Paul. I know he'll give you a fair price for the crop," Levi said. "He'd like an answer in the next few weeks so he can get his baler ready if needed."

"I would like to take him up on it after I check with Bishop Yoder."

Levi smiled. "I thought it sounded like a *goot* plan. I can check with the bishop if you'd like. I could explain the situation to him."

"*Nee*," Emma said. "*Danki*, but I can speak with him myself. I appreciate your offer, but it's my family's farm. It's my responsibility."

He hesitated only a moment before nodding. By now, Sadie and Ezekiel were meandering back to the table. It was time to move on from the conversation.

"Shelly said a lady purchased an entire case of syrup this morning." Sadie's eyes lit up with the news she shared. "She wanted gifts to give to her friends and family back home."

"*Wunderbaar*!" Emma was pleased with the news. Between syrup sales and Harvey Larson's offer to purchase the hay, her finances were looking a bit less precarious. She would need to use some of the money for their everyday expenses, but hopefully she could put aside some for the taxes as well. She sent up a silent prayer, thanking God for being such a steadfast provider.

"Emma, I thought that was you."

Emma swiveled in her seat as Rachael Esh, her dearest friend, reached their table.

"*Hallo*, Rachael."

"How are you?" Rachael asked. Her eyes skimmed the table, stopping only briefly on Levi before flitting back to Emma. "We should get together soon."

"I'm doing well," Emma said. "And I would like that."

"Did you come to town for the burgers?" Rachael teased.

Emma laughed. "Not entirely. Levi needed to go to the hardware store and asked if we'd like to ride along. Zeke's growing so quickly, I need to purchase more fabric or he'll have nothing to wear soon. I plan to pick some out today." It was an expense that could not be avoided.

Rachael's expression turned serious. "Did you hear about the Millers' barn?"

"What of it?" Levi demanded.

"One of the enormous white pines on their property fell on it. The damage was extensive," Rachael explained.

Levi winced. "It was an old barn, not very sound. If a tree of that size caused damage, it would not be salvageable."

"*Nee*, it wasn't," Rachael agreed. "It had to be torn down. A barn raising is planned for a few weeks from now. Will you be there?"

Emma nodded. "This is the first I've heard of it, but we'll be sure to make it." Joanna Miller had brought over several casseroles after Paul's passing, her kindness not going unnoticed by Emma. It would be an honor to be able to show some kindness in return.

"I should get back to the kitchen. My break is almost over. It was nice seeing you all; enjoy the rest of your day."

She scooted out of the way in time for the food to be delivered. After the blessing, they spent a few minutes eating in silence. The food was hot and delicious and everyone was ravenous after a morning of chores.

"Do we have to pick out fabric with you?" Ezekiel popped the last bite of burger into his mouth as he waited for an answer.

"You don't want to assist me? Make sure I don't pick out something soft and purple for you?" Emma teased.

The boy did not look amused.

"You could come to the hardware store with me," Levi offered. "I need to pick up an order *Daed* placed."

"Actually," Sadie said with an apologetic wrinkle of her nose, "we were wondering if we could walk to the shop down the street."

Emma gave her a knowing look. "Which shop would that be?"

"The pet shop," Ezekiel blurted. "Sadie likes the Lionhead rabbits."

Levi paused with his burger halfway to his mouth. "The what?"

"They're adorable," Sadie gushed. "The fluffiest rabbit you've ever seen."

"With a mane like a lion," Ezekiel supplied.

"Sounds…interesting." He took a bite of his burger while Emma picked up a fry.

"You may go. But you may not buy a rabbit," she said.

Sadie looked momentarily crestfallen but quickly recovered. "I won't. At least, not this time."

They finished their meals before heading their separate ways with an agreement to meet at the buggy in half an hour.

Emma went straight to the craft store that doubled as a fabric shop. The shop did well, as most of the Amish women in the area purchased their supplies there. Quilting and knitting were popular—and sometimes essential—hobbies. Emma often wished she had time to learn how to do both. As it was, she could barely keep up with clothes that fit her siblings.

A lovely bright green bolt of fabric caught her eye. It wasn't an acceptable color for a dress, but she thought it would look lovely on a quilt…a quilt she would never find the time to get around to making.

She pulled her eyes away and moved along to the darker, sturdier fabric that would be required for Ezekiel.

She felt someone edge up behind her. Tourists sometimes had no regard for privacy—as if the Amish were simply on display for their entertainment. She wasn't going to turn around, afraid she'd find a camera pointed at her face. Instead she fingered the fabric, determining that it was of good quality. She moved down the row, slowly inspecting the bolts that held colors that were acceptable. Working with a limited budget required her to find the best quality for the fairest price.

Heavy footsteps trudged along behind her, causing her spine to tingle more with frustration than apprehension. She simply wanted to shop in peace. As the footsteps continued, slowing when she slowed, speeding up when she did, she realized that would not be the case today.

The door leading to the sidewalk was within view. She hurried toward it, disappointed that her shopping would have to take place another day. Before she was even halfway, she froze in place when someone growled her name.

Instinctively she knew it was not a tourist behind her. His heavy dialect gave him away. She didn't recognize the voice, only the familiarity of the accent.

A hand clamped around her elbow. She let out a gasp of surprise as she was whirled around.

She would have preferred a tourist to the angry man staring her down.

"I've been wanting to talk with you," Amos

Stoltzfus snarled. His grip on her loosened only slightly. Even then, he stood so close as to be indecent—her back was pressed against a display of yarn, his large body caging her in. His breath was hot and foul. Emma wondered if it was the stench of stale liquor. Single Amish men were meant to remain clean-shaven, growing out a beard only after they were wed, but Amos's face was covered in stubble, as if he hadn't bothered to shave in a week.

She absently wondered what the bishop thought of his blatant disregard for the *Ordnung*, then decided it wasn't her place to wonder.

"Amos, what are you doing here?" Her voice wobbled and he grinned, seemingly enjoying her discomfort.

"I have been waiting some time to speak with you," Amos said. "It seems you're never around when I'm in town."

She straightened her spine and dared to look him in the eye. His nearness made her terribly uncomfortable. She wished he would back away but knew he would only laugh if she asked. "I didn't realize we had anything to speak about."

He leered at her. "You were to be my bride."

"That was a misunderstanding."

Amos leaned in. "There was an agreement made. My *daed* expected me to take over your farm. He expected me to have a wife."

Emma clenched her trembling hands into fists. She had never spoken with Amos before, knew him by reputation only. It seemed as if his reputation fit. Relief flooded her as she stood there, facing off with him. If not for Levi, this was the man she would've been forced to wed. She owed Levi an unending debt of gratitude for saving her from Amos.

"My aunt Naomi did not realize I am already spoken for," she said firmly.

"She should stand by her word." Amos's tone was cold and threatening. "Your farm should be mine."

"*Nee*." She shook her head. "The farm belongs to my family; it is not for sale. Naomi was in error to offer it to you and your *vadder*."

"I still say a deal was made. It is dishonest to not stand by your word." Amos sneered at her. "How do you plan to stay in *goot* standing with God if you are a liar?"

"I lied about nothing. I was no part of the discussion. However, I will not argue with you, Amos; you will simply need to find a new farm to purchase."

She took a step to the side, trying to sweep past him, but his fingers dug into her forearm once more. This time she yelped in pain as he hissed, "And what of finding a wife, Emma Ziegler? You were meant to be mine."

He jerked her forward, and she was afraid he intended to drag her from the store.

Suddenly Levi was there, wedging his body between them. He wrenched Amos's hand off Emma.

"Leave this store now," Levi said, his voice a low threat.

"And if I don't?" Amos's tone sent shivers down Emma's spine. "Are you going to fight me? Or force me out of here? I would like to see that. I don't think you have it in you to truly put up a fight."

Emma stiffened. Fighting was not their way. She

didn't want Levi to be goaded into an argument on her behalf. She was about to tell him so, but he managed to keep his senses all on his own.

"I will go to Bishop Yoder." Levi's voice was calm as he blocked Emma from Amos's view. "He will go to your *vadder*. We both know that this will not be the first time. I know the bishop has warned you about your querulous ways."

"The bishop," Amos said, "is a sanctimonious old man. Do you think I give a care about what he has to say?"

Emma frowned, having never heard anyone speak of Bishop Yoder in such a way. She wondered what altercations had taken place between the bishop and Amos for Amos to feel so strongly. She hadn't been aware of them until just now. Perhaps his standing in the community was far worse than she had imagined.

Levi confirmed her suspicion by saying, "How many more transgressions is Bishop Yoder going to allow before you find yourself under the *ban*?"

Emma schooled her expression, keeping it neutral despite her surprise. She had never heard of anyone in their district being shunned before. It was an action that was not taken lightly. If shunning was truly a possibility, that had to mean that the church elders had already spoken to Amos regarding infractions deemed serious.

If Amos had repented and agreed to change his ways, he would've been forgiven.

She realized this must not be the case if whispers of shunning were drifting about.

For most, the very thought of being shunned

would be enough to set them straight. To be shunned meant to be excommunicated. Emma could think of no punishment worse than being separated from her family, from her community.

Amos, apparently, did not agree.

"There are much finer places to live than Pine Creek," he spat.

"Stay away from Emma," Levi warned, "or you will find life here is far more miserable when you're living under the *ban*."

"I am better off without her as a wife," Amos said. "She is nothing but a nervous little mouse. It would be a chore to look at that plain face of hers across the breakfast table every morning."

Emma did not take offense at the slight. She knew they were pointless words spoken by a miserable man. Levi, however, stiffened in anger. Emma rested a hand on his shoulder as she moved to his side, and thankfully, his tension eased under her touch.

"Sadie and Ezekiel are waiting. We should go." She did not shy away from Amos. "I pray that the Lord brings you peace."

Levi nodded in agreement. Without another word, he led the way from the store, Emma following a step behind him. She dared a glance over her shoulder before they exited. Amos stared after her with a venomous look in his eye. She swiveled her gaze back around, deeply grateful for Levi and the protection he provided.

• • •

At that moment, Amos was not the only one in need of peace. Levi was so angry he was trembling. He'd never had a run-in with Amos before. He'd always been smart enough to avoid him. Stepping into the sunshine did little to ease his fury.

He didn't stop walking until he had put a block between them and Amos. Then he spun to face Emma, who had kept pace with him.

"Are you all right? Did he hurt you? I hope you don't mind that I intervened." He scanned Emma, looking for signs of distress. He knew she liked to take care of herself, but he couldn't just stand back and watch Amos accost her. She looked distraught but unharmed. He wanted to pull her into his arms, comfort her. But that was not something he could do. Not here, in plain view of any passersby. It would not be proper.

"He grabbed my arm, but you stopped him before he could truly hurt me. I'm grateful for your help. He wasn't willing to leave on his own. How did you know to look for me?"

"Ezekiel saw him enter the store. He had a bad feeling and found me. I came as quickly as I could." His *daed*'s supplies were not in yet, so he'd been walking back out when Ezekiel nearly collided with him.

"It was quick enough," Emma said soothingly. "No real damage was done."

"I think that man is unhinged." Levi clenched and unclenched his jaw. It wasn't right to manhandle a lady—or anyone for that matter. If Amos was willing to corner Emma, a woman he barely knew, in public, he cringed to think of how he would treat a wife in private.

To think that Emma had almost become that wife, it made him shudder.

"I believe it might be the drink." Emma kept her tone low, as if embarrassed to be speaking of such a thing. "I could smell it on him. I've heard it changes people, and never for the better."

Consuming alcohol was not necessarily forbidden, but it was certainly frowned upon. Moderation was expected. Amos frequently violated that expectation.

"Is it true that he has been spoken to by Bishop Yoder?" Emma asked.

"*Jah*, I believe so. I know the men like to joke about how the women gossip, but get a bunch of men together, and I think they put the women to shame." Speaking with Emma was helping to lighten his dour mood. "I first heard of it last spring, at the Weavers' barn raising. A few said he was warned of being shunned, but that could be little more than talk. It's been kept relatively quiet."

Emma's eyebrows puckered. "I've heard stories about Amos, but I didn't know that his behavior had reached the point where shunning was a possibility. If Naomi had been aware, she would not have offered to sell his *vadder* the farm, I am sure. Not for any price."

"I am guessing there is a lot that has happened with Amos that we do not know about."

"To think, Naomi wanted me to marry him."

"Your aunt has been away from Pine Creek for a lot of years. Amos's father is a reputable man. I'm sure she truly thought it would be a fine match."

She sighed. "Naomi and I have our differences, but I know she would not intentionally pair me with someone who does not live in the faith."

Levi's heart leaped when she grabbed his hand and gave it a squeeze.

"I owe you so much. If you hadn't overheard our conversation on the porch that day…" Her words faded away and she shuddered.

"You owe me nothing," he said firmly. "I care about you a great deal. I want you to be happy." What he did not want was for Emma to feel indebted to him. He knew she was grateful, but he didn't want her gratitude. He wanted much more than that.

He glanced around and realized that Emma's siblings were standing near the buggy, watching them.

"We shouldn't keep them waiting any longer," he said. "I'm sure Zeke is worried."

They hurried across the road. Levi glanced around, wondering if Amos was lurking, but he didn't spot him and he didn't care where the man had gone, as long as he was far away from Emma.

"Is everything all right?" Sadie looked at her sister worriedly.

"Everything is fine."

"But Amos…?" Sadie pressed. "He stormed out behind you. He looked so angry."

"I believe, perhaps, Amos is always angry." Levi kept his tone light. The thought of sweet, kind Emma tied for life to the likes of Amos slammed into him again. He could not let that happen. It only strengthened his resolve.

He needed to make Emma his wife.

Oblivious to his inner ramblings, Sadie gave him a contemplative look before nodding. "I suppose he is."

"We *all* ought to pray that the Lord bring him peace," Emma said.

Levi hoped the man found peace before he found a wife. If not, he feared for the poor woman.

He held out his hand to help Emma and then Sadie into the buggy. The women moved to the back, leaving the seat beside him open for Ezekiel. Levi unhitched the horse and hopped in. He held the leathers out to the young boy.

Ezekiel looked at him in confusion for a moment before the meaning of the offer dawned on him. He smiled shyly before taking the reins.

The boy was cautious, but he got the job done, and the horse responded well to him. He was careful as he guided the buggy through town. Soon enough they were on the tarred road leading south. After a few miles they'd head west on the dirt road that led to the Ziegler and Bontrager farms.

Levi decided the mood surrounding the buggy was far too somber. He glanced over his shoulder at Sadie.

"You're not sneaking one of those rabbits home, are you?" he teased. "Didn't stuff one into your apron pocket? Or hide it under Zeke's hat?"

Sadie's face broke into a smile. "Not yet. I don't have a hutch."

"What other creatures do they have in that pet shop?" Levi wondered. He'd never found a reason to enter such a place.

Sadie scooted forward, chattering so fast, he

could barely keep up. She spoke of kittens, puppies, colorful tropical fish, and a variety of rodents.

Why any *Englischer* would pay hard-earned money for rats and mice, Levi would never understand. Nor could he imagine the purpose of keeping colorful fish in one's living room. Then again, much of the *Englisch* world baffled him.

"We also stopped at the Weavers' Candy Shoppe," Sadie said. "You need to try this." She handed everyone a string of licorice. "It's their new flavor, key lime pie. Gracie came up with it." Gracie Weaver was Sadie's good friend.

"I think you could spend all your money in that place," Emma said.

Sadie nodded enthusiastically. "Gracie's family makes the best candy. Do you know what flavor they should make next?"

In unison, Emma and Ezekiel said, "Maple syrup." As if it were the most logical choice in the world.

Their answer lightened the mood, and everyone had a chuckle.

Sadie continued to chatter on and on about the many flavor possibilities of licorice and the art of making saltwater taffy.

By the time they reached the Ziegler farm, both Sadie and Ezekiel seemed to have forgotten all about Amos Stoltzfus.

Though the children had moved on, he wasn't about to. If he had anything to say about it, Amos wasn't going to get near enough to Emma to harass her ever again.

CHAPTER SEVEN

The rhythmic *clip-clop* of Ginger's hooves against the gravel soothed Emma. For weeks, she'd barely had a moment to herself. She hadn't wanted to leave Ezekiel and Sadie alone after losing their father, so she'd stuck close by them.

This morning, Amelia insisted that Emma visit her friend Rachael. At the café, Rachael had asked Amelia to invite Emma over for the afternoon. At first Emma had hesitated, but her cousin had been insistent, saying it would mean a lot to Rachael. She went so far as to say that Rachael was expecting her.

Emma supposed that if they were like the *Englisch*, and had telephones, she could have called to let her friend know she was unable to make it. She didn't want to disappoint Rachael, and other than simply not showing up, there was no way for her to decline.

She had to admit it had been quite some time since she'd visited with her friend. She missed Rachael, her easy laughter, her gentle spirit.

Now that she was on her way, she looked forward to an afternoon of visiting, even as she enjoyed the solitude of the drive to her friend's house.

With the sun shining down, and a light breeze fluttering across her face, she couldn't stop her thoughts from drifting to Levi.

Their charade was firmly in place. Already she felt guilty over the falsehood but honestly could think of no other option. Levi had a kind heart, so it certainly shouldn't surprise her that he would want to help her out of this predicament she'd found herself in. Yet she didn't like the dishonesty. However, there didn't seem to be much she could do about it at the moment.

What a mess her life had become.

Her *daed* had meant well when he set her up with Ivan, but he had made a mistake. A mistake borne of love, but a mistake all the same.

It had taken her weeks to get Ivan's anguished expression out of her mind. He'd tried to let her down gently, hadn't wanted to hurt her, but he'd been stuck in a position where he'd been left with little choice. He hadn't really wanted to marry her, and they'd both paid the price.

Now here she was with Levi, in a relationship just as fallacious but in a different way. The irony was that she thought if she pressed the matter, Levi would likely agree to marry her, too. No doubt out of a misplaced sense of chivalry.

She couldn't do that to Levi. She knew he still felt responsible over the incident with the *Englisch* boy years ago. She wouldn't take advantage of that, wouldn't allow him to give up his future for her out of guilt.

He would find love sooner or later, though it was beginning to look like later.

Truth be told, there weren't too many *maidels* left in their community, either. That thought hit her with a jolt, and she couldn't help but remember Levi's comments on the swing. When he'd first claimed to have had a crush on her when they were younger, for one silly moment she hoped that he still did.

What had he said? *There's really no one left to ask.*

As if *she* was just...what? Completely unworthy of his interest? It reminded her that he was courting her only for show. Nothing more.

"*Ach,*" she muttered under her breath. She needed to stop thinking of it. Spending time with Rachael would do her good, would help her to clear her head, think of something else.

Preferably *not* the fact that the tax deadline was looming ever closer. She had gone to Bishop Yoder's yesterday. After she had explained the situation, he had agreed to allow Harvey Larson to hay her field with his *Englisch* equipment, so she had stopped at the phone shanty at the end of the bishop's driveway to call the man, who was happy about the hay and named a price Emma knew was more than fair. The income from the hay would cover the bulk of the tax bill, but nowhere near all of it.

She pushed that thought out of her mind as well. She didn't want anything to dampen her time with her friend.

Her steadfast mare plodded along, turning into the Eshs' driveway when they reached it. The house Rachael shared with Jonah was small, but it seemed to suit them just fine for now. They could always add on to it once they got settled in life, if they needed to.

Emma ignored the slight pang of jealousy that zinged through her. If her life had been different, if *Mamm* hadn't died, if *Daed* hadn't needed her help so badly over the past years, would she be married by now?

Would she be living a life similar to Rachael's? Would she have a husband? A home? A *boppli* of her own like so many women her age? She could hardly imagine it.

No sense thinking about it. Her life had taken a different path. And there was nothing she could do about it. Though she yearned for more at times, she wouldn't change her choices, even if she could.

She loved her siblings and would never regret being there for them.

Ginger instinctively moved toward the hitching post. When the buggy came to a halt, Emma hopped down. She wasn't too proper about it, but she figured it didn't matter, as there was no one to see.

She looped the reins loosely around the post, trusting that Ginger had no desire to go exploring, and headed toward the house.

Though small, Rachael's home was tidy, well kept, and welcoming. Bright splashes of color lined the flower bed that was nestled at the base of the front porch.

Her friend opened the door, a huge grin spreading across her face.

"Emma," Rachael cried as she rushed across the porch and down the steps. "I'm so happy you decided to visit. Amelia told me she'd encourage you, but I didn't know if you would come."

"I'm so happy to see you," Emma said, returning her friend's contagious smile. "Our short visit at the café the other day wasn't nearly enough."

Rachael looped her arm through Emma's and tugged her toward the house. "I just pulled a tray of oatmeal cookies out of the oven. We can sit, have a snack, and catch up."

That sounded wonderful to Emma.

The two women quickly found themselves seated at the kitchen table, a plate of warm cookies between them. Emma realized that her friend had been married almost two years now, and while Emma had visited her on occasion, she hadn't visited nearly as often as she'd like. Now that her siblings were older, she needed to change that.

"I *canna* believe you didn't tell me about you and Levi," Rachael said as she broke her cookie in half. She continued to scold. "You're my best friend. I thought you told me everything."

"You know that we don't flaunt courting." It was the truth, even if it didn't necessarily address the issue that Rachael had raised.

"I know, I know," Rachael said impatiently. "But I told you all about Jonah and me."

Emma winced, wondering how to move the conversation forward, how to steer it away from the one person she didn't want to discuss.

Rachael noticed her discomfort and reached over to pat her hand. "I know how it is. When Jonah and I began courting, I was so afraid that it wasn't going to work out. He had just stopped seeing Natalie, and I knew she was still pining over him. I was afraid he'd go back to her. When a relationship is new, it's sometimes easier to keep it to yourself."

Emma nodded, seeing no reason to disagree. She popped a bite of warm, scrumptious cookie into her mouth.

"He was probably afraid you were still pining for Ivan," Rachael said conspiratorially.

"*Ach, nee.*" Emma shook her head, but Rachael wasn't deterred.

"At the very least," Rachael said, "I'm sure it was a bit awkward at the start. With you having been engaged to his *bruder.*"

Emma admitted, "It was a bit awkward." And still continued to be as they muddled their way forward.

"But things are nice now, *jah*?" Rachael pressed.

"I've known Levi a long time. He's kind to Sadie and Zeke. And I enjoy spending time with him."

"You know Levi and Jonah are on the same carpentry crew."

Emma nodded because she did know. Both Levi and Jonah worked for the same *Englischer*, a man who treated his Amish workers well, was fair in pay, and owned a company large enough to keep his employees as busy as they wanted to be. He was willing to allow the Amish men to work part-time, too, as many of them had obligations with their families' farms to work around.

"Jonah said he's never seen Levi so happy. Levi's typically *goot*-natured, but Jonah said some days Levi doesn't stop smiling. I wouldn't be surprised if the two of you are wed by winter."

Emma reached for another cookie. She tried to think of a way to change the conversation before she devoured the entire plate and gave herself a stomachache. She was relieved to hear that Levi was in good spirits, as she didn't want him to be burdened by his promise to her. Leave it to Levi to find joy in helping out a friend.

And the thought of a wedding before winter, it sent her stomach aflutter. Surely from nerves and not something as silly as anticipation.

"Enough about me," Emma decided. "Tell me how you are doing. Amelia said you are planning on leaving the café soon." Emma felt bad that her cousin had spent far more time with Rachael than she had lately.

A blush crept into her friend's cheeks. The ever-present sparkle in her eyes seemed to get just a bit brighter.

"I'm surprised," Emma admitted. "I thought you enjoyed working for the Hansons."

"I do," Rachael said. "But Jonah and I agreed that I would work only until we were ready to start a family. And, well…" She ducked her head bashfully, a soft smile gracing her lips.

It took Emma only a moment for her friend's words to sink in. She leaped from her chair and pulled Rachael into a tight, sideways hug. "I'm so happy for you!"

And she was.

Truly.

Yet there was that little sting of jealousy again.

She hurriedly shoved it aside, feeling terribly guilty that she would experience anything other than utter joy for her best friend.

"Thank you," Rachael said. She rested her hand on her stomach. Emma could make out only the smallest hint that her friend was carrying a baby. "It took so long," Rachael admitted, "I was afraid that it was not in God's will for us. But it's finally happened."

Emma hadn't realized that Rachael and Jonah had been hoping for a baby, though she should have—the couple had been married nearly two years. Emma felt bad that she hadn't realized her friend had been going through a difficult time.

"I'm sorry, Rachael," Emma said. "I didn't realize—"

"*Ach*." Rachael cut her off with a wave of her hand. "You have had your hands full."

Emma frowned, because even so, she should have been there for Rachael, offering her support.

Before she could say so, Rachael moved from her chair. "I would like your help with something, though, if you don't mind."

"Of course I don't mind," Emma said. Whatever her friend needed, she would gladly assist with it.

Rachael moved out of the room and Emma followed.

"I have an idea for a new quilt. For the *boppli*," Rachael said, and Emma could hear the smile in her voice. "I have a basket full of fabric and I'm hoping you can help me pick out just the right colors."

"I think I can manage that," Emma said with a laugh.

They spent the afternoon discussing quilt patterns, new recipes they'd tried recently, and reminiscing about days gone by.

"I always thought Levi would ask to court you," Rachael admitted as they sipped tea on the front porch. "I just didn't figure it would take so long."

"Why would you think that?" Emma asked.

"It was little things. The way he smiled when you were around. Sometimes he'd act all tough and strong in the silly way boys do when they're trying to impress a girl."

Emma smiled, fondly remembering the time Levi

had climbed the ancient oak tree in his yard, then yelled to her from the top. Diana had nearly fainted when she'd seen him up so high. Another time he'd wanted to show her how he could ride bareback and had taken off on Moses's buggy horse full speed. Moses had *not* been happy and had put Levi on stall-mucking duty for a month.

The other day, he'd mentioned he had a crush on her. Maybe he had.

"I can't believe you never had a crush on *him*," Rachael said. "So many of the girls did. Even me at one time."

"I know," Emma agreed. "I thought he was cute, and he was always sweet to me. But he was my friend. I didn't want to risk ruining our friendship." She frowned. "Although that ended up happening anyway."

"Darren," Rachael said knowingly. "Your *daed* was so mad when he heard you were hugging an *Englisch* boy…in public." Rachael winced. "People in our congregation have long memories, and I'm sure that's something you'd rather forget."

Emma inwardly cringed but said, "It happened years ago. Levi and I drifted apart over it, but he's apologized."

"Now look at the two of you," Rachael said happily.

Jah, Emma thought a bit sardonically, *just look at us*.

When the two friends parted, it was with a promise to get together more frequently in the future.

Emma's heart was light and joyful as Ginger trotted down the driveway. A day with her dear friend was exactly what she'd needed.

That joy fizzled just a bit when she noted that she had visitors. Levi and Ivan must've walked over from the Bontrager farm because there was no buggy in sight. They glanced Emma's way as she came down the driveway.

The brothers each lifted a hand in greeting.

She nodded back as Ezekiel came out of the barn.

"*Hallo*, Emma," he called as he plodded toward her.

"What are they doing here?" Emma asked as she pulled the buggy to a stop.

"Levi said there's a lot of fallen branches from the last storm, clogging up the maple grove," Ezekiel explained. "He said he and Ivan had some extra time today, so they decided to come over to clean it up. I've been helping, but Levi asked me to put *Daed*'s hatchet away because they just finished up with it."

Emma slid from the buggy.

"I can take care of Ginger," Ezekiel offered.

"*Danki*," Emma muttered. She would rather take care of the horse than face the brothers, but she knew Ezekiel enjoyed the task.

She made her way down the driveway toward Levi and Ivan, who were coming out of the grove to meet her.

Heat flooded Emma's cheeks at the sight of Ivan. She wished he wasn't here, then immediately felt a wave of guilt over the ungracious thought. Would she ever stop feeling shame over the way she had begged him not to break their engagement? Oh, how she had panicked, fearing that the news would upset her father. Tears had trickled down her cheeks, she had grabbed Ivan's hand—it had been the closest physical contact they'd ever shared—and she had pleaded with him to reconsider.

Despite the pained look in his eyes, he had held steadfast to his decision. Quietly, gently, he admitted that he was in love with someone else.

She'd let go of his hand then, taken a step away. Though she had hated the idea of disappointing her father, she'd known in that moment that while she might never find love, Ivan had. And she could not ask Ivan to deny his own feelings or deny him what she herself wished for so fervently.

Within days, he and Miriam had been courting. And while she'd wished he'd waited, if for no other reason than to soothe her aching ego, she understood his decision. He wanted to be happy, and Miriam clearly made him happy.

"*Hallo*, Emma," Ivan said quietly.

She nodded, scarcely able to look at him. "Ivan."

The man shuffled his feet, cleared his throat. "I best be getting back to see if *Daed* needs help with anything."

His words were aimed at his brother, and Levi nodded.

Emma bid him farewell and wished she weren't so happy to see him go.

• • •

Levi cast a glance at his brother, who was walking down the driveway. His hand clenched and unclenched at his side, and he was startled to realize he wanted to punch something. The feeling went against his nature, but he couldn't squelch it. The hitching post, the barn, the chicken coop…something. Anything to alleviate the feelings of frustration he felt.

It was impossible to miss the way Emma's cheeks had warmed at the sight of Ivan and her demeanor had changed. She became nervous, agitated, simply not herself. Was she in love with his brother? He had thought she'd considered his proposal only to please her *daed*, accepted it out of desperation. Perhaps he'd misjudged.

His heart constricted painfully. The bigger question was, did she love him still?

Guilt stabbed through him. What would Emma say, how would she feel if she knew the truth about why Ivan broke off their engagement? She knew part of the story, sure, but not the whole thing. She knew nothing of the part that Levi had played in Ivan walking away. Would she ever be able to forgive him if she knew what he'd done?

He plucked his hat off his head, raked a hand through his hair, and tried to gather some courage. He didn't want secrets standing between them, straining their relationship, so whether he wanted to or not, he needed to come clean with her.

"The grove looks *goot*," Emma said, pulling him away from his thoughts. "Thank you for working on it."

"We'll burn the brush pile when the weather isn't so dry." Cleaning out the grove was the least of what he was willing to do for Emma. When would she realize that? Was it too soon to tell her? As his gaze darted to his retreating brother, he thought perhaps it was.

Instead he asked, "Did you have a nice time with Rachael?"

"I did." A smile twitched her lips. "We picked out material for a new quilt."

He waited for her to elaborate, but when she didn't, he simply said, "That sounds nice."

"Would you like to stay for supper?"

He perked up at the thought. "*Jah*, I would." He scrubbed his palms over the thighs of his pants. "But could we talk first? There's something I need to tell you."

Her smile instantly faltered. Sensing the seriousness of his tone, she nodded.

He walked toward the wooden fence and she followed.

"What is it?" she wondered.

He leaned against a post, wondering how best to admit what he'd done.

"Emma, you can see now that you and Ivan were not a *goot* match, *jah*?"

She narrowed her eyes at him.

"We both know you were together because your *daed* wanted to be sure you were cared for," he pressed.

"It's not something I like to think about," she said.

He trudged ahead. "Ivan was in love with Miriam. Had been for years but didn't think he had a chance with her."

"I got that impression when he began courting her nearly right away." She studied him for a moment with a wry look in her eye. "Why are you bringing this up?"

"I'm the reason Ivan broke your engagement. I...I asked him to do it."

There it was. The secret he'd been keeping.

Emma's head jerked back, as if his words had physically stunned her. Her mouth opened but then snapped shut again.

He reached for her, but she took a step away.

"Emma, hear me out," he pleaded. "I've always known how Ivan felt for Miriam. He respected your *daed*, so he agreed to his request. But I knew you deserved better than being married to a man who was in love with someone else."

It was several long moments before she finally said, "Then perhaps you should have spoken to *me* about it."

"He's my *bruder*. It was easier to speak with him," Levi said.

Emma rubbed her hands over her face. "I know pride is a sin. But do you know how humiliating it was when he ended our engagement? Then within days, he was with Miriam?"

He winced. "That's probably my fault as well. I encouraged him to stop wasting time."

"My *daed* was so sick," Emma said. "I've often wondered if the stress of finding out I was on my own... I've wondered if that contributed to his death."

"No, Emma, I'm sure not." He wanted to tell her more, wanted to tell her *why* he knew that, but she didn't give him the chance.

She held her hand up, as if to ward off his

explanation. Her expression was grim. "I'm not happy with you right now; I can't believe you did such a thing. I don't want to talk about this anymore."

As she twirled away from him and stomped toward the house, his heart rattled painfully. He had known she would not appreciate his admission, but he also knew he owed her the truth. Should he go after her? Beg her to listen? Or just give her some time? As he watched her, he decided to let her go. He knew that was what she'd want him to do.

He also knew her father was more than all right with Ivan's decision. But with Emma unwilling to listen right now, he would have to save the rest of the story for another day.

CHAPTER EIGHT

Emma couldn't stop thinking about last night as she picked at her lunch at the café. The noisy chatter around her, even that of her siblings, barely penetrated her grumbly thoughts.

At first, she'd been irate with Levi for overstepping, but the more she thought about it, and though she hated to admit it, she wondered if perhaps he'd done the right thing. She didn't think Ivan would've ended their engagement without Levi's nudge. She had been so concerned about her father that she wouldn't have, either. So perhaps he had done her a favor. In a way, yet again, he had saved her.

"Is your sandwich not tasty?" Sadie asked.

"Hmm?" Emma lifted her gaze to her sister.

"You're not eating," Ezekiel pointed out.

She realized both her siblings were staring at her from across the table, wearing matching worried expressions.

"It's *appendlitch*." She picked up her turkey club and took a bite, just to prove the point, glancing around the café as she chewed. Normally it was delicious. Today, she barely tasted it.

She had decided to make the trip into town because they were running low on a few essential staples. They couldn't go long without flour, sugar, and the like. When her siblings had begged to eat at the café, she agreed because she had thought the treat would be a good distraction. She had refused to take money from Amelia for her living arrangement, so her cousin had given her a sizable gift card to the café, and today seemed like as good a day as any to use it. With the tax deadline looming, she wouldn't have made the splurge without it.

"Did you and Levi have an argument?" Ezekiel's tone was low and worried.

"Why would you ask such a thing?" Emma wondered.

Ezekiel and Sadie shared a concerned glance.

"When he left last night, he didn't look happy," Ezekiel said.

"And you've been a bit grumpy today," Sadie added.

"I have not been grumpy," Emma argued.

Sadie arched a brow. "You haven't been very *happy*."

Emma huffed out a breath because her sister was right; she *had* been acting a bit irritable all morning. And they certainly didn't deserve for her frustration to be taken out on them. She needed to turn that around right now.

She pressed a smile onto her face. "I'm happy. I'm spending the afternoon with you. We're having a lovely meal. It's a wonderfully nice day."

"What about Levi?" Ezekiel pressed. "*Are* you two arguing?"

"No," Emma said. It was the truth. She had been upset by his confession, and she had walked away, but they hadn't exactly argued. She hadn't stuck around long enough for that.

Sadie smiled. "Then he can join us for our meal?"

"You want to invite him to supper?" Emma

asked. After last night, she wasn't so sure he would want to join them for supper anytime soon. "I don't know about that."

"Not supper," Sadie corrected. "We should ask him to join us now."

"Now?" Emma echoed.

Ezekiel waved to someone over her shoulder. Emma twisted around, already suspicious of whom she might see.

Levi stood with a small mixed group of Amish and *Englisch* men, the carpenters he worked with, no doubt. Jonah Esh, Rachael's husband, was among them.

Emma forced a smile as she glanced at the group, most of whom she knew.

Levi's expression remained tentative as he acknowledged her with a nod.

"Levi," Ezekiel called. "Come join us."

"Hush," Emma gently chided, embarrassed her brother had shouted across the café. "He's with the men he works with. I'm sure he plans to eat with them."

She must have been wrong, because a moment later, Levi began winding his way through the crowded eating area. He sidled up to their table.

"Is there room for me to join you?" he asked, his gaze on Emma, clearly seeking her permission.

"*Jah*," she said. "But don't you want to eat with your work crew?"

He shrugged. "Their table will be awfully crowded."

Emma nodded in understanding. "Have a seat."

Levi pulled out the fourth chair at their round

table as the hostess seated his friends on the other
side of the dining room.

"I thought you always packed your lunch,"
Emma noted.

He shrugged. "We usually do. But it's so hot out,
we decided to come to the café to enjoy the cool air.
We're working on shingling a roof today, and it's a
scorcher up there."

A waitress stopped by the table, placing a full
glass of ice water in front of Levi. He gulped it
thirstily and then placed his lunch order.

"What brings you into town?" he asked.

"We were running low on supplies," Emma said.

"Emma said we can have haystacks for dinner,"
Ezekiel offered, noting a favorite dish of the Amish.
"Haystacks are my favorite and she asked what I'd
like to have. But she's missing some ingredients. So,
we came to town to get them." Ezekiel flashed
Emma a quick look before turning his attention
back to Levi. "Emma's haystacks are *wunderbaar*.
Her cheese sauce is the best around. You should
come for supper."

Levi shot her a cautious look, clearly a silent
question.

She nodded slowly. "You should join us. As Zeke
said, it's just haystacks. Nothing fancy."

He grinned. "I like haystacks. It's one of my favorite meals as well."

Something inside her melted at his smile, even
as she filed away that bit of information for later.
For some future dinner they might have. For now,
she needed to apologize for her abrupt behavior
the night before. But she couldn't do that with her

siblings intently listening to every word.

"Zeke, Sadie, why don't you go choose a dessert out of the case?" Emma suggested.

They gave her a curious look. Neither of them made any move to get up.

"We're never allowed dessert," Ezekiel pointed out.

It was true. Emma had never thought it was worth the expense, not to mention, like most Amish kitchens, they always had some type of dessert or another waiting for them at home.

"I'm making an exception," she said. "Levi just ordered his meal and you two are both finished with yours. We don't want him to eat alone now, do we?"

That was all the encouragement the two needed. Ezekiel and Sadie slid from their chairs and headed toward the glass case at the back, near the cash register where the desserts were displayed.

Emma glanced around. She'd prefer to have greater privacy, yet she didn't want to have last night's conversation lingering between them. She and Levi had been at odds before and it hadn't felt right. She didn't want to be in that place again.

Before she could say a word, Levi blurted, "I'm so sorry, Emma. I shouldn't have spoken to Ivan on your behalf."

"I've been thinking about that," Emma said. "It's hard for me to admit, but you probably did me a favor. Ivan as well. You probably saved us from being miserable together. He's your *bruder*—of course you want him to be happy."

Levi reached over and squeezed her hand, sending warmth spiraling through her. "I want *you* to be happy, too." He pulled his hand back and lowered his voice. "Have you come up with a solution for the other problem you are facing?"

Emma knew he was talking about the property taxes. She glanced around, assuring herself Sadie and Zeke were still checking out the desserts.

"I spoke with Marta Weaver today," she admitted. "She agreed to start selling my syrup at the candy store. I also suggested she create maple syrup licorice and she loved the idea. She thought it would be popular with tourists and bought a case of syrup from me to experiment with recipes."

"That's encouraging news," Levi said.

"It is," Emma agreed. "Usually only Pine Cone Lodge guests go into the gift shop here, but the Weavers get a lot of business. Marta thought my syrup would sell well."

The discussion ended when a voice that she couldn't help but recognize cut through the air.

"Emma, how nice to see you."

Emma twisted in her chair, her heart sinking as Mary Kurtz stood over her. Her aunt had asked Mary to check in on her. She didn't think that Mary was in the café for that reason, but if she was, it worked well that Emma was seated with Levi. She only hoped Mary hadn't overheard any part of their conversation.

She worked up what she hoped to be a pleasant smile, hiding any trace of the tension that might be lingering.

"Mary, I hope you are doing well," Emma said.

"We could pull up a chair, if you'd like to join us?" Levi offered.

"He's right, we could," Emma agreed. "Zeke and Sadie will be back with dessert soon. But Levi just ordered; you're welcome to have lunch with us."

"Thank you," Mary said. "But I didn't come in to eat. I simply stopped by for a loaf of bread."

Her words would have taken Emma by surprise—as Amish woman typically made their own bread—if she hadn't heard that Mary was struggling with arthritis. She noticed her fingers now, painfully curled. They would make kneading the dough almost impossible. Had they always been that bad? She pulled her eyes away, knowing it was rude to stare.

"I have to stop at the market, too," Mary said. "But I appreciate the offer."

Before Emma could reply, a ruckus caught the attention of the entire eatery.

Amos stood in the doorway, his grumbly voice carrying across the room as he argued with the waitress.

"My money's as *goot* as anyone else's, ain't so?" he proclaimed.

Emma doubted she was imagining the slight slur to his words. It was only midday but it seemed as if he'd been drinking already.

More words were exchanged with the waitress, and Levi rose from his seat.

"It looks like she could use some help," he said.

Emma noted that Jonah and a few other men had risen from the table across the room. The small group of men quietly, yet quickly, crossed the room to aid the waitress.

Mary sighed. "That young man can't seem to

keep himself out of trouble."

"*Nee*," Emma agreed, "he can't."

"I know your aunt meant well," Mary said somberly, "but she's been away for quite some time. Amos's dad and Naomi courted many, many years ago. He's a *goot* man who treated Naomi well. I think she believed Amos was like his *daed*. Surely, he is not."

Emma was momentarily startled by the news that Naomi had courted Amos's father.

"You've known Naomi a long time," she said.

"That I have." Mary gave Emma a knowing smile. "She's been a meddler ever since I've known her. Bless her, she means well, but she does like to stick her nose where it doesn't belong."

Emma's eyes widened in surprise.

Mary chuckled. "I know that you're aware that she asked me to keep an eye on you and Levi. She asked," Mary said, "but that doesn't mean that I have to do her bidding. You and Levi carry on with your business. Don't worry about anyone but yourselves."

"Thank you for that." Relief swept through Emma, along with a newfound respect for Mary Kurtz.

The commotion in the corner rose briefly as the men ushered Amos outside. Both women turned to see what was happening, and Emma was relieved that Levi had not confronted him alone, and she hoped that Amos didn't put up too much of a fuss.

"Levi seems a much better fit for you," Mary said, much to Emma's surprise. "I think your aunt will be happy with your choice in the end."

Emma forced a smile but didn't say a word.

Would Naomi be happy with Emma's choice?

What if, in the end, she and Levi ended their charade and went their separate ways?

• • •

"Who do you think you are?" Amos growled. "First you steal my *maidel*, then you think you can kick me out of a public place?"

"You got yourself kicked out of the restaurant permanently by not paying your bill the last time you were here," Levi corrected. "As for Emma, she was never yours."

This, apparently, was the wrong thing to say.

Amos lunged at Levi, his fist swinging, taking Levi completely by surprise. The punch connected with Levi's cheekbone, sending him reeling backward. He slammed into Jonah, who managed to keep him upright.

He wasn't a fighter, had never been and had never intended to be, but his anger surged. Not only at having been sucker punched, but at the thought that Emma had almost been pushed into marrying this man, and that he had the nerve to think of Emma as his.

Levi surged forward, prepared to take Amos down, but Jonah's arms held him fast from behind.

As Amos lunged toward him again, a few other men from their Amish crew stepped between them, cutting Amos off. Gripping him by the shoulders, they dragged him down the street, away from Levi.

The moment Amos was gone, Levi felt the heat

of regret burn his cheeks. Had he really almost gotten into an altercation? In public? Doing so would've brought such shame to his family, even if Amos had been the instigator.

"*Danki*," he muttered to Jonah, who had finally let him go.

"Amos was completely out of line," Jonah replied. "You okay?"

Levi nodded. "Fine." Amos had been unsteady on his feet, and while his swing had connected, had stunned Levi, he hadn't really done much harm.

He glanced up and down the street. Though it was midday, in the summertime, the heat was keeping most people indoors. A few onlookers began moving along again and Levi was relieved to see the altercation hadn't caused too big a stir.

"I'm sure Emma's aunt had no idea of the trouble she'd be causing by messing with Amos," Jonah said, his tone sympathetic.

"I'm sure she didn't. This isn't the first time we've run into Amos," Levi admitted.

Jonah frowned as Levi told him about the run-in with Amos at the fabric store.

He whistled under his breath. "Have you talked to Bishop Yoder?"

"*Nee*," Levi said. "Not yet. I was hoping dealing with Amos was a onetime thing. Now, after today, I'm not so sure."

"You should go to the bishop," Jonah urged. "He should be aware."

As Levi glanced down the street toward the group of men returning, he was fairly certain that somehow, someway, someone would mention the incident to the bishop. If so, he wouldn't have to. He held a deep respect for Bishop Yoder, but he was afraid the man would question him. He didn't want to admit to anyone, least of all the bishop, that his relationship with Emma wasn't what they were making it appear to be.

"I'll think on it," Levi said evasively.

"I don't think he'll be back," Thomas Miller said. "We told him that we'd be telling his *daed* about this." Thomas, a man Levi had known since their schooldays, gave him a warning look. "It seems pretty clear by the way he was shooting his mouth off that he has it in for you. I think you'd best watch your back."

The other men nodded in agreement.

"I appreciate the warning," Levi said.

The group headed back inside.

Levi returned to Emma's table, where his meal had been delivered. Sadie and Ezekiel each had a piece of lemon meringue pie placed in front of them, but neither had taken a bite.

"Is everything okay?" Emma asked.

His breathing calmed at the concern in her tone.

"Amos won't be coming back here today, if that's what you're asking." He worked up a smile for her siblings, who were staring at him with concern. "Your pie looks *appendlitch*. You best eat up."

No way was he going to go into detail about what had taken place outside. Not in front of the children, and not in front of Emma, either. He didn't want her to worry.

They obediently reached for their forks, though he could still feel their curious gazes on him. He followed his own advice, reaching for his fork so he could take a bite of his meatloaf. He froze, his fork held aloft, when Emma's fingers brushed against his cheek.

Her fingers were smooth and cool. A stark contrast to the heat he felt radiating from his own face from spending the morning in the sun. Her touch gently trailed over the tender spot where Amos's fist had connected.

"What happened?" she asked, her gaze filling with worry. As if she realized what she was doing—touching him in public—she yanked her hand away. It fell to her lap, but the memory of her touch still lingered.

He cleared his throat, trying to ignore the way his body reacted to her simple gesture. He wanted to take her hand, hold it against his cheek, feel the soft gentleness of her skin.

But he couldn't.

Instead he shrugged, as if she'd had no effect on him. "Amos got a little feisty, but he's gone now. Nothing to worry about."

He didn't like that her brow furrowed, indicating she was clearly worrying anyway.

"He hit you?" she whispered a little too loudly for his liking.

"He did?" Ezekiel gasped.

"I should wave the waitress down, see if we can get some ice," Emma said. Her gaze was already scanning the crowded room, searching out the *Englisch* woman who had served them.

"It's not necessary. I don't need ice. It was nothing," Levi assured. "The important thing is that he's not here bothering the waitress."

"Thanks to you," Emma said.

He knew that pride was a sin, but he felt his heart swell under Emma's praise anyway.

• • •

"And then he took a swing at Levi!" Ezekiel exclaimed. "But Levi just walked away. It took a whole group of men to drag Amos off, down the road. I heard Jonah telling his *bruder* Roy all about it at the hitching post."

"Zeke," Emma gasped. Her gaze darted across the table to where Levi was studiously chewing a bite of his haystack. He didn't look particularly impressed by the topic of dinner conversation—the topic being *him*.

Amelia quirked an eyebrow at Emma. "I heard a similar story. A group of men were talking about it at the café when I got off work. If I'd known you were there today, I'd have come out of the kitchen to say *hallo*."

"We didn't want to disturb you when you were working," Emma said.

"It's too bad you missed it," Ezekiel told Amelia. "I wish *I'd* gone outside. I would've liked to have seen the men take Amos away."

Emma was about to rebuke him, but Levi beat her to it.

"I'm glad you missed it all," Levi said sternly. "Fighting is never the answer."

"I know," Ezekiel quickly agreed. His head bobbed, as if to assure Levi he did know better. "But

I sure am mighty glad Amos isn't to be a part of our family."

Emma's heart clenched when she realized that Zeke's gaze drifted to Levi, relief setting across his features. Was the boy becoming too attached to Levi? Perhaps he was, but what was she to do about it?

Levi huffed a terse laugh. "You're not alone in that. The man is a challenge to be around. If he were here, I'd be worrying all the time."

If Amos were here, Emma realized, her siblings would not be. That had been the plan. For her to marry Amos and the children to move to the other end of the state.

Gratitude swelled over her like a gently rippling wave. She had Levi to thank for keeping her family intact, and that was something that meant the world to her.

He glanced at her then, likely feeling the weight of her stare, and his mouth lifted in a smile. She pulled in a shaky breath before managing to smile back.

Even though he expected nothing in return, Emma was sure she would feel forever indebted to him. How could she ever repay him?

"May I please have the lemonade?" Sadie asked, clearly unimpressed with the conversation.

Emma was grateful for the interruption. She handed the glass pitcher to her sister.

"Haystacks are my favorite," Ezekiel announced, probably in an effort to prove he'd moved on from admiring the way Levi had dealt with Amos. He began piling more food onto his plate. First rice, then corn chips, followed by taco-seasoned beef. He added some lettuce, tomatoes, onions, and a healthy serving of Emma's creamy cheese sauce.

For a small boy, Emma thought with an inward smile, *he sure has a big appetite*.

"Mary stopped by the café today," Emma said.

"How is Mary doing?" Amelia asked, genuine concern filling her tone.

Emma frowned as she remembered the painful-looking way Mary's fingers curled. "Her arthritis is acting up. She stopped by the café to buy bread."

"I wonder how she's keeping her business going?" Amelia murmured.

Emma wondered the same. Running a greenhouse could be strenuous, potting plants, lugging them around, planting seeds and nurturing them. Digging them out of the ground must be nearly impossible with her condition.

"I drove by her place a few weeks ago while I was heading to a jobsite. It wasn't looking as well kept as usual," Levi admitted. "I'm ashamed to say I didn't think a whole lot of it at the time. I sure bet she could use some help with the upkeep."

Emma thought he was probably right.

He frowned. "Now that I think about it, I'm not so sure she had her flower stand open."

Emma wondered where she was getting her income. Not that it was her business, but that didn't mean she couldn't be concerned about a spinster from their community.

"Perhaps we should pay her a visit tomorrow," Amelia suggested to Emma.

"That's a lovely idea," Emma said. "We can do

some baking tonight, bring her a few treats."

She was already taking mental inventory of what was in the pantry. Now that Mary had come up in conversation, Emma's mind started to whirl. The woman was all on her own, no family nearby, and while her greenhouse business had been successful in the past, Levi brought up a real concern. What if she'd had to close her business?

"I'll come, too," Levi announced.

Emma swung her surprised gaze his way.

His brow was furrowed. "As I mentioned, her place wasn't looking to be in the best shape. I think it would benefit from some cleaning up. I can work on the yard. Get it mowed, do some trimming. Maybe see if any repairs need to be made."

"I'll help," Ezekiel proclaimed, anxious as always to prove his use.

"I can wash floors," Sadie announced. "I'm sure that has to be difficult for her."

Emma smiled, grateful for the kind hearts of those seated at the table with her.

"It's a plan then," she said. "Tomorrow, we'll pay a visit to Mary Kurtz."

CHAPTER NINE

"Take this with you," *Mamm* told Levi as she handed him a small wooden crate. "I found some canned venison in the cellar. I'm sure Mary will enjoy it. I wonder how much gardening she's been able to manage. I had some extra peas and beans so I packed a bag of each for her."

"*Danki, Mamm*," Levi said. He knew that his mother didn't really have peas or beans to spare right now. She had picked what was available in her garden—which wasn't a lot this early in the year— and had packed it all up for Mary. "I'm sure she'll appreciate it."

His mother frowned, not looking for praise. "I feel bad I haven't thought to help her before now. She ain't one to complain, but being alone like that, it has to be tough…" Diana shook her head as she pondered the unpleasant thought. "I'm glad you realized she might be in need. It's only right to help take care of one of our own."

"It is," Levi said as he hoisted the crate into his buggy.

"It's a shame she never married," his mother continued and he grimaced, aware of what was coming next.

Levi turned to face her. "I'm sure she had her reasons."

Undeterred, she continued. "You know what the Bible tells us. Two are better than one, because they have a good reward for their toil. For if they fall, one will lift up the other." She nodded to herself, as if she had just proven a point. "I'm so glad you and Emma are figuring things out. I had a hunch you two belonged together. I'm just surprised it took *you* so long to figure it out."

Levi nodded solemnly. "If I have my way, I'll make her my wife before the snow falls."

"She'll agree," *Mamm* said firmly.

Levi didn't share his mother's confidence.

She must have noticed, because she said, "You aren't so sure." It wasn't a question.

He doubted his mother knew about the falling out that he and Emma had a few years ago. All she knew was that they had drifted apart. She had probably thought it only natural, given their ages.

"You two are courting," *Mamm* said, and he didn't have any desire to tell her the real circumstances around the arrangement. She gave him a playful nudge. "How could she resist you for long?"

Levi smiled at his mother's teasing. "You think?"

"*Jah*, I do." Her expression turned more serious when she asked, "How is her problem with the county coming along?"

"She's making progress," he said, "but she has a long way to go before she has all the funds."

"I've been discreetly encouraging members of our congregation to buy syrup," she admitted a bit sheepishly. "I know more people are asking Sadie for her goat cheese as well. Everyone wants to help the family out."

"*Danki, Mamm*." He scrubbed a hand over his

face. "I've offered to help, but she keeps turning me down."

"Then you must respect that," *Mamm* said.

He gave a noncommittal nod.

She tapped the crate. "You don't want to keep the Zieglers waiting. Enjoy your day and tell Mary I said *hallo*."

With those words of parting, she took off toward the house.

Levi headed out for the Ziegler farm. When he arrived, the yard was bustling with activity. Sadie was scurrying out of the henhouse, Ezekiel was setting a box onto the front steps—something Levi assumed was for Mary—and Emma and Amelia were coming in from the garden, both with baskets full of bounty.

"What's all this?" Levi asked as he reached the front steps.

"The girls have a bunch of stuff they want to bring to Mary," Ezekiel explained, confirming Levi's suspicion.

The boy hefted the box and made his way toward the buggy.

"Just in time," Emma called. "We were picking a few things from the garden to share."

He nodded. "*Mamm* had the same idea. She sent some peas and beans."

"Perfect," Amelia said. "We have carrots and onions and peppers."

"She will be well fed for a while," Levi said. "Are we all set to go?"

"I'm ready," Sadie said. "I was just collecting the last of the eggs. Mary used to buy them from me, but she hasn't lately. I figured she could use some."

"That's very kind of you," Levi said. "I don't know a soul who doesn't appreciate fresh eggs. Does anyone need help with anything?"

"I think we can manage," Emma replied.

They loaded their gifts and all climbed into the buggy. Amelia and the children went in first, leaving the front seat beside him open for Emma.

He was close to his own family, loved each of them dearly, but being with Emma's family like this filled him with a happiness that he'd never experienced before. He'd known Sadie and Ezekiel their whole lives. This past summer, as they'd been spending time together, his fondness for them had only grown.

He was well aware that if he and Emma were to have a future, the children would be a part of it. He had no problem with that—in fact, he relished it. He was even growing fond of Amelia, whom he barely knew. Yet he'd determined she had the same generous heart as her cousins. Lately, as all his friends had started getting married off, he'd felt as if something was missing in his life.

He knew the *something* was Emma.

He longed to marry her. Make her family his family, too.

"I hope she's happy to see us," Emma said. "It's not as if we've ever gone to visit her before. I hope she doesn't find it too odd."

"She'll be happy," Levi assured her. And if she wasn't happy, he figured she would be too polite to admit it.

Emma and Amelia discussed their strategy as he

drove. They would find a tactful way to offer any help that they deemed needed. He would tackle the lawn, which had been wildly overgrown the last time he'd gone past.

Emma let out an unhappy sigh as Mary's home came into view.

It was in even worse disrepair than Levi recalled.

"I haven't been this way in such a long time," Emma admitted. "I didn't realize things had gotten so bad. It looks like Mary could really use our help."

The house was on the eastern edge of the district, out of the way of most of their town. He figured a lot of people hadn't realized that Mary might be in need of help.

The plain wooden sign simply stating Mary's Greenhouse was nearly covered in overgrown weeds.

Levi pulled the buggy to a stop. "Zeke?" He nodded toward the weeds.

"*Jah*, I'll take care of it," he said. The boy hopped out of the buggy and set to work, tearing the weeds up by the roots. Satisfied Zeke would get the job done, he led Blaze to the fence, where he could hitch him to a rail for now.

As Zeke pulled weeds, the rest of the group moved toward the house.

Emma knocked solidly on the door.

"Come in! Come in!" Mary called from inside.

Emma and Levi shared a look before Emma reached for the knob. He assumed that perhaps it was difficult for Mary to come greet guests in her condition. As the door opened, Mary's voice carried from another room.

"I was so worried you decided not to show up! I'm so glad you're here! I have the pots all ready to go. Give me just—" She cut herself short when she appeared in the doorframe, drying her hands on a kitchen towel. "*Ach*," she said as she blinked at them in surprise. "Isn't this a pleasant surprise."

"Mary," Amelia said curiously, "who were you expecting?"

Mary sighed. "The Graber twins, Helen and Harry. I've rented a spot at Saturday Market, but I'm not *goot* at lugging pots around anymore."

Levi could imagine. Some of the plants she sold, ready to slide into the ground, were quite large and would be rather heavy.

"I hired them to run my table for me, but they aren't very reliable. It doesn't look like they are going to show up this morning." Mary waved a dish towel in the air. "Enough about them; what brings you by?"

Levi noticed that Emma had grabbed the picnic basket.

"We brought roast beef sandwiches, calico bean hot dish, and broccoli salad," Amelia told Mary as she looped her arm through that of the older woman. It looked like a friendly gesture, but Levi suspected that Amelia was taking the opportunity to help the woman stay steady on her feet. "I got to thinking, you and my *mamm* were such close friends. It's been rude of me not to pay you a visit. When I mentioned stopping by, everyone thought it was a *wunderbaar* idea. So here we are."

It was, more or less, the truth. Amelia had tactfully left out the *reason* for the visit. But every word she said was factual.

"It's so *goot* to see you all," Mary said, genuine happiness in her tone. "And for you to bring lunch, too. How nice!"

Lunch is nice, Levi thought, but as he caught Emma's eye and she gave him a small nod, he knew her thinking aligned with his own. There was something far nicer they could do for this kind lady.

• • •

"Mary," Emma said lightly, "as much as we would love to have lunch with you, how would you feel about Levi and I running your booth today?"

"I couldn't ask you to do that," Mary said firmly.

"You didn't ask. We offered, and we'd like to," Emma insisted. It was clear Mary was still going to argue, so Emma led the conversation. "Actually, truth be told, Mary, I've been considering setting up a booth of my own. I'd like to sell my syrup, but I just don't know if it would be worth my time. It would be awfully kind of you to let us run your booth today and allow me to sell my syrup along with your flowers. That should give me an idea as to whether or not it would be profitable for me to rent my own space."

"I'm sure your syrup would be a success," Mary said. "If that's what you would really like to do." Emma nodded. "Then I would appreciate it." She glanced at the clock. It was not quite eleven. "The market starts at noon today and runs until four. This is my busiest time of year because people are anxious about planting their flower beds."

"Perfect," Levi said. "If we load up right now, that will give us just enough time to stop at Emma's for a few cases of syrup."

With everyone loading various sizes of pots and trays while Mary supervised, they had the back of Levi's buggy filled in no time. Mary had large pots full of bleeding hearts, peonies, ferns, and hostas. It seemed there was an endless amount of seedling trays filled with smaller flowers. She sent along a table, two folding chairs, a price list, and her cash box to make change.

Amelia discreetly assured Emma that she, Sadie, and Zeke would get the yard mowed and help with anything else Mary would allow.

Back at the Ziegler farm, Levi hurriedly carried three cases of syrup up from the basement while Emma found paper and a marker to fashion a make-shift sign. They both tossed a quick wave to Harvey Larson who was busy haying the Zieglers' field.

They pulled into the market with not a lot of time to spare. Together, they worked at setting up the table and unloading Mary's plants. She had sent quite the variety. Large pots of perennials, small trays of mari-golds, and what seemed like everything in between.

"We did it," Emma said as she collapsed into one of the folding chairs that Mary had sent along.

"Just in time, too," Levi said. He shot her a satis-fied smile. It reminded her of their youth, back when they would help each other with chores so they'd have more time for fun.

The clear blue sky and gentle breeze made it a perfect day for shopping. Already, people were buzz-ing around, the parking lot nearly full.

Emma glanced around the market. She had come here many times as a customer. Saturday Market was always bustling, full of *Englischers* and Amish alike. This time of year, there were plenty of out-of-towners looking for unique souvenirs to bring back to family and friends.

More than a dozen booths were set up. A few sold strictly produce, one sold Amish baked goods, an *Englisch* family she knew had a booth set up with honey. Yet another Amish booth sold pot holders, placemats, and baby quilts.

It didn't take long for people to migrate toward them. Emma answered questions about the flowers, took the payments, and chatted with people while Levi often helped carry the heavier pots of flowers to people's vehicles. Emma had been a bit surprised by Mary's prices but soon realized that people were willing to pay top dollar for her high-quality plants. She apparently had a reputation around town for having the hardiest flowers available.

She had wondered how an elderly woman on her own managed with a small greenhouse. But that small greenhouse, she realized, had quite the payout. They remained so busy that she'd barely had a chance to utter a few words to Levi between customers.

Emma was delighted that her syrup sold well. It was a new product at Saturday Market, and therefore seemed to glean quite a bit of attention. The issue of the taxes kept trying to creep into her mind, but she pushed it away before the too-familiar sense of dread kicked in.

As the market finally began to wind down, she

spotted Rachael coming toward them.

"Emma! Levi! What are you doing here?"

"We're running Mary's table for her," Emma explained.

"I see that," Rachael replied. She took a bite of the powdered funnel cake she was carrying. "*Mm*, these are so *appendlitch*."

"They're my favorite," Levi admitted.

"Go get one," Emma said. "I can manage the booth. We haven't had a customer in a while."

"You should both go," Rachael said. "I watched Mary's booth a few times last summer. I'm sure she wouldn't mind. I would still do it, but I work most Saturdays."

"Aren't you here to shop?" Emma asked.

"*Nee*. I just got off work and I've had such a craving for a funnel cake all day. I came here to eat." She blushed as she raised her plate. "You two go." She made a shooing motion with her hand.

That was all the urging Levi needed. He grabbed Emma's elbow and gave her a gentle tug.

"Take your time!" Rachael called after them. She winked at Emma, clearly assuming she was doing her a favor, sending Emma off with her beau. Emma ignored the pang of unease that resulted from letting her friend believe a fib.

As they swerved through the crowd, Levi leaned in close to Emma.

"Your syrup sold well."

"*Jah*, I'm grateful." She had sold a case and a half. She would have liked to have sold more, but she would not complain about the unexpected income of the day. "It's fairly expensive to rent a spot, though. I'm not sure it would be profitable for me to have my own table."

They wandered past a booth of chain saw carvings of bears, eagles, moose, and other wildlife. While the sculptures were amazing and fascinating, Emma couldn't imagine owning something so frivolous.

"It seems you and Mary each have a unique problem," Levi said.

Emma turned from the sculptures to look at Levi.

"She needs help. You need a spot." He paused. "I think today went well. I'd be willing to help out every Saturday."

"I appreciate the offer," Emma said. "But you work all week long." She paused a moment as an idea suddenly percolated. "Sadie and Zeke are always so bored in the summer when school is out. I think they would enjoy sitting at the booth. I'll have to ask them, and Mary, of course."

She felt a small wave of panic. Despite the sale of the hay, and the extra syrup sales, she had quite a way to go before she would have enough for the payment. Yet at least she was making progress. She had mentioned her dilemma to Amelia, but she insisted Amelia not tell her siblings. She had actually hoped perhaps her cousin could help her get a job at the café. However, Amelia, unaware of Emma's desire, had admitted that she was looking forward to taking over Rachael's hours when her time was done.

There were so few options for employment for Amish women, Emma didn't know who else to ask. She knew the Weavers didn't need help at the candy shop. Their children took care of that. She didn't have the time to devote to being a nanny for the *Englisch*. There was already an Amish woman who served as seamstress, and Emma would never think of infringing upon her business.

She would somehow have to make do with her syrup. The realization only solidified her resolve to check with Mary about joining together for the upcoming Saturday Markets.

They reached the bakery booth and Levi paid for two funnel cakes. He quickly maneuvered to the edge of the market, away from the bulk of the crowd.

"I'm starving," he admitted as he handed her a plate.

"I am, too." She took a big bite. They had left in such a hurry, they hadn't thought to eat a quick lunch, and she certainly hadn't had time to pack one. The flower booth had been so busy that taking a break hadn't been an option.

The sinfully delicious concoction of deep-fried dough and sweet powdered sugar seemed to melt in her mouth. She hummed in delight. "Rachael was right. These are *appendlitch*."

Levi said nothing for a moment. His eyes seemed to be glued to her mouth. She belatedly realized she must've made a spectacle with all that powdered sugar.

"I'm a mess, aren't I?" She quickly swiped at her face. When his lips quirked, she realized she'd used the hand that had been holding the powdery funnel cake.

"Here," Levi said. "Let me help." He gently brushed one cheek, then the other. He hesitated a moment before saying, "You have some…here." His finger gently brushed the corner of her lip. Emma didn't mean to inhale sharply at his touch, but she did. "I didn't get it all," Levi admitted, his eyes still on her.

Using her pointer finger, Emma self-consciously rubbed at the sugar. She was keenly aware of the way Levi's gaze followed the movement.

"Is it gone?"

He nodded, his voice sounding gruffer than usual as he said, "*Jah*, it is."

His gaze lingered, resting on her lips. She brushed at them again, wondering why he was still staring. And staring…*like that*? Was that longing in his gaze? It couldn't be. Could it? Her heart unexpectedly leaped.

"Are you sure?" she murmured.

He nodded.

"Then what are you still looking at?" she demanded a bit breathlessly.

He lifted his eyes to hers. "You," he said with a carefree shrug. "You're just so pretty."

He said it so easily, so simply, as if it were just fact. Nothing more, nothing less. Emma was so startled she couldn't muster a response, not even a simple thank-you. She was too busy wondering at the way a delicious warmth filled her over the compliment.

Levi took a bite of his funnel cake and Emma realized that he managed to keep *his* face powder free.

"Would you like to look around a bit?" he asked. "Rachael said not to hurry."

"I...um... S-sure," she stammered.

They finished their desserts, then joined the crowd. Emma was very aware of the way Levi's hand repeatedly bumped into hers, his fingers brushing against hers ever so slightly. He would never be so bold as to hold her hand in public, but she kind of wondered if he wanted to. Somehow their day of selling flowers seemed like so much more than that.

As they moved from one booth to another, she realized she was barely paying attention to the items. She could think of nothing but Levi.

How was it that with one heated look and a simple compliment, Levi had managed to send her thoughts spinning delightfully out of control?

CHAPTER TEN

"No running in the house," Emma scolded as Ezekiel raced down the staircase and took off toward the front door.

"But Levi is here!"

"And he won't leave without you," Emma reasoned, "so slow down."

Levi was stopping by to pick up Zeke for a day of fishing. After the hard work at Mary's the day before, Emma thought the boys were due some fun. Ezekiel was so excited he'd been bouncing around the house all morning.

Emma followed him outside so she could say hello to Levi. She tried to convince herself it was only because she didn't want to be rude, but truth be told, she longed to see him, if only for a few moments.

He hopped down from the buggy with a smile on his face. "What a beautiful morning," he proclaimed.

"It is," Emma agreed, smiling at his exuberance. "It's a fine day for fishing. You and Zeke will have a nice time."

"We'll *all* have a nice time," Levi said. "Would you like to get Sadie and Amelia, or should I?"

"We should go," Ezekiel called from the buggy, fishing pole in hand. "They bite best right now."

"You heard the boy," Levi said. "We should go."

Emma laughed in confusion. "*We*? I *canna* go fishing."

"Sure you can," Levi said. He hesitated before adding, "You don't have to fish. You can just enjoy a day at the river's edge. Look at how beautiful the sky is. It's supposed to heat up later on, so the breeze off the river will feel nice."

"Levi." She shook her head. "There's much to do today."

"There's much to do every day," he argued. "Whatever needs to be done can wait." When she still hesitated, he said, "You have to come. *Mamm* packed a picnic lunch, enough for all of us. Her feelings will be hurt if it doesn't get eaten."

He gave her an imploring look, one that made her giggle. She clapped a hand over her mouth before backing away.

"I'll fetch Amelia and Sadie." She twisted around and headed back inside. They had missed a full day of doing their own chores yesterday by helping Mary. Missing another day probably wasn't wise, but oh, how she wanted to spend the day with Levi. Her time with him at Saturday Market had left her anticipating just a bit more.

She was grateful that Mary had been open to the idea of Sadie and Ezekiel running her flower stand every weekend. Today, she was feeling more light-hearted because of it. The extra income would be a blessing. While the worry over the taxes was constantly present, at least it wasn't as overwhelming as it had initially been.

"Hurry," her brother called.

Amelia and Sadie didn't need nearly as much convincing as Emma had. They were happy to postpone their chores for another day. As Levi had said, there was nothing that needed doing that couldn't wait.

As they sat on the riverbank watching Levi and Ezekiel fish, Emma was glad she let him talk her into joining them. She had brought a needlepoint pillow she was working on, while Amelia had taken along her knitting basket. Sadie had a book Mary had given her on gardening. She rotated between reading and borrowing the extra fishing pole Levi had thought to pack.

She laughed with delight when she reeled in a decent-sized bluegill. Levi added it to the creel.

"Emma," Sadie called as she skipped up the riverbank. "You should fish for a while."

"*Nee*, you were having fun. You should continue on," Emma urged.

Amelia gave her a gentle nudge. "Go down to the river's edge. Catch a few fish." She nodded toward Levi. "Spend some time with him. He was kind enough to arrange this lovely day for us; I think he'd like it if you fished with him."

"Go," Sadie urged.

Levi grinned as he motioned for her to join him.

"I suppose I could." She had loved fishing when she was younger. Now, it seemed like a frivolous activity she didn't have time for. But today, she had nothing but time. She got to her feet and carefully made her way down the riverbank. It wasn't terribly steep, but she didn't want to step on the hem of her dress and take a tumble.

"Have you ever fished before?" Ezekiel asked.

"*Jah*, a long time ago." Her eyes locked with Levi's for a moment. "When I was young, a boy who

lived down the road used to take me fishing all the
time."

Ezekiel's gaze bounced between them. "You and
Levi used to fish together?"

"We did," she confirmed, and her brother grinned.

Levi handed her the fishing pole he'd prepared
for her.

"Do you remember how to cast?" Zeke wondered.

"As I said, it's been a while, but I've been watching the two of you all morning."

"Maybe I can help refresh your memory," Levi
offered.

He slipped behind her, slid an arm around her,
and rested his palm on her waist. Emma hoped he
didn't hear the surprised little yip that slipped out
under her breath. His other hand rested over hers
on the fishing rod.

"You just reach back, push the button on the reel,
and fling the rod forward," he said. He ran through
the motion a few more times.

Emma was utterly oblivious to the rest of the in-
structions that Levi murmured in her ear. All she
could think about was that her assumption that he
had muscular arms was correct. She could feel his
biceps flexing against her arm as he guided the
movement, and the arm wrapped around her was
like iron. More than that, she was keenly aware of
his crisp scent. Some type of wonderfully fresh soap,
no doubt.

"Emma?" He chuckled in her ear.

She jerked away from him when she realized he'd
said her name more than once. What had she been
thinking, getting lost in his embrace like that? And

in front of her siblings, too. She felt her cheeks heat. More importantly, what was *he* thinking? She realized he must be putting on a show for her family, making them believe there was something between them.

Without looking at him, she said, "I think I've got it now. *Danki.*"

The first tug on her line didn't come right away. When it did, she let out a gasp of delight. The fish was a decent-sized perch that put up a bit of a fight.

Ezekiel had been right—this was fun. Over the years, she had forgotten how much she enjoyed fishing. Once her initial embarrassment wore off, she also enjoyed chatting with the two of them while they continued to fish. Her little brother, usually so quiet, had turned into a chatterbox while in Levi's presence.

Emma listened quietly as Ezekiel admitted to Levi that the Zook brothers frequently poked fun at him. They teased him about his small stature and called him names. He told Levi that a few times they'd even pushed him down, once into the mud.

Emma recalled a day last spring when Ezekiel had come home from school filthy. She had asked him what happened and he'd refused to speak at all. It had been easy to assume he'd gotten dirty while messing around, but now she knew that was not the case. She mentally cringed, remembering how she had scolded him, telling him to be more careful. She had made it clear that when he made such a mess of his clothes, it made more work for her.

"Zeke," she said gently, "why have you never told me of this?"

Her brother immediately stopped talking. He shrugged.

"Zeke," Levi gently pushed, "your *schweschter* asked you a question."

Ezekiel executed another perfect cast as he stared out at the water. She thought for sure he was going to refuse to answer. Without looking her way, he finally said, "When *Daed* was sick you never had time to talk to me. I would tell you things and you never listened. So, I stopped telling you things." He shrugged. "Levi always listens."

Her fist clenched around the pole in her hand as mixed emotions flooded her. She felt awful for not being there for Ezekiel, and so grateful that Levi had been willing to give him the attention that he so desperately needed.

Ezekiel was still so young. She was reminded yet again that he would benefit from a male in his life. One he could look up to.

"Bullying is despicable behavior," Emma said forcefully, "and it's never okay. I'm so sorry they treated you that way."

"Emma's right," Levi agreed. "Bullying is not to be tolerated."

Emma nodded, but then returned her attention to Zeke.

"I'm sorry." Her words were heartfelt. "I should have made more time for you. From this day on, I promise I will be a better *schweschter*. Can you forgive me?"

He sliced a sideways glance her way, his expression peaceful. "I already have. I know it was hard for you to be so busy all the time."

"It was hard on everyone when Paul was so ill," Levi agreed.

"I miss him," Ezekiel admitted.

"As do I." She reached over and pulled Ezekiel into a sideways hug. "I am so grateful that I have you and Sadie."

"And Levi?" Ezekiel asked.

She glanced at Levi and nodded. "I'm grateful for Levi as well." She *was* grateful that he had given so freely of himself to Ezekiel. She could add it to the ever-growing list of things for which she was grateful to him.

Eventually they decided it was time for a break. Levi lugged the picnic basket out of the buggy, and they all shifted around to make room on the quilt that was spread out under the shade of several balsam trees.

Levi's mother, Emma realized, must've approved of their choice of a way to spend the day. She'd packed a lovely lunch of sandwiches, macaroni salad, and a container of fresh melon from her garden. At the bottom of the picnic basket, Zeke had been delighted to find a container full of Diana's coveted snickerdoodle cookies.

After a nice meal filled with chatter and relaxation, Ezekiel was ready to resume his fishing. Levi joined him without a word of complaint. Emma found herself wondering if Levi really enjoyed fishing so much, or if he was intent on pleasing her brother.

She thought perhaps it was a bit of both.

Amelia rested her knitting in her lap. "I don't remember ever spending a day like this."

"Nor have I spent a day like this," Emma admitted. "I will have to thank Diana for packing such a nice meal. It was kind of Levi to think of inviting us."

"He has a lot of patience," Amelia said.

Emma nibbled her lip as she watched Levi untangle Zeke's line. Instead of scolding the boy, Levi wore a smile as he gave what Emma assumed were words of advice and encouragement.

"I always thought you two were meant to be sweethearts," Sadie proclaimed.

Emma pulled her attention away from the creek. "What do you mean?"

"Exactly what I said." Sadie gave her a knowing smile. "You and Levi belong together. You and Ivan, it just seemed, oh, I don't know," she said as she struggled for the words. "It seemed forced. We all knew that Ivan courted you only because *Daed* asked him to."

Emma scowled. She knew it as well, but she didn't like thinking about it. Arranged marriages were not exactly common in the Amish culture, but given the extenuating circumstances, she knew her *daed* had just been trying to look out for her.

"He should've asked Levi," Sadie said conspiratorially.

"Levi and I were barely speaking," Emma reminded her sister, thinking of the rift that had distanced them for a few years. All over a misunderstanding, Levi assuming she was interested in an *Englisch* boy.

"He still would've said yes," Sadie said confidently.

"He'll make a *goot* husband," Amelia said decidedly.

She hated feeling so dishonest.

Surely, courting was going to lead to nothing more.

This was *pretend* courting. It would do her well to remember that.

She couldn't get swept away by his silly flirting. It was surely all for show. At Saturday Market, there had been plenty of members of their congregation there. And today? Perhaps he hadn't been flirting. Perhaps she had only herself to blame for being swept away for no reason.

How embarrassing.

"Emma?" Amelia laid a gentle hand over Emma's. "Is everything all right? You look so unhappy all of a sudden."

"Are you worried about the wash?" Sadie wondered. "I can help with the laundry tomorrow. I know everything is getting behind. But if we all work together, it will get done."

Emma smiled at her sister's innocent query. "No, there's something far more complicated than bedsheets that's bothering me."

Amelia and Sadie looked instantly concerned.

"There's something I must confess." Emma cast a guilty glance toward Levi before returning her attention to the two sitting next to her. "Levi and I, we're not courting."

"Of course you are," Sadie said. "Why would you deny such a thing?"

"But we're not. Not really."

"I don't understand. The two of you most certainly are stepping out," Amelia said. "How else would you explain all the time you spend together?

He's come to the farm for dinner a few times and to help out. You've dined at the café together more than once. You don't do that with any old man who comes along. Who did you run to when Zeke was missing? Who came to your defense when Amos was misbehaving?"

"Levi, but—"

"It's silly to say you're not courting," Amelia gently scolded. "He's a kind and gracious man. You should be happy to have him by your side."

"I am lucky," Emma agreed. "I will say that. But things are not entirely as they seem." She reminded them that Naomi had wanted her to sell the farm and marry Amos, but Levi had interrupted the conversation. They both nodded, not surprised by this.

"What you don't know," Emma said quietly, "is that we were not courting. Levi said we were. But we were not."

"I see," Amelia said with a frown. "However, from that moment, from the moment Levi said so, you didn't disagree."

Emma blushed, her guilt eating at her. "I did not."

Amelia nodded, her brow furrowed as she reasoned out what Emma was saying. "To me it sounds like you began courting right then. Therefore, you did not tell an untruth."

Emma pursed her lips and narrowed her eyes, trying to understand Amelia's words.

"She's right," Sadie decided.

"You're not listening to what I have to say. We don't…" She struggled with finding the right words. "We don't have feelings for each other. We're courting, but we're not *really* courting. It is only for show. We both know that this, this *courtship*, will go nowhere."

Amelia laughed lightly. "I don't think Levi realizes that. I'm fairly certain he thinks he's your beau."

"He's only *pretending* to be my beau," Emma said in exasperation. Or was he? The purpose of this plan had become blurred.

"The only untruth I'm aware of," Sadie said with a smirk, "is that you're insisting you don't have feelings for him when you clearly do."

"I don't," Emma protested. But was that true? She suddenly realized that it was not. Instead of arguing about her own feelings, she feebly added, "Nor does he have feelings for me. He's being a friend. That is all."

Amelia tapped her chin in mock contemplation. "No, I don't think so. I do believe I agree with Sadie."

They shared a conspiratorial look before Amelia said, "Don't tell me there wasn't anything behind that little fishing lesson on the shore."

Emma opened her mouth to protest but quickly snapped it shut again, because what could she possibly say to that?

Sadie grinned, clearly enjoying the opportunity to tease her big sister. "I've seen the longing looks you cast his way."

Emma's cheeks flamed. "I do no such thing."

"Don't worry about being improper," Sadie said with an eye roll. "I don't think there's anything wrong with ogling the man you're courting."

"I don't ogle," Emma insisted. "Have you listened

to anything I've had to say? He agreed to court me only to buy me some time. It was a way to make Naomi happy and keep the farm."

Both her sister and cousin raised their eyebrows.

"You ogle," Amelia said. "You *canna* deny the look you gave him when he helped you into the buggy. When he took your hand, your cheeks flamed right up. You practically swooned down there on the riverbank."

"Perhaps I do give him a look from time to time," Emma relented. "But if I do, it's a look of confusion. Sometimes I *canna* decide what that man is up to."

Now that was a true statement.

"What he's up to?" Sadie scoffed. "He's trying to win your heart. That's what he's up to."

"I do believe she's right," Amelia tacked on.

"You two are impossible," Emma muttered. She couldn't help but feel that Levi was helping her only out of pity. He had a habit of barreling into her life and taking over. The incident with Darren was a perfect example, as was his interference with Ivan. Hadn't he done exactly the same thing that day on the porch? By telling Naomi they were courting, he had barged right in. Taken over. Not because of any romantic feelings, but because he clearly thought she wasn't capable of handling intense situations.

The thought needled at her.

What was worse, she realized with a wince, was that perhaps *her* feelings *were* growing. They had sort of crept up on her, to the point where there was no denying she had swooned as Amelia had accused. She would have to watch herself. Falling for Levi, when he was with her only because he thought she couldn't take care of herself, would be dreadful.

"We also happen to be right." Sadie's tone was mischievous when she said, "You two are falling in love."

Emma was growing weary of the teasing. Perhaps it would be best to not say anything and let the conversation drop. She pinched the bridge of her nose. She felt better for having told them her secret, because she hated having a lie between them.

When she lifted her eyes, they floated straight to Levi, who was staring right at her. It took him several long moments before he peeled his gaze away.

Sadie swatted her as she burst into a fit of giggles. "See." Her tone was positively triumphant. "You ogle him, and when you're not looking, he ogles you right back."

Amelia joined in with quiet laughter. "Emma, I do believe Sadie is right."

Emma shook her head and dropped her gaze. She found their stubbornness frustrating. They were wrong, both of them buying into this charade.

• • •

Levi wasn't sure what to make of Emma's behavior as he helped her out of the buggy. Or her behavior in general lately. Never would he have guessed that Emma would become so hard for him to read.

He and Zeke had caught another meal of fish while the ladies stayed busy on the shore. The morning had started out so nicely. Emma had been chipper during lunch, enjoying the food and the sunshine.

Several times he heard laughter coming from the riverbank. Whenever he looked back to see if he could figure out what was so humorous, the laughter died away.

Women, they were a bit complicated.

That's what he was thinking now as Emma acted so aloof.

"Thank you for a lovely day," she said primly. "Zeke had a great time."

"And you?" Levi asked.

She nodded. "Very nice. Thank you."

Amelia grabbed the bundled quilt and headed toward the house with the teens following her.

"I should go. Evening chores need to be done." She spun to leave but he reached out, catching her by the elbow.

"Emma, wait just a moment?" She nodded and he released her. Confusion slammed into him from all sides when she dropped her eyes to the ground. "Have I done something to offend you? Are you angry with me?"

She glanced up at him. "Why would you ask such silly questions?"

"Silly?" he scoffed. "I don't find them silly. This morning you were in a fine mood. Now you can barely get away from me fast enough. I thought today would be something you would enjoy. You did seem to enjoy it. What went wrong? Are you upset about Zeke?"

"I asked Zeke for forgiveness and promised to do better. That is all I can do."

"If you're not upset about your *bruder*, what is it then? I can tell something is eating at you."

She straightened her spine and seemed to gather some resolve. "I told Amelia and Sadie that this courtship is not real."

Levi felt as though someone had punched him in the gut. It was real to him. He had hoped it would become real to her.

"It's as real as we make it," he said quietly.

"I don't know what that means. Yes, we're courting. But for us, doesn't that just mean going through the motions?" She paused as she studied his face. "This is just a temporary arrangement. I *canna* tell you how much it means to me that you are willing to do this. But I know it will not last."

She spun and began walking away from him.

Hope sparked in his mind as a thought took hold. "Emma." He trotted along the driveway until he caught up with her. "Any chance you're upset by that?"

She skidded to a halt. "I don't understand what you're asking."

He grabbed her hand—improper or not, he wanted to feel her delicate fingers wrapped in his own. "I think you do understand. You've been moody all afternoon. What brought about that moodiness? The idea that eventually this courtship will come to an end? Does that bother you?"

She tried to tug her hand away.

"Tell me, please."

He was not surprised when she stubbornly refused. He could easily drop her hand and let her leave. If he did that, he might never know her answer.

"You don't have to assume there is an end in sight," Levi encouraged. "We could continue to court, see where this leads."

"Why? Because you fancy yourself to be my res-cuer? Always charging in to save me? You tried to rescue me from Darren, Ivan, the sale of the farm." She scoffed and shook her head. Then her hand drifted to his cheek, her thumb brushing across the scar from that out-of-control rooster. He wanted to grab her hand. Hold it. Never let it go. But all too soon it dropped away. "Even when we were *kinner*, you tried to protect me. I won't let this charade go on indefinitely because you pity me." She pivoted and hurried away, heading to the safety of her house.

She thought he pitied her? Clearly, he had not done a good job of getting his feelings across to her. He was simply going to have to try harder.

CHAPTER ELEVEN

"Did you hear that?" Amelia asked as she poked her head into Emma's bedroom.

Emma was stripping the bedding off her bed. Amelia already had her arms full of sheets.

"I didn't hear anything." She halted her task and cocked her head to the side. Her mind had been floating in the clouds. Last night, she had thought that perhaps Levi would argue with her, tell her that it was more than concern for her that he felt. He hadn't done so, and her disappointment ran deep.

A moment later, a shriek pierced the quiet morning air, yanking her thoughts from Levi completely. Amelia and Emma shared a startled glance as they both dropped the bedding and dashed out of the room. Emma reached the front door first. Her stocking feet pounded across the porch, down the steps, and over the gravel driveway.

"Emma!" Sadie shouted.

The sun cast a hazy glow over the farm as it burned its way through thick, gray clouds. Emma could see her sister standing next to the chicken coop, holding tightly to the pole that secured a side of the fence. Her sister's shoulders shook as Ezekiel stood several steps back, his hand over his mouth.

"What is it?" Emma came to an abrupt stop as she reached her sister's side.

Chicken carcasses were strewn about. Emma raised her hand to her throat. The sight of Sadie's docile Marans, torn apart, left her feeling ill.

"What happened?" Amelia cried.

"The door to the coop was open." Sadie sniffled. "I shut it, Emma. I know I did."

The Marans were sweet, tame. They roamed the yard freely during the day, but Sadie locked them up nightly. Foxes, coyotes, and raccoons were all natural predators of the defenseless hens.

A nocturnal creature had clearly gotten into the coop. The hens were so tame, they would've been no match for anything with teeth and claws. If anything, they would've tried to cower deeper inside the coop.

Emma thought it was possible that just this once, Sadie forgot to flip the latch that locked the door. The girl was so distraught, though, that she didn't see any point in making accusations. If Sadie perchance did leave the coop door open, Emma doubted that after this ordeal, she would ever do it again.

"Oh, Sadie," Emma said as she tugged her shaking sister into her arms. "I'm so sorry. Come inside."

The hens were more than part of their livelihood, they were pets to Sadie. While neither Zeke nor Emma had ever had much luck befriending the birds, Sadie could carry them around the yard, cuddled to her chest.

Sadie's feet were rooted to the spot as she scanned the carnage one final time.

"Go with Emma," Amelia ordered. "I will deal with this."

"I'll help." Ezekiel raised his chin stubbornly, assuming that he would be denied. "When we are done, I'll finish with the rest of the chores."

The goats needed to be fed and milked. The goat

pen and chicken coop needed to be cleaned out. They were tasks that Sadie and Ezekiel tackled together. This morning, Ezekiel was willing to take charge.

Emma could see this was important to him. He wanted to help Sadie. She nodded her approval.

Sadie slumped into her side as she led her into the house. Emma deposited her at the kitchen table before fetching a handkerchief for her. Sadie dabbed at her eyes before blowing her nose.

"Poor Patsy, and Mitsy, and Spotty." She sniffed, her eyes watering up again. "I didn't see the rest of them. They were probably carried off."

"I'm so sorry," Emma murmured as she rubbed her sister's back.

Sadie lifted her face to Emma's. "I always close the latch. I do. Someone had to have opened it."

"Sadie," Emma said gently, "I *canna* imagine that anyone would do such a thing. Who would want to harm your chickens?"

"I don't know," she wailed.

Emma could think of no more words of encouragement. Despite Sadie's denials, it only made sense that she forgot. Perhaps she closed the door and simply forgot to flip the latch. A raccoon, or even a fox, would figure out how to pry the door open in no time. She should have checked the latches herself. It was too late now, though; the hens were gone.

Emma's guess was that it had been raccoons. The woods were crawling with them. She had seen them at dusk many times, nosing around. The little varmints ate anything they could get their pesky little paws on. It wasn't as if the helpless chickens could fly to safety.

"I don't feel well," Sadie moaned. "Is it okay if I go lie down?"

"That's a *goot* idea. Amelia was preparing to start the wash. I don't think your bed has been stripped yet."

After Sadie tromped up the steps, Emma descended into the cellar carrying a battery-operated lantern.

On a far wall stood a battered countertop Paul had rescued from somewhere. Next to it stood shelves of canning and another shelf full of syrup. She carefully began moving the bottles of syrup to the countertop. She always ordered labels from a local print shop that simply stated Ziegler's Maple Syrup. Carefully, she peeled the backing off a label and placed it on a bottle. Then she placed the bottle in one of the special boxes with dividers she'd ordered. Each box held twelve bottles of syrup. The syrup had been selling well all over town. Community members had been buying more syrup than usual as well. Emma suspected it was their way of helping her family. She needed the money so she would not complain. Instead, she would happily put on labels and fill up the boxes so she could deliver them.

As she worked, she realized the job was too mindless. Her thoughts wandered to places she did not want them to go.

Levi. Dependable Levi.

Perhaps she *was* falling for him. Would that be so bad? It would be, if he saw himself only as her protector. She wanted more than that; she wanted someone to love, someone who could love her. It didn't matter that she could get lost in those beautiful blue eyes of his, nor did it matter that she had enjoyed his arms around her yesterday. What mattered was that Levi, apparently, had never seen her as his equal. Only someone who needed to be taken care of. And *that* did not sit well with her.

It was, in part, why she was so determined to take care of the issue of the property taxes on her own. The date—now circled in red on the calendar in the kitchen—was edging closer. Money was coming in faster than ever before for her syrup, meaning if sales continued at this rate, she would be close. Yet she just wasn't sure she would have enough.

She pressed a hand against her stomach, hoping to squelch the bundle of nerves that had settled there.

"Emma?" Sadie called down the rickety staircase. "Levi is here."

She'd been clutching the same bottle for several long moments. She hurriedly put on a label and placed it in the box. "I'll be right up."

Levi dropping in had become a common occurrence, but she was surprised that he was dropping by today. After the way they left things last night, she wasn't sure what to expect. Truth be told, she half expected him to tell her he was done with her.

She hurried up the steps to find Levi standing in the kitchen. Sadie was sniffling, telling him about the morning's catastrophe. He listened with a sympathetic look on his face.

"I thought you were going to rest," Emma said to Sadie.

Sadie's face scrunched up. Her lips trembled. "Every time I closed my eyes, I saw the chicken coop."

"It will get better with time," Levi soothed.

"What brings you over?" Emma asked.

For one frantic moment she worried that he was stopping by to end things. Her heart slammed hard against the wall of her chest. Regret coursed through her veins and she couldn't be sure of the reason. Was she upset because she would have to face Naomi? Or was she upset for another reason entirely?

She quickly realized her fear was unfounded. Levi was not about to desert her.

"Ivan asked if I'd help him out a few days this week. I'm not needed on the carpentry crew, so I said I would. His fencing on the entire east side is in pretty rough shape. He's looking to get a new bull and he needs to know the fence is secure enough to hold him."

Emma nodded, though she had no idea what that had to do with his early morning visit.

"I thought maybe I could borrow Zeke for the day. We could use the help. Do you think he'd want to come along?"

She gave him a knowing look. Fencing was hard work. The old, rotting posts needed to be pulled, new ones needed to be pounded in, then the fencing needed to be attached. Post after post after post. Ezekiel had never done anything of the sort before; she was sure he would not be a whole lot of help.

Levi's request wasn't for himself, as he had worded it. It was an offer to let Ezekiel spend the day with two men who could teach him a valuable skill. A skill she was not capable of teaching him.

"I think he would enjoy helping," Emma said, her heart melting a bit over the kind gesture. "He's outside with Amelia. I can go ask him."

"There's no need. I can find him. I only wanted to clear it with you first."

"I appreciate that."

"There's a lot to be done today. Miriam is planning on us for supper. I'll have Ezekiel home sometime after." He cast a sympathetic glance at Sadie and then left without another word.

Sadie waited until the front door gently banged shut before asking, "Is everything okay with you two?"

The question startled her, though it probably shouldn't have. The tension between them must be obvious. "Why would you ask that?"

Sadie shrugged. "You just didn't look very happy to see each other."

Emma drooped against the countertop. "We did have a bit of a spat last night."

"About what?"

Could she tell Sadie? She still thought of Sadie as her baby sister. However, her baby sister would turn seventeen shortly before the syrup harvest next spring. Before long, she'd be looking to find a beau of her own.

"I accused him of always wanting to rescue me," Emma said. "I'm afraid I wasn't very nice about it."

"So what if he does?" Sadie cocked her head to the side, seemingly perplexed by the notion. "You always take care of everyone else. Would it be so bad to let someone take care of you for a change?"

Sadie's question echoed through her mind. Was it possible that her little sister had a point?

• • •

Levi knelt down, frowning. Ezekiel and Amelia must've ventured into the woods to bury the birds. Levi had been about to shout for Ezekiel, but the coop caught his attention. Sadie had adamantly denied leaving the door unlocked. His curiosity pricked at him, forcing him to take a look.

Footprints stood out in the mud, large ones roughly the size of his. They couldn't belong to any of the Zieglers.

Had someone come during the night and opened the door? The thought seemed absurd. What would be the point? It was simply cruel.

A niggling little suspicion wormed into his mind, but he tried to ignore it. He had no proof. Yet Amos's leering smile boasted malice. He shoved the suspicion aside. It was not his place to condemn a man, even if only in his mind.

He spotted more tracks of an entirely different nature. He was certain they belonged to raccoons. It seemed that *someone* had opened the door, but the raccoons had done the damage. What a horrible waste. The Zieglers counted on the eggs the Marans laid. To have them so savagely destroyed was senseless and cruel.

Rising to his feet, he scanned the tree line, hoping to spot Ezekiel. He raised his hands, cupping his mouth, preparing to give a shout when a noise caught his attention. He froze, straining his ears to catch the sound again.

After a moment he heard it. A soft warbling coming from the flower garden. He moved forward cautiously, letting the sound guide him. He gently pried apart the thick foliage of a bleeding-heart bush. There, cowering down, was a single hen.

"Hey, there, pretty girl," he coaxed. He reached toward her. She ducked her head but didn't dart off. "It's okay. I would never hurt you."

With two hands he gently scooped her up and held her firmly to his chest. She buried her head in the crook of his arm, trying to find comfort. She still trembled, probably remembering her terror from the night before.

He let himself in the house. He could hear the clinking of dishes and water running in the kitchen.

Emma had her back to him as she scrubbed a pot.

Sadie sat at the table shelling peas. Her face was still red and splotchy, her eyes puffy. Her lips quivered as she tossed the empty pods into a scrap bucket.

The hen clucked and both Emma and Sadie jumped.

Emma spun around, splashing water.

Sadie squealed as she leaped from her chair.

"Look what I found," Levi said as he held out the hen. "She was hiding in the flower bed."

"Gretel!" Sadie tugged the hen from Levi and nestled her face into the chicken's feathers.

The bird let out another squawk of protest but Sadie didn't care. She burst into a new round of tears. Levi thought these were probably of the happy variety.

"*Danki*," she cried.

"Do not thank me," Levi said. "Thanks be to God for helping her find a safe place to hide."

Sadie nodded as she continued to hug the flustered bird.

"How did you…?" Emma started.

"I stopped to look at the coop. I heard her in the flower bed."

The front door burst open. Hurried footsteps pounded across the floor.

"Did I see Levi with"—Zeke's eyes widened— "Gretel!"

Levi grinned when Zeke's face lit up with nearly as much excitement as his sister's. Zeke moved closer, but the chicken protested his nearness.

"Sadie," Emma said gently, "could you please take Gretel outside? I'm happy she's safe, but the kitchen is no place for a *live* chicken."

Sadie nodded and the two hurried out.

"I'm so grateful you found her. I know they're just chickens," Emma said, "but she was heartbroken. Having Gretel will ease the pain a bit."

Levi grimaced. "It's not just losing them. It's the gruesome, senseless way that it happened."

"She feels terrible about leaving the door open. In all the years since she's tended to the chickens, she's never done that before. I don't think she'll ever make that mistake again."

"I'm not so sure it was her error," he admitted. "Have you had company recently? Other than me?"

"*Nee*. Why?"

"There are footprints down by the coop. They're a bit smaller than mine, but definitely a man's tread.

I couldn't track them very far because I lost them in the grass."

"Zeke?" Emma offered.

"Too big to be his."

"Perhaps someone stopped by while we were away."

"And just happened to feel the need to check out the chicken coop? Doesn't that seem like too much of a coincidence?"

She frowned at him. "What are you saying?"

"I think you know. I think someone let her chickens out."

He could see the disbelief wash across her face. But then, as she tossed the idea around, she let out a weary sigh. "Who would do such a thing?"

"I don't know."

Her brow furrowed in thought as she shook her head, not wanting to believe it was true. "Perhaps someone was stopping by to see if we were in need of anything. We had many visitors right after *Daed*'s passing. It could be someone was looking around, wondering if there was anything that needed taking care of."

Levi wasn't convinced but could tell by Emma's firm stance there would be no point in arguing. She didn't want to believe that someone could intentionally be so awful.

"It would explain why someone was walking around. Perhaps they were looking for us and were checking down by the barn?" She shrugged, but the action didn't come across as carefree. "There are other explanations. So *jah*, it could be just a coincidence."

"We have a few extra padlocks at the farm. I'll stop by and grab them before I bring Zeke back tonight." He paused. "Is that okay? Or would you like to go to town to buy your own?" He certainly didn't want to overstep again, as Emma had made it quite clear last night that he did too much of that.

"I would appreciate the locks, *danki*," she said.

He nodded. "It's better to be safe than sorry. If it was done intentionally, there's no sense in giving the person the chance to finish what they started."

"Well!" Amelia exclaimed as she breezed into the kitchen. "I do believe you have become someone's hero. I'm not sure if Sadie is going to come in again. She might not let that silly chicken out of her sight."

"It is fortunate that at least one was salvaged," Levi agreed.

"And more fortunate it was found, rather than hidden away, waiting for another attack tonight," Amelia added.

"Thank you," Emma said to Amelia, "for taking care of the mess."

Amelia nodded. "Zeke and I buried the birds. We cleaned out the coop as well. It's *goot* as new."

"It is time to move on from this, then," Emma decided.

"In all the commotion I forgot to talk to Zeke about coming with me today." He glanced at the clock on the wall. Though the time had been well spent, the excitement with the chickens had him running behind schedule.

He bid Amelia and Emma farewell before heading outside for a second time.

• • •

Scrubbing every floor in the house had not been enough busy work to clear Emma's head. Nor was the ordeal with the chickens enough of a distraction. She could not get Sadie's words out of her head. Was it time she let someone take care of her?

All her life she had put others' needs before her own. She had taken care of Ezekiel from the day he was born. She had tried to fill the void for Sadie by teaching her to do things a mother should be teaching her to do. She had taken care of her *daed* the best way she knew how. She had run the household as if it were her own.

Now her siblings were almost grown. Soon, they wouldn't need her at all anymore.

Maybe Sadie was right; maybe Emma ought to be a bit more open to receiving help. The notion was nearly foreign to her. She sighed. Yes, she *could* be more open to receiving help. But she did not want to be coddled. Well-meaning or not, Levi seemed to cross that line a bit too often.

Sadie couldn't be parted from Gretel the rest of the day, but at least her preoccupation with her favorite pet saved Emma from further inquisition. Amelia had busied herself with trying to complete the afghan she had been working on down at the river.

The three women ate a lazy supper of leftovers, each lost in her own thoughts.

A brilliant golden sunset was spilling across the western sky when Emma noted the telltale crunch of buggy wheels. She slipped out the front door before she lost her nerve.

Ezekiel hopped out of the buggy, waving to her as she descended the porch steps.

Levi had been ready to head for home, but he steadied his horse when he realized she was approaching him.

"Did you have a *goot* day?" Emma asked Ezekiel as he walked past.

"*Jah*, it was hard work." He grinned. "I hurt all over."

Emma smiled. "I'm sure you do. Go inside and clean up while I talk to Levi."

Levi was strolling toward her when she turned back around.

"He's an excellent worker." Levi motioned toward Ezekiel's retreating back. "If he's given a job, he doesn't give up until it's complete. The work was strenuous and the sun was blistering, but he didn't complain one time."

"I'll tell him you said so. I think he enjoyed himself."

"*Jah*. I think so, too. I also gave Zeke the padlocks I mentioned. I told him to put one on the barn door and on the chicken coop after evening chores."

"*Danki*."

He shifted from foot to foot, as if wondering if that was all Emma wanted to talk to him about.

She plunged ahead before she lost her nerve. "I want to apologize for last night. I am grateful for your help. I don't want to appear otherwise."

Levi cringed. "Sometimes I overstep."

"Well…sometimes," Emma agreed.

"Are you upset that I told Naomi we are court-ing?"

She thought about it a moment. "*Nee*. I don't know of another way I could have gotten her to trust me with the farm. In a few months, when she sees I've kept the place up and running, and that I've paid the taxes, she should have no reason to doubt my ability."

His lip quirked. "Until then, we're still courting?"

She gave a lighthearted shrug, but inside, her heart was racing. "I don't really see any way around it."

"Ouch." He clutched his chest. "I think you just wounded my ego."

Emma bit back a laugh. She took a step away from him. "Thank you again for thinking of Ezekiel." She turned to leave.

"Emma?" Levi called.

She pivoted back around.

"Will you go for a ride with me after the Sunday service? In my courting buggy?"

"*Jah*." She let out a little laugh. "I would like that."

This time when she hurried inside, she couldn't stop the smile that took over her face.

CHAPTER TWELVE

It was the Bontragers' turn to host Sunday services. Emma and her family were the first to arrive, eager to help their neighbors prepare. The benches had been delivered the day before. Levi and his three brothers were checking to be sure they were set up as needed. Ezekiel immediately ran off, ready to offer help.

"What can we do?" Amelia asked as they entered Diana's kitchen.

Levi's mother looked a bit frazzled. Her cheeks were rosy from scurrying about all morning.

"Nothing, really," she answered. "I think I'm ready. My only concern is having enough room for all the food."

"When people arrive, we'll adjust as needed," Emma assured her. "We always make it work."

Emma slid an enormous pot of maple baked beans onto the counter.

Women from the district all contributed food for the meal. There would be salads and meat and plenty of tasty options for dessert. Storage was often a concern but as Emma said, they always seemed to manage.

"I believe the men are finishing up with the benches," Diana said.

"They are," Emma agreed. "Ezekiel ran off to offer his help but it appeared as if the men had everything under control."

"Well then," Diana said as she smoothed back the hair at the edges of her *kapp*, "I believe that we can go outside to greet our guests."

It was a lovely day, so the service would be held outdoors. Emma, Amelia, and Sadie sat together. Ezekiel wedged himself next to Levi on the men's side.

Emma enjoyed the hymns that were sung. They were comforting and familiar, always bringing her a sense of peace. Though no instruments accompanied the songs, the melody carried by the myriad of voices was beautiful.

As the minister began the first sermon, she realized her mind had started to wander. It was all Levi Bontrager's fault. She could feel him watching her across the way. She'd met his eye a time or two, and he'd flashed his boyish grin. Was he really that excited about a buggy ride? It was utterly distracting.

It was undeniable that her feelings for him were shifting, changing, growing. Could he feel the same? Was it possible that he had romantic feelings for her? The very notion caused her heart to swirl. Levi was such a huge part of her past. It was suddenly easy to envision him in her future.

As the hours-long service drew to a close, she had the uncanny feeling someone was watching her again. She glanced up with a knowing smile, thinking it was Levi.

Her smile vanished when her gaze collided with Amos's. Somehow, she had missed him before. His eyes bore into her. Then he smirked, offered her a lecherous wink. It sent shivers of dread skittering down her spine.

The heaviness of his stare conveyed the bitterness he felt. She quickly swiveled her attention to the minister again. Perhaps it was her imagination, but her entire body tingled with apprehension. She was sure if she looked his way again, Amos would be shooting hateful daggers at her with his eyes.

When the congregation sang the final hymn, she dared another glance in Amos's direction. He wasn't sitting where he had been. Had he snuck out of the service? To do so was almost unheard of. Perhaps he'd moved to a different bench that was not in her line of sight.

"Is something wrong?" Amelia whispered as they began to file out with the rest of the women.

She forced a smile, willing herself to forget her worries. "*Nee*. Everything is fine." Today was a day of worship. She did not want to take away from that by making complaints against Amos. Besides, what had he really done, other than give her a look she didn't appreciate?

They moved into the house together to help the rest of the women prepare the meal. Most of the food was ready to go.

The men converted the benches into tables. By the time they were done, the women were ready to carry the food outside. With so many church members, it was necessary to eat in shifts. The men would eat first, then the women and children. Serving bowls would be replenished often. There would be plenty of time for visiting.

When Emma refreshed the serving bowls with the maple baked beans her family had prepared, she managed to share a few secret smiles with Levi.

"Mary has invited us for supper," Amelia told Emma as they worked together in the kitchen. It was essential to get a start on dishes so as not to get too far behind.

"I've already made plans with Levi," Emma reminded.

Amelia's eyes sparkled with delight. "I would not ask you to miss spending time with your beau. Would it be all right with you if I invited Sadie and Ezekiel to join me? Mary was hoping that I would."

"*Jah*," Emma agreed. "I'm sure they would love to go."

"We'll be home in plenty of time for evening chores," Amelia assured. "That will give you and Levi the entire afternoon to enjoy your drive."

Emma carried a pair of dessert platters out to the long tables. She jumped when she turned to find Marvin Stoltzfus in her path.

"Emma, how are you?"

She placed her hand against her heart. "I'm fine, thank you."

"Can we talk a moment?"

She was surprised by his request. Did this have to do with Amos?

"What is it?" she asked.

He glanced around surreptitiously. "My offer still stands to buy your farm for my boy. He needs something positive to focus on."

Emma's spine stiffened. "It's not for sale."

He frowned. "You've paid the taxes off, then?"

The taxes? How did he know about the taxes? Her gaze settled on Levi on the other side of the yard. Had he done this? Her heart beat out an angry rhythm as her ire began to stir.

"I ran into Paul at the courthouse some time ago," Marvin said quietly. "I overheard his conversation."

So Levi hadn't told, then. She felt a twinge of guilt over jumping to that conclusion.

Emma forced a tight smile. "It is kind of you to offer, but regardless of what you heard, the farm is not for sale."

With those words, she scurried away before he could convince her otherwise.

• • •

Levi typically enjoyed Sunday services. Today, however, he had been anxious for the day to move along. He was eager to spend some time with Emma. Stealing a few moments here and there as she bustled about wasn't enough for him.

It made matters only worse that the service was at his family's farm. Though community members helped, there was cleaning up to be done.

"I think we've got this handled," Ivan said to Levi. They had just loaded the last of the benches into the wagon. "We can finish up."

Levi's two older brothers, Joshua and Isaac, were also helping.

"Go," Joshua said with a laugh. "We know you have plans to take Emma out today. It's about time you consider settling down. Can't say I'm surprised she's the one who caught your eye."

"Jessa is hoping the two of you are wed soon," Isaac teased. His wife had grown up the only girl amid five brothers. "She's excited about the prospect of having another *schweschter*."

"As is Amanda," Joshua said, speaking of his own wife.

Levi was pleased that his sisters-in-law were so anxious to welcome Emma to the family. He had noted that Amanda and Jessa had flocked around Emma today while preparing and cleaning up after the meal, and much laughter had come from the cluster of women. He was grateful that Emma blended in with them so well, though he had no reason to think she wouldn't.

"Get going," Isaac said as he gave Levi a sturdy smack on the back. "Before we change our minds."

Levi did as he was ordered. There were still about a dozen members of their church district milling about the yard, visiting. But if his brothers were willing to entertain them and take over the rest of the cleanup, he was happy to accept their offer.

He went to the barn to retrieve his horse. In no time, he had him hitched to the courting buggy.

He strode up to the house to retrieve Emma.

Her face lit up in a smile when he rounded the back side of the house. The women were gathered here, visiting in the backyard now that the meal was done.

She said a quick goodbye to the group of women she was standing with and hurried over to him.

"Today is the perfect day for a ride," Levi said. "Don't you think?"

"*Jah*," Emma agreed. "What a beautiful day God has given us."

The sun was shining brightly. A light breeze

danced upon the air, carrying away the worst of the day's heat.

They walked side by side to where the horse was hitched to a post. A handful of other courting couples had already departed.

Levi noted a few curious glances tossed their way as he helped Emma into the open courting buggy. He felt lighthearted as they coasted down the driveway.

"I shouldn't say it," he admitted to Emma, "but I was beginning to feel as if the day was moving as slow as sap in winter." He headed north, away from the Ziegler farm.

"I was beginning to think that as well," she agreed.

"Did you have a nice visit with my *bruders'* wives?"

"I did," Emma said. "Jessa was busy chasing the twins around, but we did have a chance to talk for a little while. Amanda brought me a recipe for fudge that she's been making with our maple syrup. I'm anxious to give it a try. I didn't see much of Miriam. Your mother said she wasn't feeling well. She decided to lie down once the service was done."

"Hopefully she'll recover quickly," Levi said. If not, Ivan was sure to hurry her home to rest.

The horse plodded along. His hooves pounded out a calming, rhythmic beat.

Levi cast a few sidelong glances at Emma, causing her to fidget with the hem of her apron. Her brow was furrowed, as if she were lost in thoughts of an unpleasant nature.

"Is something troubling you?" he asked.

"I'm not sure."

"That's an odd answer." He let his knee bump into hers. "Care to share?"

"It's probably nothing," she said on a sigh. "I caught Amos's attention during the church service. He's clearly still angry with me. I thought perhaps I could speak with him after, try to smooth things over, but he was nowhere to be found."

"I'm glad you didn't find him. I don't think it's wise for you to speak with him on your own," Levi warned.

"I agree. That's why I thought today would be a *goot* day. His *daed*, the ministers, the bishop, they were all there. I didn't think he would put up a fuss. But I didn't have a chance to find out." She shrugged. "Perhaps he caught whatever bug is ailing Miriam. I think he left before the service ended." She paused a moment before adding, "That's not all. Marvin stopped me and asked about buying the farm again. He knows about the taxes."

Levi cast a quick glance her way. "He knows?"

"For just a moment, I thought you had told him," she sheepishly admitted.

Feeling affronted, he said, "I would never do that." Although, if he were to be honest with himself, he had spoken out of turn in the past. He could hardly blame Emma for her assumption.

"*Jah*, he said he heard my *daed* down at the courthouse. I'm sure he didn't mention it to Naomi. I am grateful for that."

"What did you tell him?"

"I told him the farm is not for sale."

Her tone was resolute. He was not going to ruin their day by pressing the matter.

The countryside was peaceful, a picture of God's perfect work. Brilliant green leaves trembled on the trees. Wildflowers brightened up the ditches. Gauzy clouds lazily floated across the blue sky. The Millers' field of vibrant yellow sunflowers twisted toward the afternoon sun.

Levi and Emma shared news they had heard during the meal earlier in the day. Much of the talk had circled around the Millers' barn raising, which would be held later in the week.

As they headed toward the Bontrager and Ziegler farms once more, Levi realized he wasn't ready for the afternoon to end. It was a Sunday, and as such, chores were kept to a minimum. He didn't need to return home for a while, nor did Emma.

At his suggestion they found themselves at the river. An *Englisch* family was there. Though he didn't recognize them, Levi assumed they were locals. They noted the buggy's arrival with little more than a smile and a friendly wave, which he appreciated, before returning their attention to their picnic.

Levi hitched the horse to one of the posts that was provided before helping Emma from the buggy.

They wandered down to the river so they could stroll the path that led along the river's edge. He knew some would not approve of this time alone together, but he and Emma were no longer carefree teenagers. They were both responsible adults and as such, Levi thought they deserved a bit of leeway.

"How did Saturday Market go yesterday?" Levi asked.

"It was *wunderbaar*," Emma said. "Sadie and Zeke had so much fun. Mary's flowers sold out and syrup sales were about the same as last week."

"I bet Mary was happy," Levi said.

"She was. She doesn't feel comfortable running her flower stand at home anymore. This works out well for everyone."

"And now that Harvey's baled the hay, Zeke can get new seed down for the bumper crop."

She nodded. "Everything is moving along."

Without the use of motorized farm equipment, it would take Ezekiel several days to get the seed down. But Levi was sure the boy would manage just fine. Naomi's fears about Zeke were proving to be completely unfounded.

"I'll help bring in the second crop," Levi offered. He knew the Zieglers would keep a fair share of it to get their own animals through the winter. "Zeke will need help with that, regardless of what he thinks."

"Your help will be appreciated," Emma admitted. "Once the taxes are paid, I think I'll feel a little less overwhelmed. It was a relief to have Harvey's help." She took a breath. "And yours. Hopefully by next year Zeke and I will be able to manage." She bit her bottom lip, as if she weren't so sure.

"It's a big job," Levi said gently. "You already have a household to run. There is no shame in receiving help."

Emma nodded as if in agreement, but he could see it still troubled her. She was fiercely determined, had always been independent. It was hard for her to accept help, even though to refuse would be prideful.

The river flowed at their side. As they continued

to walk, he could sense Emma's anxiety begin to fade.

He hoped that someday soon, he would be her husband. As such, taking his help would not trouble her. It would simply be an intrinsic part of married life.

• • •

The morning had gone by slowly, but the afternoon had sped past. Emma was sad to see it end. She hoped that she and Levi would have the opportunity for time together again soon. Now, both their stomachs were rumbling, so they'd decided it was time to head home.

"It doesn't look as if your family has returned yet," Levi pointed out.

The buggy was not in its usual spot next to the barn. Ginger had not been turned out to graze.

"They must be enjoying their time at Mary's," Emma said. "Perhaps you could stay for supper? It will be just me, otherwise. I was planning something light. Sandwiches and some leftover potato salad. We could eat on the porch."

"That sounds *goot*," Levi said. "I'm starving."

"We have fresh iced tea and—" Emma cut herself off with a frown. She paused a moment, straining her ears as the buggy rolled down the lane. "Do you hear that?"

"*Jah*. The goats seem to be putting up a fuss." With a gentle smack of the reins Blaze hurried his gait. The closer the buggy drew to the farm, the more apparent the commotion became.

"Oh, now what?" Emma moaned.

Gretel was distraught, running to and fro while clucking irritably. But compared to the goats, her racket was minimal.

The goats were frantically bleating. It wasn't unusual for them to create a ruckus, but a strange sense of urgency could be heard in their cries.

Levi leaped from the buggy, Emma hopping out and running after him. They hurried around the side of the barn. The goat pen was butted up against it, with the barn wall creating one side of the pen. An opening in the barn wall allowed the goats to go in and out at will.

Both of the solid white goats were outside now. Bessie paced back and forth. The other, Margie, struggled to get free from a roll of barbed wire fencing.

Emma gasped. "How did that get in there?"

Levi pulled the door of the pen open and rushed to the frantic goat. Her leg was tangled in the wire, the barbs digging in whenever she struggled.

"If I hold her still," Levi said as he gripped the goat, "can you get her untangled?"

"I think so." Emma knelt down and rubbed the goat's side. How had such a lovely day turned so troubling? She used a gentle tone that didn't belie how rattled she felt. "It's okay, Margie. We're here to help. We're going to get you out of this mess."

It was not easy going. Emma was relieved that Sadie wasn't home; she would've been heartbroken to see her goat in such distress. The large, frightened goat struggled despite Levi's best efforts to hold her still. The barbs bounced around, making it difficult for Emma to get the goat's leg free without cutting herself just as badly.

Eventually they succeeded. By the time the goat was loose, Emma's hands were scraped, but none of the injuries were too bad. The same could not be said for Margie. Bright blood stood out against her stark white coat.

"Oh, you poor thing," Emma said soothingly. "How did you get yourself into such a bind?"

They switched places. Emma held her still, a much easier task now that she was free, while Levi inspected her wounds.

"She should be all right if we get these cuts cleaned up," he said. "I'd wrap them, but I know goats. She'd just chew the bandage off and eat it."

Emma agreed. She retrieved a bucket of soapy water, rags, and a container of salve. The two of them worked together to clean Margie's wounds.

Levi held the goat still while Emma washed her wounds. For such a big man, he was surprisingly gentle. He held her firmly but took great care trying to soothe her. When she was satisfied that the wounds were clean, she spread salve over the cuts in an effort to stave off infection.

Once they were satisfied Margie was going to be okay, they checked out the rest of the property. Finding nothing else amiss, they climbed the porch steps.

"Be sure that Sadie cleans her wounds morning and night, at least for the first few days," Levi suggested. "If she continues to apply antibiotic, the cuts shouldn't get infected."

The goat was still bleating, though she didn't

sound quite so distressed.

"I don't understand how this happened." Emma slumped against the porch railing. Her appetite had faded. Now her stomach was full of knots. "The extra fencing was in the barn." She eyed the opening the goats used to go in and out, knowing there was no way they had access to the fencing on the other side. It was kept clear, away from their pen inside the barn.

"Was the door locked? Have you been using the padlocks I sent home with Zeke?" Levi asked.

"We use them at night. I don't suppose Zeke locked the barn before we left for church, though." She tugged fretfully at a string from her *kapp*. "Someone had to have tossed that roll of fencing into their pen. From now on, we'll be sure to lock up any time we leave."

Levi began to pace the short length of the porch. "I was suspicious when the chickens were slaughtered. Sadie was so sure she checked the coop door. It is more than coincidence that your goat was injured now, too."

"I agree." She was hesitant to say more, but Levi heard the accusation in her silence.

"Do you think it could have been Amos?"

She shook her head. "I shouldn't say." She remembered how her aunt had accused her of being a gossip when she had mentioned Amos's wrongdoings. She didn't want to be guilty of that by accusing him of something without proof. "I wish I could've found him after the service. It's strange that he left so quickly. I want to believe that perhaps he wasn't feeling well, like Miriam, but he seemed fine when he caught my eye."

"*Jah*," Levi grumbled, "he left quickly because he came here. He knew you would stay. The entire congregation stayed. There was no one to see him on your property."

She paused, looking contemplative. "What if it is not him? It would be wrong of us to accuse."

"Who else could it be?"

Emma shook her head. "There is no one who comes to mind. But why Sadie's chickens? Why Sadie's goats? It doesn't make sense that he's targeting her."

"Amos knows nothing of your family. It's doubtful he knows the animals are Sadie's. They're nothing more than easy targets."

"It's hard to believe that someone would do this intentionally," Emma murmured. Her mind scrambled to find a way to make sense of it, to prove that it was nothing more than a series of unfortunate coincidences. She didn't want to think the worst of anyone, not even Amos.

"I'd like your permission to speak with Bishop Yoder about this," Levi requested. "I think he would like to know."

"*Nee*. Please don't. Not until we know for sure Amos is behind this."

"Emma—"

"It's my farm," Emma reminded firmly. "It's my decision."

"But—"

She cut him off with a look.

He hesitated a moment before nodding. "Okay."

She didn't want to admit to Levi that she was

worried about what the bishop would think. What if he determined that Emma shouldn't run the farm alone? What if he sided with Naomi and thought she should sell? She would not take that chance. For as long as she could, she would keep the bishop out of it.

Levi nodded toward the road. "It looks as if your family is returning."

"I dread telling Sadie about this."

"We were fortunate that we were the first to arrive. Now the goat has calmed down some. Sadie has missed the worst of it."

"I should tell her now before she sees the damage for herself." Emma pushed away from the porch, and Levi followed. His presence gave her strength. Sadie had urged her to be more willing to accept help. She *was* willing to accept Levi's help, but she had the right to have final say in everything that pertained to her family and the farm.

Even if there was something dangerous going on.

CHAPTER THIRTEEN

Emma's heart lurched as she flew into a sitting position, her bedsheets twisted all around her. She placed a hand against her chest, unsuccessfully trying to calm herself. She blinked into the dim light of early morning.

What had awakened her?

Had it been a dream?

Had someone in the house gotten up earlier than usual?

Quickly, she slid from her bed.

A bleat cut through the quiet morning. It was one of the goats. She scurried over to the window, but shoving the curtain aside didn't help much. The sun hadn't crested the horizon yet.

Gretel squawked.

Emma hurried away from the window.

Out in the hallway, she paused for only a moment. She couldn't wake the children, but should she wake Amelia? No, she decided. Amelia would be getting up soon enough. Now that she had taken over some of Rachael's hours at the café, she was working long days. She needed her rest while she could get it.

Besides, she reasoned, she was likely letting her imagination get the better of her. It would be embarrassing to wake her cousin for no reason.

She rushed down the stairs; moving through her house by memory, she pulled open the closet near the front door. Feeling around inside, her fingers quickly wrapped around what she was looking for.

Ezekiel's baseball bat.

She slid her feet into her worn shoes and eased the front door open.

She wasn't entirely convinced that a ne'er-do-well had harmed the chickens and goats. She wanted to believe the best of people. But if someone was trespassing on her farm, it was her responsibility to figure it out.

To find out *who*.

She knew Levi suspected Amos, but she couldn't very well go to the bishop on a suspicion. She knew how that would turn out. She would be reprimanded, and rightly so—it was wrong to accuse someone when there was no proof.

She needed proof.

Maybe she wouldn't get any. It was entirely possible that Sadie had left the gate open. It was also possible that somehow the barbed wire had tumbled into the goat pen.

Not likely, but possible.

As for the animals' behavior right now, maybe they were just on edge due to the attack on the chickens. Perhaps the raccoons were stalking the yard again, hoping for more easy prey, setting the animals on edge.

She placed her hand on the doorknob, pulled in a breath to steel herself. She wasn't looking forward to heading outside, but she wanted answers. Ezekiel and Sadie needed her, were counting on her to take care of them and to keep them safe.

In order to do that, she needed to know who—if

anyone—was targeting the farm.

With one hand firmly gripped around the bat, she eased the front door open. She was grateful her father had always tried to be vigilant when it came to upkeep on the farm. The door didn't squeak, the front porch didn't creak as she made her way down it.

The morning was damp, dreary, the sky still a hazy gray.

She hustled across the yard, darting behind the overgrown lilac bush. Safely ensconced behind the shield of its branches, she began to scan the yard. She didn't detect any movement by the barn, henhouse, or goat pen. All three were locked up tight, so she didn't fear that someone had broken in.

Bessie and Margie let out sounds of frustration as they trotted toward the corner of their pen. They stood there, tails twitching, feet stamping in agitation, as they let out an occasional sound of protest.

Emma cut her eyes across the yard, to the other side of the property.

Her breath caught.

Her heart raced and her palms began to sweat.

She'd spotted what had grabbed the goats' attention.

There, in the vegetable garden, was a dark shape rooting around. Was it a bear? A stray dog? No, what would a dog be doing in the garden?

She took a tentative step back toward the porch. Then another step, hoping the animal didn't spot her or sense her presence. If it charged her, she wasn't sure she could fend it off with the baseball bat.

She suddenly felt silly for being so reckless.

Moments before she reached the step—reached safety—the figure seemed to change right before her eyes. At first, she didn't comprehend what she was seeing, so convinced it was an animal before her. When it began to lengthen, unfurl, and become taller, it took her a few moments to make sense of what she was seeing.

With a little gasp of surprise, she realized that what she was looking at was not a bear. It wasn't an animal at all. It was a man. A man who must've been crouched down, doing who knew what in the garden, before extending himself to his full height.

"Shoo!" she yelled. "Get out of here."

The words flew from her mouth without any thought. The moment they were out she realized how careless they were. Yet her innate desire to protect what was hers bubbled up strong within her.

Outraged over having her garden violated, she charged forward, baseball bat at the ready. No, she didn't think she could force herself to use the bat. But the intruder didn't need to know that.

Before she got too close to the garden, an object came hurling through the air at her. She let out a shriek as she ducked. The large rock flew over her, but it would have surely hit her square in the face if she hadn't ducked. It bounced on the ground behind her.

It took Emma only a moment to gather her wits about her. In that time, the figure darted into the cornstalks. She ran after him, but when she reached the edge of the garden, she stopped. It would be beyond silly to follow him into the corn. Chances were she wouldn't find him. And what if she did? He was bigger. He would have the advantage.

She backed away from the garden. Adrenaline making her body hum, she jogged back to the house, looking over her shoulder much of the way. She quickly let herself in and then locked the door.

"What in the world is going on?" Amelia asked as she rushed down the stairs. She held a battery-powered lantern in her hand. "I heard you cry out. What were you doing outside?"

Emma hurriedly filled her cousin in.

In the soft glow of the lantern, Emma saw Amelia's eyes widen in surprise, then horror.

"You thought the person who hurt the goats was here, so you went out to investigate? On your own?" she asked in exasperation. "What were you thinking?"

"I was thinking that Levi was wrong, that both the chickens and the goat had been injured by accident." She paused, then corrected herself. "I mean, I was *hoping* he was wrong, even though I knew he was probably right."

A banging on the door caused them both to jump.

Emma hoisted the bat as Amelia looked around for a weapon of her own. Violence was not the Amish way, but with Zeke and Sadie upstairs, they both knew they would do whatever they needed to do to be safe.

Amelia darted toward the iron fire poker near the woodstove.

"Emma?" Levi's voice boomed from the other side of the door. "Emma? Is everything okay in there?"

The women shared startled glances.

Amelia settled the poker back into the rack with the other fireplace tools. "Let him in," she commanded.

"I'm in my nightclothes," Emma hissed.

Amelia rolled her eyes. "You chased after an intruder in your nightclothes; I think you can let Levi in the house."

Emma set the bat near the door and tugged it open.

Levi stormed in. "Is everything okay? I was down at the barn feeding the horses. I heard you yell and ran all the way here." He paused. "It *was* you, wasn't it?"

"I'll go put some *kaffi* on," Amelia muttered. She shuffled toward the kitchen.

With a sigh, Emma repeated her story.

Levi began to pace. "I'm not even going to tell you how bad of an idea it was to go outside."

Emma's eyebrows scrunched in frustration. He had better not tell her that. She had done what she felt was right at the time. What was she supposed to do? Call out her upstairs window for help? Wait for a man to come to her rescue?

"But please," he implored, "did you see his face? It was Amos, wasn't it?"

"I can't honestly say," she admitted. "It was so dark. Really, I saw only a silhouette. I'm not sure what he was doing in the garden, but as I said, at first I thought it was a small bear. When he stood, it happened so quickly."

"Tell me this, at least—was he Amish?"

Emma knew where Levi was going with his line

of thinking. If the intruder was Amish, they were at least one step closer to proving it was Amos.

Unfortunately, she couldn't answer that question, either.

"I don't know. It was too dark to tell how he was dressed. And when he threw that rock at me, I ducked and he ran. It all happened in a matter of seconds, then he disappeared into the corn," Emma said.

Levi let out a little growl of frustration. "I don't like that someone is lurking on your property. This has to stop." He strode toward the door.

"Where are you going?" Emma asked. Was he angry with her? Was he going to storm out the door?

He paused. "I'm sure the man, whoever he is, is long gone. But I want to take a look at the garden. I'll come back in to tell you what I find."

Emma didn't argue; she simply watched him go.

• • •

So many emotions were coursing through Levi, he couldn't even begin to label them all. He was furious with whoever was messing with Emma. He was frustrated that she had been reckless enough to go outside. He was grateful that she was all right.

He was startled that she had answered the door in her nightclothes. A long, ivory nightgown that had flowed to her ankles. Her hair had been undone, hanging down her back, to her waist. It was a sight he would not soon forget, though he probably should. Oh, how the bishop, the community, would not approve.

Seeing an Amish woman without her *kapp*, with her hair undone, was something that should happen only behind closed doors. With a husband and a wife.

He had been overcome with such a sense of longing that it had almost left him senseless. What he wouldn't give to run his fingers through Emma's hair. To hold her close. To kiss her. Emma would be mortified if she knew.

With a firm resolve, he managed to push the image away as he strode toward the garden. Now that the sun was peeking over the horizon, he could see that some damage had been done. The man had been tearing up Emma's bean plants. While the harm wasn't extensive, it was plenty.

Satisfied nothing else seemed destroyed, he returned to the house.

Emma opened the door for him before he could knock. In the short time he'd been gone, she'd managed to change into a pale blue dress and cover her hair.

"Well?" she asked impatiently.

"He destroyed some of your beans," Levi admitted. He hesitated a moment before saying, "As much as I dislike that you went outside, you probably stopped him from doing a whole lot more damage."

Emma nodded slowly as his words sank in. "If I hadn't gone out there, he might have torn up the whole garden." She pressed a hand against her stomach and swayed.

Levi was right there, swooping an arm around her to steady her.

She pulled in a breath, shuddering in his arms.

"We count on that garden," she said. "We can the

vegetables and eat from it all year long. Without it…"

She didn't finish the sentence, but she didn't have to. He knew what she was trying to say. The garden was a staple for them, their major food supply. It was a necessity to their way of life. With the extra burden of paying the taxes, she could not afford to replace a garden full of food.

"It'll be all right," he assured her. "You stopped him in time."

She nodded, but he still felt her body trembling. He wanted to pull her closer, to assure her that everything would be okay. That he would protect her from this man. That he would always be by her side to care for her.

Before any of those promises could escape his lips, Amelia appeared.

"*Kaffi* is ready." She gave them an arched-brow look as she stood in the doorway, making no move to head back into the kitchen.

Emma stepped out of his arms.

"The man was trying to destroy the garden," Emma told her cousin.

Amelia's hand flew to her mouth, her interest in Emma and Levi's intimate position seemingly forgotten.

"Is the damage bad?" Amelia asked.

"Not too bad," Levi said with confidence. "Emma scared him away in time."

"Let's share some breakfast," Amelia suggested. "I made doughnuts yesterday and I can scramble up some eggs, fry some bacon."

"A doughnut will do just fine," Levi said. He had

plenty to do this morning, and this jaunt to Emma's house had already taken a bit of time. He wasn't in a hurry to leave, but he shouldn't stay much longer.

They settled in at the table, a plate of doughnuts and full cups of coffee among them.

"What are you doing up so early?" Amelia asked. "Do you always start your day at this hour?"

"Sometimes," Levi admitted. "*Daed* needs help with replacing some siding on the barn. I thought I should get an early start because I wanted to go to Mary's today."

"For what?" Emma asked, then took a sip of her coffee.

"I want to get her porch painted. I also noticed that one of her back steps is a bit loose. Figured I'd take care of it before it becomes a problem. She's already unsteady on her feet; no need in taking chances."

"I'll go with you," Emma said decidedly.

"You will?" Levi asked.

"If you don't mind," she quickly added.

"I don't mind at all," he said, a grin taking over his face. He'd spend time with Emma any way he could have it.

"I'd like to go, but I have to work," Amelia said. "Give her my well-wishes, will you?"

"*Jah*," Emma said. Turning to Levi, she asked, "What time should I be ready?"

"How about right after lunch?"

"That's perfect," Emma replied.

• • •

Emma had asked to go to Mary's because she had hoped to offer assistance to the older woman, but now that she was here, she realized it was a blessing, because Mary was keeping her too busy to let her mind wander.

Earlier in the morning, she couldn't keep her mind off the intruder. What if he'd run after her? What if he'd attacked her? What if the rock had hit its mark? She could have been seriously injured.

What if he came back and harmed the children? She knew she shouldn't borrow trouble. The word of God warned against worrying about tomorrow, as today had enough trouble of its own.

Can any one of you by worrying add a single hour to your life? The Bible verse had flitted through her mind more than a few times this morning.

But now, with Mary's enthusiastic chatter, her thoughts were on other things.

"I'm so grateful to you and your family," Mary was saying. "I don't know what I would do without your help at Saturday Market. Sales have been so strong the past few weeks."

"I'm not surprised," Emma said. "Your flowers are beautiful."

"*Danki,*" Mary said. "God truly blessed me with a green thumb. I'm not being prideful, mind you," she said with conviction. "I'm simply giving credit where credit is due."

"I'm not going to argue with that," Emma said. She glanced around the spotless kitchen, satisfied with her work. Upon arrival, she had placed a *yummasetti* casserole in the fridge. A loaf of freshly baked bread, courtesy of Sadie, rested on the countertop. "Is there anything else I can help you with?"

"Oh, you've done so much already," Mary said. "You and Levi both. He's spent all afternoon sanding and painting and repairing my front porch. It's going to look *goot* as new."

Emma smiled. "He's not quite done yet. If there's anything else you need help with, now's the time to ask."

"Well," Mary said hesitantly, "there is one thing. It's silly but…"

"What is it?" Emma asked, already rising from her chair, ready to jump to action.

"I'd be so grateful if you took a little treat out to the barn," Mary admitted. "There's a pretty plump cat that's been staying there. I think it's a momma, about to have babies. I'd like to give her a little something special. There's some leftover bologna in the fridge I think she'd like."

"Sure," Emma said with a smile. Mary pointed her toward a bowl and she placed the bologna inside. She went out the back door, since the front porch was wet with paint, and carefully made her way to the barn, struggling a bit with the rusty latch but finally managing to pry the door open. It grated horrendously as she tugged.

The inside of the barn smelled musty, unused. Dust motes floated through beams of sunlight that shone in via the dirty windows. Old, dry straw crackled under her feet as she moved inside.

"Kitty-kitty," she called softly. "I have a treat for you." Glancing around, there was no cat in sight. She wondered if it had moved on. Or probably, it was hiding. "Kitty-kitty," she tried again. Something skit-tered above her head. She was sure the sound was coming from the hayloft. Had the momma had her babies?

Curiosity got the best of her. Sadie wasn't the only one with a soft spot for critters. She made her way to the ladder.

Meow.

Straight above her, an orange tabby cat peeked its head over the edge, likely smelling the pungent meat.

"There you are. You smell something tasty? Let me bring it up to you, see if you have some babies up there." With one hand still holding the bowl, she managed to make her way upward. The cat darted away from the edge, then back again.

"Emma, what are you doing in here?" Levi peeked around the doorframe, a curious look on his face. He smirked when he saw she was nearly to the hayloft. "Don't tell me Mary talked you into chasing down that little rascal."

"I couldn't tell her *nee*," she said. As if to prove her point, she placed the bowl on the edge of the hayloft.

The cat, apparently having lain in wait, swiped at Emma's face as it dove for the food. Emma let out a shriek as she flung her head back, out of its reach. The sudden motion caused her to lose her grip on the ladder and she fell backward, even as the cat lunged at her again.

Shrieking, she tried to brace herself for the inevi-table impact of slamming into the floor. Instead, she slammed into Levi, who had leaped forward, trying to catch her. Tried, but stumbled backward and over a bale while she was in his arms. The two of them found themselves in a heap on the straw floor. Too stunned for words as they assessed for injuries and took in the awkwardness of the situation.

"Are you all right?" Levi finally asked, his breath coming in heavy gasps.

Staring down into his familiar blue eyes, while lying on top of him in such an *unfamiliar* position, left her speechless. She could only nod.

"Okay, then," Levi said.

She waited for him to push her off, clamber to his feet.

Perhaps he was as stunned as she was by the fall, and their position, because he made no move to get up.

"What in the world is going on in here?" Mary demanded from the doorway.

That got them both moving. Only Emma, in her haste, managed to get her feet tangled in her dress. She stumbled, slamming down onto Levi again. He grunted under her weight, and then slowly, the two of them managed to get to their feet.

Emma was horrified. What must Mary think?

"It's not what it looks like," she blurted.

Mary chuckled. "What it looks like is that you scared my cat. I saw the way she zipped like lightning, right out of the barn and across the yard. Heard you scream, too. I guess she scared you right back."

"*He*," Levi said. "That's definitely a tomcat. Got a *goot* look when he jumped over my head."

"*Ach*." Mary's eyebrows scrunched at the news.

"I guess that means there won't be any kittens scampering around my yard anytime soon."

Emma was relieved that Mary was far more interested in the cat than she was in what she had walked in on.

"I suppose that shouldn't be such surprising news. A big ol' tomcat."

"Sure is," Levi said.

"I think I'll name him Joe," Mary continued.

Emma arched a brow but didn't say a word.

"Nice name for a cat," Levi said easily.

Emma wondered if his heart was clanging nearly as hard as hers was. To hear him speak so coolly, one wouldn't think so.

"Naomi wrote me just the other day asking for assurance about you two," Mary admitted. "I believe I can, in *goot* faith, tell her I think you are doing just fine. That is, if you'd like me to. I believe your business is your own, but it might not hurt to throw your aunt a bit of positive news." She leaned forward, a conspiratorial smile on her face, a twinkle in her eye. "Are you going to make an announcement soon? You are, *jah*?"

"Mary," Emma lightly scolded with a nervous laugh.

"I know," Mary grumbled, "you young ones like to keep news like that to yourself. But I thought maybe you'd have pity on a lonely old lady. Give me something exciting to think about."

Emma was about to protest against Mary's gentle teasing, but Levi didn't give her the chance.

"Well, I sure hope so," he said. He glanced at Emma with a grin on his face. She frowned at him.

He should not give Mary false hope about any impending matrimony.

"*Wunderbaar*!" Mary exclaimed.

Her genuine excitement gave Emma pause. How could she contradict Levi? She stuffed down a sigh. She couldn't, not in front of Mary.

She would have to deal with Levi later.

"It was sure lucky you were down here to catch our Emma," Mary said.

"I didn't do such a *goot* job of that," he said with a grin. "It wasn't really luck. I was checking to see if she was about ready to go. I'm done with the porch."

Emma nodded, perhaps a bit too enthusiastically. Yes, yes, she sure was ready to leave. She wanted to get out of there before Mary asked any more probing questions. Before she got around to commenting on the cozy position in which she had caught the two of them.

The two rode home, Levi guiding the horse and buggy, amid amicable chatter. When they reached the farmhouse, Levi stopped near her front porch. He hopped down, darted around the back side of the buggy, and held out his hand to guide Emma.

Though she'd hopped from a buggy hundreds, maybe thousands of times, she gladly accepted his assistance.

"Go on a date with me," he said.

She arched an eyebrow at him. "A…a *date*?"

He grinned at her. "*Jah*. You heard me. A date."

The Amish didn't date. Not exactly. She didn't know whether to be annoyed or amused by his use of the *Englisch* word.

"I'll pick you up tomorrow before supper," he

said. "We'll do something special."

"What kind of something special?" Emma asked.

"You'll see," he said.

"Levi," Emma groaned. "You know I don't like surprises."

He winked at her, causing a flutter in her stomach. "That's because you've never had a *goot* surprise, I'm guessing."

She thought perhaps he was right.

He moved away from the porch, still wearing that pesky grin.

"See you tomorrow, Emma. Try not to think about me too much tonight."

With those infuriating words, he pivoted, hopped back into his buggy, and drove off. Emma stood gaping after him, her cheeks heated and her heart pattering in the most frustrating way.

CHAPTER FOURTEEN

What a maddening man!

Try not to think about me too much tonight.

Of course, telling her *not* to think of him would cause her to do nothing *but* think of him. Just as he'd intended. Not just last night, but all day as well.

She couldn't get those baby blue eyes out of her mind. That slow, knowing smile. The way he winked at her, sending her insides all aflutter. Nor could she stop thinking about his strong arms, and how she would love to find herself wrapped in them. She would not allow herself to think of what happened in the barn yesterday. How she had found herself draped on top of him. How, if she were a more brazen woman, she could have so easily leaned down and kissed him. No, she would not allow herself to think about that.

Not much, anyway.

That thought was one only a wife should be entertaining.

"Are you all right?" Sadie asked as she flounced into the kitchen, carrying a pail of milk.

"*Jah*, why?" Emma asked.

"Your checks are all rosy," Sadie said, studying her closely. "You almost look feverish. Are you coming down with a bug?"

"*Nee*," Emma said. "I was just doing the dishes. I guess I must've gotten warm."

"You do the dishes every day, but I've never seen

you look so flushed before," Sadie prodded.

Emma spun away from her, tugged open a cupboard door, looking for... Well, she didn't know what. Some privacy maybe.

She sure wasn't going to find that in the kitchen. Not with her little sister studying her.

Sadie clucked her tongue knowingly. Her voice rose in a teasing lilt. "You were thinking about Levi, weren't you? That's why your cheeks are so rosy."

"Sadie—" Emma whirled to face her sister, ready to scold her.

But Sadie laughed, cutting her off. "I'm not a youngster anymore." She hoisted a brow. "You don't think boys ever cross my mind?"

"*Nee*," Emma said, feeling a bit perplexed. "I didn't think they did."

Sadie laughed as she put the bucket of goat milk in the fridge to contend with later. "You have nothing to worry about. The boys I like never give me a second glance."

"*Boys*?" Emma echoed. As in more than one? "Do I need to be keeping a closer eye on you?"

Sadie only smiled and shook her head. "You and *Daed* taught me right from wrong."

"You're not sneaking around with some boy, are you?" Emma asked, the idea almost ludicrous.

Instead of being offended, Sadie simply shook her head. "*Nee*. When I finally begin courting, I want everyone to know. I don't want there to be any doubt which beau is mine."

"All right then," Emma said, still feeling a bit stunned by the conversation. "What *boys* do you have in mind?"

Sadie's lips quirked into a smile. "Oh, I don't know."

"I think you do," Emma said. "Noah Lapp?"

"What? *Nee*. Not him," Sadie said with a scowl. "He's sixteen but acts like he's six."

Emma laughed. Not because she agreed with Sadie, but because her sister looked so horrified at the thought of courting Noah. Noah, Emma knew, *was* a bit of a clown. But he was a nice boy. Polite and hardworking.

"Now *Lucas* Lapp," Sadie said with a dreamy look on her face as she mentioned Noah's older brother, "him I would like to court."

Emma's laughter quickly faded. "Lucas is nineteen."

"And very mature," Sadie said.

"He's too old for you," Emma replied.

"Don't matter," Sadie said. "Lucas wouldn't give me the time of day." She frowned, her lips almost turning into a pout. "Aiden Byler doesn't know I exist, either."

"How old is *he*?" Emma asked. She was familiar with the boy, or with his family, at least. She knew he was older than Sadie. She just wasn't sure how old.

"He's only eighteen," Sadie said.

"Only?" Emma scoffed. "Sadie, you need to pay attention to boys your own age."

She crinkled her nose in displeasure. "The boys my own age? I *canna* think of one that isn't a *dummkopf*."

A startled chuckle exploded out of Emma. "Sadie. That is unkind." But, Emma thought, a tad bit humorous and probably not at all untrue. If she remembered anything about sixteen-year-old boys, it was that they didn't always use the best judgment. Especially around girls they were trying to impress. She could understand why Sadie might not have the best impression of boys her age.

"It's true," Sadie said.

Emma fought down a smile. "When you start courting, you'll let me know, *jah*?"

"*Jah*," Sadie agreed. "Speaking of courting, you still have no idea where Levi is taking you tonight?"

Emma wasn't going to admit that she'd thought about it, wondering for a good part of the day. "He said it's a surprise. I guess it's going to be."

"That's so romantic," Sadie said with a dreamy smile. "I didn't know Levi was like that."

Emma's lips twitched. "Neither did I."

"I want to hear all about it when you get home," Sadie said. "But I need to go make sure the goats and chicken have fresh water."

She scurried out of the kitchen.

Emma wondered if she should stop her. Should she question Sadie about these boys who held her interest? She decided not to. Sadie had a good head on her shoulders. She would bring the subject up again another day. Wasn't that what sisters did? Talked about boys? Courting? Finding love? Sadie was growing up, and Emma didn't need to treat her like a child anymore. She would enjoy getting to know her sister as a friend.

The realization was another reminder of how much her life was changing.

For the better.

The children didn't need her to mother them

quite so much; they needed her to be their sister. Someone to talk to, confide in, even as she guided them.

A quick glance at the clock over the kitchen stove got her moving. Levi would be here shortly. She needed to clean up, straighten her hair, put on a clean dress. She darted from the kitchen, trying not to think of the man whose smile made her go weak in the knees.

• • •

Levi made his way into the swampy grass. There, lying just out of sight of anyone who might drive by, was a rowboat. Judd Jenkins, an *Englischer* on his work crew and a downright nice guy, had offered to lend it to Levi. He had even driven it here, hidden it out of sight, for when Levi needed it. Judd planned on coming back tonight after sunset to retrieve it.

Levi tugged at the lightweight watercraft. He pushed it toward the shore, shoved it into the river, and then guided it to the dock using the tow rope.

Emma stood on the dock grinning at him. "This is quite the surprise."

Her smile did wild things to his insides. Lit him up, brought a brightness into his life that he had never felt before. When they were younger, she'd always made his heart beat a little faster, had made his palms a little sweatier. But now? He wasn't sure how to describe what he felt for her now. The way his feelings had grown for Emma over the past months had gone way beyond boyhood crush.

He was falling in love, falling so deep, he felt it all

the way down to his soul.

"But you said you don't like surprises," he teased.

She bit her lip for a second, holding back a smile before finally setting it free. "I think I like *this* surprise."

He reached out his hand, steadying her as he guided her into the boat, and she settled onto a bench. He grabbed the picnic basket he'd left sitting on the dock. Blaze whinnied at him from the edge of the gravel parking lot, but Levi had left the horse in the shade, tied to the hitching post with a bucket of water, so he knew he'd be just fine.

He carefully maneuvered himself into the boat, shoving off with his foot as he did so. The boat wobbled under the unsteadiness of his weight but quickly settled. He dropped onto the unoccupied bench and picked up the oars.

"It's such a beautiful evening," Emma said with a happy sigh. "Do you know that I've never been in a boat before?"

He hadn't known, but he'd suspected. Not many Amish owned boats, opting to fish from the shore. Without a vehicle, they were too difficult to lug around.

"When we were younger, I used to spend a lot of time with Jonah," Levi reminded her. "His family has a large pond on their property, well stocked with fish. I spent a lot of hours rowing around that little body of water."

He had spent a lot of time swimming in that pond, too, something he knew Emma had never had the luxury of doing. He was sure she didn't know how to swim. He thought they'd be okay, though.

It had been a dry summer. The river wasn't deep
and the current wasn't strong. If they did flip—and
he sure didn't intend to—the water would be no
more than chest high. He'd never do anything to put
Emma in danger, so he'd still be cautious.

"I think I'll paddle upstream," he said. "That way
we can float back down."

He'd do all the work on the way there, then
they'd drift back, watching the sunset.

"I can help paddle," she offered.

He smiled and shook his head. "This was my
idea. I can handle the paddling."

Emma's lips drooped into a frown of disappointment.

"If you really want—"

"I do." She leaped to her feet so fast, he was
afraid they'd flip the boat after all, but after a precarious moment, she shot him a sheepish smile. Then
she so very carefully moved across the boat and
dropped down next to him on the seat. He handed
her an oar and she grinned.

She tilted her head to the side as they started to
paddle. "Where did you get this boat?"

He explained about his friend on the work crew.
"He'll be back to get it later."

They chatted about this and that, drifting up the
river, until Levi finally worked up to the one serious
item of discussion he needed to tackle.

"I spoke with Bishop Yoder today," he admitted.

Emma tilted her head to the side, curiosity evident in her expression.

"I didn't tell him about the incidents on the farm,
if that's what you're wondering," Levi assured. "*He*

approached me. He wanted to know about the incident at the diner a few weeks ago."

"Did he offer any insight?"

"*Nee*," Levi admitted. "Jonah had mentioned the incident to him. He wanted to know if I had more to say, but I told him I didn't. I wanted to tell him about the farm, but you asked me not to, and I respect that."

She quickly nodded.

Levi bolstered himself as they continued with their slow, rhythmic rowing. Gathering his courage, he said, "That's not all we spoke of."

"What else did you discuss?" Emma asked, her tone cautious as if she, once again, sensed what he was about to say.

"He asked how you were doing," Levi said. "It seems your aunt Naomi had written him a letter advising him to keep an eye on our courtship. She stated that she's particularly worried because you are living all on your own, caring for two children without the help of a man to run affairs. That's a direct quote. Or close to it."

Emma scowled.

Levi agreed. It was a bit out of line of Naomi to do such a thing.

However, it had opened the door for conversation with the bishop.

"He asked how serious I am about you," Levi blurted. He didn't miss the way Emma winced, he hoped at his brusqueness and not at the thought of them being serious.

She gripped the oar, her knuckles going white as if bracing herself for his answer. "What did you say?"

He knew he owed Emma nothing short of the truth, whether it was a truth she wanted to hear or not.

"He's worried about you, a young *maidel* with no husband and no father to look after her," he said. "I told him that I'm very serious in my intentions. I want to look after you. I want to protect you." *I want to grow old with you.*

"Because I'm a young *maidel*, with no one to look after me?" Emma asked quietly. "Levi, I know my situation is not ideal, but I think I am capable of taking care of myself."

He studied her face for a moment. Why was she always fighting him on this? "Is that what you want, Emma? Do you want to grow old as a spinster, like Mary? All alone until your neighbors finally realize that you're in need?"

"*Nee*," she said quickly. "That isn't what I want."

"What *do* you want?" he asked. He stopped rowing now and she followed suit. The rippling waves were so gentle, they weren't in danger of moving back downstream too quickly. When she didn't answer, he leaned in, his gaze intent on hers. "Tell me what you want."

Her lips trembled, as if her admission was almost painful. "I want a husband, a family. Not just my siblings to keep me company—I want children of my own. And I always want to be a part of the maple farm, even when it's rightfully turned over to Zeke."

He nodded, not breaking her gaze. "That's what I want, too. I want all of that." *With you*, he added silently. *I want all of that with you.*

He wanted to say the words, wanted to move this

courtship along, but his fears ran deep. He'd messed up with Emma before. He had a habit of barreling in and saying and doing the wrong thing. Now it made him cautious. She was giving him a second chance, but if he scared her off, would she give him another? Or was this it?

He didn't want to risk ruining it by moving too quickly.

Instead, he reached for her hands, taking them in his own.

"I care about you a great deal, Emma." There, he got the words out. It wasn't all that he wanted to say, but it was a start. "I think we could have a good life together."

"Are you saying this because you want to protect me?" Emma asked.

"Of course I want to protect you," Levi said. "But it's more than that."

"Is it?" Emma wondered. She squeezed his hands. "Or is it your concern over Amos that is driving you to want to be with me?"

"*Nee*, that isn't the reason."

"Not at all?" Emma asked.

He frowned. "I suppose that's part of it. I want to keep you safe from an intruder. But Emma, that's not the only reason. I'm…" He needed to tell her. "I care about you. As more than a friend. Much more."

Emma blinked at him before a slow smile spread across her face. "Truly?"

"Truly." Now he squeezed her hands. "I have never lied to you. Have I?"

"*Nee*. You have not ever lied to me." She paused, pulled in a tremulous breath. "Levi, I believe my feelings for you are growing as well." Her cheeks turned a lovely shade of rose at her admission.

His heart leaped. In fact, he wanted to leap right out of his seat. Wanted to scoop Emma into his arms and swing her around to show her just how joyous her words made him.

But that would likely only flip the boat.

And it was just as well, because he wasn't sure she was prepared for just how deeply his feelings ran.

"Well then," he said as he reluctantly let go of her hands, "it seems we are of one mind then."

"It seems we are," she agreed.

To his embarrassment, his stomach chose that moment to let out an angry rumble.

Emma laughed. "It seems we are in agreement about something else. I'm starving, too."

• • •

As Levi dropped the small anchor, Emma was glad for the distraction. It would have been so easy to blurt out to Levi that she thought she was falling in love with him. It would have been easy, but not wise.

It troubled her that his feelings had suddenly blossomed now that he thought she needed protection. She wanted to trust that he was truly falling in love with her. But what if those feelings were simply feelings spurned on by the desire to protect her from Amos? Or the desire to help her run her farm and raise her siblings? He was in agreement with the bishop that she needed looking after.

What if he wasn't really falling in love with her,

but simply fancying himself so because of his desire to take care of her? If only she could trust that he wanted to be with her for the right reasons. Not out of a sense of obligation that he would never admit to.

She tried to push those thoughts away, but having been through a similar situation with his brother, she was not anxious to go through it again. What if Levi came to his senses as Ivan had? What if, after she gave her heart to him, he decided that he didn't really want it?

Though that could happen in any relationship.

Yet somehow, she felt losing Levi that way would be unbearable.

"I'm glad you're hungry," Levi said. "I've packed plenty of food." He handed her a ham salad sandwich.

"You packed our meal?" Emma asked.

He nodded, grinned. "*Jah*. Well, *Mamm* made the ham salad. I just put the sandwiches together, dished up the potato salad. Cut the brownies and packed it all up."

"Everything looks *appendlitch*," Emma said. Even though Diana had prepared the food, she was touched that Levi had assembled the picnic.

They ate their dinner, chatting as they did so. Emma asked how his mother's garden was coming along, and he asked about Ezekiel and Sadie.

"Apparently Sadie has discovered an interest in boys and I'm only just finding out," Emma said.

Levi chuckled. "It was bound to happen."

Emma shook her head. "I was expecting her to like boys her own age…not a few who are older."

"A few? Sadie doesn't strike me as the sort of girl who would be so wild about boys."

"I don't think she is," Emma admitted. "I think they've just caught her interest."

"It doesn't surprise me that she's interested in older fellows," Levi said. "Sadie's always been quieter and more mature than the other girls her age. I've seen her at church and at frolics."

Levi was right. Emma had always noticed that Sadie gravitated toward the older women of the groups, though she did have a few friends. But she wasn't often found gossiping and giggling over boys.

"Losing your *mamm*, I think you all had to grow up fast," Levi said. "I know you tried to shield the young ones as best you could, but the loss still affected them."

"I know," Emma admitted. "I just wanted their lives to be as normal as possible."

"You gave up a lot so they could have that."

Emma bit her lower lip. She wouldn't complain about the life she'd led; she had no regrets, but that didn't stop her from feeling like she had missed out.

She listened with interest as Levi told her about the old Victorian they were remodeling, raving about the intricacy of the woodwork.

"I know our homes are supposed to be plain, but I can't help but admire the talent of whoever did the original woodwork on the house," Levi admitted. "It will be a fun job to work on. Something different than all the farmhouses we've been working on lately."

"Do you enjoy your work?" Emma asked.

"*Jah*." He paused. "Mostly I enjoy it. I think I like doing carpentry work because I like working with my hands. Like I told you before, I am looking forward to farming full-time." He took a swig of lemonade. "*Daed* is in no hurry to be done, though. That would give me time to help run your farm until Ezekiel is old enough to take over."

"I see you've thought about this."

"I have."

Emma found herself wondering if that was another reason for his interest. He had just admitted to missing his work on the farm. Since Moses was not ready to give up his own land, was Levi looking for something to fill those years? Was the Ziegler farm an enticing way to pass his time until he took over his father's land?

Stop, she told herself. She needed to quit looking for motive in everything that Levi did, had to learn to trust him. Even though Ivan hadn't loved her, it was possible that Levi could grow to. She had to have faith. Had to trust in that. Trust in *him*.

She forced a smile. "It sounds as if that would work out well for you."

"For *us*," he said emphatically.

Us. She liked the sound of that.

"I see nothing but *goot* things in our future, Emma." His voice was a low rumble, a soothing balm across her heart.

"I hope that is true."

"Don't just hope—believe it," he said.

As the boat bobbed on the water, as the sunset splashed a golden hue across the horizon, she wanted nothing more. Nothing more than to believe in the promise of Levi's words.

CHAPTER FIFTEEN

The Ziegler kitchen smelled divine. Emma would have to thank Amanda, Levi's sister-in-law, for passing along the maple fudge recipe. She thought it would be the perfect addition to their table at Saturday Market, then wondered how much a decent-sized square of fudge would sell for. She was certain a fair amount, and that it would be worth her while.

"I'm almost done in here," Emma told Sadie. Her first batch of fudge rested on the counter. It had already been taste tested by everyone in the family. "I need to clean up, then you may have the kitchen to yourself."

Sadie stood beside her at the counter, chopping fresh herbs from the garden.

"I've had so many orders for my goat cheese, I'm not sure my goats can keep up," she admitted.

"It is a *goot* problem to have," Emma said with a smile.

"Two new families approached me after church last Sunday. Judith Graber asked if I would be interested in trading some cheese for her pumpkins. I agreed."

"That would be a nice trade," Emma said. They hadn't planted pumpkins this year. "It would be nice to can a few pumpkins to have on hand for pies."

"That's what I thought," Sadie said. "I told her I would like to make the trade."

"Are you sure you wouldn't like me to stay and help?" Emma asked as she scrubbed a plate in soapy water.

"*Nee*," Sadie replied. "You and Zeke already have plans to pick up supplies. I can manage the cheese on my own."

"I know you can," Emma agreed.

The process was not difficult. The milk needed to be heated. An acidic mixture of vinegar and lemon juice added would cause the milk to curdle. The curds would be separated from the whey. Once the curds were properly strained with a cheesecloth, the herbs of choice could be added. The whey was typically fed to the chickens. Now that there was only Gretel, there would be an abundance of whey. They would use it to fertilize the garden.

"Is there anything you need from town?" Emma asked.

"I've already written a few things on your shopping list," Sadie replied.

Emma finished washing the dishes. Glancing out the window over the sink, she was surprised to see Levi's buggy down by the barn.

"I wasn't expecting Levi." She dried her hands on a dish towel before going to the front door.

When she pulled it open, Levi was already standing on the other side.

"*Ach*!" she exclaimed. "What is this?"

Levi held a gorgeous bouquet of peonies.

"I seem to recall you saying that peonies are your favorite."

She moved aside so he could enter. "I did?"

"*Jah*, while we were at Saturday Market. You sold

several of Mary's potted plants to a woman and you told me they were the most beautiful flower in the world."

"I don't recall saying that." She was surprised—and so touched—that he'd remembered such a thing. "They are, though. They're gorgeous." Their scent was divine as well. She laughed. "Did you take them from your *mamm*'s flower garden?"

"Hush, don't tell," he teased.

Emma took the flowers from him. She returned to the kitchen and Levi followed.

"Oh, how pretty," Sadie murmured.

"*Jah*," Emma said, "they are." She flashed Levi a thankful smile. It was kind of him to bring her such a stunning bouquet. It wasn't a common gesture among the Amish; some would probably call it improper, but Emma was pleased by his thoughtfulness.

She pulled an old mason jar out from under the kitchen sink. She filled it with water, arranged the flowers inside, and then placed it on the center of the kitchen table. Standing back, she admired her gift. Peonies had enormous blooms; these were a mixture of soft pink and the purest white. It would be a pleasure to enjoy their beauty while she worked in the kitchen.

"Levi, is something wrong?" Sadie asked.

Emma twisted around in time to notice Levi's cheeks flush. "*Nee*."

Sadie frowned before glancing at Emma and then returning her gaze to Levi. "Did you hurt your hand?"

Emma noted that Levi was clenching and un-clenching his fist.

"Let me see," she ordered.

"I've been stung by a bee," he admitted. "It wasn't happy that I took its blooms away."

She reached for his hand and held it carefully in her own. His thumb had swelled to the size of a sausage.

"This looks painful." She guided him across the room and gently pushed him into a chair. "I can still see the stinger. Give me a moment and I'll take care of it."

She hurried to the bathroom where she retrieved tweezers.

When she returned to the kitchen, Levi was inspecting his thumb. She took his hand, carefully holding it in one of hers. Without meaning to, she'd positioned herself between his knees. His body was painfully close to hers as she held his hand in place. She tried to ignore the heat spilling through her veins.

The stinger needed to be removed. There was no other way to go about it.

She held the tweezers above his thumb but hesitated.

He was watching her intently. When she looked him in the eye, her knees became weak. His proximity would likely be considered inappropriate. Emma quickly pulled her gaze away and glanced over her shoulder at Sadie. Her sister was busy working at the counter. Swiveling back around, she was determined to do what she needed to do.

Carefully, she lowered the tweezers and hoped that Levi wasn't aware of how her fingers were trembling. She managed to get hold of the barely visible end of the stinger. With a quick tug, she pulled it free.

For a moment, she was pinned in place by the intensity of Levi's gaze. She could see the navy rings around his irises. His face was freshly shaven. He smelled of that same crisp, clean scent she remembered from the riverbank. Of their own accord, her eyes dropped to his lips. Her heart began to beat a little faster.

"Take this."

She jumped back at the sound of her sister's voice. Dropping Levi's hand, she took the small jar from Sadie.

"It's a mixture of baking soda and vinegar," Sadie said. "It will help to draw out the venom. I'll get a bandage."

"There's no need," Levi said.

Sadie ignored him and went to fetch one anyway.

"Let me see your hand again," Emma said. This time when he held it up, she swabbed the mixture onto his thumb while touching him as little as possible.

Sadie returned and handed the bandage to Emma. She quickly fixed it in place.

"All set," she said, perhaps a bit too cheerily. She stepped away, grateful he couldn't hear the chaotic cadence of her heart. She had to keep her eyes averted, because she had no doubt that if she looked at him, he would not miss the longing in her gaze.

• • •

Levi cleared his throat, wondering if his cheeks were as rosy as Emma's. If he were a man with lesser control, he would've grabbed her by the waist and planted a kiss on those lips. But that would've been entirely inappropriate. He reluctantly shoved the thought aside.

"Would you like a piece of fudge?" Emma asked.

Her tone was a bit too light. Levi knew she had been as affected by their nearness as he had been. She was trying not to show it and somehow, that pleased him deeply.

Before he could answer, she began to cut him a piece. He grinned to himself. Emma offering him fudge after removing the stinger reminded him of when he was a *kinner* and his *mamm* would reward him for good behavior.

It had been a lot of years since he'd felt cared for in such a way. He could get used to having a woman tend to his needs. He wanted that. Wanted a woman to care for him, as he cared for her.

"I used Amanda's recipe," she explained. "The maple syrup gives it a delightful flavor."

"*Danki.*" He took the fudge from her and enjoyed a bite. "*Appendlitch.* The syrup really stands out."

Emma smiled appreciatively at him. A few wisps of hair were curling at the edges of her *kapp*, her dark brown eyes sparkling with appreciation. Her skin looked creamy and smooth, causing him to wonder if it was as soft as it appeared. He quickly forced his gaze away, afraid she'd be able to read his thoughts.

"I think it might be one of my favorite recipes," she admitted. She seemed like she was about to say something more, but she ducked her head and bit her lip.

"What is it?"

She lifted her eyes to him. "What?"

"You look as though you want to say something."

She hesitated a moment before admitting, "I want to add the fudge to Saturday Market." After another moment of hesitation she added, "And next summer, I want a table of my own. I plan to sell the syrup, but I also am hoping to sell treats that incorporate the syrup. And just maybe—" She stopped herself.

"What?" he gently prodded.

"Maybe I'd like to put together a small cookbook with recipes using the syrup. I spoke with the lady at the print shop who does my labels. She said they could easily print something simple like that."

"That's a *wunderbaar* idea."

She tilted her head to the side to study him. "Do you think so?"

"I do."

A soft smile lit up her face. "When we were in the boat the other night, you made me think about something. I have given up a lot of my time for Sadie and Zeke. And I don't regret it; I don't. But I started thinking that it would be nice if I could do something that *I* enjoy. It's been so long since I thought of it, I wasn't even sure what that would be. But then it came to me."

He nodded. "You enjoy the syrup. You enjoy cooking with it. Mostly, you enjoy sharing it with others."

Her eyes lit up. "*Jah*. Saturday Market would be perfect. I have a few recipe ideas I'd like to try, but we're nearly out of sugar. I was going to go into town today."

"What luck," Levi said. He stood from the table, needing to put some distance between himself and Emma. "I stopped by to ask if you needed anything. If you were going into town anyway, perhaps you'd like to ride along with me?"

"That would be nice," Emma agreed. "Amelia is working today but Ezekiel was planning to join me. Would that be all right?"

"*Jah*," he said.

Emma gathered what she needed, rounded up her brother, and they were on their way.

"Do you have much to do?" Levi asked as they neared Pine Creek.

"Not too much," Emma said. "Everything I need is at the general store. You?"

"I need to go only to the feedstore," Levi said, "to pick up a bag of oats."

"I'll go with you," Ezekiel determined. "Sadie needs chicken feed."

Levi lashed the buggy to a post near the general store, as Emma had quite a bit of shopping to do. He didn't mind carrying the heavy bag of oats down the block. It made more sense to leave the buggy close for Emma and her groceries.

"Can we eat at the café when we're done?" Ezekiel's tone was hopeful.

"We had lunch already," Emma reminded.

"It's a hot day," Levi said. "How 'bout we stop for some ice cream instead?"

"*Jah*!" Ezekiel nodded.

They parted ways with an agreement to meet at the café when they were finished.

Ezekiel chattered nonstop on the way to the

feedstore, though Levi didn't mind. Once inside, they split up to fetch what they needed.

Levi found the brand of oats he wanted. He was ready to heft a bag onto his shoulder when someone caught his eye.

Forgetting about the feed, he stormed down the aisle.

"Amos."

Amos Stoltzfus turned away from the display of heavy leather work gloves.

He cast a disinterested glance at Levi before returning his attention to the display.

"I don't suppose you've been to the Ziegler farm lately," Levi asked, his tone casual.

"Don't suppose I have," Amos replied. He kept his gaze averted as he busied himself with checking prices.

"I'm happy to hear it. Otherwise I might think you've been up to mischief."

Amos turned to Levi with a sneer. "You warned me to stay away from Emma, if I recall. I'm only doing as you said."

Levi's jaw clenched. He didn't like the condescending edge in the other man's tone. It was true that he'd kept his distance from Emma, had not confronted her. But had he decided to cause damage to her farm instead?

"I'd hate to think of the consequences if you were caught causing trouble," Levi said.

Amos grunted. "Are you accusing me of something? Doesn't sound like a very Christian thing to do. Accusing a man without proof is downright sinful."

"I'm not accusing." Levi kept his tone even. "I'm

simply warning. Stay away from the Ziegler farm or you'll come to regret it."

Amos guffawed over Levi's implied threat.

Levi pivoted and charged back down the aisle toward the feed before he said, or did, something he would regret.

He hoisted the oats onto his shoulder before meeting Ezekiel at the front of the store. The two paid for their purchases. It was all Levi could do to force himself to leave the store. He had more he wanted to say to Amos but knew it was best if he left it alone.

"What's eating at you?" Ezekiel eyed Levi curiously as he loaded the bags into the back of the buggy.

Levi shifted from one foot to the other. He scanned the street, half expecting to see Amos loitering about. "I had a little chat with Amos," he admitted. "Not that it did any *goot*."

"Did he admit to anything?"

"*Nee*," Levi said with a sharp shake of his head. "Let's keep this between us men. I don't want to upset Emma."

"*Goot* idea," Ezekiel agreed.

Levi only hoped that by confronting Amos, he hadn't poked at a sleeping bear.

• • •

"Sadie is going to be jealous she didn't come along," Ezekiel said.

"It's unfortunate we *canna* bring her some ice cream," Emma agreed. It would melt long before they arrived back at the farm.

"She'll just have to eat more fudge instead," Ezekiel decided.

The three of them were enjoying butterscotch sundaes in the air-conditioned comfort of the café.

"How is the bee sting?"

Levi held up his hand. He'd taken off the bandage. It was red but not nearly as swollen. The poultice Sadie had concocted had helped.

"I've forgotten all about it," he admitted.

"I guess that means it's doing well."

"You make a fine nursemaid."

Heat crept into her cheeks as she thought of how she had plucked out the stinger. His knowing smile alerted her that he might've felt the same sort of warmth.

"Emma's always been *goot* at making people feel better," Ezekiel chimed in.

She diverted her attention to her brother, grateful for the interruption. "You've given me plenty of cuts and scrapes to tend to."

Emma spotted Rachael in the kitchen. Her friend caught her eye and gave her a warm smile. A moment later, she bustled out of the kitchen door.

"I'm happy to see you," Rachael said. "I was looking through my *grossmammi*'s recipe cards. She had several tucked inside that are for making soap out of goat's milk. I have no intention of raising goats. Do you think Sadie would be interested?"

"I'm sure she would be," Emma said.

"I'll bring them to the Millers' tomorrow," Rachael told her. "Today is my last day here, at the café. I've been working part-time, but"—she rubbed her back—"I'm happy to be done. I'm looking forward to the barn raising tomorrow."

"It will be a fun day," Emma said.

"It always is," Rachael agreed.

"Is Amelia here still?"

"You just missed her," Rachael said. "She was in the storage room but just left for the day."

They chatted a few moments longer before Rachael returned to the kitchen.

"Would you like a ride to the Millers' tomorrow?" Levi wondered. "It's no trouble to pick you all up."

"That would be nice." Emma realized that she was anxious to spend time with Levi. A buggy ride to the Millers' and back would give her ample time to do just that.

"Are we all finished?" Levi asked.

"I'm ready," Ezekiel said.

The trio rose from the table. They left the café and were halfway down the block when Emma heard someone call her name.

She twisted around, surprised to see Amelia rushing toward her.

"Rachael said you were just at the café. I must've been outside already. I'm happy you're still in town," Amelia said. "I need to get a ride home with you."

"Of course," Emma agreed. "But why? What of the bicycle?"

Amelia frowned. "The back tires are flat. It's the strangest thing—they were fine when I came to work this morning."

"Did someone tamper with it?" Emma knew Amelia parked her bike on the backside of the building. A few other employees rode their bikes to work as well, including Rachael.

"I think it's possible," Amelia admitted, "only because it's both tires. The odds of them both going flat don't seem likely. However, no one else's bicycles seem to be touched."

Levi mumbled something under his breath that Emma didn't catch. When he caught her curious glance, his troubled features evened out. "Surely you can ride with us. I'll load the bicycle into the buggy. There's a station on the edge of town that has an air compressor available. I'll air up the tires on the way so that it is usable again."

"*Danki*. It's kind of you to go to the trouble," Amelia said.

"It is no trouble," Levi assured.

His frustrated expression said otherwise. Emma felt quite certain that his frustration was not aimed at her cousin but rather at whoever had let the air out of the tires.

She didn't have to ask him who he thought was responsible.

The answer was apparent to them all.

CHAPTER SIXTEEN

The chickens squawking in the back of his buggy could've been supremely annoying if he weren't transporting them for such a good reason.

Paul had purchased Sadie's Marans for her. Though Levi had asked around, he'd had limited luck tracking more Marans down.

Emma emerged at the side of the house. She had an empty laundry basket perched on her hip as she walked. Quilts weighed down the clothesline behind her. She waved in greeting as he drew up to the house. A smile brightened up her pretty face, causing his smile to sneak out in return.

Every day that he spent with Emma, he felt a bit more hopeful that her feelings for him would deepen. Every morning upon waking he sent a prayer up to God, asking that if it was His will, that Emma's heart would continue to open up to him.

"Is Sadie around?" he called.

"*Jah*, she's inside." Emma disappeared through the front door while he lashed the reins to the fence post.

Sadie wore a curious look when she skipped down the steps a few moments later. Emma, walking just a few steps behind, wore a similar look.

"I have something for you," Levi said.

Sadie looked at Emma. Emma shrugged. The chickens squawked from their resting place on the ground. Levi had hoisted the cage out of the buggy while Emma was fetching her sister.

"What was that?" Sadie asked. She hurried toward Levi.

He stepped back and motioned to the cage that was hidden at the back side of the buggy.

Sadie sucked in a surprised breath as her hand clapped over her mouth. She looked at Levi, the chickens, and then at Levi again.

He nodded. "They're for you. I wanted to get them to you sooner but I had some trouble tracking down more Marans. Abram Graber knew of an *Englisch* farmer who raises them. He had plenty of chicks but he had only two laying hens he was willing to part with."

"*Danki*. Oh, Levi. *Danki*!" Sadie was nearly bouncing with excitement. "Can I get them settled?"

"*Jah*. They're yours. You can do as you please with them," he said.

"Levi." Emma rested her hand on his arm, sending his heart into a pleasantly chaotic rhythm. "You didn't need to go to so much trouble."

He nodded. "I did. Look how happy she is."

Sadie opened the cage door. She placed her hand inside for the chickens to inspect before trying to pluck them out.

"I was disappointed I couldn't find more Marans," he admitted. "I got her a pair of Silkies to round things out."

While the Marans' eggs were more favorable, Silkies were known for their friendly dispositions, and he thought if anyone would be happy raising friendly chickens, it would be Sadie. He knew he was right when he watched her gently scoop the smaller

Silkie out of the cage. The bird was a bit ruffled from traveling. As Sadie murmured to it, the white ball of fluffy plumage eased against her.

"I know she's still upset about the ones she lost," Levi said.

Emma smiled. "She is. But Sadie loves animals. She'll make friends with these in no time."

Ezekiel came out of the barn and spotted the new arrivals immediately. "You got more chickens." He hurried to his sister's side, slowing as he neared her so as not to scare the birds.

"They came from Levi. I think I'll name this one Snowball," Sadie announced.

Ezekiel knelt down next to the cage to inspect the other three.

"You can name one if you like," Sadie offered.

He pointed at the other Silkie. "Let's call her Milkshake."

Levi shook his head in amusement and Emma laughed.

"Do you think the two of you can get the birds settled in the coop?" Levi asked.

"I'll help her," Ezekiel said.

"Don't take too long," Emma warned. "We should be leaving soon."

"We'll hurry," Sadie assured her. "I'll get the chickens in the coop and Zeke can lock everything up before we leave."

Amelia appeared on the front porch. She carried a large wicker basket.

"We're bringing buns and maple butter to the barn raising," Emma explained.

"The day is just getting started and I'm anxious

for lunch," Levi joked.

"It will be a lovely day," Emma said.

Barn raisings and frolics always were. The men and women worked hard—each in their own way—but even difficult tasks could be enjoyable when shared among the companionship of others. The frame of the barn had already been built. Today the men would put up the walls and the roof.

"I thought Zeke could work with me today."

Emma frowned. "He's never helped with this sort of thing before."

"All the more reason for him to learn." Levi leaned toward her as he spoke, assurance in his tone. "I'll keep a close eye on him."

"I don't doubt that you will," Emma said.

"There's plenty of reclaimed lumber that will need to have the nails stripped. I can start him off with that. It's an easy task but important; it should keep some of the younger boys busy for the morning."

"*Goot mariye*, Levi," Amelia said as she neared them.

"And to you," Levi replied.

"It is kind of you to offer to drive us today." Amelia hoisted the basket into the buggy. "I see Sadie received a nice surprise. Poor Gretel hasn't laid a single egg since her ordeal. Maybe she'll feel more comfortable with some new friends."

"I hope so," Levi said. He glanced around the farm. "Any more trouble?"

"No," Emma said quickly. "Maybe that was the end of it."

Levi's lips twisted. Emma sounded hopeful, but

he wasn't so sure. Barn raisings were a good place to catch up on gossip, though none of the men would dare call it that. He hoped to catch wind of news about Amos.

"Are we ready?" Sadie hopped up to the buggy. "I've been waiting all week for today to come."

"I have one more basket to carry out," Amelia said. "Sadie, if you'll come help with the jars of butter, we'll be all set."

The Miller farm was on the far northern edge of their district. By the time they arrived, there were already more than a dozen families gathered. The women took the food and started for the house.

Levi got Blaze settled while Ezekiel ran off to greet some friends. Levi was checking over his tools when a familiar voice greeted him.

"*Hallo*, Levi." Ivan leaned against the buggy as Levi finished his task. "It seems you've been stepping out with Emma a lot these days. Will they be announcing your marriage in the *banns* soon?"

Levi glanced at Ivan, unsure of whether his brother was teasing or serious. The smirk and mischievous look in his eye was Levi's answer.

"That remains to be seen," Levi said.

Ivan chuckled. "I think there's hope for the two of you. I pray that you find the kind of happiness I've found."

Levi narrowed his eyes. His brother, usually so serious, sounded a bit sappy. "Is there something you want to tell me?"

Ivan beamed from ear to ear. "*Jah*. I'm going to be a *daed*. The little one will be here around Christmas."

"Congratulations." Levi pulled his brother into a hug, giving Ivan's back a pounding for good measure. It was selfish, he knew, but he was grateful that Ivan had ended up with Miriam. He knew he had done the right thing by asking his brother to walk away from Emma. Ivan and Miriam would be happy raising a family together. It made him long for the same with Emma. "Does *Mamm* know?"

"*Jah*. She's so happy, I thought she might burst." Ivan leveled a look at Levi. "It's not just the *boppli* she's excited about. She's sure there's going to be a wedding this fall. She's awfully excited about gaining a new daughter-in-law."

Levi gave his brother a hesitant grin.

"Things are going well?" Ivan guessed.

"They are starting to." His smile fell a bit. "We have a long way to go."

"You've told Emma how you feel about her?" Ivan raised his eyebrows. "Does she know you've been in love with her for years?"

Levi frowned. "Not yet."

"You *dummkopf*, what are you waiting for?"

He would tell Emma everything.

When the time was right.

• • •

Emma moved between Amelia and Sadie as they helped to reset a long table for lunch. The first shift of men had finished eating. The table needed to be replenished before the second shift of men came in.

A group of women still worked in the kitchen while another group stayed busy refilling bowls and water pitchers.

The progress on the barn was already a sight to behold. The women were working just as hard in the kitchen. Platters of chicken, bowls of potatoes, and an endless array of side dishes appeared as the men trudged up to the house.

"Amelia, I've been looking high and low for you." Judith Graber's tone held a note of scolding, as if Amelia were a child who had disobeyed.

"I'm sorry," Amelia offered. "I didn't realize."

"You may not know this, but your mother and I used to be *goot* childhood friends," Judith explained.

"Judith is also Rachael's aunt," Emma volunteered.

"It's so nice to meet you," Amelia politely replied.

"You as well," Judith said. She looped her arm through Amelia's. "Your mother and I have begun writing back and forth the last few weeks. There's someone I would like for you to meet."

Amelia caught Emma's eye, a knowing scowl settling on her face. Having gotten nowhere with Mary Kurtz, Naomi had clearly enlisted the help of another old friend.

"Come," Judith ordered. "My *sohn*, Jakob, is just finishing up his meal. I'd like to introduce you before he gets back to work."

"I don't think—" Amelia started.

"Don't be silly," Judith interrupted. "I told him I would fetch you. I promised your *mamm* I would do my best to help you find a husband. Now come along." With her arm firmly looped through Amelia's, Judith towed her away.

Emma took a step after them, feeling as though she should intervene, but not sure how to do so.

"Amelia is no match for Judith."

Emma spun to find Levi standing beside her. His eyes glinted with amusement.

"I'll have to try to rescue her in a bit." Emma's heart did a little dance at the sight of Levi. "Until then I think she can hold her own against Judith. She's been holding her own against her *mamm* for years."

Levi laughed at her reasoning.

Jakob was nice enough, but he was several years younger than Amelia. He had a lot of boyish charm that caught the attention of many girls, and he didn't shy away from their notice. Still, he seemed to be nowhere near ready to settle down.

"Jakob is harmless," Levi said with a chuckle. "I know he enjoys the attention."

"His table will be getting back to work soon. Hopefully Judith won't keep them too long." Emma continued to work as she spoke. She took plates from a stack and set one at each chair. Sadie ran back into the house to fetch clean glasses for the water pitchers.

"Jakob is known to dawdle," Levi said. "I'm sure he'll take advantage of his time with Amelia."

"I'm sure Amelia can handle herself with him," Emma replied. She knew her cousin had vast experience at putting off potential suitors.

"I have no doubt," Levi agreed.

Emma spotted a clean glass at the end of the table. She retrieved it and filled it with water from the partially full pitcher.

"Drink this," she ordered. "It's warm out today."

"*Danki*."

"The barn is coming along nicely." Emma continued down the table, placing a knife and fork at each place setting.

"We have a *goot* group of men working," Levi said.

"How is Zeke doing?"

Levi flashed a proud smile. "The younger boys got all of the nails pulled. They organized the building material into piles. Some of the more experienced are taking measurements. We put Zeke to work doing some sawing."

Emma took a step away from the table, finished with her task for the moment. "He's doing well?"

"He'll be up pounding on the rafters before you know it."

Emma glanced at the barn. She knew Levi's comment was in jest, but she winced, picturing her brother so far up in the air. "Maybe someday." Hopefully a day far, far off in the future.

He chuckled. "He seems to be enjoying himself. He was already asking if he could do more."

"I'm glad to hear it." She had caught sight of her brother a few times. Some of the other boys his age were running about while a few were working on a game of catch in an open field. Not Ezekiel—he was taking the job he was given very seriously. Emma decided it was good for him to feel important and needed.

Sadie and her friend returned with the glasses. They began setting them on the table as another group of men moved in.

"You should eat," Emma said.

He nodded. "I was going to wait for Zeke, but I think he might be awhile."

Levi joined the men, and Emma moved on to the next table that needed to be cleared. She worked with a group of women who cleaned it quickly and then set it up for the next group.

Emma laughed when she spotted Amelia walking arm in arm with Rachael. Satisfied that her job was done for the moment, she wove her way around the tables.

"I don't know what Auntie Judith was thinking," Rachael said with a shake of her head. "I adore my cousin, but he is not ready for a wife. Half the time he needs his own nanny! He has a kind heart but seems to be missing out on common sense."

She released Amelia from her grip now that they were a safe distance away from Jakob.

"I hope Judith isn't too disappointed." Emma winked to let Amelia know she wasn't being serious.

"I don't think Judith will care too greatly," Amelia admitted. "Not only did she introduce me to Jakob, but on the way to her *sohn's* table she introduced me to a widower named Leroy. He seemed nice enough but..."

"But Leroy is old enough to be your *daed*," Emma supplied. Leroy had been widowed for many years and had been a friend of her *daed*'s. His children were close in age to Sadie and Ezekiel. He was a godly man, a wonderful neighbor, always a willing helper...but he was also much too old for the spirited Amelia.

"Yes," Amelia agreed, "possibly old enough to be

my *daed*. It was almost as bad as when she introduced me to Jonathon Yoder."

"The bishop's grandson," Rachael said with a giggle. "Is he even old enough to court yet?"

Emma laughed lightly with Rachael. "Judith does seem determined to help your *mamm* get her wish."

Amelia placed her hands on her heated cheeks. "I thought if I got away from my *mamm* I wouldn't have to be put through this. Now she simply has Judith doing it in her place."

"Don't worry," Rachael said assuredly. "She *canna* go on much longer. Pine Creek does have several bachelors, but most are very young or very old; not many are suitable for you. It won't be long until she runs out of men to introduce you to."

"I will find that a relief," Amelia said.

"What of you? Are you any closer to a fall wedding?" Rachael asked Emma. "The trees are so pretty that time of year. It would be perfect."

Weddings were held at the bride's home and were, like everything else, kept simple. There would be no ring, no decorations. She would sew herself a new dress, but it would be plain. But Rachael was right. The trees would create a stunning natural backdrop. Not that she should let her mind wander there...

"I don't know," Emma honestly admitted. "I believe it's still too soon to tell."

Rachael gave her a little nudge, her eyes sparkling. "Promise me I'll be one of the first to know."

"You'll be one of the first," Emma said with a laugh of her own.

The women glanced around and realized another

table full of men was clearing out. It was time for everyone to get back to work.

By the end of the day, men and women alike were weary, though the reward was a new barn for the Millers.

She was loading her empty food baskets into the buggy when she saw Marvin approaching. Oh, how she would like to dart away and pretend she hadn't seen him, but it was too late. He met her eyes and smiled.

"Have you changed your mind about the farm yet?"

She forced a tight smile. "I have not."

He patted her shoulder. "Very well. Let me know when you do."

With that, he turned and sauntered away. She bit back a growl of frustration. What would it take to prove the farm was not for sale? Reality hit quickly and she was reminded of exactly what it would take: she needed to pay off the taxes. She was getting closer. She would make it. They would be okay.

"What was that about?" Levi asked as he loped up to her. "He wasn't asking about the farm again, was he?"

"Afraid so," said Emma. "And you can guess what I told him."

He smiled. "I sure can. Let's load this buggy and get out of here."

On the ride home, Ezekiel and Sadie did most of the chattering. Sadie filled everyone in on who was now courting whom. When she finished her nuggets of news, Ezekiel spoke up.

"Levi said I did a *goot* job today," he told Emma.

"It's true," Levi agreed. "At the end we let him pound some of the siding on. He hammered the nail straight every time."

"I want to build something on my own," Ezekiel continued.

"What would you like to build?" Emma wondered.

His response was immediate. "A rabbit hutch."

"*Ach*," Sadie exclaimed. "Can he?"

"I think that's a fine idea, if it's okay with Emma," Levi said, looking over at her, so she nodded. The fact that he deferred to her warmed her heart. "It shouldn't be too difficult and is a nice-sized project to start with. I can help get it going, make sure we have the right materials and that the measurements are correct."

"You might be getting a new rabbit sooner than you thought," Amelia told Sadie.

"I hope so." The girl smiled happily.

"What is that?"

Emma looked over her shoulder at Ezekiel's strange tone. He was staring off into the distance.

"It *canna* be," Levi muttered from beside her.

Emma whipped her head back around. Her gaze honed in on the barn. Now that she was looking that way, it was impossible to miss.

"Not the barn," she moaned.

Levi gritted his teeth in frustration. The side of the Zieglers' barn was splashed with what looked like blood. "It must be red paint," he said.

Like the rest of the Amish in the community, the Zieglers took great care to keep their farm neat and tidy. Yards were always trimmed. Flower beds were weeded. The buildings were painted as needed.

It wasn't that long ago that Levi had joined a group of other men and painted the barn for Paul. Paul had been worried about the peeling paint but hadn't been able to handle the job himself. A group of men had sanded down the wood until it was smooth enough to hold a fresh coat.

Now the hard work was marred by this latest prank.

"What a terrible thing to do!" Ezekiel exclaimed. "Do you think it was Arthur and Marty Zook?"

Emma frowned. "The boys that pushed you into the mud last year?"

Ezekiel nodded. "They were making fun of me today, saying I was a show-off for working on the barn so hard. They left early."

Emma and Levi shared a look. The boys who had bullied Zeke in the past? That thought hadn't crossed her mind before. Was it possible? Levi made a face to let her know he wasn't sure what to think of it, either.

"Do they pick on you often?" Levi asked.

Zeke shrugged evasively. "I mostly ignore them."

"We talked about this," Emma said quietly. "I don't approve of bullying. I should talk to their parents."

"Please, Emma, don't," Ezekiel pleaded. "I don't let them get to me, and if you talk to their parents it might make it worse."

"I'll let it go for now," Emma agreed. She knew how it felt to want to handle something on your own, and as long as he wasn't being hurt, she'd respect Ezekiel's wishes.

Levi slowed the buggy. Up close the barn looked even worse. Someone had taken a bucketful of paint and tossed it repeatedly down the length of the barn.

"My chickens!" Sadie's voice was shrill as she realized the barn might not be the only victim today. "I need to check my chickens!"

Levi was barely able to stop the buggy before Sadie leaped out. She stumbled when she hit the ground but it didn't slow her down. Ezekiel jumped out and followed her.

Ezekiel had padlocked the coop, but padlocks could be cut. The wire fence could be torn down.

"I hope the animals are safe," Emma said quietly. "I *canna* bear to deal with more cruelty."

Ginger was grazing in the pasture. At least the horse appeared to be unharmed.

"I didn't see Amos at the Millers'," Levi pointed out. "But I never thought it could be the Zook boys, until just now. They have a reputation for being pranksters. And I know they've caused Ezekiel trouble in the past. I don't know how far they would take picking on the boy."

The trio walked the length of the barn. The paint had pooled out on the grass, but that would wash away with time. The barn, on the other hand, would require a good deal of work.

Sadie and Ezekiel rounded the side of the structure.

"All is well?" Amelia guessed.

The children appeared calm, relief etched into their features.

"The chickens are fine. So are the goats," Sadie said. "I'm glad we locked them away."

"Only this side of the barn is ruined," Ezekiel added.

It was the side visible to anyone approaching the farm. Whoever had done this had done it with the intention of making a spectacle of the Ziegler property.

"We'll have to get it cleaned up," Emma said.

"But not tomorrow," Levi added.

Tomorrow was Sunday, a visiting Sunday. Even though there would be no church service, work that was anything other than a necessity would be forbidden.

Whoever had caused the destruction would be well aware that the damage would not be dealt with immediately.

The culprit had done so with the intent to cause the Zieglers embarrassment. Emma let out a weary sigh. Oh, how she was ready for this to end. But would it end anytime soon? She didn't think so.

Not until the perpetrator was caught.

CHAPTER SEVENTEEN

As Emma stood at the kitchen sink enjoying her last sip of coffee, she couldn't help but peer out the window. The barn, with its offensive splattering of paint, was in full view. She longed to clean it up today, but it would have to wait until tomorrow.

She finished off the last of her hot brew, then rinsed the cup before setting it in the sink. They had already eaten a light breakfast of yesterday's muffins and apple slices. For lunch, they would bring a pot of leftover stew to Mary's. Mary had invited them over again today, and Emma had agreed but only on the condition that she bring the meal.

Emma was drying her hands on a dish towel when the sound of buggy wheels on gravel caught her attention through the open window. She peered back over the sink.

She couldn't stop the grimace that pressed onto her face, though she knew it was rude.

"Amelia!" She whirled around as she shouted, finding herself face-to-face with her startled cousin.

"Gracious, I'm right here," Amelia said with a laugh. "What's got you all riled up?"

"The Grabers are here," Emma said. "They're coming down the drive. It looks like just Judith and Jakob."

Amelia let out a groan. "Yesterday Judith mentioned they'd be seeing me soon. I didn't think she meant *today*."

She whirled around and Emma automatically followed as she hustled from the kitchen.

"Tell them I went to Mary's," Amelia said over her shoulder.

"I *canna* lie," Emma said apologetically. She was surprised her cousin was asking her to, despite the plight she was in.

"You won't be lying." Amelia shoved her foot into her tennis shoe. "I'm heading there now."

"You'll never get Ginger hitched up and down the driveway in time. They'll see you," Emma warned.

"I'm not taking Ginger," Amelia said. She took off toward the kitchen again.

Emma pivoted to follow her.

"I'm taking the bicycle. It's parked in the barn, and if I ride out the small door on the back side, they won't see me."

"They won't see you if I keep them busy in the sitting room," Emma corrected.

"Yes, exactly. Thank you," Amelia replied.

It hadn't been an offer coming from Emma's lips. She was none too thrilled about entertaining Judith and her son. Then she instantly felt a bit of guilt because she should be hospitable, regardless of who her guests were.

"I'll tell Mary you and the children will be by later," Amelia said. She tugged open the kitchen door and slipped outside.

Emma let out a little huff of frustration.

She heard the boards creak as Amelia made her way across the porch. The very same porch where Levi had told Naomi they were courting. Oh, how she'd rather be spending the time with Levi than with the Grabers. But no time to think of that now.

She peered out the window again.

Jakob was lashing the horse's reins to the hitching post while Judith was striding purposefully to the front door. Emma spotted a flash of white slipping across the window on the other corner of the kitchen—Amelia's prayer *kapp*, no doubt. A small burst of laughter escaped from Emma's lips; she couldn't help it. She couldn't see her cousin but could imagine her skulking along the side of the house, just waiting for the Grabers to come inside so she could make a mad dash for the barn.

All so Amelia could avoid finding a potential beau.

Maybe I shouldn't laugh, Emma thought as her smile slipped away. It was really sort of sad, the lengths that Amelia was apparently willing to go in a effort to avoid being matched with a man.

A sharp knock on the door pulled Emma from the kitchen. She couldn't see Amelia but had a hunch she was out of sight on the side of the house.

She forced a welcoming smile onto her face as she tugged the front door open.

"*Hallo*, Emma," Judith said as she sidestepped her hostess and walked into the house. "We've come to visit. I'm sure you don't mind."

"Of course not," Emma said, both women knowing full well that Emma would never say anything to the contrary. "But this is quite the surprise."

Judith's eyebrows arched. "I told Amelia that we would be stopping by."

That wasn't what Amelia had said, and Emma doubted that Judith had been very clear.

Jakob came inside to join them. After a quick greeting, Emma thought it best to point out the inevitable.

"If you're hoping to visit with Amelia, you've missed her."

"Missed her?" Judith echoed. "But we came to see her."

"I'm afraid there's been a misunderstanding," Emma replied. Actually, she was fairly certain that Judith had not been up-front with her intentions of an immediate visit. "She's left to visit Mary for the day."

Judith's brow crinkled. Jakob shuffled his feet.

Emma thought perhaps they would leave.

She thought wrong.

Judith simply turned to her.

Oh. Emma realized she was waiting to be invited to have a seat.

"Would you like to visit in the sitting room? I could put a new pot of *kaffi* on."

"That would be fine," Judith agreed. She nodded to her son, and the two of them took a seat in the living room. Judith dropped down onto the sofa. Emma had the disturbing impression that Judith had something other than just Amelia on her mind.

The woman was studying the walls, the floor, the woodwork, even seemed to take a good look at the windows.

What is going on? Emma wondered. If she was looking for Amelia, she surely was not going to find her in the window trim.

Jakob sat in a side chair, his long legs spread out before him, wearing a decidedly uninterested expression on his face.

Emma took her time filling the stove-top perco-
lator with fresh grounds and cold water. She turned
on the gas burner and contemplated hiding out in
the kitchen until the coffee had brewed. Curiosity
brought her back to the living room where Judith
was gently tapping on a wall.

"This house looks sturdily built, *jah*?" Judith said.

"My grandfather built it," Emma replied, not
sure if the comment was a compliment or simply a
bizarre acknowledgment.

"What do you think, Jakob?" Judith asked her
son. "Does it look well built to you?"

Jakob wore an amused expression that Emma
didn't quite understand. "It looks well enough built."

Well enough for what?

Judith resumed her seat on the sofa. "Emma," she
said, "I've been speaking with your aunt Naomi."

Emma stuffed down a groan. It seemed nothing
good ever came of conversations with her meddling
aunt.

"Writing to her weekly," Judith clarified.

"How nice," Emma said.

She did not miss the way Jakob's eyebrows
quirked as he wore an expression suspiciously close
to a smirk.

"It's my understanding that Levi will take over
his father's farm," Judith declared.

"*Jah*, I believe you are correct," Emma said.
"Though that's not my business to discuss."

"*Nee*, I wouldn't ask you to," Judith hastily
agreed. "However, if he takes over his *daed*'s farm,"
she continued, "he will not be able to run this farm."
She paused a beat before saying, "Jakob would like

to buy it."

Emma felt her mouth drop open. She slammed it shut again. Whatever gave this woman the impression that the farm was for sale?

She turned to Jakob, who simply gave her a lazy shrug.

Emma realized that it was Judith driving this decision. "I'm afraid it's not for sale," Emma said to her.

"Hear me out," Judith urged. "I know you and Levi are courting. He'll inherit the farm from Moses, and he *canna* possibly run two. My Jakob needs to settle down soon. He'll need a farm of his own."

"The farm will go to Zeke," Emma said firmly. As the youngest son—and in this case, the only son—it was his birthright. "Moses is not ready to hand over his farm anytime soon." Not that it was any of Judith's business. "And regardless," Emma said, "*I* am running the farm."

"It'll be many years before Zeke is old enough to take over," Judith argued. "Just think about it. Speak with your aunt and she will give you the guidance you need. Selling this farm would be in the best interest of everyone."

"The farm is not for sale," Zeke said as he stood in the doorway, a horrified look on his face. "It's not for sale, is it?" His imploring gaze dug into Emma's.

She hadn't heard him come inside from checking on the animals.

"It certainly is not," Emma confirmed. "I'm not sure what Naomi has told you, but the farm is not her concern."

Judith's brows furrowed in disapproval, but Emma didn't care.

"Emma," Judith said, her tone maddeningly calm and conciliatory, "your aunt wants only what's best for you. Don't you think you should at least give selling a thought?"

• • •

"What do we have here?" *Daed* asked, his tone completely perplexed.

Levi glanced over his shoulder, his eyes nearly popping as he spotted what had caught his father's attention. He abandoned the horse they'd been hitching to the buggy, assuming his father would see to finishing the task. It certainly wasn't a two-person job, but he'd offered to help while he and *Daed* discussed cattle prices and the best direction to take in the future. Not just the Bontrager farm, but the Ziegler farm as well.

Not that he would make any decisions without consulting Emma and, eventually, Zeke. The boy would take over the farm one day, so he needed to be included in every decision. It would give him a solid foundation to build upon someday.

No time for that now as he stepped away from the buggy.

An Amish woman on a bicycle was tearing down the driveway, pedaling so fast that dust was flying. He recognized the bike right away, and it took only a moment longer to figure out which of the three women was riding it. He took off at a jog to meet Amelia.

"Is everything all right?" he demanded.

"*Jah*, I think so," Amelia said as she skidded to a

stop. "Well, mostly."

He arched a brow. "Mostly?"

She nodded. "Judith Graber just showed up at the farm." She explained the connection between Judith and Naomi. "I think because Mary wasn't keen on the idea of sending her updates about you and Emma, she's enlisted Judith."

"I see."

"I thought you may want to head over to the farm to offer Emma some support."

"You rode over here just to tell me this? Didn't Judith wonder where you were going?"

"She didn't see me because I'm on my way to Mary's."

Levi nodded, though he was a bit confused as to how Amelia had slipped past Judith. There was only one road in and out of the Ziegler place.

"I'm sure Judith is visiting so she can tell my *mamm* how she thinks you and Emma are faring," Amelia said as she cast a suspicious glance over her shoulder. "I best be on my way in case they don't visit long. Because I also think she wants me to marry her son."

She looped around Levi and then pedaled off down the driveway.

Levi watched her go with a bemused expression on his face.

"That woman always was a meddler," his father muttered.

Levi hadn't realized his father had followed him out of the barn. They had been hitching the buggy so they could visit Levi's brother Joshua and his family.

"Which woman?" Levi asked with a shake of his

head. "Judith or Naomi?"

Daed chuckled. "I've known the pair since we were *kinner*. *Jah*, they are both meddlers." He clapped Levi on the shoulder. "I don't think your *mamm* is quite ready to go yet. How about I drive you over to Emma's? You can visit Joshua and Amanda another day."

Levi took him up on the offer. He could walk, but with the buggy hitched and ready to go, it would be faster if he accepted the ride.

He and *Daed* shared shocked expressions when they neared the Zieglers' front porch and could hear raised voices coming from inside.

His father cast a wary glance at the Zieglers' front door. The voice that carried had to be that of Judith. "I'll leave you to it," he said as he clenched the reins.

Levi gave his father a wry smile. Moses had never been much for confrontation, and he certainly wasn't much for confrontation among womenfolk. It didn't surprise Levi one bit that his dad was anxious to be on his way.

"Wish me luck," he said as he hopped down.

"You'll need more than luck," *Daed* grumbled. "May God be with you."

With a nudge of the reins, his horse trotted away.

Levi shook his head as he hurried to the door. It swung open before he could knock.

"Judith thinks Jakob should buy the farm," Ezekiel announced.

"What farm?" Levi demanded as he stepped inside. "This farm?"

"*Jah*," Judith proclaimed as she stepped into Levi's view. "This farm. Naomi agrees with me."

Levi wondered if Naomi was hoping for a cut of the sale, as she had been last time. He didn't dare ask, nor did he have the chance.

"You should talk some sense into this *maidel*," Judith said.

Emma gasped.

Jakob, who had sidled up to his mother, winced. "I think I'm going to go wait in the buggy. It was nice seeing you, Emma."

He wore an amused look as he walked out the door.

Levi leveled his gaze on Judith. "Emma is a capable woman, and she owns this farm. Paul saw to that. He's entrusted her to pass it along to Ezekiel when the time is right."

"This really is a family affair and not up for discussion," Emma told Judith.

"Naomi is your family. She discussed it with me," Judith persisted. She gave a little sniff. "But I see that you did not inherit your aunt's *goot* sense."

"Hey, now," Levi said. "There's no need—"

"Naomi believes there is a need," Judith said. "I'm just trying to be a *goot* friend." She cut her gaze to Ezekiel but quickly looked away. "Once Levi takes over for Moses, he won't have time for this place. If you two even wed," she said almost accusingly. "Naomi is afraid there will be no one capable to run the place. I'm only trying to help out."

And help her son to the farm, apparently.

"I believe I shall leave before I overstay my welcome," Judith announced.

Levi thought it was probably far too late for that but bit his tongue.

The woman left without a goodbye.

Once she was gone, Emma slumped against the door.

"What was that all about?" Levi asked. "She thinks she can just waltz in here to buy the farm for Jakob?"

"If Naomi gave her that impression, I can hardly blame Judith," Emma said with a sigh.

Levi hadn't been present for the entire conversation, but he was able to fit together the missing pieces easily enough. Naomi had no faith in Ezekiel and didn't believe he'd be able to handle the farm one day. She hadn't given up on the notion that it was best to sell the place.

Levi knew the woman was wrong.

He placed a hand on Zeke's shoulder. "No one is going to take the farm from you. It will be yours. And you're going to run this place every bit as well as Paul did."

"*Danki*, Levi," Ezekiel said. "I'm going to find Sadie, let her know that the Grabers left and probably won't be back." As he marched out the back door, he muttered, "I hope."

"*Jah*, *danki*," Emma said, "for making Zeke feel better."

"I spoke only the truth," Levi said.

"I appreciate you standing up for me. Thank you for telling Judith I'm capable."

He smiled. "You *are*."

"How did you have such perfect timing?" Emma asked.

"Amelia stopped by on her way to Mary's. She thought you might need some support, though I don't think fighting to keep the farm is what she had in mind."

Emma pinched the bridge of her nose. "I love my aunt, but I've had enough of Naomi's interfering. I wish she would trust me to do what is best."

"She should," Levi said. "Paul did. He trusted you, and she should trust his judgment."

Emma's lip trembled, and he feared he had said the wrong thing.

"This place should belong to Zeke, and I'm determined to make that happen." She sighed. "Enough nonsense talk. The farm is not for sale and that is that. I think we need to talk about something else, anything else."

Levi's lips quirked. "Your *kaffi* sure smells *goot*."

"*Ach*," Emma said, looking a bit surprised. "I forgot I brewed a new pot. I had offered a cup to Judith but never got around to serving it. Would you like some?"

"I would," he said. What he would really like was to linger, stay for a visit.

She motioned him toward the kitchen. "I thought you were to visit your *bruder's* family today."

"We were going to. I got sidetracked by coming over here," he admitted. He smirked, remembering how Moses had hightailed it away from the farm. "I'm pretty sure that they left without me."

Emma poured them each a mug. "Since they left without you, perhaps you should stay and visit us."

She gave him a shy smile and his heart leaped at the sight.

"I'd like that."

"We told Mary we would be over later, in time

for lunch." She paused before saying, "You can join us if you'd like."

"I would like to visit with her." It was true. He was growing fond of the spinster. Meanwhile, he was simply going to enjoy this rare, quiet time with Emma.

She poured cups of coffee for both of them, and they took them out onto the back porch. In the not-so-far distance, the maple leaves fluttered in the breeze. They took a seat in the porch swing.

It swayed gently under their weight.

"Amelia seemed a bit desperate to get away," Levi said.

Emma sighed. "She was. She isn't the least bit interested in courting."

"Apparently not." Levi grimaced as he remembered how the dust had kicked up around her as she'd frantically pedaled away.

"I pray for her," Emma said. "I know that now she's hurting, and I pray for her heart to heal." She sipped her coffee, then turned to look at Levi. "I think deep down, she doesn't want to be alone. I believe that even though she's not ready to admit it, she wants to find love again someday. That's what we all want, isn't it?"

Levi's heart leaped at the look in Emma's eyes. Was it hope he was seeing? Perhaps even love? Oh, how he prayed it to be so.

"Yes," he agreed. "That's what we all want in the end."

CHAPTER EIGHTEEN

"Where are you running off to?" Emma demanded. It had been several days since the barn had been tampered with, and so far, there didn't appear to be any more destruction. Levi had been busy with his carpentry job and hadn't had enough time in the evenings to work on painting over the damage.

Ezekiel had come in from his chores, washed up, but then Emma heard him pounding down the staircase running to the front door. He whirled around to face her.

"Amelia almost has breakfast on the table," she said. "You already did your chores."

"I'm not hungry. I need to go."

Emma frowned. "Not so fast. Where are you going *to*?"

He motioned to the door. "Just to the barn. Levi's here; he brought some paint and said he needs my help to make the barn look like new again. It's going to be a big job."

Emma bit back a smile. Perhaps Ezekiel had grown a few inches since she last checked, or perhaps he was just standing taller. Spending time with Levi had given him confidence he never had before.

He shifted anxiously from one foot to the other. "May I go? Levi needs me."

"And you," she said, "need to eat." She motioned to the door. "Run outside and invite him in. Tell him Amelia made cinnamon rolls. He will not want to pass those up."

Ezekiel darted off.

Emma returned to the kitchen to help Amelia. She moved the cinnamon rolls from the counter to the table while Amelia finished scrambling the eggs. Sadie moved between them, retrieving what she needed to set the table.

Minutes later, Levi and Zeke returned.

"Sit, have some breakfast," Emma ordered.

"I don't always expect you to feed me. I ate already. But I would not turn down a cup of *kaffi*."

"You should not turn down Amelia's cinnamon rolls," Sadie warned. "Tourists pay *goot* money for them at the Pine Cone Café. You may have one simply for sitting at our table. Besides, the rolls she makes here are even better. She puts maple syrup in the icing."

Levi chuckled. "An offer I *canna* refuse."

Emma poured coffee for all but Ezekiel. After their blessings were said and the food passed around, the conversation flowed.

"I could paint the barn," Emma said. "You don't need to trouble yourself with it."

"Have you painted before?" Levi asked pointedly.

"Not really," she admitted. She'd watched men paint barns before. How hard could it be?

"The paint was splattered against the barn. It dried in thick streams," Levi said. "That will need to be sanded down before painting over it. It will take a while to get the barn done."

"I could at least help," she pressed.

"Zeke mentioned your plans with Rachael."

Emma frowned. She did have plans—Rachael had invited them to her family's farm. The berries were ripe, prime for picking. Emma had been picking berries at the farm since she and Rachael were young children.

"Perhaps we can meet with Rachael tomorrow," Emma said.

"No need, honestly." Levi waved her off. "Go pick your berries. Hopefully by the time you return, Zeke and I will have the barn looking fine as new."

"If you're sure," Emma said hesitantly.

He nodded. "Sure as can be."

"When are we leaving for the berry farm?" Sadie asked.

"As soon as dishes are done," Emma said.

"We'll need the afternoon to clean the berries and make a pie or two," Amelia replied.

Levi finally managed to take a bite of his cinnamon roll. "This is the best cinnamon roll I've ever had. Putting syrup in the icing was a wise idea."

Amelia blushed. "*Danki*. I'm trying to convince the Hansons to let me use syrup in the rolls we serve at the café." She flashed Emma a smile. "I figure it can only help with the syrup sales."

Ezekiel was the first one done. He fidgeted in his chair as he waited for Levi to finish off his coffee, and as soon as he did, the two went outside to set to work.

"It's kind of Levi to do so much around here," Amelia said as they cleared the table.

Emma nodded. "It is. He's also been spending a lot of time with Zeke. I only hope it isn't too much. I don't want to take advantage of his kindness."

"Zeke loves spending time with Levi," Sadie chimed in. "And I think Levi feels the same. I don't believe he's doing it simply out of kindness."

"Levi has a gentle way about him," Amelia noted. "He always makes Zeke feel important, even when he's helping with the smallest thing. I know pride is a sin, but I also think it's sinful to think too lowly of yourself. I'm pleased that Levi has been able to help Zeke see past the unkind words my *mamm* said."

Emma's thoughts were similar to Amelia's. She was also pleased that Ezekiel's self-esteem had risen since spending time with Levi. The more time they spent together, the clearer it became to Emma that Ezekiel would only continue to benefit from having Levi in his life.

"My *mamm* is often critical of those she loves most," Amelia continued. "I believe it's *because* she loves them and wants what's best. But oftentimes she goes about pushing ahead in an unkind manner."

Sadie continued to wash the dishes but spoke over her shoulder. "Is she that way with you?"

"*Jah*," Amelia said. "She is especially that way with me. I think it hurts her to know that I am still grieving. I believe she wants only for me to be happy."

"But happiness *canna* be forced." Emma gave her cousin's shoulder an understanding squeeze.

"No. It *canna*," Amelia agreed. "*Mamm* seems to think if I find another husband, he'll immediately take over Gideon's place in my heart. But it doesn't work that way."

Emma's chest twisted with sadness for her cousin. Amelia had paused in her dish drying, lost in thought. She wore a wistful expression laced with pain and longing.

"Gideon and I were childhood friends," she admitted, "much like you and Levi. I was just a *kinner* the first time he told me he was going to marry me someday." A sad smile broke free. "His *mamm* was my *mamm*'s best friend. When he passed, I not only lost my husband but a dear, dear friend."

"I'm so sorry." Emma's words were heartfelt. This was the most Amelia had opened up to her about Gideon, and it was all too easy to put herself in her cousin's place. If something happened to Levi, she imagined she would feel much the same way. Losing him would cause a huge, gaping hole in her heart. She imagined the pain of that loss would be nearly unbearable.

She craned her head and caught a glimpse of Levi and Ezekiel. They both had their backs to her as they worked at sanding the barn.

"I'm sorry." Amelia shook her head. "I don't know what got into me. Forgive me for being so melancholy when I have much to be grateful for. I must remember that the next time I let myself get lost in downhearted thoughts."

"Please don't apologize," Emma said. "You've suffered a great loss. Your pain is understandable."

"Perhaps, yet I refuse to wallow any more today." She hesitated, giving Emma a gentle look. "I know you believe your relationship with Levi is tentative, but I don't see it that way. Please keep an open heart and an open mind."

Emma nodded, knowing she shared something special with Levi. She had a chance for a future with him, and that was not something to be taken lightly. Not when she knew how fragile a future could be. Amelia's confession only proved that point.

When the kitchen was spotless Sadie hurried outside to hitch Ginger.

"How are the syrup sales coming along?" Amelia asked as she leaned against the countertop.

Emma knew what she was really wondering: whether she was going to make the tax deadline.

"I think we will make it," Emma said. "There won't be much to spare, but I think we're going to be okay." She felt a sense of lightness as she said the words. It was as if God was assuring her that He would provide, as long as she retained her trust in Him.

"I'm relieved to hear that," Amelia said.

The pair headed to the door to catch up with Sadie.

The moment she stepped outside, she knew something wasn't right. Ezekiel spoke with Levi, his shoulders slumped. He looked utterly dejected.

Emma frowned, wondering if Levi had scolded the boy. She knew if he had, it would've been with good reason. She trusted Levi's judgment, but curiosity nipped at her.

"I'll be back in a moment," she told Amelia. She quickly covered the distance to the barn.

Her eyes met Levi's and she immediately detected the frustration swimming in them.

"Is something wrong?"

Ezekiel nodded as he twisted around to face her. "They came back during the night."

"Who?" The question was automatic, though

Emma was sure she knew of whom Ezekiel was speaking.

"Whoever painted the barn," Ezekiel said.

"How do you know?" Emma demanded.

"I worked on the hutch last night before dark," Ezekiel said. Levi had come over the past few evenings to help Ezekiel along on his project. "I didn't look at it again until just now. I wanted to show Levi the work I'd done without him, but someone tore it apart. It's in pieces."

"That's the third time damage has been done during the night," Sadie said as she joined them. She shuddered.

"Do you think it was Marty and Arthur?" Ezekiel asked. "I told them I was building a hutch and they laughed at me. They told me it was going to be a piece of junk."

"The truth is, we aren't sure who it is." Levi grimaced. "But I think someone needs to talk to those boys' parents."

"*Nee*!" Ezekiel shook his head. "Please. I can handle them. They're not nice, but mostly I ignore them."

"It's true," Sadie said. "Those boys pick on everyone."

"Don't worry about the hutch," Levi told Ezekiel as he clapped him on the back. "We'll fix it." To Emma he said, "Perhaps it's time to speak with the bishop."

Emma didn't want to discuss her hesitation. She was afraid the bishop would think she couldn't handle the farm. Instead she just said, "I'll think on it."

Levi seemed to understand her hesitation. "Go,"

he ordered. "Enjoy your berry picking. There's nothing to be done about the trouble right now."

"Levi is right," Amelia agreed. "We should go. Rachael is expecting to meet us at her parents' farm soon."

"We ought not let whoever is doing this ruin our day," Sadie said decidedly. "Whether it be Amos or those bratty Zook boys."

"You're right," Emma agreed. "God will help us to deal with it when it is time."

• • •

"Emma!" Diana Bontrager greeted her with a smile. "Come in."

"*Goot nammidaag*, Diana. Is Levi here?" Emma lifted the pie plate she held in her hands. "We picked strawberries today while he painted my barn. The season is winding down, but we still harvested our fill, and he was gone by the time I got back. I brought him a pie, though it hardly seems an even trade."

Diana took the dessert from Emma's hands. "I'll see to it that he gets it. He's out in the pasture with Moses, checking on some fencing. Are you in a hurry or do you have time to visit for a while?"

"I have some time."

Emma followed Diana into the kitchen. Diana took two glasses from the cupboard and filled them with lemonade, then motioned for Emma to take a seat at the table.

"I've missed having you stop by," Diana admitted. "I don't see you nearly often enough."

Emma wasn't sure how to reply to that. When she

and Ivan were courting, Diana had insisted that Emma come for supper once a week.

"I've already told Levi that I'd like to see more of you," she continued. "I'd love to have you start coming for supper again. I'd be pleased if you brought the rest of your family as well."

"That's a generous offer." Emma took a sip of her lemonade.

"Nonsense," Diana said. "You know you and your siblings are like family. I've spoken with Amelia only a few times, but I would like to get to know her better."

"I'm sure she would enjoy that as well."

"I was pleased when I thought I would have you as a daughter-in-law," Diana said softly. "Don't get me wrong, I love Miriam. I'm happy my *sohn* is so happy. Yet a part of me was disappointed that we wouldn't be welcoming you into our family. I've known you since you were a *boppli*. I watched you grow up along with my own children."

Emma smiled at the memories her words elicited. After her mother died, Diana had stepped in as a surrogate mother of sorts for Emma. She often helped *Daed* when he was working the fields and needed someone to watch the children. Emma had spent many hours in Diana's cozy kitchen, learning to cook and the art of canning.

Part of the appeal of courting Ivan had been thinking she would gain Diana as a mother-in-law. It had crossed her mind that the same could be said for courting Levi. With each passing day, it seemed as if a new reason for wanting Levi in her life permanently took root in her mind.

"It troubled me when you and Levi stopped speaking. I *canna* tell you how happy I am that the two of you moved past whatever was troubling you." She reached over and squeezed Emma's hand. "I would love for you to join our family. It makes me happy to know there's still a chance."

Emma's heart swelled. She loved Diana as if she were already family. "You have always been so *goot* to me."

The sound of the front door closing stopped Emma from saying more.

Levi appeared in the threshold. The sight of him taking her in with those baby blue eyes, flashing her a charming smile, made Emma's heart do a little dance in her chest. There was no denying it. She was falling in love with this man.

• • •

"Am I interrupting?" Levi asked from the kitchen doorway. There was something reassuring about seeing his mother and Emma seated together at the kitchen table, smiling and lost in conversation.

"*Nee*," his mother said. "Join us."

He had chores to do, having spent so much of the day working on the Zieglers' barn, but Emma's welcoming smile made it impossible to refuse.

"Did you pick all the berries you wanted?" he asked.

"*Jah*." Emma chuckled. "I thought we picked more than enough, but once we got home, Zeke couldn't keep his hands off them. I think he ate an entire bucketful already."

"He worked hard today. The boy was hungry." He laughed along with Emma.

"We still have enough for a few pies. We might need to pick more if we plan on making jam."

"*Ach*!" Diana exclaimed. "I should serve the pie."

"I can do it," Emma offered.

Diana waved her offer aside. "You sit and visit." She patted Levi's shoulder as she rose to her feet. "Emma baked a pie for you. I hope you don't mind sharing it."

"*Nee*." Levi winked at Emma. "If it goes too quickly, I'll just have to beg her for another one."

"I will make you as many pies as you like," Emma readily agreed. "It's the least I could do. I looked at the barn earlier—it looks *goot* as new."

Levi nodded. "I'm happy with how it turned out, and it didn't take as long as I expected. Zeke is a fast learner."

Diana placed plates of pie in front of them.

"Levi has spoken highly of Zeke." Diana returned to her seat with a knowing smile on her face. "I think he enjoys having a young one to teach things to. As the youngest of the family, he finally has the chance to be a big *bruder*."

"I appreciate that," Emma said. "Zeke needs guidance right now—he's at an impressionable age. I *canna* think of anyone I would rather have him spend time with."

Her words stirred something deep within Levi. It was rewarding to see the boy's eyes light up when he learned something new, and *Mamm* was right: as the youngest in the family, he'd never had the opportunity to guide someone. He'd never had someone look up to him, not the way Ezekiel did. It made him yearn for something even greater. Having a son to teach, to guide, was something that he longed for.

When his mother requested that Emma stay for supper, Emma politely declined, telling her that her family was probably wondering where she was. *Mamm* insisted that Emma and her family come to supper one day soon. Emma agreed, telling her they would choose a time in the upcoming week.

"I'll walk you out," Levi said.

She did not refuse his offer.

Once outside, Levi turned to Emma as they walked down the driveway. "I've been thinking about Amos and what's been happening at your farm."

"What about it?" Emma asked.

"Do you think his *daed* told him about the taxes?"

Emma frowned. "I've no idea."

"What if he did? The deadline is coming quickly. What if Amos thinks causing problems will make you more likely to sell to his *daed*? When we were in town, Amos made it clear he feels cheated out of the farm." Levi looked at her expectantly. "I think we need to talk to the bishop."

"*Nee*," Emma said firmly. "We can't go to him with accusations and no proof. Besides, what if it really is the Zook boys? It would make sense that they went after the rabbit hutch."

"Do you think it is?" he asked.

"I don't know," Emma said, "and that's the problem."

Levi studied her face for a moment. "And if I'm

able to get proof that it's Amos? Then may we speak with the bishop?"

"Only then would it make sense to go to the bishop." She paused, seeming to think it over. "The taxes are due at the end of next week. *If* that's what this is about—and I'm not sure that it is—then he should stop when the bill is paid, don't you think?"

He nodded slowly. "I suppose." *If* he was right, and *if* that was what Amos's plan was. There was always the possibility the man was just a miserable miscreant. And of course, there was the possibility it was Marty and Arthur, though his instincts were telling him it wasn't them.

Emma was right. They needed proof, one way or another.

Whether it was Amos or someone else, it worried him that the person had not stopped yet. Concern ate at him. What if this person became arrogant enough to break into the house? He could cause untold damage. Or worse, what if he broke in at night, while they slept? What if he harmed them? He couldn't let that happen.

"Levi? You look like your head is elsewhere." She touched his arm, and his mind reeled back to the present. He cupped his hand over hers, slowly entwining his callused fingers with her dainty ones.

"I'm sorry." He didn't want to tell her where his mind had gone. Thoughts of a man breaking into her home were not something he would burden her with.

"There's nothing to apologize for."

Their hands slipped until they were dangling between them. He was grateful for the dense copse of spruce trees that surrounded the property. Though his mother adored Emma, she might not approve of such closeness.

Emma gave his hand a gentle squeeze. "I feel as though I should be the one apologizing. You've done so much for us. I'm afraid we're going to become a burden to you."

A burden? How could she think such a thing?

"It is no burden. I enjoy helping you when I can. I wish I could do more."

"More?" She shook her head. "What more could you possibly do? You have spent more time with Zeke than I have; you have taken the time to teach him things I never could. You've painted my barn, found Sadie's chicken, and even bought her new ones. I could go on and on."

He was surprised when he realized tears were seeping into her eyes.

"I feel like Naomi was right. Now that *Daed* is gone, I could not run the farm alone. If not for you and Amelia…" She faded off as she fought back tears. "I miss him terribly and I feel as though I am failing."

"Failing? Why would you think that?" He was baffled as he waited for her response.

"If *Daed* were here, no one would be trying to sabotage our farm."

"You don't know that," Levi warned. "The Zook boys have always picked on Ezekiel."

She shook her head. "I don't think it's them, not really. My instincts tell me it's Amos. Maybe that's wrong; I shouldn't condemn without proof. But that's how I feel. Teens might play a prank one time, but this person keeps returning. It feels personal."

A tear slipped down her cheek and she hastily wiped it away with her free hand.

Levi's heart wrenched. He knew that she was still grieving, but he had not seen her cry since Paul's death. Her tears tore at him.

He tucked Emma into his arms, letting her softly weep against his shoulder. He was again grateful for the privacy of the trees, where no buggy would drive by and no errant person out for a walk would spot them. He realized even if they were elsewhere, he would still want to comfort her. That he was too besotted to care what anyone thought.

There were times when compassion had to win over discretion.

It seemed too soon that Emma regained her composure. She gently pushed herself away from him. "I'm so sorry," she murmured. "I behaved inappropriately."

"You did no such thing," Levi assured. "You've faced so many changes recently and have been dealing with so much. I admire your strength."

"I don't feel strong," she admitted. "I feel as though I've come to depend on you so much."

She was so distraught, he couldn't admit that her words made his heart soar. It pleased him that she needed him. He wanted to be needed. He wanted to be wanted.

"I'm happy to be here for you. In any way I can. And, Emma…depending on others isn't a weakness. It takes real strength to accept help sometimes."

"Thank you for that." Her expression softened; some of her distress seemed to melt away. I really should be getting home," she said. "Amelia has probably started supper without me."

"I'll walk you."

"That's not necessary. You don't—"

"Emma." He gently lifted her chin with his fingers until she was looking into his eyes. "I want to. When are you going to accept the fact that I *want* to?" *I want to spend every minute with you*, he added silently.

"If you're sure."

"I'm sure."

As they headed toward the Ziegler farm, one thought was at the forefront of Levi's mind. Emma did not need the stress the vandal was causing.

Emma said he could go to the bishop only if he had proof. So, fine, then. He would have to catch Amos in the act.

There was only one way he could think of to do that.

CHAPTER NINETEEN

For three straight nights, Levi crept through the darkness and planted himself on the Zieglers' back porch. He was a light sleeper and was certain the barn animals—especially those noisy goats of Sadie's—would put up a fuss if a stranger disturbed them at night.

For three straight mornings, Levi awoke before sunrise, bundled up the blanket he'd wrapped himself in, and hurried home. Each time he wondered if he was being ridiculous, but he was unable to stop himself from returning.

On the fourth night, he awoke to the sound of the chickens clucking. He tossed the blanket aside and scrambled to his feet, instantly alert. It took only a moment for his eyes to adjust to the darkness. A shadowed figure, with a tall, bulky silhouette barely visible in the moonlight, was moving toward the tree line.

One of the goats bleated.

He heard a horse whinny in the distance.

Amos—and he now had no doubt it *was* Amos—must've come by buggy but hitched the horse to a tree or a post down the road.

Levi crept off the porch. Even though he was certain it was Amos, he couldn't figure out what the man was up to. As Levi's eyes adjusted to the darkness, he realized the man was stumbling a bit and also carried something in one hand. A pail? Levi couldn't tell. It was too big to be a paint pail.

He followed at a distance, sticking to the shadows on the edge of the yard. When Amos moved into the tree line, Levi was stumped. He hurried to catch up, afraid if Amos gained too much of a lead, he would lose him in the darkness.

As he got closer, a familiar scent tickled his nose. The stench of gasoline clung to the air. It became apparent that what Amos trudged along with was a gas can. Levi assumed Amos had not remembered to put the cap back on the can and was probably splashing himself as he walked along. Levi grimaced, knowing what a catastrophe it would be if Amos lit a match. The *dummkopf* was going to set himself on fire.

Levi no longer worried about Amos hearing him. The man was clearly intoxicated, not in possession of his senses—a herd of cattle could've probably stormed by and Levi doubted Amos would notice. The man kept stumbling. The can he was holding splashed its contents each time he pitched forward.

Amos stopped abruptly and swayed, as if his own movements were disorienting to him.

"Don't do it." Levi's voice carried through the empty woods.

The man twisted around to face him as Levi closed the distance between them. Moonlight shone down on his face, confirming what Levi had known all along.

"Don't do it," he ordered again. "I know you're angry with Emma. But think before you set fire to these trees. You could burn all of Pine Creek to the ground."

Amos laughed, a harsh, cold sound. "Do you think I care what becomes of this place? Let it all burn."

Levi edged closer.

Amos paid no attention to him as he splashed the gasoline all around. Levi jumped back to avoid being doused.

"Do you realize you've been splashing yourself as well?" Levi warned. "You light a match, and this grove is not the only thing that will go up in flames."

"This farm was to be mine," Amos said, as if not hearing a word from Levi's mouth. "*Mine*. You had no right to it." He dropped the can and began to dig in his pocket.

Levi knew he needed to distract him. As worried as he was about the maples, and as much as he disliked Amos, he could not bear to see the man burn himself alive.

"I had every right," Levi ground out as he strode closer. "Emma didn't deserve to be married to a man like you. You are nothing but a drunk, a disgrace to this community."

Amos froze.

Levi didn't revel in using the harsh words, but they grabbed Amos's attention. Levi wanted Amos's attention on *anything* other than the matches in his pocket.

He took another step forward and forced a laugh. "It's no wonder Bishop Yoder wants to put you under the *Meidung*. I've heard tell even your own *daed* wants you gone."

The words were cruel, but there was a whisper of truth to them. After the way Amos had been behaving in town, his own father had become fed up with him. Or at least, that's what the men were saying over coffee.

Amos lunged at him, but he was unsteady. Levi easily stepped out of the way, causing Amos to stumble to the ground. He landed on his knees, sucked in a few breaths, uttered words that an Amish man should never say. Slowly, he managed to stagger to his feet.

Despite all he had done, Levi felt sorry for the man. How had he sunk this low, drifted this far from God and his community? God had given man free will, and Amos had clearly chosen wrong far too many times.

God and the community would forgive, if only Amos would ask. But Levi knew that would not happen. Not anytime soon, given the state Amos was in.

"Go home." Levi did not want to fight Amos; it was not his way. But he couldn't allow him to start the fire. He feared for not only the maple trees, but the entire town, as well as Amos's life.

"I won't take orders from my *daed*," Amos said threateningly. "I won't take orders from the bishop. I surely am not going to take orders from *you*."

He charged Levi, but Levi was ready. He dodged to the side again, this time catching Amos by the arm, giving him a shove, and Amos fell to the ground, harder this time. Before he could get to his feet, Levi leaped onto his back. He quickly unhooked his own suspenders, wrapped them around Amos's wrists. He managed to tear Amos's suspenders off, too, and wrapped them around his ankles.

When the troublemaker was trussed up like a

turkey, Levi took a step back.

They'd needed proof.

And Levi was about to deliver.

• • •

"Were you expecting Levi?" Amelia asked. Emma shook her head. "He's here."

Emma frowned and glanced at the clock. The sun had only barely crested the sky. She had time to do little more than dress herself and put the coffee on. These early morning visits of his were becoming a habit she could get used to.

"I hope nothing has happened." She felt along the edges of her *kapp* to be sure she had secured it tightly enough. Her stocking feet padded across the floor as she walked to meet Levi at the door.

She pulled it open, her heart lurching when she noted the seriousness of his features.

"What brings you by so early?" she asked. "What's happened?"

He had shadows under his eyes and smudges of dirt on his neck and cheek. His clothes were wrinkled. Emma was certain they were the exact clothes he'd worn the day before, and it caused anxiety to skitter down her spine.

"May I come in?"

She stepped aside. "Of course. Would you like some *kaffi*?"

"Please," he accepted. "It would be much appreciated."

She led the way to the kitchen, and Levi dropped into a chair at the table. She poured him a cup of coffee while Amelia silently placed a strawberry-cream muffin on a plate.

"Would you like me to leave the room?" Amelia asked as she set the plate in front of their guest.

"*Nee*," Levi said. "What I have to say, you should hear as well. Sadie and Zeke?"

"Not up quite yet," Emma said.

She and Amelia sat down with their own cups of coffee. Emma wished whatever Levi had to say, no matter how bad, he would just get on with it. Her nerves were getting the better of her.

"Did something happen?" she tried again.

"It did," Levi admitted. "I finally have proof that Amos was behind sabotaging the farm."

Emma sat up straighter, her fingers laced around the hot mug of coffee. Her voice wobbled when she asked, "What sort of proof?"

Levi sheepishly admitted that he had been sleeping on their back porch for several nights. Emma blinked in surprise.

"You said if I could get proof, we could go to the bishop, so that's why I did it. It's a *goot* thing I did it," he said firmly. "Last night, Amos came back."

"You've been sleeping on my porch, trying to catch Amos," Emma said, stuck on that detail. Surprise battled with appreciation as she tried to grasp what he had done for her.

"*Jah*," Levi said. "Are you angry that I didn't let you know?"

She was about to say that he *should* have let her know, but Amelia's hand landed on her shoulder and gave a squeeze. She blew out a breath.

"As a matter of fact, I'm working on accepting

help these days," Emma said. "I'm trying to be a bit less independent."

Levi's eyebrows hitched.

Emma's lips quirked. "Don't look so surprised. I believe you gave me that very advice."

"Well, it was *goot* advice," Levi said lightly.

Emma cleared her throat and moved the conversation along. "You were obviously able to catch him."

"*Jah.*"

"What was he up to this time?" Amelia asked with a grim look on her face.

Levi's gaze darted to Emma. "He'd had a lot to drink. He drove up, hitched his buggy down the road a ways. When I first spotted him, he was heading into the woods."

"The woods?" Emma echoed with a frown. She couldn't fathom what he would be doing in the woods.

Levi grimaced. "He carried a gas can."

Both women gasped.

"He wouldn't!" Amelia scoffed in outrage.

"He was going to burn down the maples?" Emma's voice was tight. She clasped her fingers more tightly around the mug to keep her hands from shaking.

"It appears so."

"You stopped him," Amelia said quietly. "Thanks be to God you stopped him. If he had set fire to the trees, there is no telling how much damage could have been done or how long it would've taken to put the fire out."

"If he was using accelerant, and at that time of

night, when the fire would've gone unnoticed, he could've burned the whole town down." Emma slumped in her chair, the weight of what could've happened pressing in on her.

"I told him that. He said he didn't care. It is hard to say if he meant it or if it was the liquor talking."

"It seems I owe you another debt of gratitude," Emma said, the feeling of relief swelling up inside her.

Levi shook his head. "*Nee*. I was happy to finally catch him. He was sloppy, in pretty bad shape. He lunged at me but it didn't go well for him. When he hit the ground, I managed to restrain him, then loaded him into his own buggy and drove him, gas can and all, to the bishop's house this morning."

"What will happen?" Amelia asked. "Surely, after all he has done, he will be shunned. This sort of behavior is dangerous."

"That will be for the bishop and the church elders to decide," Levi said. "But *jah*, I assume he will be asked to leave Pine Creek. I asked him why he'd been doing this. He was upset because he feels the farm should be his. I guess if he couldn't have it, he felt you shouldn't have it, either."

Emma's head was swimming. She had been fairly sure it was Amos all along, but having proof that someone from their community was responsible still stung.

"If my *mamm* hadn't interfered," Amelia said with a sad shake of her head, "none of this would have happened."

"We mustn't blame Naomi," Levi said. "It's true that he probably wouldn't have targeted the farm if

Emma hadn't been brought to his attention, but he's caused plenty of trouble elsewhere. It was bound to catch up with him." Levi shook his head in disgust. "The bishop admitted that Amos's own mother had come to him with concerns. It appears she found boxes full of *Englisch* goods in their woodshed; she believes Amos has been stealing from *Englischers* and was just waiting for the right time to pawn everything. His *daed* is in denial, though, saying Amos is innocent of it all. I'm sure it's not sitting well with him that his wife went to the bishop, but she must have been feeling desperate."

"Because he's *not* innocent, is he?"

Emma twisted around to see Sadie standing in the doorway. Her *kapp* was askew, wisps of hair poked out from under it. It looked as if she had dressed quickly, trying to make herself presentable for their early-morning guest, but hadn't quite succeeded. She held her apron over her arm and wore a deep frown on her face.

"It was," Levi said gently.

"He killed my chickens," Sadie said, disbelief coloring her tone. "He hurt Margie." She wandered into the kitchen and slumped into a chair.

Emma reached over to squeeze her sister's hand. "I know it is hard to understand why he did what he did. We do not know the pain he felt in his life, or what provoked him to act in such a way. We must find it in our hearts to forgive him."

Sadie nodded, her voice still trembling. "I know. I will pray that God will help me to forgive. Right now, I don't feel very forgiving." She hung her head and fidgeted with the apron that was now draped over her lap. "I miss Spotty and Mitsy. I know they were just chickens, but they were *mine*. I raised them from tiny chicks."

"I know it doesn't change what has already happened," Levi said, "but at least it's over. He *canna* cause any more trouble."

"He almost burned down the maples." Sadie shook her head. "What kind of person would do that?"

"A very unhappy one," Amelia said decisively. "When people are suffering, they tend to do hurtful things. I do not pretend to know what he was feeling, but from what I've seen, he is a very unhappy man. May God's unending love heal his soul."

Emma slid her chair away from the table. She was finding it difficult to sit still. If not for Levi and God's amazing grace, everything could have been lost. Not only the trees, but the house, the barn, the entire farm.

They could have lost their lives.

"I should get breakfast started." She had to do something, had to keep busy. It was the only way to keep her mind free of the horrors of what might have been. "Levi, you'll stay, won't you?" She reached out and touched his arm, part of her feeling so overwhelmed by the realization he quite possibly had saved their lives. She simply wanted to collapse against him but wouldn't allow herself to do so.

He put his hand over hers, gave it a gentle squeeze, but shook his head regretfully. "I need to get back to help my *daed*." With a sheepish smile he admitted, "And then I might try to sneak in a few hours of rest. I have not managed much sleep the last few nights."

"All right then, I'll walk you out."

Emma followed Levi from the kitchen. She could hear Sadie and Amelia set to work.

As she stepped onto the front porch, she knew it was going to be a sweltering day. The sun had climbed up the horizon. The sky was a hazy gray. Not the sort that brought rain clouds, but the kind that brought incessant heat.

Levi stopped at the porch's edge. He turned to study her face. "Are you upset with me?" he asked.

His surprising question caught her off guard.

"How could you think such a thing?" After all he had done for her family?

"I saw your face when I said I'd been sleeping on your porch. I realized maybe I should not have done that without permission. You did say I could try to get proof, but I didn't let you know how I planned on going about that. I'm sure it wasn't proper." He scratched at the back of his neck. "I wasn't sure that I would catch Amos, so I didn't want to mention it in case my plan was in vain."

"I wasn't upset," Emma assured him. "I was simply surprised." She smiled. "I'm not sure *why* I'm surprised—it seems there is no end to what you are willing to do to help my family."

"Emma." He reached over and took her hand.

His touch was magnetic. He moved toward her and she felt drawn to him, so much so that she wanted to place herself in his arms, to relish the security she knew she would feel there. She took a step back, surprised by the magnitude of her feelings.

Confusion flashed across his face, and she

instantly felt guilt sizzle through her. He had been so kind. Yet she always seemed to repay him by behaving erratically.

He recovered quickly. "There *is* no end to what I would do. You and your family mean a great deal to me."

"You mean a great deal to us as well." She gazed up at him, studying his face. It was a face she knew well, knew by heart. But today something seemed different. The way he looked at her brought about a softness to his features. Was that love in his eyes? She was instantly overcome by a heated blush. She shouldn't be thinking something so presumptuous.

When his hand drifted across her cheek, she realized maybe she wasn't being presumptuous after all.

The magnetism she'd felt before was intensified by his touch. Without thought, she pressed up on her toes, and her mouth met his. What could have been little more than lips brushing against lips turned into something more powerful when one hand drifted to the small of her back, the other to the nape of her neck, holding her in place.

With nowhere to go—and no desire to go anywhere—she gave in to the feelings she'd been fighting for weeks. Maybe longer.

A *bang* from inside the house—probably a door caught by a gust of wind slamming closed—caused her to jump back. If one of her siblings, or even Amelia, happened to look out the window, she would be mortified.

Levi's hands slowly slid away. For a moment she couldn't look at him. When she did, he was studying her face.

"Was that okay? I should've asked before I—"

"It was fine," she quickly assured him. It was more than fine. It had been wondrous. Her knees were quivering and she felt a tremble in the pit of her stomach. She wanted nothing more than to wrap her arms around him and kiss him again.

She took a step back, trying to put some space between herself and the dangerous thought.

"Please don't be upset," Levi softly requested. "I wanted to kiss you, Emma. And I want for you to want to kiss me, too."

Did she want that?

Apparently, she did, because with a glance over her shoulder to make sure no one was peering out the window, she darted forward and kissed him again. This time, it was light and quick, but full of intent.

The smile it brought to his face was not a memory she would soon forget.

"*Mamm* is hoping you will come for supper tonight," he said, still grinning. "She's preparing a ham. Please say you'll come. Bring the rest of your family. It will make her happy."

"We would love to. It is kind of her to ask." She appreciated the thoughtful request. Would she be able to sit at the same table as Levi without her cheeks blazing? "Tell Diana that I will bring dessert."

Levi nodded as he started backing away. "See you this evening."

• • •

Levi needed to try to get a grip on his emotions. As he worked in the barn, he found himself humming. Humming of all things!

"Is it true?" Ivan asked as he strode into the barn. "I heard you caught Amos trying to burn down the Zieglers' trees."

Levi rose from the desk his *daed* kept in the backroom of the barn, his makeshift office. He had been going over some paperwork, checking over his *daed*'s books. *Daed* wasn't good about updating his cattle sales. Unlike his sons, he didn't see the point in it. It was one of the few things that Levi would change when he took over the farm. Someday. When his father was ready to retire and hand it down to him.

"*Jah*," Levi said. "It's true. How did you hear about it? It happened only this morning."

Ivan grinned. "News travels."

Levi laughed. "*Jah*, it sure does."

"His *daed* blames Amos's behavior on not having a wife." Ivan shook his head. "I heard that's why he was so anxious to take Naomi up on her offer. He feels that if Amos were married, he'd settle down. I heard he's none too happy about you and Emma stepping out together. Blames this last bit of trouble on Amos's broken heart."

"Broken heart?" Levi scoffed.

"That's the excuse his *daed* is using. Says Emma broke his heart and he's been beside himself."

Levi frowned. He didn't believe that was true. If anything, Emma had wounded only his pride. But it was not his place to accuse Marvin Stoltzfus of dishonesty. He was a father trying to keep his son out of trouble; the man's words were between himself and God. Levi was just relieved that Amos had been caught.

"Speaking of needing a wife," Ivan started, "how are things between you and Emma?"

"*Goot.*" Levi turned around and absently began flipping through sales receipts.

Ivan knew him well and chuckled at his discomfort. "How *goot*?"

Levi had a quick mental debate about confiding something so personal to his brother. The kiss should be between himself and Emma. Yet, he valued his brother's opinion and desperately needed some advice.

He twisted back around, the receipts forgotten. "I kissed her today."

Instead of the teasing he had assumed his brother would bestow upon him, Ivan simply nodded. "I'm happy for you. You've loved Emma a long time."

"I have had feelings for her as long as I can remember." He paused before saying, "I always thought I loved her. But I don't think I really knew what love was until just lately. Spending time with her again, I've gotten to know Emma in a way I've never known before. Sometimes, the way I feel about her"—he held his hands out to the side and then dropped them—"I don't even know how to describe it."

"*Jah.* Sounds like love to me." Apparently tired of the sappy talk, Ivan said, "*Mamm* said the Zieglers are coming to supper."

"Will you and Miriam be joining us?" Levi asked.

"Not tonight. Miriam has been so tired lately. I

like to see her rest in the evenings."

"Is everything okay?" Levi asked. "With the *bop-pli*, I mean?"

"Everything looks *goot*. The midwife said her energy should be returning soon. When it does, we will have to have a big family meal."

They visited for a while longer before Levi announced he needed to go in so he could clean up for supper.

Though he'd courted in the past, he'd never invited a girl to supper before. It wasn't for lack of his mother offering; there had just never been anyone special enough.

Emma fit in so well with his family. It was as if she were already part of it.

When she arrived, it was all he could do to contain a ridiculous grin. Having her here, with his family, was worth the wait. His mother ushered everyone into the kitchen where the table was set. She placed Emma directly across from him, which suited him just fine.

His father, usually a quiet man, easily became wrapped up in conversation with Ezekiel. The boy was curious about cattle and wanted to know about the herd.

His mother chatted with the women, jumping from one topic to the next.

He joined the conversation intermittently, but for the most part he was happy to sit back and watch Emma. He enjoyed the lilting sound of her voice; he warmed at her laughter. When their eyes met across the table every now and again, his heart jolted at what he hoped was a flicker of adoration in her gaze.

When dessert was served, his *mamm* raved over it.

"This peanut butter pie is absolutely *wunderbaar*."

"Thank you. It was my *mamm*'s recipe," Emma confessed.

"Barbara was an excellent cook," *Mamm* praised. "Always the first to bring a casserole to a family in need. She would be so pleased with the three of you."

The three Ziegler siblings looked melancholy for a moment, but *Mamm* quickly moved the conversation along.

"You know," she said, leaning in conspiratorially, "she and I used to tease each other about the two of you." Her gaze sparkled with amusement as it bounced between Emma and Levi. "You were so close when you were children, spent so much time together."

"*Jah*," *Daed* agreed with a chortle. "You two were like each other's shadows. Where one was, the other always followed."

Emma wore a soft smile, as if her mind had wandered to the past. To simpler times. Following Ezekiel's birth—and her mother's death—Levi knew she'd had to grow up quickly, bear a lot of responsibility. Running through the fields and traipsing through the woods became distant memories.

"We always thought the two of you would wed." A wistful smile appeared on his mother's lips. "I know Barbara would be so pleased."

Levi glanced at Emma and found she was already looking at him. A hint of sadness tinged her expression, but something else as well. He hoped it pleased her that this was something her mother would've wanted.

"I never knew that," she said to *Mamm*.

"Some things are just meant to be," *Mamm* said.

Yes, Levi thought. *God willing, some things are just meant to be.*

CHAPTER TWENTY

The sweet aroma of strawberries melded enticingly with the scent of rhubarb. Emma stood in front of the stove, stirring an enormous pot of jam that was being prepared for canning.

"My *mamm* feels terrible about the trouble she riled up with Amos," Amelia said as she reached for another piece of rhubarb to dice. "I think she's horrified that she tried to marry you off to a man with such loose morals. She shouldn't have been so hasty in trying to find you a groom."

"You shouldn't have troubled her with the news," Emma said. "It wasn't her fault. She couldn't have known."

Amelia gave her an arch look. "I didn't tell her. You can thank her friend Judith for that—she's been sending *Mamm* letters with updates. *Mamm* knows all about Amos, you and Levi, and she thinks she knows all about me, too."

"What about you?" Emma sensed a note of frustration in Amelia's tone.

"That I'm hopeless." Amelia forced a shrug.

"You're not hopeless," Emma said with a twinkle in her eye, "you're just stubborn."

"I guess I take after my *mamm* more than I care to admit," Amelia said lightly. "Not only can my stubbornness match hers, but I've been honing my matchmaking skills while living in Pine Creek."

Emma laughed. "Your matchmaking skills?

Please explain that to me."

Amelia flashed a sly grin. "I assume you know Ruth Stoltzfus."

"*Jah*." Emma knew she was a distant relative of Amos's. She was a soft-spoken woman with gray hair and an ample figure who worked at the Pine Cone Café and had for as long as Emma could remember. Her husband had died shortly after they were married. They hadn't any children and she never remarried. "I know Ruth. What of her?"

"Leroy came into the café last week," she said, mentioning the much older man Judith had tried to match her up with earlier in the summer. "He looked so lonely, and I told Ruth so. She took pity on him and invited him to supper with her family— she lives with her *schweschter*—and it turns out they had a fine time. He's been back for supper several times since."

"How nice for both of them." Emma was genuinely happy for the pair.

"I might work in the back," Amelia said with a smirk, "but I see plenty of what goes on up front. I hear chatter. Rachael's so sure her cousin Jakob is too immature to marry, but I don't think that's the problem. He's smitten with Daisy Miller. I told Daisy so when she came into the café one day, and though she said she wasn't interested because he's too much of a goof, I convinced her to let him try to prove himself. He just didn't know what to do with himself while he waited for her to come around. There was a singing last weekend at the Graber farm."

Emma shook her head in amusement. "Let me

guess. Daisy decided to give Jakob a chance."

"They took some time to talk there. He asked if he could drive her home from church next Sunday and she agreed." Amelia looked pleased with herself.

"You're enjoying this, aren't you?" Emma laughed. "You find it pleasing to spoil your *mamm*'s plans." Both men were bachelors whom Judith had introduced Amelia to as prospects for herself.

"*Nee*," Amelia said with a gentle shake of her head. "It is not spoiling her plans that I'm growing fond of. I enjoy knowing that these couples are experiencing a bit of happiness."

She was quiet for a moment, and Emma knew she was thinking of Gideon.

Amelia shook off the melancholy moment. "It won't be long before our Sadie is courting."

Emma winced at the thought. She was not ready to see her sister stepping out, but Amelia was right—time moved swiftly.

Emma moved away from the stove to let her concoction simmer. "It was strange, listening to Diana speak of my mother the other night. She's been gone so long, and *Daed* didn't really talk about her. I think it was too painful."

"It sounds as if she and Diana were close."

"I had forgotten how close. They often did their canning together after fall harvest." Just as she and Amelia were beginning to do. "I can recall them quilting and preparing meals together." Her mind wandered, thinking of days when her mother and Diana would sit at the kitchen table, drinking coffee while she and Levi would sometimes cause mischief. More often than not, though, their mothers would put them to work. She could fondly recall traipsing through the woods with pails. There was always an abundance of blueberries and chokecherries waiting to be picked.

"It sounded like your *mamm* thought you two were a *goot* pair," Amelia said with a wry smile.

"We were children," Emma reminded. "It was all in jest."

Even so, the thought did warm her heart. She had noted Levi's bemused smile at supper when Diana spoke of the past. Meanwhile, she had barely been able to get his kiss out of her head. She wondered if he thought of it often as well.

She took a look at the recipe, though she knew it by heart. Thoughts of Levi had become far too distracting lately. Not only was she thinking of the kisses they'd shared, but she couldn't seem to stop thinking about when she would be able to kiss him again.

"You look lost in thought," Amelia mused.

Emma snapped out of her reverie and returned to the stove to check the fruit mixture. "I was just thinking. Wondering, actually, who will you be finding a beau for next?"

"It's funny that you should ask," Amelia teased. "Because I've decided to use my matchmaking skills to give my favorite couple a nudge."

Emma narrowed her eyes at her cousin. Was that what all this talk about romance had been about? "What are you up to?"

"Levi will be here shortly."

"Amelia, we have so much work to do today," Emma scolded.

"The work will get done. Sadie will help me with the jam." Amelia wiped her hands on her apron. "Fall harvest will be upon us soon. Once it is, there will be very little free time."

"When will he be here?" Emma asked.

"Soon," Amelia said evasively. "He suggested the two of you take a walk through the woods. He said you frequently did that when you were younger. It would be a fine time to check on the trees."

"You're sending us off alone?"

"Is there a reason I shouldn't? Are you trying to tell me that you two are not trustworthy?" Amelia teased.

Emma swatted her with a towel. "You know we are." Emma was tempted to tell Amelia about the sweet kiss they had shared but decided not to. That should remain private, between her and Levi.

"Well, then, I see no problem. Truth be told, most couples sneak off every now and again. It's to be expected."

Emma laughed. "Expected by whom? Surely not your *mamm*? And surely Judith Graber would not approve."

"I don't suspect Judith will show up on your property again, so I don't foresee her having a problem with this. Of course," Amelia said airily, "I'm sure that Zeke and Sadie would gladly tag along if you'd like them to."

"That's a terrible idea," Sadie said from the doorway. "I'm helping with the jam, and Levi's here already and brought some more lumber for Zeke. Zeke wants to make a climbing platform for the goats. They're getting bored in their pen. They need more obstacles to keep them entertained."

"Zeke has gotten *goot* with his hands," Emma said. "I think I'll go see what it is he plans to build."

"She's really going down to the barn to see her sweetheart." Sadie's tone was smug as she loudly whispered to their cousin.

Emma heard them both giggle as she left the kitchen. She shook her head but her lips twitched in a smile.

She found Levi beside the goat pen with Ezekiel. The two nosy goats stood on the other side of the fence watching the pair. Emma took her lead from the goats and slowed her pace. Watching Levi with her brother always stirred something within her—his patience and commitment were so admirable. They were the sort of traits she hoped for in a husband, in a father to the children she hoped to have someday.

She allowed herself a few more moments of observation before interrupting them. Levi had his back to her. Sadie would smirk if she knew how Emma was admiring the breadth of his shoulders, the contour of the muscles she could see past his rolled-up shirtsleeves. It was easy to get lost in thoughts of Levi's arms around her. The few times he had held her, she'd felt so safe. So secure. She forced her feet to move before her mind took off, skipping down a path that was indecent.

"What do we have here?" she asked as she closed in on them.

Levi grinned when he saw her. "We're not sure yet. I told Zeke I had some extra lumber. It's mostly scraps, but there's some larger pieces, too. It's up to him to decide what he wants to do with it."

Ezekiel studied the pile of wood spread out on the ground. Emma could practically hear the gears of his brain setting to work.

"I have a few ideas," he finally said.

Levi handed him a tool belt. "I *canna* wait to see what you come up with. Anything else you might need should be in the back of the buggy. Help yourself."

Ezekiel nodded absently as he narrowed his eyes and studied the pile of wood.

Emma began to back away and Levi followed.

"I think the boy has found his calling," Levi said. "Did he show you the hutch?"

"He did." Emma smiled as she recalled the elaborate creation. Ezekiel had produced a new hutch in a few days' time. His second attempt was more complex than his first had been. "I told him the rabbit will feel like royalty. Sadie was giddy with excitement. Now she's searching for the perfect rabbit."

Levi laughed as they wandered toward the tree line. "With the hutch complete, Zeke has it in his head that the goats need more things to play on. I think really, he was looking for an excuse to build something."

Emma thought it was a bit of both. The goats did become easily bored. They liked to climb on things and they liked to play. It was to her advantage that Ezekiel's new hobby could help them out with that.

"It's a useful skill to master. Thank you for being so patient with everything."

"I enjoy my time with him."

"Sadie has been pestering him about expanding the goat pen," Emma admitted. "Rachael gave her recipes for making soap out of goat's milk, and Sadie has experimented with a few batches. They've turned out well."

"So will she need more goats to milk?" Levi guessed.

"*Jah*. Sadie is a little entrepreneur. Who would've guessed?" Emma smiled, admiring Sadie's ambition. "She's hoping the Pine Cone Lodge will sell them in the gift shop. If not, the *Englisch* are always around checking out the farmers markets in the area. I'm sure she'll have no problem making a go of it."

"I would be happy to help Zeke with enlarging the pen. I'll take a look at it when we get back, figure out the best way to go about it."

"I didn't mention it because I was expecting you would offer to help," Emma said. "I hope you didn't take it that way. Still, I am grateful." She looked him in the eye. "Thank you for your help."

"You are welcome," Levi assured her. "But I just might have to charge Sadie for my services. I'm thinking a sample of cheese every once in a while."

"I think we can manage that. I might even throw in a batch of fudge here and there," Emma teased.

"Even better."

All teasing aside, Emma said, "I do wish I had a way to repay you."

"Spending time with you is all the payment I need."

She gave his shoulder a nudge. "Levi. I never knew you were such a charmer."

"I speak only the truth."

His voice was low, and it warmed her insides. Her heart gave a little flutter when she caught his eye.

The way he looked at her, it reminded her of the way Ivan looked at Miriam. She had longed to have someone look at her just that way.

Could it be that Levi was God's plan for her life? Was that why he had placed Levi in her path the day Naomi tried to tie her to Amos?

Distracted by her thoughts, and the look in Levi's eye, she tripped over a fallen branch that stuck up, tangling in the hem of her dress. Though she stumbled, Levi did not let her fall. He caught her as her body slammed into his.

"Are you all right?"

She nodded as his hands held her upright.

Thoughts of their shared kiss washed over her. How easy it would be to kiss him again. Levi's arms circled her waist, holding her steady, his lips oh so close. If she was not mistaken, he was overtaken with the same thought, seeing as his gaze drifted to her mouth. Seconds floated by, neither of them daring to move. Oh, how she longed to kiss him again.

The *whack* of a hammer against nail made her jump. The repetition let them know her brother had set to work.

Levi dropped his hands from her waist, allowing her to slip away. She glanced over her shoulder. Ezekiel had his back to them, no doubt lost in his imagination as he worked out his project. But it would've been all too easy for him to turn around.

Her cheeks flushed. It would be inappropriate for them to kiss with her brother watching. How horrifying that would be.

Levi apparently came to the same conclusion.

He cleared his throat as they began to walk again.

"I'm anxious to see what he comes up with."

"As am I." Ezekiel's project was the last thing on Emma's mind, but it was a safe topic, so she was happy for the distraction.

As they reached the edge of the maples, the familiar scent greeted Emma. Damp foliage and the sharp, crisp smell of a forest.

"I haven't taken the time to walk through here in so long," she admitted. "I love the forest in the fall. If I have time, I like to enjoy a cup of *kaffi* on the porch. The air is always so refreshing, the changing leaves just so beautiful. Those are my favorite mornings."

"Sounds *wunderbaar*," Levi said, his tone husky.

She paused, enjoying the view, thinking about the future, and unable to stop from picturing herself and Levi at the center of it all.

• • •

"What's on your mind?" Levi asked Emma as they followed a worn footpath through the trees. She wore a wistful look and he was curious, wanting to know what brought it about.

"I was thinking of the syrup. It's so much work to process, but I enjoy it so much."

"We've always had a *goot* time." Levi's family had helped Paul for as long as he could remember. His mother and Emma would prepare good food; the men would watch the fires. Over the years there had been plenty of laughs. It was always time well spent.

"It will seem so strange without *Daed* here." She

shuddered as she turned to face Levi. "I *canna* stop thinking of how close we came to losing it all. If you hadn't stopped Amos the other night…" It wasn't as if the trees could simply be replanted. They would have to grow for many decades before maturing enough to tap for syrup.

Amos could've destroyed everything, with no chance for years of rebuilding what was lost.

"Don't think about it. God was watching over you."

Emma smiled. "*You* were watching over me as well."

"Fortunately, you no longer have to worry about Amos. I heard that he left Pine Creek of his own accord."

"I suppose that shouldn't surprise me."

They began walking again, weaving around the trees.

Levi cleared his throat, alerting Emma that there was something he had to say.

"The taxes are due tomorrow," he said carefully. He hadn't wanted to press her on the matter, but with the deadline looming, he couldn't help himself. "Are you going to make it? If you're short, I can help. I have money that I've set aside to buy my own place, but I'd gladly give it to you—"

"*Nee*," she said firmly. "That's not necessary. I won't take your money."

"But—"

"Levi, I have it handled," she said. "I have almost the full amount at home. I spoke to Marta Weaver and she let me know that my syrup has done well. *Very* well. We've made arrangements, and I plan on stopping at her shop tomorrow. She has a payment for me that will cover what I'm short on the taxes, with even a bit to spare."

Relief filled her eyes, and perhaps just a bit of pride.

"That's *wunderbaar*, Emma," he said. "I'm proud of you."

She smiled shyly. "*Danki*. I was afraid for a while, but it feels so *goot* to have accomplished this on my own."

They slowed as Levi helped her over a fallen tree.

"*Mamm* was so happy you came to supper the other night," he confessed.

"I had a lovely time." Emma smiled and slid a glance his way. "It is so rare that anyone talks about my *mudder*. I enjoyed hearing of her. She's been gone so long that I've forgotten what she looks like. I don't remember the sound of her voice. I have faint memories of things we did together, but those are fading as well."

She stopped walking and rested her hand against a maple, letting her fingers brush over the rough bark. "I *canna* help but wonder how long it will be before I forget my *daed*. Every day I think of him, picture his face, imagine his voice. I know he is in a better, happier place, with *Mamm* and God. It's selfish of me to wish he were here, but I do."

"It's not selfish," Levi assured. "Of course you miss him. I don't believe you will forget him. You were so young when your *mamm* passed."

She nodded. "I was. I'm grateful for the memories I do have. Sadie has far fewer, and Zeke did not get to know her at all."

"They are so fortunate to have you."

"And I was fortunate to have Diana," Emma admitted. "I could barely scramble an egg. She brought me into her kitchen, into her home. She taught me so much."

"She considers you family."

"I feel the same way about her," Emma assured him.

Levi's heart pounded as he reached for Emma's hand. She let him take it. He'd asked Amelia for some time alone with Emma, and she'd been happy to arrange it. There was something he desperately wanted to talk to Emma about.

Now that he had the chance, he was having a hard time finding the words.

What was it about this woman that caused him to fumble so?

He loved her. That's what it was.

He had always harbored feelings for her, yes. But these new feelings over the past few weeks, these were real, true love.

Her opinion mattered to him more than anyone else's. Because of that, because of his fear of rejection, he had a hard time getting his words out. But he must. He'd remained quiet for far too long.

"What is it?" Emma's tone was gentle as she studied his face. "You look as if you're lost in thought."

He forced a smile, trying to appear more light-hearted than he felt. What he was about to ask would change his life—both their lives—in an irreversible fashion. He hesitated, wondering if he should give Emma more time. Glancing over his shoulder, he realized they had walked for a while, meaning Ezekiel was now out of sight. If Emma rejected him, he could wallow in the woods for a while to gather himself.

He looked into her eyes and got lost in their familiar depths.

"Emma." He squeezed her hand, drawing strength from her that she didn't even realize she was giving. "I would like to marry you. If you feel the same, I plan to speak with Bishop Yoder. I would like for him to announce it in the *banns*."

Her eyelids fluttered, her expression unreadable. Her fingers trembled slightly in his hand while she remained silent.

He fought the urge to take a step away from her. The idea that she was about to reject him was almost more than he could bear. He should've waited. This, *this* was why he'd always been afraid of telling her his feelings.

Her rejection would rip out his heart.

"You want to speak to Bishop Yoder?" Her tone was careful, even.

"*Nee*. Perhaps it's too soon," he backtracked. He gave himself a mental lashing for not taking things slower. He had plenty of time to speak to the bishop before the fall wedding season took place. He shouldn't pressure her.

"*Nee*?" Her mouth drooped into a frown.

Now he found he was the one hesitating again. Was that disappointment etched across her face?

"What would you like?" he asked. Perhaps that was how he should've approached the topic in the first place.

She pulled in a breath, as if to steady herself. "I

think," she said slowly, "that I would like to be your wife."

"You would?" Had all of his worrying truly been in vain? The Bible proclaimed that one should not worry. He should've known better.

She laughed at his surprise. "I wasn't expecting you to ask just yet, but *jah*, I believe I would."

"Okay." The grin that broke out across his face was so huge, it made his cheeks ache. "I would like that very much."

"Amelia and Sadie will be so excited," Emma said. "Ezekiel, too."

"As will my family."

Emma smiled happily. It lifted his spirits to see a smile on her face. They had been too few over the past year. He silently vowed to find a way to make this lovely woman smile every day. He could hardly wait for the day that Emma became his wife.

"Levi?" Her query was soft, tentative.

"What is it?"

Rosy splotches bloomed on her cheeks. "Do you think you could kiss me now?"

He laughed, but it was cut short as he pulled her close. "I think I certainly can."

CHAPTER TWENTY-ONE

Emma stared at the stacks of bills on the table and wondered how this could have happened. How could she be so close? Yet due to unforeseen circumstances, she was just too far away. With the hay sale, gift shop sales, Saturday Market, and Weavers' Candy Shoppe, she should've had enough.

Oh, the Weavers.

She placed her face in her hands and let out a miserable groan.

Stella Murphy, the kindly—if somewhat nosy—*Englisch* owner of the consignment store next door, had seen Emma pacing in front of the candy shop. She'd hurried out to let her know that she'd received a call earlier that morning from Marta Weaver. There had been some sort of family emergency, and they were closing the candy shop but didn't know for how long.

So now Emma was worried about the Weavers as well as her own family.

"I would have had enough," she said to the empty kitchen, her tone holding equal amounts of sadness and disbelief. When she last spoke to Marta, the woman had given her an estimate of her sales. Added in with her other sales, Emma had felt a sense of relief. She would have enough, and some left over.

But not now. Not yet, when she didn't have access to it.

What was she going to do?

When she'd passed Levi's, she'd noted that his buggy was missing, as he was surely at work already. His offer from the night before had speared through her mind. She hadn't wanted his help. For once, she wanted him to see she could take care of herself. Now that she had no way to reach out to him, it wasn't even an option to contemplate.

She stifled a sob. They were going to lose the farm that should rightfully be Ezekiel's one day. She felt like an utter failure as a big sister. No, she felt like a failure as an adult.

"Emma?"

She dropped her hands to the table as Sadie padded across the kitchen on bare feet. A look of worry marred her young face, and Emma hated that she had put it there. All her life, she'd felt responsible for her siblings—knowing she had failed them broke her heart. How was she going to tell them that they were going to lose their home?

How could she marry Levi now? And where would they live? His father wasn't ready to give up his farm. The day on the swings, Levi had said he hadn't saved up quite enough for his own place yet.

Would they have to move away and live with Aunt Naomi?

When Emma had told Sadie and Ezekiel about Levi's proposal last night, they had whooped with joy. Ezekiel seemed especially elated at the prospect of not being the only male in the house come fall.

Now Emma would have to tell them that it was not to be.

And worse, that their world was crumbling around them.

"What's wrong?" Sadie slipped into the chair across the table from Emma. She glanced at the neatly organized piles of bills on the table. "I have never seen someone look so sad over so much money."

Emma tried to shoo her away. "It's nothing for you to worry about."

Sadie narrowed her eyes at her sister. When she spoke, her tone was the firmest she'd ever taken with Emma. "Something is wrong. I'm not a child anymore and you don't need to protect me; I'm almost seventeen. Tell me what's going on."

Emma didn't want to burden her, yet what was the point in putting it off? She'd have to delve into the truth sooner rather than later when the county came after their home.

She took a deep breath, then said, "*Daed* got a bit behind on property taxes."

Sadie's gaze slid to the stacks on the table, then cut back to Emma. "How far behind?"

Emma named the amount. "There were back taxes, and fees, and interest."

Sadie's eyes widened. "Goodness. I see why you're so upset. That's a lot of money to part with."

"The reason I'm upset," Emma said slowly, "is that despite what I've managed to scrounge up, I don't have enough to pay off the bill."

Sadie was quiet a moment, as if she needed some time to process what she was hearing. Finally, she asked, "What does that mean?"

"It means that unless I come up with the money

by the end of the day, the county is going to take the farm," Emma said flatly.

"No!" Sadie gasped. "Emma, they can't."

She nodded. "They can, and they will."

Sadie glanced at the money, then back at Emma again. "Then we just need to come up with the rest of the money. How much are you short?"

"A lot," Emma admitted.

"How much?" Sadie demanded.

Emma felt ashamed at this detail, but she knew Sadie wouldn't be deterred. "Five hundred and sixty-three dollars."

"I see." Sadie tapped her fingers against the table for a moment, her expression calm. Emma was surprised at the resolve Sadie showed as she slid from her seat. She left the kitchen without saying another word.

Knowing she had just broken her sister's heart, Emma didn't have the energy to call after her.

She was surprised when Sadie returned only a few minutes later carrying a cardboard shoebox.

"I want to help," she said simply.

When she took the lid off, Emma felt her eyes pop. Bills of a variety of denominations filled the box.

"How... Wh-Where..." Emma spluttered. "How did you get so much money?"

Her sister shrugged. "Emma, I've been selling eggs since I was ten, selling my goat cheese for years. What did you think I was doing with all the money? Wasting it on pretty fabric and licorice from the candy shop?"

Emma realized that yes, she had thought that.

But only because she hadn't realized how much her little sister was making.

"Let me help," Sadie said. "Let me contribute the last portion."

"Absolutely not." Emma shook her head. "I can't let you do that."

Even as she said the words, though, she knew it wasn't true. She needed the money, but habit had her refusing. Still, Levi had taught her that there was strength in accepting help.

Sadie jabbed a fist into her hip, an uncharacteristically defiant gesture for her. "*Jah*, you can. You just told me that we're going to lose our home. I'm not a child anymore, Emma—I *want* to do this. I want to help. You've been taking care of Zeke and me for as long as I can remember. Let me help you.

"I want to stay here where my goats have their pen and my chickens have their coop." She gestured toward the box. "It's only money, Emma; I can make more. But this is our home and it's not replaceable. I live here, too, and should have some say in the matter. Please, let me help."

"D-Do you actually have enough?" Emma hesitantly asked.

"I have enough and then some. I'll have enough left over to buy all the pretty fabric and licorice I could ever want," Sadie said wryly. "You need to let me do this."

It was the determination in Sadie's plea that swayed her. Sadie was right; she wasn't a child anymore.

"You came up with most of the money on your own," Sadie continued. "Let me contribute the last portion. *Please*."

"Okay." Emma whispered the word. Her eyes stung with tears—tears of relief. "Thank you."

"*Nee*, Emma. Thank you." Sadie reached for her hand. "Thank you for giving up so much of your life to take care of us. Thank you for finally letting me help."

Emma could only nod.

"Now, let's get this money counted out," Sadie said. "I think we'll both feel better once you get to the courthouse and get this bill paid."

"*Jah*," Emma said with a laugh, "that is the truth."

"Would you like me to go to town with you?" Sadie asked.

"*Nee*, you and Zeke were planning on picking blueberries. I won't be gone long."

An hour later, she hitched up Ginger and drove into town with a lightness in her heart. She actually felt lighter for having taken Sadie's money, knowing she was no longer alone in running the farm and that Sadie had given the money willingly. With Sadie's help, she had done it.

She had saved the farm.

She strode purposefully into the courthouse, but her exhilaration was quickly replaced with confusion.

Emma blinked at the woman on the other side of the counter at the county office. She couldn't have possibly heard her correctly.

"Please check your records," Emma said. "They *canna* possibly be right."

A wrinkle of irritation dented the other woman's forehead. "I assure you, our records are correct.

Your back taxes were paid in full this morning. You don't owe a penny."

Emma shook her head. "I have the money right here. I didn't pay yet."

"Excuse me." An older lady scooted up to the window, subtly nudging aside the younger woman who'd been helping Emma. "I couldn't help but overhear. You said you're trying to make a payment on the Ziegler property?"

"Yes," Emma confirmed. "I had until today to pay. But this woman refuses to take my money."

"That's because you don't owe anything," the older woman said.

Emma fought down a growl of frustration. She had hoped that with this lady, she would actually get somewhere.

"You see," the woman continued, "your bill was paid this morning as soon as we opened. I recognized the name because I took the money myself. Took it from a good-looking Amish fellow. Your husband, perhaps?"

A good-looking Amish fellow?

My husband?

Ach, nee!

"Maybe he forgot to tell you he was paying the bill so you wouldn't have to come in," the lady continued. "He was really nice. So polite."

"Is that so?" Emma asked through clenched teeth. "Was he about this tall?" She raised her hand to approximately Levi's height. "With dark hair? Pale blue eyes?"

The woman smiled. "Oh, yes. I remember the eyes for sure. Such pretty eyes."

"Thank you for your assistance," Emma said. She pivoted and scurried out of the building, her heart pounding as frustration coursed through her. How could Levi do this to her? First, all those years ago he had to stick his nose in her business with Darren and made a mess of things. He talked his brother into *not* marrying her. And now this?

"He had no right," she muttered under her breath. "I told him I did not want his help. I *canna* believe he did this."

Ginger let out a concerned whinny as Emma neared.

"Don't mind me, girl," Emma said to the horse. "I'm not mad at *you*." She clambered into the buggy. Instead of calming down on the way home, she found she was simply getting more worked up.

Why was it that Levi couldn't trust her to take care of anything?

What right did he have to always take over?

Why couldn't he just trust her?

Or at least *talk* to her. But no, he yet again did what he pleased without discussing it with her.

She was still fuming when she returned home.

After caring for Ginger, she marched into the house. She and Levi had plans to go to the river today. Glancing at the clock hanging on the kitchen wall, she realized he was supposed to be there any moment. If he thought she was spending today, or any other day, at the river with him, he was wildly mistaken.

She knew she needed to keep herself busy or she would lose her mind. Ezekiel had been working so hard all summer. Custard was his favorite dessert, so she decided she should make some to have with the evening meal. She marched outside and headed toward the chicken coop for the required eggs.

Even the friendly Silkies scurried out of her way when she entered their domain. She let herself into the henhouse and earned an annoyed squawk from Gretel.

"What have you got for me, girl?"

The hen gave her a distrustful look, clearly not impressed with Emma's tone. She moved toward the chicken, and though Gretel made another sound of protest, she still scooted out of Emma's way, and Emma was rewarded with an egg. She moved on to the other nests and found three more. She gently nestled them into the basket she carried.

The unmistakable sound of a buggy rolling down the lane reached Emma's ears. She leaned against the wall of the chicken coop, her chest heaving in frustration. She didn't trust herself to talk to Levi right now. If he knew what was good for him, he would be on his way.

Of course, he had no idea what was in store for him, so after pounding on the farmhouse door, he stuck around.

He shouted Emma's name as he moved toward the barn.

His voice grew louder as he neared the chicken coop.

Emma clenched her teeth and prepared herself to confront her *former* friend.

· · ·

Levi wondered if he had gotten the time wrong. It wasn't like Emma to keep him waiting. He knew her siblings and Amelia had other plans for the day. Ginger was grazing in the pasture, so he was sure Emma must be around somewhere.

He'd pounded on the front door. He'd even taken the liberty of letting himself into the foyer to call her name. There had been no response. He glanced toward the stand of maples, wondering if she'd gone for a walk. He was so excited to find her, couldn't wait to share the good news with her of how her farm was saved.

He had stopped at Weavers' Candy Shoppe this morning, hoping to leave a note with Marta, asking Emma to meet him for lunch to celebrate paying off her taxes. He'd been surprised to see the closed sign on the door. As he stood there, contemplating what to do, Stella from next door had poked her head out of her shop. She'd seen him with Emma a time or two and had figured he was looking for her. To his surprise, she told him that the Weavers were away, and that yes, Emma had stopped by first thing that morning. Stella said Emma seemed terribly distraught, though she hadn't been sure why.

Levi had a hunch that *he* knew why. He had made a quick loop through town, hoping to spot her. He'd been sure to pass all the usual places she shopped, but there was no sign of her buggy. He had to get to work, so feeling he had no other recourse, next he had stopped at the bank to withdraw cash from his savings. Then he'd gone to the courthouse where, sure enough, Emma's bill had remained unpaid.

What a relief it had been to pay it for her. And as her future husband, it had not only felt right, but necessary. Now if only he could find her so he could tell her what he'd done.

He cupped his hands around his mouth and shouted once more. "Emma?"

The commotion he was making flustered the Silkies. Their gentle clucking was the only response he received.

He was about to turn around, plant himself on the front porch, but he was met with an unexpected greeting.

Splat.

He let out a very unmanly sound of surprise. Glancing down, he saw the slimy remnants of an egg plastered to his chest. Bits of shell stuck to the mucky mess. He stumbled backward, even more surprised by the look of pure outrage that marred Emma's pretty face. She stalked out of the chicken coop, unkempt hair shooting past the hem of her crooked *kapp*.

"Don't you *dare* take another step," she warned. She held a basket of eggs in one hand, a single egg in the other. "I have an entire basket…and I'm not afraid to use them. This time, I'll be sure to have much better aim."

He held his hands up. "What is going on?"

She shook her head and glared at him. "How could you?" she asked slowly, deliberately.

He wanted to ask how could he *what*? But he was pretty sure he knew.

Instead he hazarded to ask, "Why are you so angry?"

That, apparently, was the wrong thing to say.

"W-Why?" she sputtered. Her eyes widened and heat colored her cheeks. "Because you are a bully, Levi Bontrager. That's why! I didn't ask for your money. I didn't need it. In fact, I clearly remember telling you I didn't *want* it."

A bully? Oh, that hurt.

He winced and said, "Emma, I care about you. I...thought you'd be pleased. I was just trying to help."

"I didn't *ask* for your help." She heaved out a breath. "You didn't bother to ask me if I wanted help. You just took over like you have a habit of doing. First with Darren all those years ago, then with Ivan. With Naomi. Now this?" She shook her head. "You clearly don't think me capable."

"It's not that—"

"*Ach*," she said, "but it is. I think you should leave," she added. "And it would probably be best if you didn't come back."

The feeling in his heart was pure anguish. "You... you *canna* mean that."

She nodded briskly. "I do. I do mean it."

"B-But we're getting married," he said feebly. Disbelief slammed into him. What was happening here? How had his good deed gone so terribly wrong? He reached out to her.

"*Nee*." She backed away from him, and he felt his world crashing in. "I *canna* imagine being married to someone who doesn't trust my judgment. I won't marry someone who goes behind my back."

He wanted to argue, tell her he loved her, but he wasn't sure what more he could say.

"I'm sorry, Emma. I'm sorry I'm such a *bully*," he said in frustration. "I thought it would be a nice surprise to celebrate our engagement. I just wanted to do something nice to help you."

"I didn't ask for your help!" she cried.

Frustrated, heartbroken, and afraid he'd say something harsh that he couldn't take back, he pivoted then and strode to his buggy. In a blur of emotions he left the Ziegler farm, wondering if he were ever going to be welcome there again.

When he returned home, he nearly crashed into Ivan, who was coming out of the front door.

Ivan took a step back, realizing Levi was covered in splattered eggs and broken shells. He burst into robust laughter.

"What's happened to you?" he demanded.

"Emma," Levi said. His voice was flat, a cover for the tumultuous emotions roaring within him. He still couldn't wrap his head around how things had gone so terribly wrong. Hadn't she *just* said she was going to try to accept more help? Well, she was doing a terrible job of it!

Ivan's laughter faded but his grin remained. "What did you do to deserve that woman's ire this time?"

"I helped her out," Levi said a bit bitterly. Ivan raised a brow in question. Levi sighed and told him what he'd done.

With a frown, Ivan said, "It sounds like you did overstep."

"To save her farm," Levi ground out. "How was I to know she'd found the money? Stella Murphy made it sound as if Emma had given up."

"Perhaps she just needs time to cool off," Ivan offered.

Levi shrugged. "I'm not sure it'll matter. She called me a bully, said she doesn't think she can marry me. And you know what? Maybe I don't want to marry someone who is so stubborn. So *prideful*."

Did he mean that? He swiped another chunk of eggshell off his chest. Yes, in that moment he sure did.

• • •

Emma had thought she would need to hide her misery from her siblings and Amelia during dinner. Instead, Sadie and Ezekiel seemed as downtrodden as she felt. Amelia continuously glanced around the table at the dreary group. Forks clanked against the dinner plates, but no one seemed to be eating the tuna noodle casserole.

Amelia had just returned home from work, and Emma hadn't had a chance to tell her about Levi yet. She was not looking forward to telling Sadie and Ezekiel, either. They already looked unhappy enough. She knew she should ask them what was wrong, but her own heart ached so badly, she just couldn't bear the thought of taking on more burdens at the moment.

She couldn't get the vision of Levi's face out of her head. First surprise, then regret, then sadness mixed with anger as he finally turned and walked away. But what had he expected? She was sure she'd made it clear that she hadn't wanted his help with the money.

He hadn't taken her wishes into consideration. He'd just trampled right over them.

Finally, Amelia set her fork down. Her concerned gaze skipped around the table. "I can't take this anymore. Has something awful happened that no one has told me about?"

Emma studied her siblings, then she cleared her throat. "Sadie? Zeke? Is something wrong?"

"*Is* something wrong?" Ezekiel echoed with a frown. He gave Sadie a knowing look.

"Well," Emma pressed as she set her own fork down, "is there?"

"Yes," Zeke said quietly, "there is. We heard you and Levi arguing when we came back from picking blueberries."

"Arguing?" Amelia gave Emma a questioning look.

Emma leaned back in her chair. "I'm sorry you heard that."

"*That's* what you're sorry about?" Ezekiel muttered.

"Yes, I'm sorry you heard us arguing. That was a terrible way to find out that Levi will not be joining our family," Emma said, speaking past the lump in her throat.

She heard Amelia gasp, but it was her sister who spoke first.

"Emma Ziegler," Sadie ground out, "I have spent my whole life looking up to you. But right now, I'm so mad at you I could...I could j-just..." she sputtered. "*Ach!* I don't even know. I'm so angry."

"You're angry with *me*?" Emma asked, completely bewildered. Sadie had always been so calm, so subdued. Even as a child she'd never thrown a tantrum. Emma was completely baffled by her behavior. She was so surprised she wasn't even offended.

"*Jah*, you!"

"What did *I* do?" Emma wanted to know.

"What did *you* do?" Sadie echoed. "Emma. Do you really not know?"

She shook her head. "I really do not."

"How could you end your engagement to Levi?" Sadie moaned. "Why would you do that?"

Emma bristled. "You know why. He went behind my back."

"To save our home," Sadie said forcefully. "Do you know why he went behind your back? Because he knows you. He knows how stubborn you are." She flung her hands up in the air. "He believed that all other avenues were lost to us, and he knew you wouldn't accept his money. You'd rather lose our home than accept his help."

"That's not true— I would have taken it. But he did it behind my back when he should have asked me first," Emma said stubbornly.

"You know he was afraid you'd say no."

"All the more reason for him to have asked first," Emma insisted.

Sadie shook her head. "I love you, Emma. You're the best big sister anyone could ever hope for, but you're wrong about this. You're wrong to shut Levi out. You're wrong to let your pride get in your way. All he wanted to do was take care of you because he loves you, but you are so prideful that you won't even let him."

"I accepted money from *you*, didn't I?" Emma pointed out.

"Only because I practically *begged* you," Sadie said. "And because this is my home, too. I have a lot at stake here as well, and you know it. But would you really have taken money from Levi?"

"I should have been given a choice."

"Stop being so selfish, Emma," Sadie said quietly. "This isn't only about you. We love Levi, too."

Ezekiel nodded.

"We want him to be part of our family. We like having him around. He cares about us. He makes you happy." Sadie heaved out a sigh. "You ruined everything." She pushed away from the table and leaped from her chair. Emma gaped after her as she raced up the stairs.

Emma's gaze swung to her brother, who had gotten to his feet as well.

Ezekiel shook his head, his pitying gaze nearly breaking Emma's heart. "I'm not happy with you either, Emma. Not happy at all."

He walked away, slouched over as if he carried the weight of the world on his young shoulders. Or perhaps, just the weight of Emma's very bad behavior.

CHAPTER TWENTY-TWO

Emma stared listlessly out the window over the kitchen sink. Rain was pouring down, thunder rumbling above, with the occasional streak of lightning splitting the sky.

The last few days had been dreary, gloomy, just like her mood.

It had been nine days since she'd last seen Levi. This past Sunday hadn't been a church Sunday but a visiting Sunday, so they had spent it with Mary Kurtz. It had been a nice distraction, but Emma had thought about Levi throughout the visit. She had found herself wondering if his family was hosting company, or were they out visiting others?

Sadie, who had always been so happy and easygoing, looked sad much of the time.

And she had not seen Ezekiel so sullen since Naomi had stayed with them.

The pair had barely spoken to her, and then, only when they had to. They were polite but distant. Emma wasn't used to the strain between them. She didn't like it one bit.

Having essentially raised her siblings, the rift between them was nearly as painful as the rift between herself and Levi. The only reason it wasn't as bad was because she knew eventually her siblings would forgive her. She knew that if she was patient, life would go back to normal.

That wasn't the case with Levi.

They were over for good.

She rinsed off the skillet she'd been scrubbing for the last few minutes. As she placed it on the drying rack, a car came down the driveway. Chloe, one of the waitresses at the Pine Cone Café, had been driving Amelia in the inclement weather.

Emma pulled the sink plug. She rinsed off her hands as the water burbled and drained. Grabbing the dish towel, she dried her hands as Amelia breezed into the kitchen.

"I'm so grateful for Chloe. I would not want to ride the bike in the rain, and it would be unkind to have Ginger stand outside in this weather waiting for me," Amelia said.

"It's very kind of her," Emma agreed.

Her cousin looked around. "It's so quiet in here. Where are Sadie and Zeke?"

Avoiding me, she wanted to say. Instead she replied, "Sadie is in her room reading her way through a stack of library books. I think she found a few on making soap, to help with the recipes from Rachael's grandma. Zeke is in the barn, busy building more birdhouses."

Ezekiel had been making good use of the pile of lumber scraps Levi had brought over. He'd begun fashioning birdhouses in a variety of styles and sizes. It was an excellent way to hone his carpentry skills.

Emma had mentioned that she would like her own booth at Saturday Market next year, and Ezekiel and Sadie had loved the idea. Sadie wanted to sell the goat soap she'd begun dabbling in, thanks to the recipes from Rachael, and Ezekiel was hoping to sell the birdhouses. Emma thought it was wonderful that the booth would be a family affair.

It also gave Ezekiel an excuse to stay in the barn and far away from Emma at the moment.

"Are they still upset with you?" Amelia ventured.

Emma's expression was forlorn when she said, "They certainly are."

Amelia gave her arm a gentle squeeze, then took a glass out of the cupboard and filled it with water. Her cousin had offered to listen if she wanted to talk about Levi, but she hadn't pressed. And Emma hadn't been ready to talk.

She thought now, perhaps, she was.

"Amelia," she began. "Do you think I've made a terrible mistake?"

Amelia studied her as she took a sip of water. Finally she said, "I don't think my opinion matters here. What do *you* think?"

Emma wished she were a child again so someone, perhaps her father, could tell her what to do. She didn't miss the bitter irony of that thought. She was in this mess precisely because she had the desire to be wildly independent.

What this past week had taught her was that she didn't want to go it alone. With her siblings angry and Levi missing from her life, she was miserable.

"Do you think I overreacted?" she asked, hoping Amelia would help her out.

Amelia seemed to be pressing back a smile. "Emma, what do you think the answer is?"

Emma let out a little growl of frustration.

"Maybe *I* should ask *you* a few questions," Amelia said. "Are you happy right now?"

"As a matter of fact," Emma said tartly, "I'm not."

"Do you miss Levi?"

"Of course," Emma said. "I got used to him being in my life."

"Do you really want to spend the rest of your life without him, then?" Amelia raised her eyebrows and waited for Emma's answer. When she didn't respond, she continued. "How happy do you think you'll be when you see him with a *frau*? With *kinner*? When you bump into him at Sunday service with his new family?" She paused a moment, letting the words sink in. "If you are unhappy now, Emma, how will you feel then?"

"I don't suppose I would be happy at all," Emma admitted.

"Do you love him? I know you are upset with him right now," Amelia added, "but the real question is, do you love him?"

"*Jah*," Emma moaned. She leaned back against the counter. "I do love him."

Amelia pressed ahead. "Can you forgive him?"

They were both well aware that to forgive was the Amish way. The Lord forgives a multitude of sins and commands that they love and forgive one another.

Emma realized she hadn't done a very good job of that.

She winced. "I think I've been holding a grudge."

Amelia made a face as if silently asking *Oh, you really think so?*

"I can forgive Levi," she said quietly. "But I wonder if he can forgive me."

"Well," Amelia said, "I believe there's only one way to find out."

• • •

Levi stared at the numbers he'd just jotted down in the ledger. He was trying to come up with a budget for the farm for the upcoming year. His father wanted to add a dozen more heifers to eventually contribute to the breeding chain. He was trying to calculate what that would mean for pasture capacity. And the feed supply. But the numbers that he'd just calculated swam before his eyes.

He blamed his lack of focus on the thunder rumbling overhead. Rain pounded against the barn roof. He had to use a battery-operated lantern for his bookwork because the sky was so gray, the day so dark and dreary.

This blasted weather had dragged on for days, and it was wearing on him. He hadn't been needed on the carpentry crew all week. It gave him far too much time to mope around.

Maybe he was in the wrong. He didn't feel remorse for helping Emma, but now that he'd had days to think about it, he should have given her the choice. Even if she had turned down his offer to help, it should have been her choice. Though it would've taken some time, he *could* have driven to the farm to ask her permission. Living without telephones, that was the sort of inconvenience they were accustomed to.

He tapped his pencil against the ledger. So much for writing up a business plan. He couldn't concentrate on much of anything these days.

He propped his chin in his palm as he gazed out

the office window. The rain pelted against the window, blurring the world beyond. It was because of his limited vision that he didn't realize that someone was racing down the driveway in the storm. He couldn't tell who. The person looked like a distorted blob through the sheets of rain.

He didn't know if the person was male or female.

What he did know was that the Zieglers were his closest neighbor. They were the only ones within walking distance.

His heart instantly catapulted into his stomach. Had something awful happened? He couldn't imagine why else one of them would be racing down his driveway in this deluge. Instantly, he shoved the chair back, causing it to nearly topple as he bolted from the office. He raced through the barn and tugged open the barn door.

He could hardly believe his eyes when he saw that it was Emma. She wore galoshes and carried an umbrella that wasn't doing much good in the wind. She was hurrying toward the porch, toward the front door of his parents' house. But he stepped out into the rain and called to her.

She nearly skidded to a stop, then whirled to face him.

"Emma!" He darted out after her. "What is it? What's wrong?"

Surely there had to be a disaster of some magnitude for her to have reason to come here. After all, she'd avoided him for over a week now. She'd told him not to visit her farm anymore. Now here she was, in a thunderstorm no less.

She seemed frozen for a moment, rain pouring

down on her, her dress soaked despite the umbrella, the hem muddy. Rivulets ran down her face. A stray lock of hair was plastered to her cheek. Oh, how he longed to tuck it behind her ear.

"Levi."

His name was breathless on her lips. She seemed to relax when she saw him, and some of his tension eased.

Again, he asked, "What's wrong?"

"Everything." She quickly closed the distance between them. "I need to speak with you."

He motioned to the barn and they hurried inside. Once they were out of the rain, Emma couldn't seem to talk fast enough.

"I'm sorry, Levi. I overreacted. I know you were only trying to help," she said. "I'm still not happy that you went behind my back, but I am sorry I was so angry. Can you forgive me?"

He blinked at her in surprise. It took a moment for his mind to wrap around and sort out all that she had said. "Was that supposed to be an apology?"

She nodded. "I think so."

"You think so?" He shook his head. "Emma, you called me a bully. That, well...that hurt."

She winced and hung her head. "I know. I shouldn't have said such a thing."

He paused a moment, thinking it over. "You *shouldn't* have said that. But did you *mean* it?"

She hesitated a moment longer than he would've liked. "I may have meant it in the moment, but that's not how I really feel."

"I see." Actually, he didn't. She either thought he was a bully, or she didn't. Her answer was not making that clear.

She pressed her fingers to her lips, as if to keep herself from saying more until she'd thoroughly thought it through. Finally she said, "I'm sorry. I'm making a mess of this. I came over here because I wanted to ask for your forgiveness."

Forgiveness. Of course, that would be important to her. It was important to all Amish to not only forgive but to be forgiven.

"I forgive you," he said a bit woodenly. "And I hope you can forgive me. I interfered, as I apparently have a habit of doing."

His heart sank a bit. He had hoped that she was coming over to ask for a whole lot more than forgiveness. He wanted to move past this ordeal, repair their relationship, and still build a future together. But clearly, she wasn't as brokenhearted by this breakup as he.

"I do forgive you," she said.

"Well, *goot*." He realized his voice was a bit gruff, but he was struggling with his own emotions.

She stood gazing at him, as if she expected him to say something. He wasn't sure what he was supposed to say. He wasn't sure what she wanted from him. Apparently nothing, because she turned to leave.

"Goodbye, then, Levi."

"Goodbye, Emma."

She reached for the barn door. She paused for a moment and he thought she'd turn back around. He contemplated going after her.

He should go after her. His heart ached and his brain was shouting at him to not let her go. But no, she'd said her piece and maybe they really were too

different. He didn't want to be a bully. He didn't
want to be the one chasing after her—again. He
wanted a wife who adored him the way he adored
her. She didn't have to bend to his whims, but he had
an innate desire to protect, to provide. Like his father did, and his brothers, too.

He didn't go after her, and then she slipped out
the door without looking back, and the moment was
gone.

* * *

Emma stood in the rain for a moment. She was already so drenched that at this point, it didn't matter.
She had done what she'd intended to do—she'd apologized to Levi. She had hoped for more, but his re-
served demeanor had caused her to hesitate to do
more than apologize. What she had wanted to do was
to ask if they could put the whole mess behind them.

Looking at Levi, she knew, she just knew they
were meant to be together.

She whirled around, determined to tell him.
Before she could push the door, it swung open.

Levi stood there, looking as startled as she felt to
suddenly be face-to-face.

He said, "Emma," the same moment she said,
"Levi."

"I was hoping to catch you," he said. "Come in
out of the rain." He took her elbow and gently
guided her in.

"I couldn't leave," Emma said as he closed the
door behind her. "Not when I feel like we had more
to say."

Did Levi feel as if there was more to say as well? Was that why he had followed her?

She wasn't sure, but she wanted to find out. She wanted him to speak, to tell her what was on his mind. But after all that had happened, after demanding that she be treated as his equal, it was only fair that she speak first. It was only right that she put herself out there.

"Do you have more to say?" Levi asked, his tone carefully controlled.

"I do." She wished his expression weren't so unreadable. "I need you to understand something. It's not because you paid my bill, not really." She tilted her head to the side as she rethought that. "More than that, it's that you did it without *asking* me. You didn't check in to see if I could do it on my own. Levi, I had most of the money. We could have worked together to pay it off. I could have maybe borrowed the rest from you and paid you back as soon as I was able. But you didn't give me that choice. You just barreled in and took over."

"I assumed I knew best and didn't take your feelings into consideration," Levi said.

She nodded. "I know I can be stubborn. I'm used to having to be independent. But I also know that sometimes, even if I don't like to admit it, I need help."

His lip quirked up. "I never thought I'd hear you say that."

"The problem," she said a bit crossly, "is that you *always* seem to think I need help. For *years*, you have refused to let me handle situations on my own. You don't trust my judgment."

"*Nee*," he said firmly. "That's not it at all."

"But it is," she insisted. She needed him to see that. Her memory flashed back to all of the times that Levi had been there, meddling. If he couldn't admit to that, she felt as if he hadn't learned anything from this ordeal. And if that were the case, where would that leave them?

He scrubbed a hand across his face; then his gaze landed on her, an unreadable look in his eye. "Emma," he began, "that's not—"

She opened her mouth to protest, but he placed a finger over her lips.

"Would you just hush and let me speak?" he asked sternly.

She frowned but nodded, and his finger slipped away.

"I will admit, I have interfered in your life a few too many times," he said. "What you are mistaken about is why. It's *not* because I don't think you capable."

Confusion washed over her. She wanted to demand he tell her why, right now, but she remembered his request that she hush so she shuffled her feet instead.

"I've loved you for years, Emma." The words seemed to flow from him in a rush, flooding Emma with such a feeling of surprise it nearly took her breath away. "I've loved you for as long as I can remember." He paused. "*Nee.* That's not right. I've had feelings for you for as long as I can remember, but it's been only these past few months that I realized what love is."

She sucked in a startled breath.

"Emma, all the times I stepped in, it was because I cared about you. I worried about you. When I saw you with Darren all those years ago, I was jealous, but more than that, I was afraid. I was afraid he'd take you away and I'd never have a chance with you." He took her hands, causing a rush of warmth to swirl through her as his words took root in her mind. "The thought of you marrying my *bruder*, it was like a knife through my heart. That's why I asked Ivan not to marry you."

"What?" Could it be?

All the times he'd interfered had been because he'd cared, perhaps too much?

"It's true." He gave her hands a squeeze. "I know you worry that your *daed*'s health declined because of his concern for you after Ivan broke off your engagement. I can tell you, that was not true."

Her voice was barely more than a whisper when she said, "How can you possibly know that?"

"Because I went to him. I told him of my feelings." His gaze bore into her, as if searching her soul. "I told him I loved you, and I intended to court you, and I hoped that someday, I would be blessed enough to marry you."

Tears filled her eyes, but words evaded her.

"He gave us his blessing."

She looked at him in disbelief. "Levi—"

"It's true," he said. "I promise you, it is."

Her voice was choked when she said, "My *daed* truly gave us his blessing?"

"*Jah*," he sighed. "He did. But then he became gravely ill. He passed, we had his funeral, and it didn't seem like a decent time to tell you that we'd spoken. But then I heard your conversation with Naomi. I couldn't let you lose your farm and all that you loved."

"So, you stepped in."

"Because I love you."

"Because you love me." She paused, her mind reeling with all that he had said. "And you've loved me for a while."

"I have," he said solemnly.

She placed a hand over her racing heart. Waves of intense emotions coursed through her. She thought about Levi, his past actions, and she saw everything from a different perspective now. When you loved someone, you wanted to care for them. You wanted to help them. Wasn't that what she'd done with her siblings her whole life?

Feeling emboldened by all that he had confessed, she pushed ahead with what she had wanted to say since coming back through the barn door.

"Levi, I'm not satisfied leaving here as your friend."

His eyebrows twitched but he remained silent.

She raised her chin defiantly. "I love you, too."

His lips quirked. "You do?"

"*Jah*," she said firmly. "I do."

He opened his mouth but she rushed ahead, cutting him off.

"I love that you care so much for Zeke and Sadie. I finally understand that you are so protective of me not because you think I'm incapable, but because you care so much." She brushed her thumb against the scar on his cheek. "I want to be your wife. But I want to be your equal. I want to be a part of the decisions that involve me, the decisions that will involve our home and our future family."

This time he waited, as if he thought she had more to add. She did.

"Is that," she said cautiously, "something you still want, too?"

"That is something I want very much. I know I am not perfect. I am only human and bound to make mistakes. I promise that I will do my best to always take your feelings into account. But Emma," he said firmly, "I want to take care of you. Almost your whole life you've given so much of yourself to others. It's one of the many things I love about you. I think we can find a balance. Don't you?"

She nodded vigorously. "I do. Does that mean you will be my husband?"

He laughed as he pulled her into his arms. "There's nothing in this world that I would like more."

With those words filling her mind, he bent down and gave her a kiss that promised a future together, love, and a lifetime of commitment.

EPILOGUE

Emma readjusted the scarf around her neck. The blue scarf was her first attempt at knitting. It had turned out a little lopsided, just a bit crooked. But after practicing with countless dishcloths and hot pads, she'd made vast improvements in the craft over the winter. She was thrilled to finally have the time to work on a hobby that she enjoyed. Amelia was a patient teacher, and Emma hoped to learn much from her.

She was, after so many years, spending time on herself. She had whiled away the winter in her cozy, warm kitchen trying countless recipes, tasting them, perfecting them, and sharing them. She had an outline for a cookbook ready to go next summer and a small menu planned for the space she intended to rent.

Now the weather was warming up, the sap was flowing, but early mornings still held the chill of an occasional snowfall. She stood on the back porch, scanning the maple forest. It was sugaring season. Galvanized buckets still hung from most of the trees, collecting the sap that seeped out. It would take nearly forty gallons of sap to make a single gallon of syrup. First the sap needed to be strained to rid it of unwanted debris, then it was boiled down in the sugar house over one of the special woodstoves. The tops of the stoves held several long metal pans. When the sap was boiled the extra moisture—there was much extra—would be removed, leaving only sugary syrup behind.

"I never knew the air could smell so sweet."

Emma twisted around to face Amelia. Her cousin wore a content smile.

"It's *wunderbaar*, isn't it?" Emma asked.

Hundreds of buckets of sap had been collected and were in the midst of being processed. Steam rose from the sugar shack as the excess water was boiled from the syrup. The steam scented the air in the most enticing way. The process would take weeks and then they would be finished for another year.

"I never knew what a process this was," Amelia admitted.

"It is, but Levi and Zeke seem to be having a fine time with it."

Speaking of her husband, he emerged from the sugar house. He spotted her standing on the porch and headed her way.

"I think I'll go inside for another cup of *kaffi*," Amelia said.

Emma gave Amelia a smile as she left. Naomi had tried to convince Amelia to return to Harmony, but Amelia wouldn't hear of it. Emma was relieved her cousin had decided to stay. She was still honing her matchmaking skills. She enjoyed seeing other couples fall in love, despite insisting *she* was perfectly happy to be on her own.

The farmhouse was full of family and fun these days. That wasn't to say that they still didn't work hard, because they did. But even the most arduous of tasks was more enjoyable with loved ones by your side.

She watched as Levi strode across the yard. They had been married last fall, not quite half a year ago, and she thanked the Good Lord daily for blessing her with such a wonderful man. His family had welcomed her with open arms. Despite the bumpy start, she and Miriam had become good friends. In fact, Emma had become close to Levi's sisters-in-law. She cherished her new family and was grateful for their love and support.

True to his word, Levi treated her as his equal in marriage. That wasn't to say that he wasn't still overprotective, but she had changed, too. She was more accepting of receiving help. Whenever a decision needed to be made about the farm—such as the herd of cows they were planning to acquire this spring—they made it as a family.

"Zeke is turning into a stubborn one." Levi's tone held a hint of humor as he clomped up the steps; Emma knew he was proud of the boy. He was turning into a fine young man. "He told me he can watch the fire on his own. Said I should head into town because the feed supply is running low."

"Did he? He's being a bit bossy, is he?" Emma asked in amusement. Levi oversaw the farm, but Ezekiel was learning all he could, stepping up every chance he got, though it would be quite some time before he took over. In the meantime, he was learning from Levi, who had given up his carpentry job. His time was split between the two farms, and they were both thriving.

"It is a *goot* thing Sadie's goats earn their keep. They sure do eat a lot."

Emma laughed, nodding her agreement. "They do."

Sadie now had half a dozen goats and a blooming business because of them. Her goat soap had become quite popular in the gift shop, plus news of her cheese had spread throughout the community. She spent a fair amount of time in the kitchen these days. Emma knew a few boys had asked to court her, but Sadie had turned them down. Emma was sure she knew why. Sadie was holding out for a certain boy. She was interested in Jonathon Yoder, the bishop's grandson, and was unwilling to consider anyone else.

"I think maybe I will go into town as Zeke advised," Levi said. "Would you like to ride into Pine Creek with me?"

"That sounds like a fine idea." She moved in close to her husband, taking his hands in her own. Hers were chilled from standing on the porch while his were warm from the fires. "I would like to ride along. I need to buy another skein of yarn."

"What project are you working on this time?" Levi wondered.

Emma's eyes sparkled, barely able to contain her happiness. "This time I'll be knitting an afghan for a *boppli*."

Levi's brow furrowed in thought. "A gift for someone?"

"*Nee*." She shook her head. "This afghan will be special. This will be one that we keep."

Emma enjoyed watching his expression flicker from confusion into that of realization. His eyes grew big, his lips dancing with the promise of a smile.

"Are you saying…?" He swallowed, as if needing a few more moments to wrap his mind around the possibility. "Are you saying that I'm going to be a *daed*?"

She nodded, her own smile taking over her face. "*Jah*. That is what I'm saying."

"This is such wonderful news." A joyful laugh broke free. He picked up Emma, swinging her around the porch. "God has blessed us in so many ways. You have just made me the happiest man in all the world!"

ACKNOWLEDGMENTS

Thank you to my agent, Jessica Alvarez, for your patience and guidance. I'm so grateful you suggested this project. A heartfelt thank-you to Stacy Abrams for taking a chance on me in this new venture. It was wonderful to work with you again. I'm delighted to have been given this opportunity with Entangled Publishing. Thanks so much to Heather Riccio for always being so helpful. And, Nancy Cantor, thank you for your help in fine-tuning this story. I appreciated the sweet side notes along the way! Curtis Svehlak, I'm so grateful for all of your work in getting everything finalized. Last but absolutely not least, a huge thank-you to Elizabeth Turner Stokes for such a gorgeous cover.

*What happens when a female horse whisperer butts
heads with a traditional male wrangler within the
quiet Amish community of Honey Brook?*

Turn the page to start reading The Amish
Cowboy's Homecoming *by* USA Today
bestselling author Ophelia London

the
AMISH
COWBOY'S
HOMECOMING

USA TODAY BESTSELLING AUTHOR
OPHELIA
LONDON

On sale April 27, 2021

CHAPTER 1

Isaac King slowly ran his finger down the center of her nose, ever so gently.

"Morning, sweetheart."

He felt her take in a breath, responding to his simple touch. When she made a sound, he stepped closer, placing a hand on the side of her face. "I know, I know," he whispered, looking into her eyes. "I hate to leave, but it's something I have to do." With both hands now, he gently caressed all the way down her neck. Then, when there was nothing more to say, he touched his forehead to hers, taking in a deep breath. She smelled of earth and energy but mostly like…oats and molasses.

"Easy there, girl." Isaac laughed as the sure-footed, petite Haflingers horse shook her head. "You know I could never leave you for long. It's just a day or two, and then we'll see what happens—probably nothing." He exhaled, trying to stay optimistic. He looked up into the blue-sky morning, feeling a slight flutter in his stomach.

This could be it, he thought, though not wanting to get his hopes up too high. *This could be my way out. Our way out.* Feeling a lump in his throat, he glanced toward the house. No one was awake yet. That was good. He'd said his goodbyes to Sadie last night before he tucked her in bed. That had been hard enough—he didn't want to go through it again.

After giving his gaul—the one he'd had since he was

just a boy—one more stroke down her nose, he knew it was time to stop procrastinating. Sunny wouldn't be coming with him on this trip, though she'd accompanied him everywhere else he'd ever gone. She was getting on in age, and this time, he wouldn't be needing a horse to just pull a buggy. Scout would be his travel mate.

From just thinking the fella's name, he heard the deep *neigh* coming from two stalls over.

Isaac grabbed his saddle, reins, and the rest of the tack off the back of the gate. "*Jah, jah*," he said while approaching his white mount. "You excited, boy?" He laughed, patting his strongest, hardest-working horse—the one he could always count on. The one who would see him through one of the most important moments of his life.

After leading Scout out of the barn, Isaac gave him a few extra minutes of brushing. Yes, he was stalling again. "Okay, time to go." He threw another glance toward the house. If he didn't hurry, his in-laws would be waking up soon and maybe try to talk him out of this. The buggy was already packed for an overnight stay if needed, and he had a fresh change of clothes on a sturdy wooden hanger in the way back of the carriage. He smoothed the front of his hair down and slid on his favorite straw hat. The one shaped more like an Englisher "cowboy" hat than a traditional Amish one, with the round brim.

He easily recalled when that hat had been given to him as a gift. As he clicked his tongue, prompting Scout to walk, he pulled down the front brim, ready for business. He could've had one of his Mennonite friends drive him the thirty miles in a car, but the four-hour buggy ride would give him time to think, more time to mentally prepare.

He'd been over every angle dozens of times. He'd sought counsel from his brother and good friends, but mostly he'd prayed his heart out. This route, this very road he was on right now was the path that felt right. This brought a certain amount of peace to his heart, though the thought of taking his little family away from home might be the hardest thing he'd ever have to do.

The early-morning spring sunshine shone down an hour or so later—time to give Scout a break, and Isaac needed to stretch his legs. Maybe do some jumping jacks, try to pop that tight area on his lower back. He might've worked the new draft horse too hard yesterday. If Isaac himself was sore, Nelly would be, too. His stomach dropped slightly, always regretting when he overworked a horse—he cared so much about the animals, especially the ones that had come to him from rescue situations. Those were always extra special to Isaac. He gave Scout a few additional rubs and scratches down his neck. When the retired racer had first been brought to him, the poor horse had been worked nearly to death. Even though violence had never been a part of his personality, Isaac would've loved five minutes alone with the person who'd done that to a helpless gaul.

All these thoughts were still going through his mind when he arrived in Honey Brook. Following the careful directions given to him, he took the last stretch down a long, windy road past several well-kept dairy farms. While at the top of the hill, Isaac easily saw the horse ranch—the large, telltale pasture ring in the front of the property giving it away. As he drew nearer, he noticed someone was in that ring with a horse. Probably John Zook, the owner of the property and the man who just might be his future boss.

Wanting to quietly observe the man's technique— wondering how well it would match up with his own— Isaac slowed the buggy, then tied Scout to a nearby hitch. The closer he got, the more he noticed how tall the horse was. The caramel-colored gelding looked to be about twenty hands high. A giant.

Isaac neared the white fence, his curiosity getting the better of him. But now, the closer he got, he noticed it wasn't that the horse was tall; it was that John Zook was short. Very short and quite slim, more like a teenage boy than a grown man. Isaac tilted his head. Was John Zook wearing a…dress? That was definitely a blue top with a long black apron. The skirt of the dress, however, was hiked up, tied in the back. And were those pants underneath?

Isaac felt a smile slowly spread across his face when he realized it wasn't a grown man or a boy working with the horse but a young woman, though she was petite and probably no more than nineteen years old at most.

"Good day," he said, using the common Englisher greeting instead of "*guder daag,*" the traditional Amish phrase, though he was pretty sure she was Amish. She dropped the long stick she was holding and spun around. He hadn't meant to startle her. Even her horse let out a little whinny.

"Oh," she said, sounding out of breath while trying to push back the loose strands of hair that had fallen out of her *kapp.* "Morning." She looked at him for another moment while attempting to dust off the layer of dirt from the front of her dress. After probably realizing it was no use, she lowered her chin and smiled—but it seemed that smile hadn't been meant for Isaac. By the way she was looking off to the side, she was smiling at something personal. A private memory?

For some reason, this intrigued Isaac even more.

Without speaking again, she returned to her work, trying to get the pretty gelding to trot in a circle.

Isaac leaned an elbow on the top rung of the fence and watched, a bit captivated, for she seemed to know what she was doing. Though the stick never touched the horse, she kept it right at his peripheral vision, so he would know it was there but receiving no harm.

"This the Zook farm?" Isaac asked.

"Aye," the woman said without looking at him. The ties of her black prayer *kapp* were caught in a breeze as more of her hair came spilling out. It was brown, reminding Isaac of someone else in his life—someone who used to be in his life. "If you're looking for John Zook," she added, "he's in the house."

She switched the stick to her left hand so she was holding the lead rope in her right. Without missing a beat, the obedient horse did an elegant turn, his hoofs keeping perfect time, and he began trotting in the other direction, steps high.

Isaac was taken aback. He hadn't known many Amish who preferred the English style of riding over the more common Western, especially if all you needed was a strong horse to pull a plow or an obedient one to lead a buggy.

"Impressive," he couldn't help saying. "How did this gaul come to you?"

"Pardon?" she said, tossing back her skirt in an unexpectedly feminine way.

Isaac stepped onto the bottom rung of the fence so he was closer to her. "Where did you get this horse?"

Before replying, the woman began slowing the gelding's speed, gently pulling the lead in one inch at a time. When he was close to her, she leaned in and whispered something Isaac couldn't hear.

"Honey Pot came as a new foal," she answered, leading the horse toward the fence.

Isaac couldn't help lifting his brows. "Honey Pot?"

The woman was close enough now that when she smiled again, he could see a dimple in her right cheek, making her look…maybe not younger but much more innocent…and rather pretty, despite her tomboy exterior.

Though even simply noticing that another woman was attractive caused a knot to form in Isaac's stomach.

"I think it fits him quite well," she replied, turning to the horse and running a hand down his neck. "Though I didn't name him."

"So he didn't come like that?"

"Like what?"

He was about to say "so well trained" but didn't. "Nothing," he said instead, not wanting to insult her if she'd been the one who'd trained him in the English style. But how likely was that? Isaac knew very few—if any!—Amish women who took more than a passing interest in horse training.

Martha didn't, he couldn't help thinking, that knot in his stomach returning. But then he forced a smile, thinking of Sadie. There wasn't a bigger horse lover than her, and she'd always seemed very interested in what he did.

"What's the joke?"

He looked over at the woman. She was shading her eyes from the bright afternoon sun. "Joke?" he asked.

"*Jah*." She patted Honey Pot. "The way you're smiling, like you're thinking of something funny."

"Not funny exactly," he replied, noticing that the loose strands of her hair had flashes of red. And her eyes were blue. Why did he have the impulse to wipe the streak of dirt off her cheek?

Not wanting to reveal what he was suddenly thinking, he blurted, "I was remembering a joke."

She tilted her head, one corner of her mouth lifting. "*Jah*?"

Isaac dusted off his hands. "Ever heard the one about the Mennonite and his favorite cow?"

After a short pause, the woman lifted her chin and started laughing. It was loud but also feminine in a way, maybe because her voice was high like a bell. "Oh, gracious!" she said, still laughing. "You sound like my brother." She waved a hand in the air. "And all his friends." She cleared her throat and dusted off one shoulder. "Aye, I know all about the Mennonite and his cow."

While watching her, Isaac grew even more intrigued. Who was this woman? And how could she be both feminine *and* act like one of the guys?

"Anyway," she said when silence stretched on for too long. "Best be getting back to work."

Isaac nodded. He needed to pull his thoughts together so he would be prepared for his meeting with John Zook. Last thing he needed was to be preoccupied by a dimple and jovial blue eyes.